Bolan retrieved the motorcycle and kicked it to life

"I thought...you do not...fight cop."

"I don't. I clotheslined a cop. Hang on."

Bolan aimed the bike toward the on-ramp, nearly losing it as Ramzin sagged to one side and toppled to the pavement. The Executioner spun the bike to a stop and jumped off.

The Russian's mouth hung slack. Clear fluid leaked from the corners of his eyes. His pupils were blown. Major Pietor Ramzin was gone.

Mack Bolan gazed down at one of the most dangerous men he had ever faced. The truth would be covered up. Bolan knew Ramzin would be crucified posthumously.

But there was one thing that couldn't be taken from the man, even in death. Bolan took Ramzin's Hero of the Soviet Union medal and pinned it to the dead veteran's chest.

D0978368

Don Pendleton's Mack Bolan®

Mission: Apocalypse

A GOLD EAGLE BOOK FROM

W☸RLDWIDE®

TORONTO • NEW YORK • LONDON
AMSTERDAM • PARIS • SYDNEY • HAMBURG
STOCKHOLM • ATHENS • TOKYO • MILAN
MADRID • WARSAW • BUDAPEST • AUCKLAND

Recycling programs
for this product may
not exist in your area.

First edition September 2009

ISBN-13: 978-0-373-61531-5

Special thanks and acknowledgment to
Charles Rogers for his contribution to this work.

MISSION: APOCALYPSE

Printed in U.S.A.

The Old Testament teems with prophecies of the Messiah, but nowhere is it intimated that that Messiah is to stand as a God to be worshipped. He is to bring peace to the earth, to build up the waste places—to comfort the broken-hearted…

—Olympia Brown
1835–1926

Gavi Arkhangelov is no messiah. Bring peace to earth? He seeks war. Build up waste places? He plans to level cities with nuclear bombs. Comfort the broken-hearted? The man intends to sow pain and sorrow. But the best-laid plans can be destroyed. And they will be.

—Mack Bolan

For my friend, Billy C.

CHAPTER ONE

State of Sinaloa, Mexico

The Executioner's fist crashed across the sentry's jaw.

Guard duty was dull duty the world over. The man had spent more time and attention lighting his cigarette than he had the darkness around him. The flare of the lighter had instantly killed his night vision. In the same instant Bolan was on him. Teeth and tobacco went flying. In the sentry's defense he was deep in his homeland, deep in the desert, the roads were all watched and all military and police units in the area had been thoroughly penetrated and bribed to alert his organization to any movement.

No one was expecting a single, hostile American to come floating down out of the sky six hundred miles south of the border into Mexico.

Bolan hit the guard again. This time his open hand chopped into the side of the sentry's neck like an ax. The Executioner raised his hand for a third blow but the man was already falling unconscious to the ground with a concussion and half of his carotid arteries and nerves crushed. Bolan let him fall and caught the man's rifle before it could clatter to the pavement. The G3 assault weapon was Mexican Army issue and probably stolen. The man was most likely ex-Mexican Army issue, as well. Bolan knelt over the sentry and found that he was indeed wearing Mexican military dog tags beneath his windbreaker. Gasca, Victor, was a private. Private Gasca was out of uniform. Mexican military officers and enlisted men moonlighting to do work for the cartels was as old as the war on drugs. Gasca was also wearing a white card key around his neck. Bolan removed the key and ran it through the lock on the warehouse door. The light on the lock blinked green. Bolan pulled his night-vision goggles down over his eyes and slid inside into the darkness. The light-enhancing optics took the barely discernible glow of the stars shining through the skylights and magnified it thousands of times, turning the inky blackness of the warehouse interior into a harsh, grainy, gray-green world.

Bolan subvocalized into the microphone taped to his throat. "I'm in."

Fourteen hundred miles away in Virginia Aaron "the Bear" Kurtzman sat in Stony Man Farm's Computer Room and gazed at satellite imaging of Bolan's position in Sinaloa. "Copy that, Striker. Begin radiological survey."

"Copy that. Commencing survey." Bolan pulled the Geiger counter out of his web gear and powered it up. The IDR-Monitor 4 was a simple Geiger-Müller type that measured alpha, beta, gamma and x-radiation and was about the size of an old style walkie-talkie. The device's main component was a tube filled with argon gas. Argon was inert, but it would briefly conduct electricity when a particle or photon of radiation passed through it. The tube amplified the current into a pulse. The pulse was what created the typical clicking, static sound Geiger counters made. The faster, uglier and more staticky the sound was, the more radiologically uglier the ambient environment was.

This night, gamma radiation was the subatomic particle of choice.

Gamma radiation was always around. It was constantly bouncing around the cosmos, but usually in amounts a human being would consider infinitesimal. However, gamma rays were the most dangerous form of radiation emitted during a nuclear explosion. Unlike solar radiation, gamma rays were not stopped at the skin level. They passed completely through the body like a freight train, damaging every cell in their path and creating breaks in the DNA strands. Victims of exposure suffered horribly before they died, and survivors would pass on their damaged DNA in the form of birth defects to their children. You didn't need a nuclear explosion to get gamma radiation. It was emitted from spent nuclear reactor fuel at very lethal levels. Mixed with conventional explosives, nuclear material would go on killing long after the effects of the explosives had been dealt with.

Gamma radiation was the "dirty" in dirty bombs.

Bolan muted the audio signal on the IDR-4 and began running his sweep through the warehouse. He waved the counter slowly over and around each pallet and crate, keeping his eye on the tiny dial to see if the needle jumped. It was barely twitching, but it was twitching. "Bear, I have slightly elevated levels of gamma radiation."

"Give me a count," Kurtzman replied.

Bolan watched the needle tremble at the very lowest end of detection. It was far less than the exposure one would get from an X-ray imaging at the doctor's office, but it was still abnormally high for a nonmedical or nonindustrial warehouse in the middle of Sinaloa. "I've got ten kV." Bolan shook his head. "Maybe less."

Kurtzman echoed Bolan's thoughts. "It's residual. The material has moved."

"Continuing sweep." Bolan slid from pallet to pallet and stack to stack. Ostensibly the warehouse was used in the transshipment of beans and soya out of the Mexican highlands to the south. Bolan knew that any dope-sniffing dog worth his salt would be doing backflips from the scent of the residual Mexican brown heroin and Colombian cocaine that had spent the night on its way to the United States border. Gun-sniffing dogs would have recognized the scent of Cosmoline, Russian military lubricants and high-explosive blocks. As far as Bolan knew, there were no uranium-sniffing dogs, and if there were they had very short life spans. But the needle of the electrical sniffer in his hand began to twitch like a nose as it scented the air. "Reading getting stronger."

"Maintain safety protocols, Striker," Kurtzman warned.

"Readings still far below danger levels." Bolan knelt on the warehouse floor as the needle shook like a leaf in the wind. His eyes narrowed beneath his night-vision gear. The needle was still vibrating against the low-end peg. He traced his fingers on the outline in the floor where pallets had obviously rested for years. Bolan passed the IDR-4 over the scratched square, and the needle twitched up a hairbreadth. Something radioactive had indeed rested here. The fact that there was still a distinctive radiation signature told Bolan that the bad guys had either breached the original containment vessel or they had transferred the materials to a new container whose shielding was not up to spec. "Confirmed, material was in the warehouse, and has since been moved."

Kurtzman's silence spoke volumes. Nuclear material had gotten within six hundred miles of the U.S. and was still presumably heading north.

They both knew there was only one option left.

"Bear, I'm heading up to the hacienda for some Q and A."

"Copy that, Striker. Will advise the Man."

Kurtzman was going to inform the president that the mission had progressed from reconnaissance to search and destroy. Bolan finished sweeping the warehouse, but the strongest reading continued to be the suspiciously empty space. He stepped back over the stricken sentry. The man was alive but wouldn't be raising the alarm anytime soon. Bolan's boots crunched on the gravel road as he moved up toward the house. In the distance the Tamazula River gleamed with reflected starlight. Oswaldo "Pinto" Salcido seemed an unlikely trafficker in nuclear materials. He had gotten his nickname for the continent-shaped wine stains that streaked his left cheek and temple and had a vicious reputation in an already vicious line of work. He was still lower echelon, a regional warlord who exploited his locals and took a taste of goods moving through his territory rather than a major player in the Mexican crime cartels. If he was moving nuclear material, then he had moved up to the big leagues.

Bolan was about to give Pinto some big-league attention.

The Executioner raised his night-vision goggles and unslung his SCAR rifle. The weapon had a 40 mm grenade launcher mounted and loaded beneath the barrel, but he reached over his shoulder into his pack and drew forth a GREMs barricade breaching rifle grenade and clicked it on his muzzle. Salcido's place was standard twentieth-century Mexican crime lord. High pink adobe walls surrounded a sprawling hacienda. Bolan closed within twenty yards of the automatic iron gate, peered through his rifle's optic and fired. The assault rifle bucked against his shoulder as the rifle grenade flew from the muzzle. The grenade slammed into the gate's locking plate and ripped the entire wrought-iron fence right off its tracks and left it twisted and lying in the driveway.

Bolan squinted as the hacienda's security floodlights snapped on and threw the entire front of the house into shadowless glare. The front door flew open and three men with AKs charged down the steps. Bolan leveled his rifle but pulled the trigger on the grenade launcher. Pale yellow fire belched from the 40 mm muzzle, and a bee swarm of buckshot expanded and enveloped the charging men in an invisible cloud of lead ball bearings that passed through their bodies like a withering wind. The three men twisted and fell.

Bolan raised his rifle and fired six quick bursts into the arc of floodlights, and the front and sides of the hacienda plunged back into darkness. He pulled his night-vision goggles back down, jacked a tear gas grenade into his launcher and slid a fresh magazine into his rifle.

Within the hacienda men were shouting, women were screaming and dogs were barking.

A man leaned out of an upstairs window and sprayed the grounds with submachine-gun fire, but he was firing blind into the darkness. He showed up perfectly in Bolan's optics and the Executioner's burst blasted him from the window and dropped him down to the patio below. Bolan sent his tear gas round spiraling through the vacated window and sent a second one through the front door into the house a few seconds later. He took a moment to don his gas mask and clip it to his night-vision gear. Bolan moved up to the hacienda. Ignoring the open front door, he stepped onto the patio, picked up a wrought-iron patio chair and hurled it through the French windows. Shattered shards of glass cascaded to the tiles. Fresh feminine screaming broke out, as well as several gunshots, but none were aimed at Bolan. He jacked another buckshot round into his grenade launcher.

Glass crunched beneath his boots as the Executioner entered Casa de Salcido.

The gas was spreading nicely from room to room. Bolan went to the kitchen and took the stairs into the basement. He raised his rifle and burned a magazine on full-auto in the fuse box. The rest of the Salcido household plunged into darkness. Bolan strode back upstairs. Everything was chaos. People ran throughout the house shouting, screaming, choking and cursing. He could see everyone and everything through his optics, but to the inhabitants of the house he was just one more dark shape in the gloom and gas. Men with guns, Bolan shot. Men without guns, Bolan gave a lick with the butt of his rifle and dropped them. He grasped women firmly by their shoulders, told them "Get out" in Spanish and shoved them toward the closest exit. No one Bolan had encountered so far matched Pinto's description. The soldier finished sweeping the ground floor of the hacienda and began to suspect Señor Salcido was upstairs.

Bolan went to find him.

Things were slightly more organized on the second floor. Flashlight beams were sweeping wildly about while some-one—Bolan suspected Salcido—was bellowing orders at the top of his lungs. A man appeared at the head of the stairs waving a flashlight and a pistol. Bolan stitched him with a burst and he tumbled down the steps. The rest of the gunners upstairs finally found some focus, and salvos of gunfire erupted and tore across the top of the landing. Bolan drew two flash-bang grenades from his bandolier, pulled the pins and lobbed the bombs over the landing. He prudently closed his eyes beneath his goggles and stuck fingers in his ears. Twin incandescent flashes lit up the upstairs landing and twin booms rocked the house like thunder.

Bolan came to the top of the stairs.

Two men with rifles staggered like drunks in half-blind, half-deaf disorientation. Hundreds of winking, pyrotechnic aftereffects flitted about like fireflies. A third man was holding himself up with one hand on the wall and desperately shaking his head to clear it from the effects of the stun grenade. In the gray-green world of the night-vision goggles the wine stains on the man's face looked black. Bolan put a burst into each of the riflemen and put them down. Salcido pushed himself away from the wall and tried to raise a pistol.

Bolan closed in three strides and snapped the butt of his rifle on Salcido's wrist. The man screamed as his wrist fractured and the pistol thudded to the carpet. Whipping the butt up, Bolan cracked Salcido across the cheek. As his adversary staggered back under the assault, the Executioner slung his rifle and buried his fist into the man's guts. The drug lord doubled over and then screamed and stiffened like a board as Bolan dropped his fist across each kidney as if he were hammering nails. The big American seized him by the collar and belt, and marched him into the master bedroom. More French doors opened onto a balcony. Pinto howled as Bolan accelerated from a fast walk to a run and gave him the bum's rush right off the balcony.

Salcido screamed as he plummeted through the darkness.

His screams were cut short as he hit the swimming pool with a splash. Bolan climbed over the balustrade, hung by his hands for a moment and then dropped down in the backyard below. He went to the pool and hauled Salcido out by the hair and hurled him onto the pool deck. Bolan unslung his rifle and aimed at Salcido's face. He activated the tactical light mounted on the side of his rifle and strobed Salcido with 75,000 candlepower at sixty blinks per minute. Salcido moaned and tried to raise his hands in front of his face. Bolan kicked them away, killed the light and planted a knee on Salcido's chest. "Pinto, where is it?"

"Where's...what?" Between the flash-stun, the beating,

the impromptu skydive and swim and the strobing, Salcido was at an all-time moral low. "Where's what? I got money, I got drugs.... Whatever you want."

"I want the material."

Salcido gasped. "What...material?"

Bolan frowned beneath his mask. It was possible that Salcido had no idea just what had been stored in his warehouse. "You had a very important consignment in the warehouse. Now it's gone." Bolan leaned more weight into his knee. "Where is it now?"

"Shit...I don't know. I was just paid to sit on it until pickup."

"Who picked it up?"

"I don't know, some guys. I didn't know them."

Bolan sighed inwardly. Unfortunately he was fairly certain Salcido was speaking the truth. "When did the plane leave the airstrip?"

Salcido suddenly became reticent.

Bolan dialed the light up to 150,000 candlepower and hammered Salcido with the strobe. The man groaned and twitched feebly. At this level some individuals were known to have seizures and the drug lord had already had a hard night. "They left by truck! They took the road north!"

Bolan killed the light. "How many men?"

"Three."

"Who were they?"

"I told you! I don't know!"

"Describe them."

"One was Mexican. He did all the talking, and he didn't talk much. The other two were white boys."

Bolan cocked his head. "Americans?"

"I don't know...I don't think so."

"Why?"

"I don't know. They didn't say anything, but they acted all cool and European and shit. They were all dressed down, but you could tell they were suits."

"How long ago did they leave?"

"This morning."

Bolan nodded. He might have caught a break. It was 650 miles to the closest point of the border. That was a long haul through a lot of rural Mexico. "What kind of truck?"

"I don't know what kind of truck!"

A man lurched onto the back patio coughing and hacking. He carried a revolver in one hand and machete in the other. Salcido screamed as Bolan put a burst into the interloper's chest and hammered him back into the hacienda. Bolan waited a moment to make sure he stayed down and then returned his attention to Salcido.

"What kind of truck?" he repeated.

"I don't know!"

"Describe it."

"I don't know! A flatbed! Like farmers use! The cab was blue!"

"How big was the load?" Bolan persisted.

"It was like six packing crates."

"How big?"

"Like the size of coffins. I didn't ask any questions. I got paid not to ask questions. My men loaded it up and they took off."

"How was it loaded?"

"In a pyramid, three on the bottom, two in the middle and one on top. They're tied down and have a tarp over them."

"Were they heavy?"

Salcido considered this. "My boy Chivo says it felt like they were loaded with rocks."

"Any of your boys feeling sick?"

Salcido seemed confused by the question. "Sick? No, no one is sick. Why?"

Bolan ignored the question. "You say you don't know who picked the load up or where they went?"

"No."

"Who sent it?"

Salcido got reticent again.

Bolan strobed him.

"*Hey!* Shit! Man! I—"

"Talk to me and you live." Bolan was implacable. "You don't, I shoot you and ask someone else."

"I don't know who sent it! I'm just part of the pipeline!"

"Who was the part behind you?"

Salcido trembled. Bolan gave him a bit more knee in the sternum.

"King Solomon! He sent it up from Mexico City!"

It was a name Bolan had heard of in Mexican crime. He heaved Salcido to his feet and handcuffed him. "Let's go for a walk."

"A walk? Where?"

Bolan gave him an encouraging shove. "Into the hills."

"Aw, shit, aw, shit…you promised. You promised!"

Bolan marched Salcido whimpering, blubbering and begging for mercy into the Sinaloan night. By the time they had gone two miles the drug lord had fallen five times and thrown up twice. Once out of fear and the second time out of exhaustion. Bolan stopped at the drop point. "On your knees."

"*Por favor, amigo!* Please! Plea—"

Bolan kicked Salcido's legs out from under him and swiftly manacled his feet and hog-tied him. Bolan stripped out of his raid suit and pulled on jeans and a leather jacket, then put most of his weapons and gear into a large duffel. He clicked on the GPS transponder. A pair of Sinaloan CIA assets would come and pick up Salcido and the gear. They would get descriptions of the three men in the truck and get police sketches out and sit on the drug lord. Bolan heaved up the BMW Dakar motorcycle he had jumped with and kicked it into life. The nuclear materials were heading north. The Executioner had only one lead, and it was forcing him to turn south. Back to Mexico City.

Back to where the whole thing had started.

CHAPTER TWO

Culiacán

Bolan plugged his laptop into his satellite link and typed in his codes. Lights blinked on the link and told him the line was secure. Moments later Aaron Kurtzman, Stony Man Farm's genius in residence and lord of the Computer Room, blinked into life on an inset screen in real time. "What have you got for me?"

"A name," Bolan replied. "King Solomon."

"Guillermo 'King Solomon' Dominico?" It was a name Kurtzman was familiar with. He clicked keys on his side of North America and brought up DEA and FBI files. "Smuggling nuclear materials seems to be a bit out of his normal purview."

Bolan had never personally run up against Dominico, but he knew him by reputation. "I would have said the same thing about Pinto Salcido, but Geiger counters didn't lie and when he and I had our little talk I don't think he was, either."

"Well, as drug dealers go he's a pretty interesting cat," Kurtzman stated.

Bolan scanned the DEA files and they agreed with what

he'd heard. Guillermo Dominico had appeared on the smuggling scene literally out of nowhere with a couple of planes and respectable war chest of seed money to start his business. His father had been a crop duster in the State of Nayarit who went on to buy some land and become a fairly successful grain farmer. Dominico had taken the skills he'd learned from his father and earned a reputation as a daredevil pilot who could land a plane anywhere. From the very beginning he had liked to spread his money around in the string of little towns he operated out of. Rather than a trafficker of poison he had been regarded as a kind of Robin Hood figure who snuck under the FBI's and the DEA's noses and brought back wealth for the people. The *corrido* musicians had written dozens of songs about him and turned him into a folk hero.

It wasn't long before he had moved up into management.

"King Solomon" Dominico had become famous for his biblical and, by drug-smuggling standards, merciful judgment and punishment of those who transgressed against him. Most drug dealers simply slaughtered anyone who got in their way, and threw in some torture and atrocity to add fun and fear to the mix. Dominico had an Old-Testament, eye-for-an-eye, yet live-and-let-live philosophy. Anyone who stole from him? He cut off their left hand. Second time? Their right. Third time? Their head. To date there was no record of a second or a third transgression. If you informed on him, he tore out your tongue with tongs. As for DEA undercover agents or informants, nothing pleased him more than kidnapping them, keeping them as guests for a week or two at one of his haciendas deep in the desert and then dropping them off on the northern side of the border naked and hallucinating from violent heroin withdrawal.

Over the course of the last decade and a half he had carved himself a somewhat small, but tidy and quite profitable corner in Mexican organized crime.

He was big on Mexican pride and insisted on selling his wares north of the border. Anyone who worked for him who he caught selling locally received his judgment. Even other drug dealers liked and respected him and on several occasions "King Solomon" had been called upon to mediate disputes between the cartels. Dominico was a walking anomaly, a drug kingpin who had a code and actually walked his walk as he talked his talk. Bolan looked at the DEA file photo that Kurtzman had brought up on the screen.

Dominico bore a disturbing resemblance to a smiling, Mexican Sylvester Stallone with a beer gut.

Kurtzman was right. Smuggling nuclear materials for terrorists was not the sort of thing Guillermo Dominico would normally be involved with. Drugs, guns and kidnapping were things to be inflicted upon the *yanquis,* his neighbors north of the Rio Grande. For Dominico, Mexico was holy ground. Bolan just couldn't see him trafficking in radioactive poison even if it was heading north. The other very interesting thing was that unlike most crime lords who ended up in prison or dead, according to the FBI Dominico appeared to have gone into retirement several years ago, left the state of Sinaloa and moved to Mexico City.

"I think maybe I need to go have words with King Solomon."

Kurtzman had been afraid of that. "Well, here's something about the boy you might not know."

"Do tell."

"Many people believe that King Solomon the drug lord was once the masked wrestler Santo Solomon."

Bolan raised a bemused eyebrow. "Really."

Bolan knew just enough about the wonderful world of *Lucha Libre,* or Mexican professional wrestling, to know that the original masked wrestler named Santo ran a close second to Jesus as most popular person on Earth with the previous three generations of Mexican citizenry. Untold legions of *luchadors* had attached the name Santo to themselves to ride his rep.

Kurtzman called up more files. "At first he called himself Silver Solomon, and his gimmick was to come into the ring tossing peso coins to the crowd as he made his entrance." He pulled up a grainy screen capture from Mexican cable television. A man in silver tights and a silver mask stood atop the second rope of a wrestling ring. His fists were cocked on his hips and his chin lifted like Superman as he absorbed the adulation of the crowd. He was wearing a silver cape. A twenty, a five and a one peso coin were sewn in descending order on the forehead of his mask with the one set between the mask's stylized eyebrows. He was strong-looking, with impossibly broad shoulders, but was built more like a gymnast than his freakishly muscled wrestling counterparts north of the border. Mexican *luchadors* engaged in a lot of high-flying maneuvers and needed a higher power-to-weight ratio.

"So then he started dedicating matches to this church, or that charity or this orphan," Kurtzman went on, "and people started calling him Santo Solomon."

"So what happened to him?"

"The Santo Solomon gimmick just disappeared. Some people say the guy behind the mask took on a new persona, others say he got injured and had to quit. Being unmasked is a grave dishonor in the ring, and a lot of these guys retire without anyone knowing their true identities."

"If it's true he'd have the seed money to buy his own planes and start his own business. Can you link them?"

"I'm working on it."

"You say Dominico is currently in Mexico City?"

"Nice little house in the hills."

Bolan nodded. The nuclear material was still on its way north. He didn't have much time. "I'm on a plane."

Mexico City

KING SOLOMON'S KINGDOM was humble by most drug-lord-estate standards. It wasn't the usual Latin crime-king sprawling rancho or fortresslike hacienda. It was a modest Eichler-style house of mostly glass walls and open floor plan. The most opulent thing about it was the prime hillside real estate it rested upon. The altitude put it above the horrendous air pollution and afforded a sea-of-stars view of urban Mexico City below. The house itself didn't have much in the way of security, but most of the homes up in the hills were part of gated enclaves each with their own security station and armed guards. The raven-black 2008 Cadillac STS-V Bolan drove told most onlookers that Bolan belonged in these hills, and he wasn't going to bother with trying to bluff his way past the gate. Bolan parked at a turnoff located about a hundred feet below the cliff that King Solomon's house perched upon.

It wasn't a particularly technical climb, but a hundred feet of rock was still a hundred feet of rock and Bolan was making his ascent at night. The soldier shrugged out of his sport jacket and took off his tie. He rolled up the sleeves of the black silk shirt he wore and strapped his silenced Beretta machine pistol to the thigh of his black climbing pants. Bolan put handcuffs and a few other odds and ends in a fanny pack and looped a coil of rope over his shoulder. He kicked out of his Italian loafers, laced into his rock shoes, powered up his night-vision goggles and started to climb.

Even at midnight the rock still radiated heat from the summer day, but a warm, dry rock face was the climber's friend. He had scouted the cliff in the morning, and he climbed more by feel than what his goggles revealed. Only one overhang provided much of an obstacle, and for a few moments Bolan hung in space seventy-five feet above the road. However, he had photographed the ledge and committed its surface to memory, so the crevices and knobs were where he expected them to be.

Bolan was at the top a full five minutes under the time he had allotted himself.

He looped his rope around a tree trunk and cast the coil down the cliffside in case he needed to make a fast rope extraction. Satellite surveillance from the Farm had informed Bolan that Dominico's girlfriend had left at noon and not returned. The gardener had gone home around 4:00 p.m. and the maid-cook had left at 10:00 p.m. It was now 12:15 a.m., and it appeared that Guillermo Dominico was alone. Bolan scouted the outside of the house. It was literally perched on a cliff and the glass walls had been designed to take full advantage of the view. Dominico had just enough of a back porch to include a long, narrow pool lined with black lava rock with an attached hot tub. There was a barbecue area off to one side, but no walls or fence to interfere with the vistas of the Anáhuac plateau below. Bolan spent long moments watching. Through his goggles he didn't see the ghostly beams of any laser motion sensors. It appeared Dominico felt fairly secure in his aerie and the gates and guards on the periphery that kept out the riffraff and unwanted visitors from his past.

No one had planned on some American pulling a Spider-Man in the middle of the night.

Most of the rooms were dark. The master suite glowed blue from the light of a television. Bolan stepped into the shadows of the eaves and peered into the bedroom. One look told Bolan that Guillermo Dominico and the *luchador* Santo Solomon were the same man. King Solomon had been working out. He hadn't quite reclaimed the fighting physique of his *luchador* days, but the barn-door shoulders were no

longer sagging and the paunch and jowls from his DEA surveillance photos were gone. The coin-embossed, silver wrestling mask mounted behind glass on the wall surrounded by
wrestling photos and newspaper clippings were something of
a giveaway, as well. Dominico sat on a folded blue yoga mat
wearing a pair of sausage-casing tight biking shorts; he was
sheened with sweat and twitching and grimacing as he tried
to hold a very forced and uncomfortable-looking half-lotus
pose in front of his seventy-two-inch HDTV. Bolan paused a
moment. It wasn't something you saw drug kingpins do every
day, even supposedly retired ones.

Up on the screen a man wearing nothing but a white loin-
cloth sat in a full-lotus position and lectured in obviously
dubbed Spanish. He looked like Yul Brynner, if the actor was
a six-foot-six Special Forces operator moonlighting as a yoga
instructor. Beneath his dais three beautiful blond women dem-
onstrated poses at various levels of difficulty as he lectured.
Bolan bided his time and silently picked the lock on the sliding-
glass door.

He had run up against some wrestlers gone bad before, and
anyone who had the capacity to fake that kind of physical
carnage day in and day out without using wires or computer-
generated special effects could also inflict it for real outside
the ring. Bolan grimaced at the tiny click the latch made as
he lifted it with his pick. Dominico was oblivious. His attention was equally divided between his DVD guru and his own
straining knee joints. Bolan watched as the women on the
giant TV unfolded themselves effortlessly from their sitting
positions and flicked out their legs into full-forward splits.
Dominico's groan was audible through the sliding glass as he
made a very impressive attempt at following suit.

Bolan slid back the door and it closed behind him as he
strode into the room.

Dominico's head snapped around and he rose an inch out of his splits. "Hey!"

Bolan slammed his hands down on Dominico's shoulders. The former crime lord groaned as the soldier leaned his two hundred plus pounds into his attack and pushed Dominico a little deeper into the splits than he'd ever gone before. He could almost hear the groin muscles and tendons pulling like piano strings being tuned to the breaking point. Dominico's shoulders suddenly heaved as he tried to push himself up. He was a powerful man, and it was a mighty attempt but Bolan had all the leverage. Dominico was pinned in place like a bug. The only direction for him to go was down. Bolan spoke quietly from his position of moral advantage. "Try that again and you're going to sing soprano, Santo."

Dominico couldn't rise and he sure as hell didn't want to go any lower. He snarled, suspended in yogic purgatory. "Don't call me Santo!"

Bolan raised an intrigued eyebrow. For a man about to be snapped like a wishbone Dominico was remarkably defiant. Bolan leaned a little harder. "You'd prefer King Solomon?"

"No!" Dominico's triceps stood out like horseshoes as he bore the weight of both of them. "It's just Memo now!" he gritted.

"Memo" was the diminutive of Guillermo, like Billy for William. Bolan decided to give it to him. He didn't have a partner to play good cop-bad cop with so he was going to have to play both roles; that and Guillermo Dominico was giving off just about the weirdest vibe of any crime lord Bolan had ever encountered. It was going to require more study than just a quick beat down for intel. "Okay, Memo, let's talk."

"Hey, man…" Dominico groaned in counterpoint. "Do I know you?"

"I want to know about the operation in Culiacán."

"What are you? FBI? DEA?"

Bolan shoved down a little harder. "Talk to me or make a wish."

Every muscle in Dominico's body tensed with strain. "I haven't been to Culiacán in years!"

"There's a farm up in the hills. Near the Tamazula River. It has a hacienda and a warehouse and an airstrip. There was a time when you flew out of it. From what I know you used to own it."

"I got nothing going on in Sinaloa! I'm retired!"

"Drug dealers don't retire, Memo." Bolan leaned hard. "They just change their M.O."

"Jesus!" Dominico shuddered with effort. "I'm retired! Ask anybody!"

"That's not what I hear, Memo."

"Heard from who!" Dominico probed.

"Your old buddy, Oswaldo Salcido, for one," Bolan replied.

"Pinto!" A geyser of Spanish profanities erupted from Dominico's mouth. "That prick? You took his word? I set him up in business! I gave him a piece of my territory when I retired as a gift! Now he fingers me? *Pinche chingaso* mother…" Dominico dropped back into profanity.

Bolan shut it off by giving the crime lord an extra millimeter of unwanted flexibility. "You are going to talk to me."

"Listen…" Dominico's elbows bent as his muscles began to give out and his crotch moved inexorably toward the floor. He hissed through clenched teeth. "You gotta let me up, man…before I never have children!"

Bolan relented a couple of inches. "Come up slow."

Dominico didn't rise. He suddenly dropped beneath Bolan's grip and spun on his back like a break-dancer. His legs scythed upward and his ankles locked behind Bolan's head. The soldier's feet left the ground as he found himself in a scissors hold. The glass walls shook as Bolan hit the floor flat on his back and the air blasted out of his lungs. He clawed for the Beretta 93R strapped to his thigh, but Dominico grabbed his wrist in both hands. "Gonna snap you like a toothpick, motherfucker!" Dominico began pulling back to straighten Bolan's arm and break his elbow.

Bolan found himself wrestling with a professional *luchador,* and he had no illusions about who was going to win a match between them. Dominico's legs felt like two pieces of oak as they vised down on Bolan's carotids for the strangle.

The soldier's temples pounded as he felt the blood shut off to his brain. His only advantage was that wrestling, whether real or fake, was played by rules and most people in an emergency did what they had practiced, and a lot of wrestling holds had weaknesses for those willing to cheat. Bolan managed to turn his head two inches. Dominico howled and released the scissors hold and Bolan's arm as the big American sank his teeth into his calf. Bolan shook his head against the head rush as he lurched to his feet. Dominico popped up and came in snarling and limping. "You dirty son of a bitch! I'm gonna—"

Bolan faked a right-hand lead but Dominico lowered his head and came in, willing to take a punch so he could get his hands on Bolan again and resume trying to snap him like kindling. Bolan fired his right hand for real—except that rather than going for a fist to the jaw he corkscrewed his thumb into the hollow of Dominico's throat. His adversary's eyes flew wide, and his tongue popped out as his trachea compressed. Bolan slammed his fist into the ex-drug dealer's solar plexus, and the guy's diaphragm spasmed against his already deflated lungs. Dominico's face drained of blood, and he sat down on his yoga mat gasping like a landed fish. Bolan stepped in and threw an uppercut as if he were bowling to pick up a spare. His knuckles looped into the point of

Dominico's chin like a wrecking ball and ironed him out flat on the floor.

Bolan drew his Beretta 93-R machine pistol. The laser sight blazed into life as he squeezed, and it painted a ruby red dot between Dominico's eyebrows. Dominico gazed up into the muzzle of the machine pistol dazedly and sucked for air. Bolan took a couple of long breaths himself and shook his head to clear it. "Memo? I'm done playing with you."

"You aren't DEA," Dominico gasped. "And FBI doesn't work like this. You aren't cartel, either. Who the fuck are you?"

Bolan gazed down on Dominico. He had taken down more bad guys than most people had eaten hot meals. A lot of those bad guys had been drug traffickers. At this point most drug dealers would be screaming for mercy or screaming for their lawyer. For a former professional wrestler who'd just gotten his ass kicked and a drug dealer staring down the muzzle of a machine pistol, Dominico was remarkably calm and collected.

Bolan raised an eyebrow at the Yul Brynner look-alike lecturing in dubbed Spanish on the screen. "Memo, what is that stuff?"

"You gotta be kidding me, man." Dominico genuinely looked shocked that Bolan didn't know. "That's Cielo Ahora."

Bolan watched the bald man gesture gracefully with hands the size of catcher's mitts while his nubile assistants twisted like dreamy-eyed circus contortionists. "Heaven Now?"

"Change your life, man," Dominico confirmed. "Changed mine."

Bolan peered down at Dominico with sudden intuition. "This is why you retired from the life?"

"Hey, man, everybody's got to grow up sometime. I been a legend twice. But Santo Solomon had two cracked vertebrae in his neck, and the doctors told him if he wrestled again he'd end up in a wheelchair. No one needed to tell King

Solomon that he was going to wind up dead or in prison. Not that I cared, until a couple of years ago. Gavi helped me get my head right."

"Gavi?"

Dominico grunted up at the screen and the bald man with the piercing eyes. "Gavi."

"So you quit the life because you found God?"

"Found Gavi." Dominico grinned. "The rest I'm working on."

Bolan gave Dominico a long, calculating look. "Memo, you want to go for a ride?"

Dominico's face went flat. "I've seen that movie, man."

Bolan shrugged. The ruby dot of the laser never wavered from Dominico's forehead. "I can kill you now."

Dominico weighed the steel in Bolan's blue eyes. "A ride is good."

CHAPTER THREE

Campo Militar No. 1

"Uhh..." Dominico looked unhappily at the gates of Mexico City's military base. "You know me and the military don't get along so good."

"Relax, you're with me." Bolan tossed Dominico the keys to his handcuffs. "And I won't tell them who you are if you don't."

Dominico removed his manacles and rubbed his wrists. "You know this is kidnapping."

Bolan nodded through the Caddy's tinted glass at the Mexican military policemen with assault rifles guarding the gate. "Take it up with them." Bolan rolled down the window and displayed an ID card and a pass. The guard nodded and waved them in.

Dominico watched barracks and military buildings pass by. "Man, just who the fuck are you?"

Bolan ignored the question. *Campo Militar No. 1* was a sprawling establishment with many of the Mexican Army's branches having headquarters. Bolan knew exactly where he was going. He had already been there once earlier in the week. He drove up to a complex of tents that had the universal medical Red Cross flag flying over them. "We get out here."

"A hospital? Why are we—"

Bolan got out and went into the tent complex with Dominico muttering and reluctantly following on his heels. Two guards with subdued Special Forces flashes on the sleeves of their uniforms were smoking cigarettes in the foyer tent. Both nodded at Bolan in recognition. They're hands moved vaguely toward the grips of their FX-05 Fire Serpent assault rifles as they eyed Dominico. "Who's he?"

Bolan smiled. "You wouldn't believe me if I told you."

The Special Forces corporal's eyes narrowed suspiciously. "Try me."

"You don't recognize him?" Bolan shrugged. "That's Santo Solomon."

The guard's jaw dropped. "No fucking way!"

Dominico was appalled.

"Do it!" the guards begged in unison. "Do it!"

Dominico shot Bolan a look, sighed, put his fists on his hips, flexed his pecs, flared his lats, turned his head and lifted his chin as he seemed to lean slightly into a wind only he was aware of. The profile was unmistakable. You could almost see the silver cape flowing behind him. "Santo!" the guards cried. "Santo Solomon!" Both men snatched up pens and paper from the desk and demanded autographs. Bolan and Dominico were both given neck badges and proceeded past the checkpoint while the guards stopped just short of squealing like schoolgirls and fainting in Dominico's wake.

"I can't believe you told them who I was, man. You never reveal masked wrestlers," Dominico muttered. "It isn't cool."

"I had to tell them something. I could have told them you were King Solomon the notorious drug smuggler instead.

You saw the patches on their uniforms? Those young gentlemen are Special Forces and trained specifically to kill people like your other alter ego."

"Man…" Dominico wasn't mollified. "What am I doing here?"

"There's something I want you to see." They passed through a canvas corridor and came into a large medical tent. "And some people I want you to meet."

A short, fat bald man in a white lab coat waddled forward quickly. He was followed by a short, lean man in Mexican military camouflage with the subdued three-star insignia of a colonel. The doctor stared at Dominico in awe. "It's true!"

Dominico sighed heavily. Bolan suspected the guards had gotten on their cell phones. Bolan made introductions. "Dr. Corso, Colonel Llosa, meet Memo Dominico."

The doctor giddily pumped Dominico's hand. "You know, I grew up watching El Santo, the original."

"Who didn't?" Dominico admitted diplomatically.

"But you? Santo Solomon? When my boys were young? You were their hero. I took them to see you wrestle El Monstro Rojo when you won the title." Corso managed to curb his hero worship slightly. "Forgive me, but may I ask why you are here?"

Colonel Llosa stared at Dominico with a professional interest that had nothing to do with wrestling. "I also must admit I am intrigued."

"It's somewhat complicated," Bolan said. "Dr. Corso, may I show him your patients?"

"Of course." There were sixteen beds in the tent but only two were occupied, and monitors, drips and machines surrounded them. Dominico jarred to a halt as they got close. The two men inhabiting the beds hardly looked human. Neither was conscious and their breath was so shallow that only the mournful beeps of the vital signs monitor indicated they were alive. Dozens of tubes and wires were busy carrying out their most basic bodily functions for them while other machines monitored their impending death. They were as stick-thin as famine victims and open sores covered their bald, sunken skulls.

"You know what's killing these guys, Memo?" Bolan inquired.

"I don't know." Dominico stared at the two dying men greenly. "AIDS?"

Bolan read Dominico's body language and saw no deception. "No, radiation poisoning."

"Radiation poisoning?" Again Dominico was clearly both confused and appalled. "How did they get radiation poisoning?"

"They were exposed to radioactive material," Llosa answered dryly. "Dr. Corso is the head of Nuclear Medicine at the American British Cowdray Hospital Cancer Center here in Mexico City. Doctor?"

Corso tapped his chart. "Both men were exposed to lethal levels of radiation. Given the rapid onset of symptoms and the searing of the lungs I believe they breathed in contaminated dust, most likely from spent nuclear fuel rods that had been stored improperly. We will most likely never know. Both men were in an advanced state when they were dropped off in the parking lot at Mexico City General. Neither man was conscious at the time of admission and neither has regained consciousness since. They were initially misdiagnosed as victims of some sort of virus and put under quarantine. Luckily the head virologist had received federal nuclear, biological and chemical emergency training and recognized the symptoms of radiation poisoning. It then became a military matter. I was called in and the United States government contacted."

"Any luck IDing them?" Bolan asked.

The colonel shook his head grimly. "As you know, neither

man had any identification on their person. The federal police ran their prints and came up empty. Your FBI had no record of them, either. They lack any of the usual gang tattoos. If I had to bet? These men are *campesinos* from the countryside, day laborers who came to Mexico City looking for work. I would also wager neither man was told what he was handling and neither were any safety or decontamination protocols observed." He shook his head sadly. "They were used and then thrown away."

"There isn't any radioactive material in Mexico!" Dominico objected.

"Not normally," Bolan agreed. "In this case Mexico is a transshipment point."

The colonel gave Dominico a severe look. "And you know all about transshipment points, don't you, Memo?"

Dominico flinched.

Bolan steered the conversation back to business. "I believe these men were exposed to the same radioactive material that was being stored at your warehouse outside of Culiacán."

"I told you man! It isn't my warehouse anymore!"

Bolan gave Dominico a long, hard look. "Someone is using your routes and your contacts to smuggle nuclear materials through Mexico."

Dominico shook his head vehemently. "No one is using my routes, man!"

"Yeah?" Bolan leaned in close. "Well, someone used the warehouse and the airstrip outside of Culiacán. Your old stomping grounds. You said yourself you gave out your territory when you retired."

Dominico backed up a step. "No way, man! I said I gave up my piece of the action! I never gave up my routes, and I sure as hell never gave up my people or my contacts! I took care of my own!"

"You're routes and your people are being used, Memo, and they're going to start dying if this stuff is still being stored improperly. We don't know where the material came from. All we know is that it was in Mexico City and then it was in Culiacán. It's moving north, Memo, and at the end of the trail someone is going to build a bomb."

Dominico gaped.

Bolan locked eyes with him. "I want your people, I want your old routes, I want your contacts and for that matter I want you. Everyone involved will go to ground when I start hunting, but they just might talk to King Solomon. You're going to open some doors for me. With luck we might just stop something terrible from happening, and we might just save the lives of some people you care about along the way." Bolan locked eyes with him. "You in or out?"

Dominico broke eye contact and stared over at the blistered, emaciated dying men in the beds. He looked back at Bolan and met his burning gaze. "I want a gun."

Bolan shrugged. "What kind do you want?"

He blinked. "Uhh...an Uzi?"

"A bit old-fashioned these days."

"First gun I had, when I started flying routes in the eighties. Nothing wrong with Hebrew steel."

Bolan nodded at the wisdom of the statement. "Nothing at all."

Culiacán New Airport

BOLAN PULLED AN UZI out of his gear bag. They were in a private hangar and Dominico had flown the Piper-Aztec from Mexico City. They were back in Sinaloa. Bolan had done some shopping at the CIA Mexico City station before their flight. "Here you go."

"Damn, you weren't kidding!" Dominico took the submachine and eyed the shortened barrel critically. "Why is it sawed off?"

"It's an ex-U.S. Secret Service weapon. They removed a couple of inches of barrel so it would fit into their standard-issue briefcases. They called it 'The Rabbi' model."

"Circumcised." Dominico grinned and racked the action. The padded case Bolan handed him held the gun, an ex-Secret Service shoulder rig, six loaded magazines and a couple of boxes of spare ammo. Bolan pulled out a plain black windbreaker that had been cut to help conceal the rig.

They hadn't spoken much on the flight. Bolan had given the man time to think things through. He'd been intimidated at the army medical facility, but Bolan didn't want Memo Dominico intimidated or just turned. He wanted him dedicated to the fight. "So what are you thinking?"

Dominico scratched his chin. "I'm thinking we should go see a guy—Varjo. You said Salcido thought he was working for me. Any orders he's taking these days would've probably have come through Varjo. I think maybe we should ask Varjo where he thinks his orders were coming from."

"Varjo's an old buddy of yours?"

"No way, man." Dominico shook his head. "Varjo is a serious asshole, but when I was running things he always owed me a taste. When I left Sinaloa I heard he moved up. He's one of the reasons I never gave anyone my contacts or my routes. He would have used them up, ripped them off and spent them like water, but he and Salcido were always thick. Both were always a little too dumb, and tried to make up for it by being too brutal. Salcido I could work with. He didn't have any delusions of adequacy. Varjo on the other hand? He's seen too many movies."

Bolan got the picture.

"I figure we just drive right up and surprise him. You're my bodyguard. If Varjo thinks he's working for me, he should be a fucking gold mine of information. If he isn't—" Dominico spread his hands as if casting their future to fate "—we'll find out real quick."

It wasn't a bad plan.

The DEA presence in Sinaloa had been kind enough to have an unmarked Ford Bronco waiting for them on the tarmac, and the Farm had arranged for a full war load of equipment to be loaded in the back while Bolan had been in Mexico City. Bolan checked his weapons and put a Desert Eagle semiautomatic pistol in one shoulder holster and his machine pistol in the other. He pulled a leather jacket over his hardware and let Dominico drive.

Bolan scanned DEA files on his laptop.

Varjo Amilcar's nickname was "El Martillo" or "The Hammer." He had been a cruiserweight boxer of little distinction in the professional ranks but had taken what skills he had and traded them in as a freelance collection agent for various loan sharks in Sinaloa. His method was simple. His partner would hold a debtor in place while Amilcar worked them like a heavy bag. He had beaten several men to death and done a nickel standing on his head at the penal colony on Maria Madre Island. With his reputation made, he had used similar brutality and the connections he had made in prison to move into the drug trade. However Dominico's estimation of Amilcar seemed accurate. In the drug war Amilcar just wasn't officer material. Despite his elevated status he was still more of a muscle and go-to guy rather than a man who ran his own routes or had his own suppliers. Amilcar was strictly middle management. Dominico regarded him with professional contempt as well as the disdain most wrestlers had for boxers. Despite that both Bolan and Dominico were disturbed by the idea that Amilcar had somehow broken into Dominico's old business circle.

He couldn't have done it without help.

They drove north out of the city and paralleled the Humaya River. "I want to make a call," Dominico said.

Bolan took out his phone and put it on speaker. "Go ahead."

Dominico was surprised as he took the phone. He dialed some numbers and the phone rang for long moments before a wary female voice spoke. *"¿Hola?"*

"Najelli," Dominico said. "It's Memo. What's up?"

"What's up?" The woman exploded. "I tell you what's up! Everything is fucked, Memo! What do you think is up! And why are you talking English?"

Dominico looked at Bolan and was at a loss. "I'm...in town."

This was met with a long silence. "Why?"

Dominico blinked. "Why am I in town?"

"No, why are you speaking in English and why am I on speaker— Cabrón!" Najelli hung up violently.

"Girlfriend?" Bolan inquired.

"I wish." Dominico sighed. "More like the big sister I never had. She might be able to give us the lay of the land and some backup."

Intel was good. Backup was intriguing. "Try again."

The phone rang until Dominico got the answering machine. He waited patiently for the beep. "Najelli, pick up."

The line picked up. "Memo, I—" The woman exploded again. "You motherfucker! I'm still on speaker!"

"Listen, Najelli, you—"

"Memo..." The woman sounded like she was about to start crying. "Tell me you haven't sold me out. Tell me you're not sitting next to some American DEA prick."

"Uhh..." Dominico was at a loss again. "He's not DEA, and I'm pretty sure he's no prick."

"Memo, give me the phone," Bolan said.

Dominico handed back the phone sheepishly. Bolan covered the receiver and whispered. "Last name?"

"Busto."

Bolan raised the phone to his ear. "Miss Busto? My name is Cooper."

The invectives flew. *"Yanqui federale chingaso cabrón—"*

Bolan interrupted and threw a card on the table. "Miss Busto? I'm not a cop. You are not under surveillance. You are not under arrest and you are not a suspect. I'm here in Culiacán to help Memo kick Varjo Amilcar's ass."

That tidbit of information was met with a profound silence. A tense ten seconds passed. "Put Memo back on."

Bolan covered the receiver with his hand as he passed the phone back. "Don't mess this up."

"Man…" Dominico took the phone. "Najelli, whatever is happening, it isn't me. I gave no orders. I'm coming out of retirement to fix this, understand?"

"Okay, so who's the American?" she retorted.

Dominico ad-libbed. "I didn't know who I could trust. I hired a Special Forces mercenary. He's all professional and shit. Real badass."

Bolan shrugged.

Silence reigned for a long time before Busto spoke. "Memo? I'm telling you. Things are bad."

"I know. Let me pick you up. We'll talk. If you want out, I got a plane."

"You got room for my mother? And my daughter?"

Dominico looked to Bolan, who nodded.

"Yeah. I got room. You're family, Najelli."

"Then come and meet me at Davilo's shrine."

"When?"

"Now, *chico*." The line clicked dead.

"Who's Davilo?" Bolan asked.

"Davilo Fonseca, fellow pilot. He was Busto's boyfriend. She learned a lot from him. Then the *federales* punched holes in his ride on the way back from the U.S.A. and he made a smoking hole in the ground. Man, I tell you, I tried to steal her from Davilo a thousand times, but she was in love. After he died, a lot of guys wanted her. Some were bad, including Varjo. I let everyone know they had to go through me. You know, I offered to marry her. Instead she asked me to teach her how to shoot. Then she up and left to Mexico City to became a bodyguard. There's more call for women guards there than you think. You know, rich guys want someone who can stay with the women and children and girlfriends twenty-four-seven. Someone the hombres feel safe with operating in their harem. Then she got pregnant. Word is it was one of her clients. One of her married clients. He denied it and she got fired and moved back here to Culiacán. She didn't think Mexico City was a place to raise a kid. Like any place is anymore."

"It's not *where* you raise a kid but *how*."

Dominico shot Bolan a look and then suddenly pointed at a dirt turnoff. "We go there." The road wound for another ten minutes through the hills and they came to a tiny valley. Dominico sighed in memory. "They call it El Corona."

Bolan examined the ring of hills that formed "The Crown."

Weeds overgrew the floor of the vale, but it was clear that it had once been leveled into an airstrip. It was a picture-perfect, hidden landing zone for a daredevil *narcotraficante* willing to risk everything, but it was short. Very short. For a pilot with a damaged aircraft the Crown would turn a hairy descent into suicide. Dominico pulled up beside a cairn of stones covered with tarnished religious medals, faded ribbons and burned-out votive candles.

It was the last resting place of Davilo Fonseca.

Bolan could see unshed tears in Dominico's eyes by the glare of the Bronco's headlights. "I taught him everything he knew." Dominico scraped the back of his hand across his face. "She won't be long. Her mother and father were farmers. She took over the old place. It's not far from here."

Bolan found a courtesy Thermos of DEA coffee and a foam box laden with street-vendor tamales wrapped in corn husks. He and Dominico leaned against the Bronco and ate and waited. Dominico was right. It wasn't long before headlights showed up on the dirt road. Bolan drank coffee as a primer gray and rust red Mercury Grand Marquis pulled up in front of the Bronco. A woman got out from behind the wheel. She wore old cargo pants, a man's cardigan sweater a few sizes too big for her and some ancient-looking cowboy boots. She was runway-model thin with brown hair worn in two braids. Her brown eyes were huge above a little ski-jump nose and bow lips.

Najelli Busto looked like a lost waif from the streets of Rome rather than a Mexican gun moll—except for the stainless-steel Ruger pistol thrust into the front of her pants. She wore a scowl on her face and was smoking the stub of a cigarette. Bolan could tell by the sweet smell of the rice paper binder that it was an unfiltered Mexican Faros. She chain-lit another as she and Bolan sized each other up in the glow of the headlights. She spoke to Dominico without taking her eyes off Bolan. "You look good, Memo."

"You, too, baby!" Dominico grinned.

Busto made a bemused noise.

"Miss Busto, you said everything in Culiacán is messed up. May I ask what you meant?"

"Well, you're a polite son of a bitch, I'll give you that." Busto looked warily to Dominico.

He nodded. "You can talk to him. He's cool."

"I am cool," Bolan agreed. "Tell me what's messed up, Miss Busto."

Some pent-up anger began to simmer to the surface. "You want to talk about messed up? First you got Pinto and Varjo acting like they own the place, and they don't play nice. What's worse is even guys who don't normally sweat guys like Pinto and Varjo, men of reputation, are acting like they're scared. That gets everybody scared. Some people disappeared and suddenly Varjo and Pinto can get away with just about anything. Then Pinto gets hit—"

"That was me," Bolan admitted.

Busto's big brown eyes blinked. "That was you?"

"Yeah."

"You and Memo took out Pinto?"

"No, just me."

Busto was incredulous. "Memo, who the hell is this guy?"

Dominico sighed. "I stopped asking."

Busto struggled with it all. "So you kicked Pinto's ass? And all of his men? By yourself?"

Bolan nodded. "Yeah, and now I'm gonna do the same to Amilcar. You in?"

Busto just stared.

"Listen," Bolan went on, "I've gotten to know Memo a little bit. I believe he's on the up-and-up. I also believe he's being set up for a big fall. When I spoke with Pinto, he didn't know who the head of the operation was, but he thought Dominico was calling the shots from the Mexico City leg. I want to know if Varjo believes the same thing and if he knows anything more than Pinto did."

"What kind of fall?"

Bolan weighed how much to tell the woman. "The kind where Memo wakes up in a subbasement in Kazakhstan."

"Jesus, you're talking like the war on terror and shit."

"That's right." Bolan nodded. "The bad guys didn't expect to get discovered, but they got sloppy with their packaging and we caught a break. But if they did get discovered, King Solomon would take the rap. No one believes in drug dealers who retire. Think about it, he drops a profitable business in drugs, leaves for the capital and goes dark for two years. On paper it sounds shady as hell. He'd be the perfect fall guy. Memo would be shipped off to a secret prison someplace, someplace dark and deep, and by the time the Ukrainian interrogators got done with him and figured out he really didn't know anything, whatever ugliness the bad guys are planning would have already happened."

"So who are the bad guys?" Busto asked.

Bolan shook his head. "I don't know."

"What are they planning?"

"I don't know, but something involving a flatbed-load of radioactive material."

"Jesus…"

"Najelli," Dominico said very quietly, "some *campesinos* in Mexico City are already dying from just moving this stuff. I've seen what it's going to do to people. I signed up with the hombre here. We're gonna stop it. We got to."

Busto looked back and forth between the two men. "Jesus, Memo, you know I heard you joined some cult and gotten religion or something."

Dominico rolled his eyes. "It's not a cult, it's—"

Bolan cut him off. "We're going to go pay a visit to Varjo Amilcar. You in or not?"

"Oh, I'm in." Busto dropped her cigarette butt to the ground and crushed it beneath her heel. "But how are you going to play it?"

Bolan had been considering his approach. "The element of surprise is always good."

"Surprise is good," Dominico agreed. "And I think Varjo will be very surprised to hear from me, but I don't think it will be a good kind of surprise. I'm thinking we don't even make it through the gate."

Bolan smiled slyly at Busto. "How surprised would Varjo be if you called him and said you wanted to see him?"

Busto snorted. "He'd be surprised. He's always wanted a piece of me." She chewed her lip and shook her head. "But I don't know if he'd buy it. He knows I hate him. He'd suspect something."

Bolan weighed what he knew about the Hammer. "You said people have disappeared. People in Culiacán are scared. Everything is messed up and now he's the top dog. What if you called Varjo and told him you're lonely, scared and out of money? That you're scared for your mother and daughter."

Busto smiled bitterly. "Well, that would all be true, wouldn't it?" Her smile grew predatory as she thought about it. "But he'd like that. He'd like that a lot. Varjo has a real sick cruel streak. He'd love me to come to him begging. He'd love to break me."

Dominico looked at Bolan with renewed respect. "Jesus, you're all Machiavellian and shit."

"It's what I do," Bolan agreed. He looked to Busto. "How soon can you be ready for your big date?"

VARJO AMILCAR was ready for his big date.

He was ready for it tonight. Bolan had smelled the sadism behind his reassurances when Busto had started crying and saying she didn't know what to do anymore. Busto could have had a job in Mexican soap operas. She was that good. They sat in her parents' old farmhouse. The walls were made out of adobe bricks, and Busto said the place was at least a hundred years old. They'd put her mother and her daughter in the Bronco and sent them on to the next town where her mother had friends. Bolan and Dominico drank coffee and ate red beans while they watched Busto doll herself up for her date. She'd looked cute in her knock-around clothes in the glare of the headlights.

Now she was a knockout.

Skintight jeans sheathed her lower body. Bolan suspected she'd had some surgical enhancements, and her upper half was doing its utmost to explode out of the camisole she wore. She'd brushed out her braids and her brown hair fells in waves around her shoulders. She draped a man's sport coat that had been cut to fit her frame over it and began judiciously applying makeup to emphasize her features.

Now she really looked like she belonged in Mexican soap operas.

Bolan watched as she checked the loads in her 9 mm Ruger and stuffed spare magazines into her pockets. "You any good with that?"

Dominico stabbed a proud thumb into his chest. "I taught her everything she knows!"

"You any good with that?" Bolan repeated.

Dominico rolled his eyes. "Man…"

Busto checked the loads in a snub-nosed .38 and tucked the little revolver into the top of her boot. "When I went to Mexico City the security service that hired me put me through a course to teach me right."

Dominico deflated. "Man…"

Bolan turned on Dominico. "You said you always had an Uzi, ever since you started flying?"

"Yeah." Dominico thrust out his jaw defiantly. "That's right."

"You ever fire it?"

"Of course I fired it!"

"In anger?" Bolan prodded.

"Yeah! Yeah, I did as a matter of fact! I was in a firefight! With Colombians in Baja!"

Bolan probed further. "Did you hit anything?"

"I…" Dominico's shoulders sagged. "I don't know, man. It was dark, and across an airstrip."

"I see."

A city map and satellite photos were spread out across the table. Bolan tapped the spot where Amilcar had a house on the Culiacán River. "Najelli, you're going to drive right up. Memo and I will be in the trunk. All eyes will be on you and I doubt they'll search the car. They will probably search you for a wire. They'll find your gun, but Varjo probably expects you to have one. Expect to have it taken from you. Ask for a drink, start crying again and then tell him you want to be alone with him. I want Varjo separated from the rest of the household, so try to get him into the bedroom as soon as possible."

Busto grinned. "That shouldn't be hard."

"No." Bolan gave her an appreciative glance. "No, it shouldn't. Once you're inside Memo and I will extract ourselves from the car and make our way to you. With luck we'll achieve total surprise."

"And then?"

"Then we have a quiet talk with the man."

DOMINICO LAUGHED in the darkness. The trunk of Busto's Grand Marquis was pitch-black, but it was cavernous. Both Bolan and Dominico were able to recline on their sides on piles of blankets in relative claustrophobic comfort as the sedan bounced over the potholed streets of Culiacán.

"What?" Bolan inquired.

"The song."

Bolan perked an ear. Busto had her stereo cranked up playing cassettes of old school *narcocorrido* music. The *corrido* was a form of Mexican *norteño* folk music. The *nar-*

cocorridos were folk songs about various drug smugglers and their exploits. They had become popular in the sixties when the American drug culture had exploded and enterprising Mexican criminals had exploited it. Today it was a music industry unto itself in Mexico. The music was fast and the Mexican slang so thick Bolan couldn't make much of it. "What about it?"

Dominico laughed again. "It's about me. That song is ten years old. It never made it to CD, not that I know of. It's called *'De Las Alas Hasta el Rey.'*"

Bolan flexed his Spanish. *"On the wings until the king."*

"Very good, man." Bolan could almost hear Dominico grinning in the dark. "The song is about a lowly *narcotraficante* flyboy who rose on angel wings to become the great King Solomon."

Bolan raised a bemused eyebrow. "Angel wings?"

"I didn't write it, man! Anyway. Najelli? She's my friend. She's playing it to give me courage."

Bolan hoped it was working. Dominico had been twitchy since Busto had slammed the lid shut. It wasn't locked. Bolan was holding it shut with a piece of twine, but on every continent on Earth with a drug trade, being put in the trunk of a car was a death sentence, and this mission was starting to turn into a suicide run. "How you holding up?"

"I'm okay." Dominico was silent for a moment. "Can I ask you a question?"

"Sure."

"Who are you? I mean…you're not a cop."

"No," Bolan agreed.

"You're not a soldier."

"I was," Bolan admitted.

"But not anymore."

"No."

Dominico spent long moments digesting this. "So…what the fuck, man?"

Bolan gave him the short and sanitized version. "I was in a war. That was bad enough, but when I came back I found that some bad people had gotten into my world. They got close to me and mine. They got too close, they did damage and it got ugly."

"So, what did you do?"

"I killed them, Memo. I killed them all."

"Jesus… So you're the Terminator?"

Bolan chose his words carefully. "You remember those *campesinos* dying of radiation poisoning in Mexico City?"

"I'm having nightmares about it."

"I'm here to stop it if I can. If you're not down with that, then knock on the trunk and Najelli can let you out. As far as I'm concerned you've done your bit, and we're square."

"No way, man. I'm down, and I'm not going to let Najelli down. I have your back. I've been trying to get my head right. I've been trying to reject violence. But some shit, like nuclear radiation shit, has to be resisted."

"Righteous enough." Bolan nodded. "But do me one favor."

"What's that, *amigo?*"

"That thing at the back of your Uzi?"

"What thing at the back of my Uzi?"

"The folding stock."

"What about it?"

"Deploy it."

"Man?" Dominico made a dismissive noise. "I never use that thing."

Bolan sighed. "That's what I figured."

Busto knocked three times on the roof. It was the signal that they were arriving. Bolan aimed his Beretta at the trunk lid as he felt the ancient car slow. The safety on Dominico's Uzi clicked off in the darkness and the weapon clicked again as he slapped the folding stock into place. Dominico radiated renewed tension in the trunk's pitch-black confines. "Shit," he said. "Here we go."

Bolan spoke quietly. "Memo."

"Yeah?"

"Relax, shut up and don't shoot unless I do."

Dominico absorbed the sage advice. "Right."

The Mercury came to a halt and Bolan heard muffled talk as Busto spoke to the gate guard. She was expected and the car moved ahead once more within seconds. The Mercury turned left, then right and came to a stop again. Bolan's mental map from the satellite photos told him they had parked by the northern side of the house. He heard two sets of shoes crunch up in the gravel. Busto got out, the door slammed shut and he heard her follow the two men back the way they had come.

Bolan spent long moments listening.

"Hey, man," Dominico said. "We—"

"Quiet." Bolan let up a few ounces of slack of the twine around his little finger. The trunk lid cracked open an inch and light flooded into the trunk. Bolan waited and the light suddenly disappeared. The floodlights were slaved to a motion sensor. Bolan figured it was three minutes since the car had parked and Busto had walked away. Inch by inch Bolan let the trunk lid up. "Stay low by the side of the car. I think we're inside the motion sensor's guard. We hug wall and move to the back. Got it?"

"Got it."

Bolan paid out twine until the trunk was open. The floodlights still stayed off. "Follow me."

The soldier unfolded out of the trunk and crouched by the side of the car. He drew his Desert Eagle to fill both hands with steel. Dominico followed him but the lights stayed off, no alarms sounded and no attack dogs came slavering out of the dark. Bolan took the lead as they moved toward the river. Amilcar had a nice spot. Culiacán was a city of three rivers. The Humaya and the Tamazula met in the city to form the Culiacán River that flowed all the way to the Pacific Ocean. Amilcar had a little pier with a pontoon boat for parties, a couple of river boats clearly dedicated to fishing and a sleek cigarette boat Bolan suspected was for high-speed exits to the sea.

Bolan didn't see any guards on duty. It was late, it was a school night and Amilcar was gearing up for a private night of romance and revenge. It looked like they might have caught a break. The backyard was a wide expanse of lawn with the obligatory fountain, gazebo and arena-sized barbecue pit.

Bolan glanced up as light spilled out across the balcony of the master bedroom. Dominico frowned upward. "Varjo works fast."

"So should we." Amilcar's vast living room overlooked the backyard and the river, and the lights were still on. Bolan peered in and counted four men. They all wore white track-suits and were failing to conceal the fact they were carrying pistols beneath their clothes. They were all drinking beer and watching a soccer game on a plasma-screen TV the size of a drive-in. Bolan nodded at Dominico. They walked past the glass door and none of the four men looked up. Bolan and his partner moved back into the shadows. Amilcar's house was newly built, and rather than gutters he had installed some very chic, Japanese-style iron rain chains. The Executioner holstered his pistols and clambered hand over hand to the roof. Dominico took the chain with the facility of a spider. Bolan walked across the roof tiles one slow, carefully placed step at a time and then lowered himself to the master balcony. His comrade alit beside him a moment later, and they crouched behind a pair of potted palm trees. In the master suite Busto lay back on the king-size bed while Amilcar pulled off her cowboy boots. The drug enforcer paused as he felt the steel she was concealing in her right boot. He drew the little blue steel Smith & Wesson and tossed it onto a love seat in the corner. "You don't need that anymore, baby." Amilcar raised his arms and flexed his biceps. "*El Martillo* protects you now."

Busto let out a credible giggle and sat up. "Baby, I'm going to—"

Amilcar's hand cracked across her face like a gunshot and slapped her back down to the bed. "You're going to do what I tell you, bitch." He yanked her back up by the hair. "You tell me to fuck off? Humiliate me in front of my friends and go off to Mexico City like you're hot shit and then come back here dragging someone else's kid? And now that I'm the man in Culiacán, you come begging for me to take care of you, your old whore of a mother and your snot-nosed kid? Oh, I'm going to take care of you, baby. I'm going to take care of you in ways your boyfriend Davilo was afraid to try."

Busto hissed in rage and threw a very credible straight right hand at Amilcar's face, but Amilcar had been a professional boxer and he swatted it aside easily. His hand whipped across her face twice more, forehand and back. Only his fistful of hair kept her from collapsing. The Hammer had heavy hands.

His smile was ugly as he dropped her back to the bed. "Go ahead, baby. You were the hot shit bodyguard in the big city. Fight me. Get up and fight me." Amilcar cracked his knuckles and warmed to his task. "Man or woman, business or pleasure. I love it when they try and fight back."

Busto let out a whimper and Bolan didn't think she was faking.

Amilcar laughed. "What's the matter, baby? King Solomon

isn't here to protect you anymore? Guess you aren't so tough after all. On your knees."

Dominico tensed, but Bolan put a restraining hand on his shoulder. "Wait for it," he whispered.

Busto reached out with shaking hands and began to unbuckle Amilcar's belt. Bolan stood up as Amilcar's pants went down around his ankles, then stepped into the bedroom as Amilcar's underwear followed. The drug enforcer had a split second to gape as the man in black appeared as if by magic. The Hammer might have been a professional boxer, but Bolan had literally caught him with his pants down. Amilcar should have put up his fists and shouted for his men, but instinct trumped his training. He made a strangled noise of shock and consternation and snatched for his pants.

Bolan's right hand sent Amilcar's front teeth down his throat. Then he stepped forward and threw his cupped hand across the man's face like a tennis forehand shot and slapped him onto his back. Bolan's Beretta was in his hand and the machine pistol's laser sight tracked between Amilcar's legs.

"Let's talk quietly," Bolan suggested.

Amilcar drooled blood and teeth while he twitched in pain, shame and shock. He desperately wanted to pull up his pants. He desperately wanted to do anything but the laser beam painting his manhood kept him pinned in place like an insect. His hands were brutal weapons, but now they twitched at his sides like injured birds afraid to rise. Bolan didn't use laser sights to aim very often but one nice feature they had going for them was that they scared the hell out of people.

"Where did the material go?" Bolan asked.

"What material? I— Hey!"

Bolan knelt and screwed the muzzle of the Beretta's sound suppressor beneath the Hammer's scrotum. Varjo Amilcar's genitalia immediately tried to retreat into his body. Bolan lifted his head and looked around the room in mock concern. "Is there a draft in here?"

Amilcar started to sit up and found himself staring down the .50-caliber muzzle of the immense Desert Eagle pistol that had appeared in Bolan's other hand. The soldier twitched the muzzle toward the floor and Amilcar flopped back with a noise that presaged crying. Amilcar was a genuine tough guy, and he could have undoubtedly stood up to a great deal of physical torture in the same fashion that he had taken poundings in the ring; but Mexico was a macho culture and Bolan had usurped the Hammer's machismo in the worst way possible.

Bolan's face was a mask of stone. "I'm not going to kill you, Hammer, but if you don't tell me what I want to know they're going to start calling you El Buey."

Buey was Spanish for bullock or castrated bull.

Busto had risen from the bed. Her cheeks were turning purple and inflating like balloons. Her slitted eyes gleamed with palpable hatred out of the swelling. She reached into her left boot and pulled out a straight razor that Amilcar had not detected. "Let me do it."

"Watch the door," Bolan ordered.

Busto drew on her boots, scooped up her pistol and cracked the bedroom door to watch the hall.

Bolan decided to go with some simpler warm-up questions. "Who gave you your orders?"

"It was King Solomon!" Amilcar squeaked.

"King Solomon sent you the material?"

Amilcar grabbed for it like a lifeline. "*Sí!* I mean, yes!"

"He gave you orders in person?"

"Yes!"

"He gave you his routes?"

"His routes! His contacts! Everything! He called the shots!"

Bolan raised a questioning eyebrow. "Are you willing to testify against him?"

"King Solomon is a whore! He gave orders like he really thinks he's king and then sat back in Mexico City while we did all the work! You get him? I'll testify against him!"

Bolan let out a long breath. "You hear that, Memo? El Martillo is prepared to testify against you."

Guillermo Dominico stalked into the room from the balcony as if he were entering a wrestling ring. His head was lowered and his hands curled into claws by his sides. "Let him talk."

"Oh, shit…oh, shit…oh, shit…" Amilcar muttered it under his breath like it was his mantra.

Bolan rose. "I'm not a torturer. It's not what I do. But you're lying to me, and Mexican citizens are dying as we speak. Soon United States citizens will be dying, and I think you know something about it. So it's like this. I'm going to leave you here with Memo and Najelli. I'm going to step out into the hall and kill anyone who tries to come up while you testify. You know Memo well, Varjo. From back in the day. You know the judgment of Solomon, and you know what he does to those who lie and inform on him."

Amilcar knew full well that back in the day they'd have their tongues torn out.

Bolan stared down at Amilcar's shriveled sack. "I think you can guess what he'll do to a man who messed with a woman under his protection."

Amilcar made a mewling noise.

"Your choice, Varjo." Bolan holstered his pistols. "Pull up your pants and talk to me, or testify as God made you in King Solomon's court."

CHAPTER FOUR

Varjo Amilcar spilled everything and Bolan recorded it.
Names, routes, contacts—everything. Dominico grew increasingly agitated as Amilcar gave up the entire King
Solomon machine from Sinaloa to Baja. It was Dominico's
former machine, but he had taken pains to protect the people
he had left behind when he had turned over his new leaf. He
thought he had buried his past. Someone had handed Amilcar
King Solomon's criminal gold mine, and Amilcar had glee-
fully dug up everything and everyone. Many of Dominico's
old accomplices had been forced back to work, sold out or
killed. Dominico's voice dropped to an ugly hiss. "How the
fuck did you get all this!"

Amilcar cringed.

Dominico beseeched the ceiling. "How the fuck did I forget
to bring tongs!"

Bolan's blue eyes burned down upon Amilcar and they
were pitiless. "The man asked you a question. Make him ask
again and I take that walk."

Amilcar babbled. "I...I...I..."

Busto whispered urgently. "Someone's coming!"

Bolan raised his pistols. "How many?"

"Two!"

Bolan rose from Amilcar's side. "Memo, watch him."

Amilcar suddenly shrieked. "Rudi! Tucho! *Aquí! Aquí—!*"

Dominico drove the steel strut of the Uzi's folding stock between Amilcar's eyes. The drug dealer flopped to the floor like he'd been shot. Dominico smiled happily at Bolan. "You're right! The stock! It works!"

Busto slammed the door shut. "Here they come!"

Bolan wasn't in the mood for a blind exchange of fire through the door with Busto and an intelligence asset in the room. Fists pounded on the door and the men outside were shouting. "Varjo! Varjo!"

Bolan charged the door. Busto's eyes flew wide. "What are you—!" Busto shrieked and threw herself aside as Bolan hit the door like a fullback going up the middle. The door shattered off its hinges and Rudi and Tucho were smashed back with it. Bolan hurdled the fallen men and spun about, pistols in hand. Tucho had taken the brunt of the blow and was flat on his back. Rudi popped back up with a revolver in his hand. Bolan leveled the front sight of the Desert Eagle on Rudi's chest and fired. The report of the big fifty in the confines of the hall sounded like a cannon. Rudi flapped his arms like a broken bird as he flew backward. Tucho struggled to sit up and draw his pistol. Busto had stepped into the hallway. She kicked Tucho in the chest to put him back down and shot him in the face.

Amilcar roared behind them. "Prick! I'll—" Bolan glanced back. The drug dealer had bounced up and the ex-boxer had taken a swing at Dominico. The ex-wrestler held Amilcar's arm out straight with his elbow and wrist locked. His adversary howled as Dominico held him in a standing arm bar. "I'll kill you! I'll kill everyone who ever worked for you! I'll shank

Najelli's little—" Amilcar gasped as Dominico scissored his arms savagely and Amilcar's elbow and wrist snapped. Dominico let go of his foe's arm and the man sagged to his knees, mewling and cradling his shattered limb. Dominico gave him a thunderous slap to the back of the head that pitched him forward. "What did you say?"

Bolan looked at his ally warningly. "Memo…"

"He can still talk!" Dominico spit.

Bolan sighed inwardly. This was what happened when you took amateurs for allies. With a broken arm there was no way to get Amilcar down from the balcony except to throw him. Renewed shouting was echoing up the stairs. This was a nice neighborhood and private security would be responding soon and the *federales* wouldn't be far behind them. "You cripple him, you carry him. I still need him and we're out of here!"

"Don't wait on me!" Dominico reached down and Amilcar screamed as he was yanked to his feet. Dominico chicken-winged Amilcar's remaining arm into a come-along grip and pushed the muzzle of his Uzi into the back of his head. *"Ándale!"* Dominico marched him toward the shattered door. Bolan moved down the hallway. Someone had trained Busto right. She stayed back on Bolan's six with her pistol held in both hands. Bolan moved to the banister and the twin detonations of a double-barrel shotgun printed a moonscape of craters across his shadow on the wall. Bolan leaned out over the landing and his pistols rolled in his hands. The killer took a .50-caliber slug and a 9 mm triburst simultaneously and the chest of his tracksuit exploded in red. Bolan leaned back out of the line of fire as an automatic rifle cracked and tore splinters from the top of the railing. Bolan rolled down three stairs and shoved his machine pistol out between two of the railing spindles. His triburst tore off the top of the rifleman's head. The man behind him screamed as he was sprayed with brains and blood. Bolan rose and the big fifty ended the man's hysterics with a single boom.

The house was suddenly very quiet.

Bolan spoke low. "That's five. How many more do you have, Varjo?"

The man blubbered something unintelligible and then squealed as Dominico cranked the chicken-wing. "Two! Gal and H!"

Gal and H were conspicuously absent. No one downstairs was shooting or screaming. If they had run outside, the motion sensors would have come on and it was still dark outside. Bolan suddenly had a very unpleasant suspicion. "Who owns the houses on either side of you?"

Amilcar's voice went from terrified squeak to suicide-run ugly. "I do, motherfucker, and they're full of my men. So is the house across the street."

"Shit," Busto cursed.

Despite having a broken arm and no pants Amilcar laughed. "*Shit* is right, and I own the cops around here. You better rethink your situation. You better think about your family. I'll make you a deal. Memo? Kill the *yanqui*. You can take Najelli and disappear again."

The hallway got even quieter.

Busto's gun wasn't quite pointed at Bolan, but she was looking back at Dominico.

Amilcar's voice was sick with twisted triumph. "I got at least five guys who want to take over the operation. We go outside? You can't use me as a shield. They'll cut us all down. So I tell you what. You call me King Amilcar and kill the *yanqui?* You can fuck off, Memo, and take the bitch with you. But you better decide real quick."

Bolan considered the shot. Dominico had cover behind

Amilcar. He'd have to cross pistols and blast through Amilcar with the fifty and burn down Busto with the Beretta.

Amilcar's smile was sickening. "You don't love me, Memo, but you know I never break my word. You know I'll—"

Dominico squeezed his Uzi's trigger.

Varjo Amilcar's cranium came apart like a water balloon under the onslaught.

Dominico dropped the half-decapitated drug dealer and reloaded with a shrug. "Fuck him. I never liked him anyway."

Busto sagged against the wall with visible relief. "So what now?"

Bolan had really wanted to ask Amilcar a few more questions, but there was no point in crying over split skulls. "The river. We take his speedboat and go."

Busto nodded. "Nice."

Bolan advanced down the stairs. No bullets came. Gal and H had drawn back into either side of the house. They probably had the bottom of the stairs in a cross fire and were prudently waiting for reinforcements. Bolan took the second flight of stairs four at a time and threw himself into a diving roll across the foyer. Pistols barked in his wake and Gal and H shouted back and forth at each other. Bolan came up and saw muzzle-flash at shoulder height in the next room. Gal or H quickly jumped back around the corner. Bolan leveled the big .50 at the interior wall and it jumped three times in his hand as he let loose the thunder. Three silver-dollar-sized craters impacted and behind the wall a man screamed. A track-shoed foot suddenly slid out from cover as the man fell.

"Gal!" The man on the other side of the foyer was screaming. "Gal!"

Bolan used the foot as an index. He lowered his aim, tracked sideways and fired three more times where he thought

Gal's head and upper torso should be. The foot jumped with all three shots and flopped twitching to the tiles.

"Gal!"

Bolan fired his last shot the other way to keep H down and reloaded. "Najelli! Covering fire."

Busto swung just enough of her body around the landing to aim and began to fire, her Ruger discharging rounds methodically. Bolan marched across the foyer and down the short hall as the woman's shots made little sonic booms in passing. She stopped as Bolan stepped into the line of fire. He took up the slack and touched off tribursts from the Beretta as he entered the vaultlike living room.

The best cover that had line of sight on the stairs was the wet bar. Bolan shot out the mirror behind it and was rewarded as H screamed. H's pistol snaked over the top of the bar and popped off several blind shots. The Executioner took a heartbeat to steady his aim and squeezed off a burst that sent the pistol and several fingers spinning away across the bar. H shrieked and what remained of his hand disappeared. Bolan fired off two more bursts at the top of the bar, and his Beretta racked open on a smoking empty chamber with a conspicuous *clack!*

"I heard that!" H lurched up. He was big and bald and had a machete in his good hand. "You're dead, motherfucker! You're…" H's rant tapered off as he stared down the loaded .50 in Bolan's other hand.

Bolan idly wondered what kind of people kept machetes behind the bar, but the obvious answer was that drug dealers did. A smart drug dealer would have stocked his bar with shotguns. "Yo, H." Bolan motioned with the Beretta while he kept the Desert Eagle on the man. "Come on out. We need to talk."

H stumbled out from behind the bar.

"Leave the machete," Bolan advised.

The machete clanged to the tiles.

"You want to live?" Bolan asked.

"Yes."

"Where are the keys to the speedboat?"

"What?"

"The speedboat, at the dock. Where are the keys?"

Fists began pounding on the front door. Busto whispered, "We have company!"

Bolan put the front sight between H's eyes. "Keys."

"In the kitchen! By the door!"

Bolan jerked his head. "Najelli! Go!"

Busto ran for the kitchen. The fist blows turned into the thuds of men hurling themselves against the heavy oaken door. Dominico leaned against the foyer with his Uzi pointed at the front door. "It won't hold!"

Busto skidded back into the room waving a key attached to a little yellow float. "Got it!"

"Memo! Najelli! Run for the docks." Bolan nodded at H as they ran past. "You did good." Bolan pistol-whipped him to his knees as the front door failed. He reloaded the Beretta and roared at the top of his lungs in Spanish, *"Upstairs! They're upstairs! They have the boss!"*

Bolan hightailed it as more than a dozen men flooded in through the foyer. It was time to break contact. He reached into his jacket and pulled out a white-phosphorous grenade. The cotter lever pinged away as he reached the kitchen and Bolan tossed the grenade onto the kitchen island as he went out the door. Dominico and Busto had tripped the motion sensors as they made their escape, and Bolan ran out into the lunar glare. He holstered the Desert Eagle and slid the Beretta's folding stock from its shoulder sheath. The Willie Pete detonated behind him, and the kitchen window blew out in streams of white smoke and burning phosphorus element.

Bolan extended the stock with a snap of his wrist and clicked it onto the butt of the machine pistol as he ran. At the dock two 500-horsepower diesels roared like dinosaurs arising from their ancient sleep. Busto waved at him frantically. Bolan had closed the door behind them but men were coming over the walls. Busto banged off return fire, but the range was long for the woman and her handgun.

Bolan had transformed his machine pistol into a carbine.

He dropped to one knee and flicked the selector switch to semiauto. Two men were straddling the western wall and trying to bring Mexican Army rifles to bear. Bolan shouldered the Beretta and put the glowing dot of the front sight on the closer man's chest. He squeezed the trigger and the rifleman jerked, dropped his rifle and pulled a Humpty Dumpty as Bolan's bullet opened his throat. The Executioner tracked his sights as the second man on the wall exchanged fire with Busto. The throttles on the cigarette boat suddenly cut back ominously. Bolan ignored the dock and aimed. He squeezed the Beretta's trigger, and the man on the wall dropped back like a shooting gallery target. Busto was running down the dock shouting Dominico's name.

Bolan rose and ran.

The men at the western wall had ceased their siege.

The guys at the eastern one were just getting into gear. A bullet cracked past Bolan's head as he ran. He cleared the back lawn, and boards thudded beneath his boots as he ran down the dock. Dominico was sprawled backward in the cigarette boat. Blood painted the white leather of the driver's seat and fiberglass of the cockpit. Busto was bent over him.

"Go! Go! Go!" Bolan boomed.

Busto looked back over her shoulder desperately. "I don't know how to drive a boat!"

Bolan took three more running steps and jumped as bullets

whined and whipped past him. The cigarette boat lurched and the fiberglass floor made an ugly crackling noise as Bolan hit. He hauled Dominico out of the driver's seat and rammed the throttles forward. The cigarette boat shot ahead like an arrow and screamed down the river. "Get down!"

Bolan dropped down and negotiated the next hundred yards of the river from snap memory. He had discouraged the men in the western house from attempting the wall. Now the cigarette boat took a broadside of lead in passing. Bullets walked across the prow, shot out the windscreen and tore into the stern. One of the diesels shrieked as something big enough to tear into the engine block gutted it. Bolan rose up as gunfire crackled, but the hull no longer shuddered with bullet strikes. He rose up just in time to violently swerve the boat away from the bank and aim it westward. The port diesel clanked and howled and died as Bolan throttled it back. The starboard engine still had five hundred horses, and Bolan kept the hammer down. Gunfire still crackled and sirens wailed along the river. Bolan could see the blue-and-red flashes of police lights strobing through the trees, but they were all heading east toward Amilcar's house.

Bolan burned westward for the sea.

CHAPTER FIVE

Altata, Sinaloa, Mexico

Dominico had bled up a storm. A bullet had ripped through his left bicep. The local tissue destruction was minimal but it had zipped through close to the bone and had nicked his femoral artery. Bolan's medical kit was minimal, but he had managed to clamp it and close it. Now he was closing the entry and exit wounds. Busto applied pressure above the wound as Bolan stitched beneath the light of the veranda's bare 100-watt bulb. Dominico lay back in a hammock and drank tequila straight from the bottle with his good arm. They had checked into a camp that consisted of a cluster of adobes along the beach. Each had a reed-covered patio and was less than ten yards from the water. Altata was one of Sinaloa's hidden gems. Most tourists beelined for Mazatlán. Altata was a sleepy little fishing village in Ensenada de Pabellones. Only the most ardent tourists reached it and did so by motorcycle through the endless dunes. The camp had a number of advantages. One was that almost no one came here. Two was that if an army of drug muscle came driving down the dirt road, they would see them a long way off and they could head straight back out to sea, and three, one of the nice things about clay-brick adobes was that short of heavy machine-gun fire they were pretty much bulletproof.

Busto nodded as Bolan worked. "You're good."

Bolan wished he had a medical stapler but his knitting skills would have to do. "Thanks."

"I couldn't do what you did inside his arm."

Bolan shrugged. "That's okay. Bandanna."

Busto mopped Bolan's brow with her bandanna. "But what you're doing now?"

"Yeah?"

"I can do better."

Bolan accepted that. Dominico groaned as he dug his thumb higher up on the femoral artery and let Busto get to sewing. "How's it hanging, tough guy?"

"Pain I don't mind. I've had plenty of that, but my fingers feel funny. Like my foot. It went tingly and numb when I hurt my back and had to quit wrestling."

Bolan had been afraid of that. If a bullet damaged the femoral artery, it generally damaged the femoral nerve, as well. The question was whether the nerve had been nicked or just traumatized. The fact was Dominico needed a doctor. "I'm thinking of sending you back to Mexico City."

"Fuck that, man. I'm just a quart low and need a nap."

Busto sat back from her suturing and wiped a sweating brown tequila bottle across her brow. Dominico flinched as she took the tequila, poured some over the entry and exit wounds and gave herself a chaser before winding a bandage around his arm. Busto sighed as she sat on the ice chest and reached for her cigarettes. Her right cheek was purple; her left one was turning black. She grabbed ice from the hotel bucket and held it against her face with a sigh. Dominico took another long swig from the bottle and closed his eyes. The whole team needed a nap.

The problem was a nuclear time bomb was ticking.

Dominico began to snore.

"Najelli, I'm going to give him a couple hours' rest. I need to contact my people."

Busto opened the chest and cracked herself a fresh beer. "I'll stay by him and watch."

Bolan went in and plugged in his laptop and satellite link. He punched in his access codes and Aaron Kurtzman was online instantly. "You've been busy, Striker."

Bolan took a seat on the cabin's single rope bed. "Yeah, well, you know."

"Culiacán local and federal police have been lighting up all night."

"How bad is it?"

"Well, officially there's a manhunt going on."

Bolan had expected nothing less. "And unofficially?"

"Everyone thinks it was a cartel assassination, and with Varjo Amilcar dead there's a sudden power vacuum in Culiacán. No one has any idea who did it but territory is territory. The major cartels moved northward into Baja and along the Texas border in the last decade, but Culiacán is still considered the old alma mater of Mexican crime and being acknowledged as boss there has prestige. On top of that Amilcar wasn't popular. No one is crying over him."

"What's the situation on the coast like?"

"The Mexican Navy and Coast Guard are watching for Varjo's boat, but they figured whoever stole it went out to sea and are burning north. They're putting up a cordon around Baja."

"No mention of Memo officially or otherwise?"

"You caught a break on that one. Anyone who recognized

him during your raid on Amilcar's place is currently deceased. The police are looking for two suspects, a *yanqui* vaguely matching your description, a man described as little more than a Mexican national, and unfortunately Señora Najelli Busto is wanted by name for questioning."

Bolan had been afraid of that. Amilcar had undoubtedly bragged about his impending conquest and there had been survivors in the battle on the river. "She and her family are going to need asylum in the United States."

"We're already putting in the paperwork, Striker."

"Thanks, Bear."

"What have you got on your end?"

"Somehow Amilcar got a hold of all of Memo's old routes and contacts. How is still a mystery. Apparently Dominico took pains to cover his tracks when he got out of the life. He says he doesn't know how this could happen."

Kurtzman frowned on the video link. "You think Dominico is lying?"

"If I was reading this in a report I'd say yes, but I've been hanging with him for three days now. He's had his chances to turn on me or make a break for it, and unless he's one hell of an actor he is genuinely mystified and appalled at what's happened to his old machine. He sure as hell wasn't faking his reaction to the men with radiation sickness at Camp One."

Kurtzman sighed unhappily. "We've heard from Dr. Corso. The surviving radiation victims have died."

Bolan shook his head. "I don't suppose they got any information out of them?"

"Sorry, Striker. They never woke up."

"What did the interrogation team get out of Pinto Salcido?"

"Not much more than he already told you. Whoever is behind all this kept him pretty ignorant. We're going to have to figure they have cutouts all the way up the chain. The good news is the team did work up some pretty decent police sketches from his descriptions of the men who took the material off his hands. I'm sending them now."

Bolan clicked on the jpeg files and three police sketches appeared on the screen. The first was Caucasian. His receding hair, beard and mustache had all been trimmed to a matching one-millimeter of stubble. His nose was broken and he had a lateral scar going through his left eyebrow. The stats read six feet and two hundred pounds and he smelled like muscle to Bolan. The second sketch was of a Mexican man sporting dark glasses, a short mullet, sideburns and a Vandyke beard. He was two inches shorter and twenty pounds heavier than the first suspect. The third man was thin-faced, with a long nose and curly black hair pulled into a short ponytail. Bolan had to agree with Pinto Salcido's initial impression. The two Caucasians definitely smelled Euro. "We get anything on the descriptions?"

"No, but we're distributing them to the border patrol and posting them at all U.S. checkpoints. Homeland Security is sending them to all the airports. We can expect full distribution within forty-eight hours."

It wasn't enough. The material could switch hands anytime before the attempt was made to smuggle it into the United States, and it was anyone's guess whether that would be by land, sea or air. The opposition would have to be complete idiots to have the same three men try to ride the material all the way, and Bolan had the feeling he wasn't dealing with stupid men. At the moment the suspects were most likely bribing their way across Mexico, where they didn't already have complicit help from the authorities.

Kurtzman read Bolan's mind. "Speaking of the authorities, we've been getting increasingly urgent messages from Colonel Llosa. He wants to know where you are and what information you've acquired."

Bolan had weighing that option. Colonel Cesar Llosa was a Mexican Special Forces commander and a twenty-year veteran of the war on drugs. The Mexican cartels had a five-million-dollar bounty on his head and numerous attempts to collect had been made. He had surrounded himself with a cadre of men personally loyal to him. Bolan trusted the colonel, and if Bolan needed helicopters and Mexican Military assistance Llosa would be the man to go through. The problem was that Mexico was riddled with corruption from top to bottom, including the police and the military. The minute Colonel Llosa and his strike teams left Camp One in force, everyone would know it, and any move Bolan made in coordination risked being leaked somewhere along the line.

At the end of the day? The best chance Bolan had was to continue acting independently and try to make the intercept happen in Mexico.

"Tell Colonel Llosa I'm operating in the field and I'll send him a full report ASAP."

"Okay, but he won't like it. What's your next move?"

"Memo took a bullet and lost some blood. As soon as he wakes up, we're going to figure the most likely route the materials would have taken based on his old smuggling machine and what we know about Amilcar. I need extraction out of Altata, and I want to avoid any roadblocks or checkpoints. I need a plane with a legit flight plan in and out of here. Oh, and there isn't landing strip anywhere nearby."

"Way ahead of you, Striker. Jack is on his way to your position in a floatplane as we speak. ETA is two and half to three hours. Sit tight. Get some rest. He should be there right around dawn."

"Thanks, Bear. Striker out."

Bolan stepped out onto the patio. Dominico was blissfully snoring away. Busto was smoking and staring out at the lagoon. She turned and gave him a smile out of her battered face. "We leaving?"

"Not yet. I have a friend bringing a plane. We have an ETA of about two hours." Bolan stretched and grabbed a bottle of water from the bucket. "I'll watch if you want to go in and grab some shut-eye."

"You know, I would rather go stick my feet in the water." Busto gave Bolan a sad, mutilated smile. "Culiacán is only fifty-five meters above sea level, and only eighty kilometers from the sea, but most people there have never seen the Pacific. I love the water, but like most people in the city I almost never go."

Bolan dropped his water back in the bucket and grabbed two bottles of beer. "Whatever baby wants, baby gets."

"You say all the right things."

Bolan kicked off his boots, peeled off his socks, and he and Busto walked down to the water. The night breeze off the Pacific was the best thing that had happened to either of them in the last twenty-four hours. "Najelli is a beautiful name," Bolan mused. "Is it Aztec?"

"Very good. It is Aztec." Busto beamed at Bolan. "You even pronounced it correctly."

"What does it mean?"

"Love."

"Nice." Bolan stepped into the surf and the waters of the Pacific lapped around his ankles. Busto followed him into the water. They walked a few dozen yards until they came upon a hump of rock sticking up out the water and sat down. They spent long moments silently sipping beer and looking up at the stars. Busto spoke very quietly. "I can't go back home, can I?"

"No, there are too many people who know you were at Amilcar's when he was killed. He wasn't exactly Mr. Popularity in Culiacán, but Varjo was a made man. Now he's dead and the cartels know you were involved."

"So, what happens to me and my family?"

"Witness protection. I'll set you up."

Busto sighed.

"You don't want to leave Mexico, do you?"

Busto thumped her hand over her heart in solidarity with her homeland. "I'm a *mexicana. La raza*—born and raised. I don't want to drive a school bus or bus tables in...Minnesota."

"You say you like the water. Florida is nice for that."

"Oh, so the U.S. government is going to set me up in a beach house in Florida?" Busto lit a cigarette and blew smoke bitterly into the ocean breeze. "Is that what you're promising?"

"I said I'm setting you up. That's what I'm promising." Bolan shrugged. "Me? I like Hawaii, myself. Of course there aren't a lot of Mexicans on Molokai. Your daughter will have to learn how to surf if she wants to fit in."

Busto's hand slid into Bolan's and gave it a squeeze.

Mack Bolan and Najelli Busto sat with their feet in the Pacific drinking beer as they waited for the sun.

CHAPTER SIX

Bolan rose onto his elbows as he heard the drone of a twin-engine aircraft. Busto made a noise and lifted her head from his chest. Bolan shielded his eyes against the rising sun and saw the plane coming straight out of the orange ball. It banked to land in the lagoon and the dark silhouette dissolved into the sleek lines of a blue-and-white Piper Aztec Nomad float-plane. The water on the lagoon was as flat as glass and the plane threw up graceful, twin white-water rooster tails in its wake as the pontoons cut the surface. The plane turned toward them across the lagoon and cut its engines. A familiar face was grinning behind the water-spattered windscreen and blue-mirrored aviator sunglasses. The pontoons gently ground to a halt against the sand, and Jack Grimaldi popped out of the cockpit. He stepped out onto the pontoon and tossed a small anchor into the sand. He looked at Bolan, looked at Busto, and looked back at Bolan again. "Nice."

Bolan glanced at his watch. "You made good time."

"I had a good tailwind out of Baja, and if you're going to fly an amphibian—" Jack Grimaldi, ace Stony Man pilot, grinned at his plane "—you can't beat an Aztec Nomad."

Busto perked at the name. "An Aztec Nomad?"

Bolan smiled and gave Busto's shoulder a squeeze. "It's what you are now."

Busto giggled.

Grimaldi nodded. "It's a plush ride."

The sound of the plane had brought Dominico wandering down the beach. His arm was in the sling Busto had rigged for him. He staggered a little bit with blood loss and hangover. He clutched the tequila bottle and took some hair of the dog to brace himself. He looked Grimaldi up and down noncommittally. "Who's this guy?"

"Fellow pilot," Bolan said. "You'll like him."

Grimaldi shoved out his hand. "Jack."

Dominico stuck out his hand and noticed there was a bottle of tequila in it. "Uhh…"

Grimaldi took the bottle and took a swig without batting an eye. "Top of the morning, Memo." He handed the bottle to Bolan. "This would go better with coffee."

Bolan agreed. They needed a strategy session and everyone needed food. Altata was a fishing pueblo, and the cantina was open late for the boats that had stayed out night-fishing for squid and stayed open to feed other fishermen who headed out before dawn. Mexican fishermen had long ago learned to reserve comment about strange boats and planes arriving or departing in the wee hours, but Bolan didn't want Dominico, Grimaldi or his own descriptions floating around for anyone who came after them. "Najelli, do me a favor. Go to the cantina and get us some food. A lot of it." He handed her a wad of pesos.

"You got it." Busto took the money, dusted the sand from her clothes and trotted off.

Dominico gave Bolan a strange look. "Can I talk to you for a minute?"

"Sure. Jack, I'll be back in a second." They walked down the beach a few yards. "What's on your mind, Memo?"

"I'm thinking of asking Najelli to marry me when this is over."

Bolan smiled. "Again?"

Dominico scowled. "Yeah, again. So tell me one thing, man to man."

Bolan locked eyes with Dominico in deadly seriousness. "I didn't sleep with her."

"It sure looked like you slept with her."

"I promised her I would set her and her family up in witness protection, then we had a beer, then we had a nap."

"A nap?"

"Memo, I'm not going to lie to you. We held hands."

"You held hands?"

"We held hands."

"That's it?"

"That's it."

"Well, okay." Dominico let out a long breath. "Promise me you won't do it again."

"No." Bolan shook his head.

"No?" Dominico spluttered in shock. "What the f—"

"At your wedding I'm going to lay a big old sloppy wet one on her."

Dominico actually blushed. "Man…"

Busto came out of the cantina carrying a massive basket. They all returned to the cabin and she spread out paper plates and began heaping them with rice, yellow *azufrado* beans and fried sardines, and buried it all in the local *salsa fresca*. The two Thermoses of coffee were steaming hot and laced with cinnamon and nutmeg. The team spent long moments attacking the feast by the light of dawn through the window. Bolan waited for the first round to be finished and then spread out the police sketches as the team reloaded their plates.

"You recognize these guys, Memo? Pinto said they took the material off his hands."

Dominico shook his head over the alleged Europeans. "Never seen baldy. Curly-top? Maybe, someplace, but I can't place him." He tapped the sketch of the bearded Hispanic man sporting the mullet. "But him? That's Rubino Mankita."

"What's his story?"

Dominico shook his head. "Manny? He kills people."

"For which cartel?" Bolan asked.

Dominico snorted. "The Libertad Onza cartel."

Grimaldi shook his head. "Never heard of them."

Bolan drank coffee and mulled that over. The Libertad Onza was the Mexican mint's current one-ounce gold coin. "He's freelance?"

"That's what they say, and they say he takes payment in gold. He does his work bloody and he likes to do it in public."

Busto rolled a sardine in a tortilla and bit it in two. "When I was doing security work in Mexico City? Mankita had a real bad reputation. They say when the assassination business was slow he had a sideline in kidnapping, only he wasn't too good at it because half the time the kidnapping turned into a slaughter and even when he pulled it off the other half of the time he would kill the hostages when things didn't go fast enough. Everyone was afraid of him."

"Real bad hombre," Dominico agreed.

"How come Pinto Salcido didn't recognize him?"

"Pinto was always local West Coast. He never operated in Mexico City. He'd undoubtedly heard of Manny but wouldn't know him by sight."

That was probably the way the bad guys had wanted it, and it was a very interesting bit of intel. The Mexican cartels, the

Russian *Mafiya*, the Chinese triads, all criminal organizations had their killers, but generally they were part of the extended family. Even if they were raping women and slaughtering children in their beds they were still considered soldiers rather than assassins. They did it for the profit or defense of their cartel, clan or syndicate. A man who killed for nothing more than money was a sociopath, and rightly feared and despised even by other criminals.

Whoever the bad guys were they were transporting nuclear material across Mexico. Bolan found it very intriguing that they would use a psychopath, much less put him in such a position of trust. More than intriguing, it made no sense, but too many things on this one made no sense. Bolan suspected there was madness involved, but a deadly serious machine was in motion, and he knew the pieces had no meaning because he didn't have enough of the puzzle.

"Memo, best guess. Which way do you think they went?"

"Well, they aren't transporting fifty kilos of cocaine or marijuana. If what you say is true they're moving over a ton of metal and the goons guarding it. I'd go to Baja. Sparse population and you can buy an entire pueblo's silence easy. By the same token, you got lots of airstrips, lots of ports, and Tijuana and Mexicali if you need a big-city connection. If things start to get too hot? Shit, man, you could just dump the stuff into the Sea of Cortez and come back for it later. I did that once. I'm sure salvaging uranium would be harder, but what the hell, man? These guys have money, and uranium doesn't rust, does it?"

"It oxidizes, but that wouldn't effect its radioactivity. It would just make it more dangerous to handle, and it would probably help spread the nuclear material out from the explosion." Bolan frowned over a map of the Baja Peninsula. Dominico had called it the same way he would. "Still, over a ton of crated material plus the men guarding it. That pretty much precludes a light plane."

Dominico nodded. "And bigger transports draw bigger attention."

That would leave train, truck or boat. The only train line clipped the top eastern corner of the state and stopped dead in Mexicali without crossing the U.S. border. However it did come up all the way from Sinaloa with dozens of stops in between. The material could have been offloaded from the truck and loaded into a container car anytime within the past twenty-four hours. Bolan's instincts spoke to him. A train was a lock. Once the material was on board there was no way to quickly offload it. Trains had regular stops and all of them could be filled with *federales* at a moment's notice. Bolan felt sure the material was still in a truck heading north for the border or had headed for the coast and was on a boat rounding Baja. Guillermo Dominico's alter ego King Solomon was the key.

"Memo, it's still on a truck and it's in Baja, probably getting close to the border. Where are you taking it?"

"That would depend on the situation."

"You know that the dying men in Mexico City were discovered. You know Pinto Salcido and Varjo Amilcar got hit, but you don't know if it was cartel-sanctioned or not." Bolan's spine spoke to him. "In fact assume that you don't have inroads with the cartels. Let's assume you're using cartel outsiders. You have King Solomon's routes. You're working through guys like Amilcar and Rubino Mankita and you're assuming King Solomon, whose machine you stole, is still fat, dumb and happy studying Scientology and doing yoga in tight pants in Mexico City."

"It's not Scientology!"

Busto raised an incredulous eyebrow. "You're doing yoga?"

"Man…" Dominico rolled his eyes. "Okay? You want best

guess? You aren't going to like it. I'd take that load up into Sierra de Juárez."

Bolan peered at the map. The peninsular mountain chain ran right up to the border. Baja was almost all desert. Bolan had operated in it before, and the mountains that rose up out of it were often brutal, blazing-hot labyrinths. Bolan smiled dryly. "You got bandits up in those hills?"

"Oh, we got bandits all right. Mexican bandits straight out of the movies. There're pueblos up there that aren't on any map, and the mountains are riddled with hidden canyons and caves. The cartels took over the drug smuggling trade except for the smallest, playground-level stuff. So the *bandidos* in the mountains take whatever piece of the action they can get. Smuggling illegals, hijacking trucks, kidnapping rich Mexicans on holiday, setting up fake checkpoints on the road for a few hours and extorting bribes out of tourists, you name it. Targets of opportunity, and they aren't above ripping off a drug shipment from the cartels if they learn about it and can put the odds in their favor. Whatever they do, they do it quick and then fade back up into the mountains. Most of their stuff is so small-scale the *federales* don't care, and they bribe the locals to care even less. Oh, they piss off the cartels, but the cartel men aren't dumb enough to go up into the mountains after them. Shit, man, even your buddy Colonel Llosa isn't dumb enough to go up there unless he's got at least a company of soldiers with him and air support. You watch the news? Those mountains are like Afghanistan, man, except hotter."

Bolan didn't bother to keep the smile off his face. "And you know so much about this because…"

Dominico shrugged grudgingly. "Yeah, I got some friends up there."

"You think your bandit friends would help out terrorists?"

"These terrorists have my routes. If they dropped my name

and paid good money, they'd be treated right and no one would be the wiser. I'm thinking Rubino and his Euro-trash amigos have probably broken down the load into two or three four-by-fours and have headed into the hills."

Bolan really saw only two choices. Go in with Colonel Llosa shock-and-awe style or head into the hills with his own little team and make some discreet inquiries. Jack Grimaldi waggled his eyebrows at Bolan over his plate of beans. He already knew which way Bolan was leaning. The soldier decided. "Memo, I need you to drop a dime on some of your friends."

Dominico shook his head. "The people in the mountains spook easy. They won't say much besides *'hola'* over the phone, and that's assuming they pick up. All the numbers I have are old. If I say one thing and it doesn't match up with what the other assholes said, they'll know something is up and their first instinct will be to bug out, and like you said, we're running out of time."

Bolan didn't doubt any of that. "Fine, we'll just have to drop in, then. Najelli, pack your bag. We're going to drop you someplace where you can link up with your family."

Busto smirked. "I got a better idea, why don't you take me along?"

Bolan smiled back but his eyes narrowed. "I think this is about you missing the action."

"I won't lie to you, but like Memo said, the mountain *bandidos* spook easier, and trust me, everyone relaxes a little when there is a girl around. Dominico bringing strangers into the mountains is going to raise eyebrows, no way around that, but if he brings his girl, too, at least no one is going to think he came for war."

She had a point, and Bolan had seen her shoot. "What about your black eye?"

Busto sighed from very long experience. "Mexico is a macho culture, Memo is a known drug dealer—trust me, no one will bat an eye. They'll be looking at my ass anyway."

Grimaldi grinned in agreement. "I can't take my eyes off it."

Busto favored the pilot with a smile and locked eyes with Bolan. "You need every gun you can get, and I'll need a rifle, by the way. A folding-stock Ruger. That's what the agency issued whenever we knew we were in a high-risk situation."

Bolan didn't like putting Busto in harm's way again but she was right. "Well, I've seen Memo shoot."

"You saw me at Amilcar's!" Dominico protested.

"I saw you behead a guy at six inches with an Uzi," Bolan countered.

"Man…"

Bolan scanned the map again. Most of Baja was desert, but up at the higher elevations there were lots of little lakes and pockets of pine forest. Bolan tapped the map on his laptop and the mountains of Baja Norte got bigger and bigger. "Memo, pick a contact, then pick the closest lake. I'll organize an equipment and transportation drop to be there when we touch down."

Dominico poked a tiny lake on Bolan's plasma screen. "There. There's a landing strip I used further north but since we have a float plane we can almost drop straight in."

Bolan pushed himself away from the table. "We're out of here."

CHAPTER SEVEN

Sierra de Juárez

The Aztec Nomad skimmed to a halt on a blindingly blue mountain lake with no name on any map. Dominico was flying in case anyone was watching the landing. He was famous for his flying exploits, and if anyone but him had gotten out of the pilot's seat Bolan and Grimaldi would instantly be figured as feds. They probably already had been but with any luck Dominico behind the stick and his girlfriend riding co-pilot would at least throw some doubt. With any luck Bolan and Grimaldi might be mistaken for muscle. Bolan surveyed the local scenery. The mountain lake was a little slice of heaven. Much of Baja's terrain was brutal, but the lake was surrounded by a green skirt of Spanish grass and surrounded by stately, ancient pines. The pilot of the U.S. military transport that had preceded them in the night had been good. He had flown in low over the lake and drogue-chuted his payload onto the grass-covered shore without getting it wet and still managed to climb back above the trees in what had to have been a harrowing ride. Still, they had burned twenty-four hours arranging the drop, flying from Sinaloa, refueling and then flying into the mountains.

The clock was ticking.

Bolan stepped out onto the pontoon as Dominico cut the engines and jumped into the shallows. The container was the size of a minibus and sat strapped to its drop pallet. Bolan keyed in the combination the Farm had given him, swung open the double doors and looked at their ride. The United States military had gone over to Hummers long ago but they still had thousands of surplus Ford M151 MUTT jeeps. This one had obviously seen some hard miles over the years and was painted a scratched desert beige Bolan recognized from Operation Desert Storm under George Bush senior. The Executioner clambered into the container's metal interior and checked the jeep. It looked sound, the tank was full and it had all the mounting brackets he'd asked for. Crates of requested equipment were tied down in the bed, across the seats and on the hood, and two jerricans of gas had been strapped to the bumper. Bolan slid into the driver's seat. He stepped on the starter button and the jeep coughed three times and revved into life like a champ. Gears ground as Bolan put the jeep into Reverse and rolled out of the drop container.

"Haven't seen one of those in a while," Grimaldi stated.

Bolan hopped out, and he and Grimaldi manhandled crates under the pines.

Dominico popped some painkillers and eyed the crates. "What have you got in there, man?"

"Stuff for now." Bolan took up a crowbar. "Stuff for later." He cracked open a crate and took out Busto's Ruger carbine and a pair of twelve-mag bandoliers for it. "For the lady." Busto checked the weapon like a trained pro as Bolan handed Dominico a belt and stuffed ammo pouches for his Uzi. Grimaldi had already packed himself a full war load in the plane. Bolan took out his own weapon. In his experience, mountain fighting was all about reaching out and touching people. He drew forth a SCAR rifle like the one he'd hit Pinto's place with, except this model was up-gunned to .30 caliber, had higher-powered optics and a twenty-inch barrel threaded for a sound suppressor. With the grenade launcher mounted beneath, it was heavy and a handful, but Bolan wanted range and firepower. The other crates contained other sorts of ugliness but they were for later, if there ever was a later. Right now they were in scouting mode rather than assault.

"So, Memo, where are your buddies?"

"Probably watching us right now, but they'll wait until we move out and they can put us into a decent ambush position before they come out and talk."

Bolan offered Dominico the wheel. "By all means, let's not disappoint them." Busto grabbed a shotgun and Bolan and Grimaldi got in the back with their weapons across their knees. Dominico shoved the jeep into gear and they drove toward the southern end of the lake. A river fed into it from the mountains higher up, but it was midsummer and the river was at low ebb and about a foot deep. Dominico drove straight up through a twisting gully. The walls were about six yards high, and anyone at any time could have stood up and shot them to pieces as they passed. Their only real defense was Dominico. King Solomon had been a drug smuggler but he had spread his money around, and through generosity and the power of myth he had become beloved.

Bolan was crossing his fingers that the *bandidos* of the Sierra de Juárez hadn't lost that loving feeling.

Dominico stopped the jeep at a fork in the gully.

The *bandidos* rose up from behind the rocks and trees and lined the lips of the gully like Robin Hood's merry men. Still more filled the immediate horizon like Zulus at the dawn of attack. Bolan counted thirty men and boys, and all were carrying rifles. Dominico grinned like an idiot and waved his good arm happily. *"Hola, amigos!"*

Dominico's salutation was met by profound silence, but Bolan was gratified to notice that while all the bandits had guns none of them were pointing them directly at the jeep yet. Moments of stony silence passed, and then a boy who couldn't be more than twelve picked his way through the creek. The battered FN assault rifle he carried looked almost as big as he was, and someone had stuck a bowl on his head and cut all the hair that had stuck out. An old man rode a horse beside him. His denim jacket, sheepskin vest and John Deere baseball cap looked as old as he was. One look told Bolan that the man was nearly blind. Dominico slowly stood up behind the wheel and draped his empty hand over the windshield. "Hey, Omaro! You look good! How are you?"

The old man turned rheumy eyes on Dominico and seemed to spend long moments considering this greeting. "Memo, why are you speaking to me in English?"

"Oh, you know. These gringo friends of mine don't speak much Spanish. I don't want them getting nervous."

"So now you love gringos?"

"You know, Omaro, you and me both made a lot of money off gringos, and I love everybody, until they show me it's time not to love them. You know that. You taught me that."

Omaro grunted and then squinted at the jeep. "Who is the woman?"

Busto waved from the passenger seat. "Najelli Busto, *jefe!*"

Jefe meant chief in Spanish and was a particular honorific among Latin criminals. The old man sat up straighter in the saddle. "Davilo's girl?"

"Sí, jefe."

"Davilo was a good man." The old man peered into the past. "I was sad to hear of his passing."

"The people in Culiacán gave him a shrine, and the *corridos* gave him a song. He is smiling down on us." Busto's voice dropped modestly. "I am with Memo now."

Omaro smiled into the middle distance for a moment. He suddenly twitched his shoulders and shook off memories like he was shaking off a chill. The bandit was all business once more. "What do you want, Memo?"

"I want to ask you a question, Omaro."

"You come up here with gringos to ask me questions?" The men lining the gully stayed silent, but the hostility level radiated up a notch and baked down into the gully.

"Yes, Omaro, with permission. I have only one. Anything after that is up to you."

Omaro sighed like a sympathetic judge who was nonetheless passing a death sentence. "What is your question for me, Memo?"

"Did three men come up here in trucks saying they worked for me?"

"Yes, Memo. They did."

"Well, just between you and me, old friend, they don't work for me, and they're not friends of mine." Dominico let out a long breath. "Or yours."

The old man took a long time to shake a cigarette from a pack and light it with a match. "You know, Memo, I was afraid of that. But the money was good, they said all the right things and I could not get ahold of you."

It was cards-on-the-table time, and Bolan knew there was no point in holding back. In this gully with Omaro they would live or die by the truth. "Memo, tell him the whole story. Tell him everything."

Dominico walked over to Omaro and began speaking low,

fast Spanish and it went on for several minutes. Omaro asked perhaps three short clarifying questions and then closed his failing eyes as Dominico drew him the picture of the team's past seventy-two hours. Omaro's already stooped shoulders sagged as if an invisible cross had been laid across them for him to bear.

Bolan rose slowly from the backseat and left his rifle on the seat. "Omaro, you spoke with these strangers?"

"Yes."

"There were three of them?"

"Yes."

Bolan hopped down into the creek. He took the DEA sketches from inside his shirt and walked up to the mounted man. "With your permission, Omaro."

"Yes."

Bolan handed the sketches to the boy. The boy looked up to the old man and Omaro nodded. "*Sí*, Leobardo."

Young Leobardo quickly rifled through the sketches. He nodded in recognition at each one and handed them back to Bolan. "*Sí.*"

Bolan tucked them away. "Omaro, did you speak with these men? Could you tell anything about them?"

"Yes." Omaro took a long drag on his cigarette. "I am going blind, but I can tell you what I heard. One was Mexican, from Mexico City. One spoke his Spanish with a *Cubano* accent, and it was not his first language. The other spoke Castilian like he was born there."

In Bolan's experience the vast majority of Caucasians who spoke Cuban Spanish as a second language were Russians and more often than not soldiers. The question of the day was what were a Mexican assassin, a Russian soldier and a Spaniard doing transporting nuclear materials across Mexico? "Do you know which way they went?"

Omaro shrugged. "North."

Bolan could have guessed that. "You have no one shadowing them?"

"They told me it would be best for me and my people if I didn't." The old man sighed. "I believed them."

"You weren't worried about the military coming after them and you?"

Omaro stared at Bolan. His half-blind eyes were frank. "They said they owned the military, and the *federales*. It was *yanquis* we were to watch for."

Bolan's blood went cold. "The load they carried, was it broken up into separate trucks?"

"Three Toyotas," Omaro confirmed. "And they are not alone."

"No?"

"No, Leobardo was on watch last night. He heard planes."

Grimaldi shook his head. "That was our people."

"He saw things drop from the sky."

"That was us," Grimaldi reiterated.

"Did your people come in two planes? One at midnight and then another at four?"

Bolan was starting to get an ugly feeling. "My people dropped the jeep in a single container. That would have been the 4:00 a.m. drop. Leobardo, what did you see at midnight?"

Leobardo spoke in thickly accented, broken English. "Men, falling from the sky."

"Parachutes?" Bolan flexed his Spanish. "*¿Paracaidistas?*"

"*Sí.*" Leobardo grinned. He couldn't have been more than twelve but already his mouth was full of gold teeth. "Men in…parachutes."

Bolan needed a number. "*¿Cuántos?*"

"Eight?" Leobardo held up his hands. "More, maybe."

Grimaldi drummed his fingers on the side of the jeep. "I'm betting at least twelve. A squad. Maybe a reinforced one. Broken up to guard the trucks."

Bolan had the same feeling. Twelve to eighteen men, broken into fire teams assigned to each load. It would—

Omaro cleared his throat.

Bolan suspected he knew why. "You were paid to let no one follow?"

Omaro nodded grimly. "Money changed hands. Honor is honor. A deal is a deal."

The men lining the gully shifted on their feet and hefted their weapons.

"I respect you, Omaro." Bolan shook his head. "But these men? They are *terroristas*. Animals."

"Yes," Omaro agreed. "It complicates things."

"Whatever they paid you—" Bolan spread his hands "—I'll pay double."

Omaro snorted. "You do not know what they paid."

"I don't care."

Omaro's eyebrows rose. "You know, *señor?* I believe you don't."

Bolan stripped off his money belt and tossed it to Leobardo. "There's fifty thousand dollars. Is it enough?"

Omaro took the belt. His fingers walked from pouch to pouch like an ancient spider and riffled wads of American green. *"Madre de Dios..."*

Bolan struck while the iron was hot and the cash was cold. The key was to find their landing zone. "Leobardo."

"Sí, señor?"

"Men who parachuted," Bolan said in Spanish. "They need a flat place, and a soft place, grass, sand, for twelve men to land on, understand?"

"Sí!" Leobardo nodded eagerly. "I understand!"

Dominico rolled his eyes. "Your Spanish isn't bad, but I could have asked him all that."

"Leobardo and I are bonding." Bolan shot the young man the thumbs-up. *"Sí?"*

Leobardo jerked his thumb skyward. *"Sí!"*

"Where, Leobardo. Can you find it?"

Omaro cackled. "Leobardo can track rabbits across rocks!"

Leobardo puffed up with pride. *"Sí,* I know a place."

"Can you take us?" Bolan asked.

Leobardo's smile vanished and he held up his open palm. Omaro had taken Bolan's money not to kill them. Hiring Leobardo as a tracker was a separate deal.

Bolan started the bidding. "A thousand dollars?"

Leobardo's palm stayed outstretched.

Bolan upped the ante. "Two thousand."

Leobardo shook his palm like he was jingling coins.

Bolan considered what was left of his war chest. "Two thousand and my jeep when I'm done with it. That's all I got on me, deal?"

Leobardo gazed eagerly at the jeep. It was said that if you had a straight screwdriver, a Phillips, a wrench and some wire you could fix anything on an M151. For a young man living in the mountains of Mexico, it would be hard to imagine a sweeter first ride. Leobardo clenched his hand into a fist. "Deal."

Bolan turned to Dominico. "Let's get back to the lake. Jack and I need to make some modifications on the jeep and we need to armor and gear up."

"Modifications?"

"Yeah, and I want to be on the trail in half an hour."

Dominico shrugged. "Okay," he said, and started to climb back into the jeep.

"Hey, Memo?"

"What?"

Bolan jerked his head at Leobardo. "Let him drive."

Leobardo stopped just short of bursting into flames.

CHAPTER EIGHT

Bolan loped along the trail behind Leobardo. Grimaldi was in command of the jeep, and it was staying several hundred yards behind while Leobardo and Bolan tracked. Leobardo had taken them to a sandy glade higher up in the mountains and found the airborne unit's landing zone. Bolan counted boot prints and estimated a fifteen-man unit had parachuted in. Leobardo agreed. The men had moved out at a fast pace and in a textbook arrow formation that screamed military. Half a mile down the mountain they had linked up with vehicles and begun proceeding northward through the canyons. Bolan knew he was gaining. The going through the river canyons was rough and slow. Twice he found deep drag marks in the mud where one of the trucks had bogged down and another had pulled it free.

Bolan was beginning to wonder where the rear guard might be.

He pointed to the top of the canyon. "Me high, you low. *Comprende?*"

"*Sí, señor.*" The young bandit knew exactly what Bolan intended. Bolan dug his fingers into the cracks in the rock and clawed his way to the rim of the canyon. Below him Leobardo continued shadowing the convoy.

Bolan shadowed the youth.

It wasn't long before the young man stopped. Bolan glanced through his optics and saw that Leobardo was kneeling beside foot tracks that had broken away from the path of the vehicles. He glanced up in alarm as two men appeared as if by magic out of the rocks.

Bolan subvocalized into his throat mike. "Jack, we have contact. Hold position."

"Copy that, Striker."

The two men were Caucasians and wearing civvies. Their boots, pants, shirts and vests looked to have come straight from an upscale, online outdoor catalog. Mountaineering sunglasses hid their eyes, and both men wore Mexican soccer team Cruz Azul baseball caps. They could have easily passed for well-heeled ecotourists except for the folding-stock Chinese Type 81 assault rifles they cradled. Both weapons had been modified with aftermarket optics and tactical lights. The larger of the two men had a grenade launcher mounted beneath his weapon. Leobardo rose slowly and the closer man jerked the muzzle of his weapon back to the creek bed. Leobardo knelt in the mud. Both men wore tactical radios. The shorter man seemed to be in command and spoke into his radio for a few moments before nodding and then turning his attention back to Leobardo. He had a short conversation with the young man and then nodded at the taller man with the grenade launcher. The man in command kept his weapon leveled at Leobardo's head while the other man tossed Leobardo's rifle away into the mud. He drew a pistol with a suppressor tube attached and stepped behind Leobardo.

Bolan raised his rifle.

His weapon had a suppressor tube, as well, and the magazine was loaded with heavy, subsonic bullets. Bolan put his crosshairs on the man in command. The range was less than fifty meters. Bolan squeezed his trigger three times in rapid succession. Red dust flew from the talker's vest and he collapsed backward with a splash into the creek. The big man stared in shock for a fatal split second. As he started to spin about, Bolan put three bullets between his shoulder blades. The would-be assassin dropped to his knees and Bolan's fourth bullet shoved him facedown into the mud, where he lay, unmoving.

Bolan descended to the canyon floor while Leobardo began stripping the two men of their weapons. Both men were beyond caring. "You okay?"

Leobardo presented Bolan with his open palm again.

Leobardo was fine, and Bolan suspected he owed the young man another thousand. Bolan nodded and clicked his tactical radio. "Jack, two hostiles down. Hold position. Will contact you when I have joy."

"Copy that, Striker. Be advised, we have company."

Bolan could hear his old friend grinning across the tactical. "What kind of company?"

"The cavalry. One coming ahead."

"Copy that." Bolan held position while Leobardo stashed his loot from the corpses and exchanged his battered old ex-army rifle for one of the fallen men's tricked-out AK. A horseman came up the gully. Facially he looked like a younger version of Omaro but with an untamed Albert Einstein haircut and a Pancho Villa mustache. He rode a small, shaggy horse. A hunting rifle and a machete hung from saddle scabbards. He had a .45 tucked into the front of his belt. Leobardo waved his new rifle. "Papa!"

The man nodded at his son but kept his dark eyes on Bolan. "My name is Isidoro."

"Striker."

Isidoro looked down upon the dead men. "Is it true? They have nuclear bombs?"

What they had was spent nuclear fuel but Bolan didn't try to explain the difference. He countered instead. "Have any of your people gotten sick?"

"Sick?"

"Did any of your men help with the contraband, loading, unloading or breaking up the loads? There was a radiation leak in the south. *Campesinos* were poisoned. They sickened and died."

Years of hard living and hard thieving in a hard land had left Isidoro with a permanent scowl. Eyes that had been burned into a permanent squint by wind and sun flared and went ugly as the bandit leader realized the men he had aided had brought poison among his people. "None yet."

Bolan hoped Isidoro was properly motivated. "What can I do for you?"

"We have come to help."

Bolan could use the guns, but he wondered what it would cost him. Leobardo was twelve and he had already commanded a fairly hefty tab. Isidoro seemed to read his mind. "You have already paid us enough. I have brought ten men. They are all good shots. They are all reliable. They are all volunteers."

"Good. Tell me, is there a path down the mountain that you can take with your horses that will let you get ahead of the trucks following the river?"

"Yes, it can be done with ease."

"Then I need you to get ahead of them and block their path. However, I warn you, you must pick your shots. If you hit the loads the trucks carry, some of what they contain could spill. Even just dust or pieces of their inner container could be lethal. If the material is in pellet form and it spills into the river, then the water and any pueblo dependant on it will be poisoned for years. Even tiny amounts are fatal. If you shoot at the vehicles, shoot out the tires. Shoot up the engine blocks. Go for head shots on the men."

"I understand." Isidoro gave Bolan a sly look. "In my saddlebag I happen to have dynamite."

"How much?"

"Not enough to bring down the canyon, but I could drop enough rock so that trucks could not pass, and give my men cover."

"Go for it."

Isidoro handed Bolan a cell phone. "I will call you when we are ready."

"Leave me two of your men."

Isidoro gave Bolan a suspicious look.

"You saw my jeep?"

The bandit nodded in grudging admiration. "Yes."

"I'm driving it straight down the creek at them, but I want a man on top of each canyon wall to put them in a cross fire from above." Bolan glanced over at Leobardo. "And someone should probably keep an eye on him."

"I will send you Luis and Missael." Isidoro spun his horse about and galloped back the way he had come.

Leobardo waggled his eyebrows. "That's my papa."

Bolan was dealing with three generations of *bandidos*. Grimaldi's voice crackled across the tactical. "Striker, I'm coming ahead with the gun jeep and a couple of *caballeros*."

"Copy that, Jack. Come ahead."

BOLAN WAITED as the cavalry arrived. Luis and Missael were of a type; lean and leathery dressed in cowboy boots, cowboy hats and denim jeans and jackets. Both men had hunting rifles in their saddle scabbards. Hunting still made a valuable contribution to the daily diet in the mountains of Mexico, and Bolan took it as a good sign that the two men could shoot. The jeep came to a halt in the middle of the creek. Bolan and Grimaldi had made some modifications by the lake and the old surplus jeep had definitely taken on a more hostile mien. They had pedestal-mounted an M2 .50-caliber machine gun in the back bed and then removed the windscreen to attach a .30-caliber M60 to cleats in the hood for the man riding shotgun. Leobardo gazed dreamily at his promised ride. Bolan shook his head at Leobardo. "The machine guns are mine."

Leobardo sighed for what might have been.

Bolan pointed to the top of the canyon walls. "I want you up on the west wall with Missael, and stay well back. Najelli, you go up on the east wall with Luis. Memo? You're driving the jeep. Jack, you take shotgun." Bolan clambered into the back of the jeep and got behind the grips of "Ma Deuce." Missael and Luis tied up their horses and clambered up either side of the wall. The wait for Isidoro's call began. Missael and Luis squatted on their heels as silent and still as stones. Leobardo did a credible job of imitating his elders. Busto leaned against a rock, smoked and kept her own thoughts. Grimaldi put his feet up on the dash and laced his fingers behind his head. Bolan got on his satellite link and made a call. Colonel Llosa answered instantly.

"Striker!"

"Colonel, we're in the Sierra de Juárez. Near the border. I'm sending you the coordinates now. We're attacking. Send in your strike team."

Colonel Llosa launched an impressive eruption of Spanish profanity. "My closest team is in Sonora! It will take over an hour to get there! You have—"

"I advise you throw a cordon twenty kilometers ahead of my position. Be advised targets are in three pickup trucks and following the smuggling routes through the canyons. They have been reinforced by mercenaries, presumed Russian, heavily armed and at squad strength."

"Russians! What—"

"Be advised they are being led by the men from the police sketches. One has been positively identified as the Mexico City criminal Rubino Mankita."

"Mankita! You have—"

"Godspeed, Colonel." Bolan cut the line.

Grimaldi waggled his eyebrows. "Oh, he's mad."

Bolan nodded. He was going to do some fast talking if he lived through the next hour. There was nothing he wanted more than Llosa's heliborne strike force, but if the bad guys had informants as high as they claimed, within ten minutes the nuclear caravan was going to know the colonel was coming. Bolan and his team were going to have to depend on surprise.

Dominico began fidgeting. "Man, when is this shit going to go dow—"

Thunder rumbled across the clear blue sky. The horses reared against their tethers and red dust rolled down the canyon sides in streamers with the vibration of the dynamite blast. Bolan had been hoping Isidoro might call first, but then again Bolan had long ago learned that these sort of situations often took on a life of their own. "Memo, move it out."

Dominico shoved the jeep into gear and they splashed forward through the streambed. Missael and Luis paced them above on either side. Rifle shots began crackling and popping in the distance. Bolan racked the bolt on the M2 once to start the feed and the second time to bring a round the size of cigar into the chamber. It wasn't long before Bolan heard engine noise. The four-wheel-drive trucks ahead were roaring into overdrive in reverse gear as they tried to retreat backward up the winding river canyon. Missael could see them coming from his vantage and waved, and shrugged at Bolan in question. Bolan motioned to let them come. Grimaldi racked the bolt of his M60 on a live round.

Two men on foot came around the bend. Their adventure clothes and Kalashnikovs branded them bad guys. They snapped their weapons up with alacrity, but Bolan's team had them dead to rights. The Executioner put a hand on Grimaldi's shoulder. "Wait for it." Luis's and Missael's hunting rifles cracked and the two scouts fell dead into the stream. The bad guys kept bulling forward. They had no place to go except backward to find a place they could get out of the killing box of the canyon. The first truck came around the bend. The white Toyota Tacoma leaped and bucked over rocks and ruts and swerved in reverse. The four gunmen in the back were all shouting directions in a mix of Spanish and Russian and spraying wild bursts at the canyon rim. Luis and Missael had already faded back.

The bad guys just weren't expecting a MUTT in gun-jeep configuration blocking their path.

Bolan cut loose. The spade grips in his hands shook as the heavy machine gun jackhammered bursts into the Toyota. Bolan fired low and the huge, off-road tires exploded under the .50-caliber onslaught. The rear bumper dropped into the riverbed with a splash, and Grimaldi fired high. Two men literally lost their heads. The other two men prudently leaped from the truck. Bolan caught one in flight and cut him in two. Grimaldi put a burst into both sides of the cab rear window. The glass instantly spiderwebbed and went red, and the engine died. The sole survivor leaped up out of the stream and ran back for the bend, waving and screaming at the oncoming trucks. Bolan and Grimaldi put him in a cross fire and ripped him into rags.

The next truck slammed into the truck blocking the path. Bolan grimaced as the loads strapped down in the stricken and listing truck shifted precipitously. The two trucks locked bumpers and the second truck stalled. The four gunmen in the bed of the second truck leaped off to take cover behind rocks and the body of the first vehicle.

Dominico fired a burst from his Uzi one-handed. "Surrender, motherfuckers!"

Automatic rifles ripped back in response.

"Jack, suppressive fire." Bolan and Grimaldi cut loose, stitching the sides, the roofs and the surrounding rocks with machine-gun fire. The gunmen huddled down beneath their cover as Bolan and Grimaldi rained on them with half a belt each. Bolan took his finger off the trigger paddle and shouted out a choice phrase in Russian.

"You are surrounded! Surrender or die!"

The canyon suddenly grew very quiet except for the idling engines of the jeep and the truck still behind the bend. Someone shouted something in Russian from behind cover, but it was well beyond Bolan's comprehension. He shouted back in English. "Surrender! Now!"

The voice snarled back with a heavy Russian accent. "Each truck contains four hundred and fifty-four kilos of nuclear material!"

The bad guys had three thousand pounds of poison. "Surrender, now! Or I will—"

"Trucks also contain two hundred and twenty-seven kilos of Amatol high explosive!" the Russian interrupted. "I have detonator!"

Bolan's knuckles whitened around the .50's grips. It wasn't the most effective mix for a dirty bomb. This was an insurance policy until they could get the material to a safe place and assemble a doozy, but it would be enough to leave this little corner of Mexico unlivable for a hundred years, and the streams that flowed out of the Sierra de Juárez to irrigate crops below would bring down poison for a generation.

The Russian knew what Bolan was thinking. "We can have nuclear incident right now!"

Bolan scanned the load of the tipped truck to try to calculate if the man was bluffing. The load was shaped like a pyramid of coffins covered by a tarp and strapped down with webbing. Fifteen hundred pounds was about the maximum load for a Toyota and by the roar of the engines it had been clear they had been supercharged and maximized for off-road hauling. Bolan's phone rang. "Yeah?"

"Rocket!" Isidoro shouted in panic over the phone. "They have a rocket!"

Bolan dropped the phone. "Abandon the jeep!" Bolan began burning the rest of his belt as Dominico leaped from behind the wheel. Grimaldi yanked the locking pin out of the M60's mount and ran for the rocks toting the machine gun. The big .50 in Bolan's hands suddenly locked open on a smoking empty chamber. There was no time to reload. The RPG antitank rocket hissed from between a pair of boulders at the canyon bend. Bolan seized a gear bag and dived off the back of the jeep for a patch of deep water in the river. Cold water closed over his head, and Leobardo's promised ride blew sky-high. Bolan ate gravel as the blast wave shoved him along the bottom. Chunks of burning metal sizzled and whooshed through the water and something hit Bolan in the back like a kidney punch and drove the air out of his lungs. Bolan rose up while smaller pieces of jeep rained from the sky. He threw himself behind a tombstone of rock and ripped open his gear bag. Grimaldi was on the other side of the river with Dominico firing from cover. Bullets were flying in all directions. Bolan yanked out his grenade launcher and a bandolier of shells. "Jack! What are they doing?"

"They're untangling the trucks! I make it they still have about a dozen guys! Soon as they unlock those bumpers they're gonna rush us! I can feel it!"

Bolan grimaced in agreement. It's what he would do. The good news was the bad guys hadn't lit up the mountains yet. Bolan wasn't sure if these guys were ready for one last act of defiance, but if they were at least they were keeping it as plan Z. He broke open the launcher's cylinder and scanned his belt of grenades. Dropping high explosives into nuclear-fuel and explosive-laden trucks was out of the question. Bolan made a grim choice and plucked four grenades from the bandolier. The two smoke grenades had been tasked to mark the bad guys for an air strike. That air strike wasn't coming. The two tear-gas grenades had been in case they needed to break contact. There wasn't going to be any breaking contact. Someone was going to get their hash settled in this canyon one way or the other.

"You say a dozen?"

Grimaldi rattled off another burst. "I'd say!"

Dominico was cursing a blue streak as he tried to reload his Uzi with a wounded arm.

Bolan raised the grenade launcher. "We take them now! Before they get the trucks moving again! We take them hand to hand!"

Grimaldi stared for an unblinking, incredulous moment. "Hand to hand?"

Bolan glanced around. His tomahawk, his rifle and his bayonet were God knew where. He spied the jeep's blackened front bumper and part of the grille still attached to it lying beside his rock. The entrenching tool that had been cleated to it was still in place. Bolan nearly got his hand shot off as he reached out from behind cover and yanked the tool free. It was an old model. Bolan snapped the shovel blade open at a right angle and did the same to the folding spike of the pick. It was the best battle-ax he could manage at the moment. "We take them! We take them in the smoke!"

Grimaldi grabbed his M60's bipod and unlocked the quick-change barrel. He bobbled the smoking hot steel and dunked it into the shallows to quench it. Grimaldi grinned like a maniac as he raised the twenty-two-inch truncheon. "Let's do it!"

Bolan yanked a bandanna from his pocket, dunked it into the shallows and tied it over his face. It wasn't much of a gas mask, but it would give him a few seconds' advantage over their adversaries.

Dominico dropped his Uzi and drew his machete.

Bolan rose from behind his rock and fired the two tear gas and two marking smoke canisters into the cluster of pickups. The gunmen trying to separate the two trucks shouted in alarm, and the men standing guard sprayed their weapons in return as thick gray gas expanded to fill the bend in the canyon. The marking grenades bloomed into swirling clouds of yellow and purple smoke. Bolan dropped the grenade launcher and drew his Beretta. Dominico roared loud enough to be heard up in the cheap seats at a wrestling arena. *"Ataque!"*

Bolan, Grimaldi and Dominico went over the top. They would know in a few seconds if Isidoro and ten of his forty thieves would meet them in the middle. Two men came staggering and choking out of the gas and smoke. Bolan put a burst into each one. A third man came up from behind a rock and shoved out his AK. Bolan whipped his pistol around, but Dominico leaped into the line of fire. The gunman screamed as Dominico's machete skidded down his rifle, slicing off fingers as it went. Dominico chopped his blade twice into the man's chest and dropped him to the shallows. Beyond the bend a cacophony of whooping and yelling like a Mexican rodeo sounded as Isidoro and his men attacked.

Bolan took a deep breath and entered the fog of war.

The fog was purple and yellow intermixed with the burning gray mist of tear gas. Bolan's eyes instantly started to sting. A man before him was on his knees in the river dunking his head. He rose just in time to take Bolan's entrenching tool in the face. Bolan took a breath as he ripped the shovel blade free, and he felt the lachrymal agent pass through his feeble cotton filter and the tear gas burn began. He had been exposed to tear gas many times. He couldn't keep his eyes from tearing or prevent the searing of his sinuses and lungs, but he could ignore the natural panic and confusion that choking and eye pain caused. Bolan took the pain and continued his attack.

Everything was panic inside the cloud. Men were hacking, choking, staggering and firing their weapons toward the sound of the charging mob of bandits. A few determined souls were still struggling to pry the trucks apart. Bolan gave a ragged shout as he spotted the RPG man across the creek. "Jack! Rocket!" The rocketeer had reloaded, and he coughed and wept as he aimed his weapon down the bend at the charging bandits. Grimaldi bounded up with his machine-gun barrel and swatted the rocket launcher off the operator's shoulder. The man spun and fell, clawing for his pistol. He began to scream and flail as Grimaldi beat him like a rug.

Isidoro's bandits hit the bend howling like banshees.

The battle went hand to hand among the trucks and boulders. Isidoro had taken Bolan's warning about the nuclear material to heart. Nearly every bandit had a machete, and those that didn't carried a knife big enough to skin a buffalo. Blades chopped the Russians apart and the bandits were chopped apart by point-blank bursts from automatic weapons. When the rifles ran dry there was no time to reload and the

Russians swung them like clubs. Bolan put his pick blade through a screaming man's temple and hunted for detonators. Dominico knelt in the river and roared in ragged triumph. "I got him!" The bullet-headed man they had identified in the sketches as "The Russian" floated past with Dominico's machete in his head. Dominico plunged his hand into the river and scrabbled along the bottom. He shoved a small plastic box skyward. "I got it!"

Bolan blinked and swept his gaze across the choked and swirling battlefield. "Where's Mankita?"

"I don't know! I—shit!"

The third pickup's engine roared as it ripped itself free and accelerated. Dominico bounced off the bumper and fell backward into the water. Mankita was behind the wheel, head craned back as he drove in reverse to break through Bolan's very thin battle line. Bolan flung his entrenching tool as Mankita came alongside. The folding shovel shattered the driver's window and clubbed into the side of Mankita's face. The Executioner stalked forward through the shallows. He took hold of Mankita by his mullet and bodily hauled him out the window. Mankita hit the water with a splash and Bolan put a foot on his chest to keep him there.

Bolan spun as a half-blind Russian charged him, swinging his AK by the barrel like a baseball bat. The soldier emptied the Beretta into him and avoided the rifle blow, but he fell off his perch on top of Mankita as the Russian plowed into him. They fell in a tangle into the river, and it took vital seconds for Bolan to wrestle the deadweight of the Russian corpse off him. He kept his eyes open beneath the surface to take what advantage he could and clear the tear gas out of them. Bolan rose. His Beretta was gone but the entrenching tool hung off the window of the stalled pickup by the pick spike. Mankita had crawled to shore and was having a heavy go of it crawling through the gravel and mud, and puking up river water as he tried to get out of the gas cloud.

Bolan slogged up behind him and raised the entrenching tool with the pick end leading. Mankita looked over his shoulder with bloodshot eyes. His left hand turned over in the dirt. It was clutching a black box. His thumb flicked at a plastic safety shield.

Bolan swung the pick down with both hands and pinned Mankita's hand to the sand like an insect. The man howled as his hand spasmed open and the detonator spilled off his fingertips. Bolan left the pick where it was and kicked the detonator away. Mankita feebly tried to pull the pick blade out of his hand, and Bolan gave him a boot to the face by way of discouragement. Mankita collapsed to the sand, temporarily content to just cough, retch and bleed.

Bolan picked up a shot-put-sized rock and looked for another opponent.

Other than the moans of the wounded and dying it had grown quiet. The air was still gray and purple and yellow, but the mix of gas and smoke was dispersing. The little river was a red tide of blood and floating corpses. Bolan dropped his rock, found a rifle, took a magazine off a dead Russian and reloaded. Dominico trudged up coughing raggedly. "We…we got them! We got—" Dominico coughed so hard he fell to his knees and puked.

"Yeah." Bolan nodded wearily. "We got them."

Dominico's hand slipped from its sling and dangled bloody by his side. It looked like he'd ripped out his stitches rather than gotten shot again. Grimaldi waggled the bent barrel of his machine gun. Other than appearing to have had a good cry the pilot looked as fresh as a daisy. Isidoro's men had faired far worse. Only five were standing, and two were badly wounded. Isidoro was not among them. Bolan went back into the cloud. He found Isidoro facedown between the wheels of one of the pickups with half a dozen exit wounds in his back. Bolan dragged the bandit leader back to shore and out of the gas, then the soldier redunked his head in the river to clear it. He looked down at Isidoro as his men gathered around. The man was a smuggler and bandit, but he had died to protect his people. His people would build him a shrine. The *corridos* would give him his song, and Isidoro of the Sierra de Juárez would become another legend of the Mexican frontier.

Leobardo came forward with Luis and Busto. Missael had stayed topside as a lookout. He looked down upon his father and did not cry.

"Leobardo," Bolan said, "the army will be here soon. In helicopters. *Comprende?*"

The young man nodded gravely. *"Sí."*

"Take the guns, equipment and money and get your people out of here. Ride hard. Disperse. I will speak for you, but it may not be enough."

"Sí." Leobardo spoke quietly and the men that were still standing gathered up the horses and went to work.

Bolan nodded at Grimaldi. "Let's check it out." His Geiger counter had gone up with the jeep, but Bolan examined the first two trucks and was relieved to find that the loads were all still in place and none seemed to be riddled with bullet holes. Grimaldi gave him the thumbs-up from the third. They had caught a break. Bolan jumped down and found Dominico staring long and hard into the shattered cab of the first truck. Bolan took a look at the driver. Grimaldi's machine-gun burst had blown out the back of his head and come out his face. It wasn't a pretty picture, but despite the grotesque, death-mask distortion, Bolan recognized the man from the three police sketches he had designated as the Spaniard. "You know this guy?"

"I swear, I've seen him somewhere before, man." Dominico gazed upon the dead man with streaming, gas-reddened eyes. "But I don't know any Spaniards, and I never been to Spain."

"No pressure, Memo." Bolan put a hand on his shoulder. "But I need you to think real hard."

"I am."

"We'll get fingerprints and dental off of him. That may help."

Leobardo rode up on his father's horse followed by the rest of the bandits. The horses were loaded down with AKs and ammo, and the saddlebags were stuffed with phones, radios and everything else of value the Russians had had on them. The other horses were strung together with the bodies of their dead owners tied across the saddles. Leobardo looked down at Bolan with a good approximation of his father's laconic mountain-man stare. He seemed to have aged ten years in the last ten minutes. "We ride, for my grandpapa. Then we… disperse."

"Good. I'll wait here for the army and try to keep them off your back."

Leobardo jerked his head and the bandits rode back the way they came. He lingered just a moment and spoke quietly as he spun his horse. "You owe me a jeep."

CHAPTER NINE

The War Room, Stony Man Farm, Virginia

"The Mexican government isn't happy." Aaron Kurtzman's facial expression spoke volumes as Bolan walked into the War Room.

Bolan could well imagine. Colonel Llosa had jumped out of his helicopter and promptly had a hissy fit right on the spot. Llosa was a Special Forces officer, and he was quite accustomed to yelling. It had been quite a dressing down. Short of excommunication from the Holy Church, there was nothing that he hadn't threatened Bolan and his team with. Bolan had stood at attention and taken it. No one liked a renegade foreign intelligence operation on their own sovereign soil, and Bolan could empathize. He didn't bother to apologize, but once Llosa had begun to wind down Bolan had begun the mollification process. All of the radioactive material was accounted for and would be turned over to the Mexican government. They had Mankita and two of the wounded, presumed to be Russian mercs, and they were all Llosa's, as well. Llosa got a "No shit, Sherlock" look on his face, but Bolan knew that somewhere down deep the colonel was relieved there would be no row with the CIA. Then Bolan told the colonel the collar was all his, and he would be happy to sign the after-action report any way that Llosa cared to write it up.

Llosa didn't exactly smile but things got more cordial after that.

Bolan held nothing back, and short of Stony Man Farm's existence and address gave him a full report of everything that had happened from the moment Bolan had set foot into Mexico. Bolan was an excellent storyteller. As an operator himself, Llosa couldn't help but be sucked in by the tale and be fascinated by the way Bolan had run the mission. Then the negotiating began. Both Bolan and Llosa agreed to the exchange of information as the investigation continued. The colonel agreed to let Najelli Busto, her daughter and her mother cross the border into the United States. Llosa had very reluctantly agreed to leave the bandit clans alone for the moment.

Negotiations bogged down with Dominico.

King Solomon the drug dealer was a wanted man who had managed to disappear. Colonel Llosa's unit was tasked with drug interdiction, and Llosa wanted the collar as the feather in his cap for this bust. Bolan pointed out that Dominico had decided to serve his country and had done so bravely even after being wounded. Llosa countered that scum was scum, and he wanted King Solomon's head on a platter to present to his superiors.

Bolan didn't leave people behind.

He wrote a phone number on a piece of paper and gave it to Llosa, telling him that if he ever needed more cooperation from the U.S. military, police or government than he was getting through normal channels to call it. Llosa had frowned. Then Bolan leaned in close and wrote a second number. He told Llosa that if he ever felt he or his family was in danger and he needed help outside of normal channels to call the number. The United States government owed Llosa a favor, and so did he. He would come personally. He would bring friends.

Llosa had stared at the paper for a long time. The Mexican government, military and police were in a violent war with the drug cartels. Half of the soldiers, cops and politicians were on the take. Those who weren't were targets. In Mexico's battle with the cartels, men like Llosa were the tip of the spear, and every day soldiers, cops and judges were being murdered in the streets. Llosa had a bull's-eye on his back 24/7 and they both knew it. Llosa had folded the piece of paper and put it in his pocket. He had put Bolan, Dominico and Busto in a helicopter and flown them to the border city of Mexicali. At the border he had told Dominico to never be seen in Mexico again.

They had taken a rental car to San Diego where Dominico's arm had gotten proper medical attention at the naval hospital. Bolan had put Busto on a flight to Molokai, where her mother and daughter were already waiting. Dominico had been turned over to the CIA. He was probably going through some pretty hard questioning and debriefing about his past operations, but in the end he would be freed and put in witness protection.

Bolan had returned to the Farm and spent the past twenty-four hours eating and sleeping and horseback riding in the hills by way of downtime while various intelligence agencies worked on what he'd accomplished. He took a seat across from Kurtzman. "I know they're angry, but are they still cooperating?"

"Yeah, grudgingly. I think they know they dodged a bullet on this one, and I believe Llosa put in the good word. They allowed a pair of CIA observers to be present during the interrogation of the prisoners."

"So what do we have on this Mankita?"

"Oh, everything Memo and Najelli told you checks out. Stone-cold killer. Total psychopath."

That probably wasn't good. "How's he responding to interrogation?"

"He's not."

"You said he's a psychopath. There has to be some way to push his buttons."

Kurtzman sat back in his wheelchair. "Well, amigo, therein lies the problem. He's a psychopath."

"The man cuts up kidnapped children with machetes when their parents don't pay up with Mexican gold doubloons, Bear. You don't have to tell me he's a nut job."

"Let me put it like this." Kurtzman warmed to the subject. "No matter what anyone tells you, psychology is not an exact science. Sociopath? Psychopath? Maniac? These terms are often interchangeable. Let's start with what Rubino Mankita is not. Take your serial rapist. Their…predations have very little to do with the sexual act. They have to do with subjugation, humiliation and empowerment. Usually in direct reaction to similar predations they observed being inflicted on family members or having been inflicted on themselves in childhood. They literally have a movie in their head they need to enact and reenact. They need the empowerment of inflicting onto others what was done unto them or theirs. That's why women who fight their rapists very often get hurt but don't get raped. Women who scream, swear and bite and gouge ruin the movie, and the rapists very quickly break contact."

This was all stuff Bolan knew. "And that's not our boy Rubino."

"No, Mankita doesn't have a movie in his head. He's altogether different. He's more like your cartoon maniac who thinks he's Napoleon. You can put him in an institution, and he'll just think he's in exile on the island of Elba and write letters to his field marshals."

"And?"

"Well, that's the funny thing about Rubino Mankita."

"What's that?"

"Like I said, you put a sociopath in prison and he really doesn't care. He just keeps acting out his gig. Plus? Once you have them incarcerated, they can't shut up. They love talking about themselves and their gig. They can't stop themselves."

Bolan saw it. "And Mankita has gone stone cold on us."

"That's right. He's a sociopath who isn't talking."

Bolan smiled. "Mankita's gig is still going on outside of incarceration and he knows it. He's an outwardly motivated maniac. A maniac with a cause."

"You know you really do have a way with words, Mack. You should write a book."

"Yeah, right. When I have the time. So what's motivating Mankita?"

"Well, that's the million-dollar, spent-nuclear-fuel question. If we figure that out, we have the key to pushing all of his maladjusted little red buttons. Right now he's buttoned his lip and just sits in the interrogation room flexing his mangled hand like it's the red badge of courage."

"What did we get out of forensics on the bodies?"

"We got some. The Russians aren't cooperating with the investigation, but we got lucky with the guy from the Pinto Salcido sketches you designated the Russian. His name is Kirill Kuzin. He's ex-Russian Air Force, and achieved the rank of sergeant in the Russian Eighth Air Division for Special Purposes."

"Where did he learn Spanish?"

"Like you guessed, Cuba."

"Let me guess, their equivalent of search and rescue."

"Nice, Mack." Kurtzman pushed a file across the table. "Kuzin went to Cuba in 2002 for tropical warfare training. Russian SAR guys are a lot like ours. They don't just go in and rescue their own, they also go in to secure landing fields behind enemy lines. Of course I don't need to tell you this, but you know the Russians. Anyone in any service branch with what you and I would call Special Forces training is often thrown into the front lines during any conflict and used as shock troops."

Bolan knew all about militaries squandering their best and brightest. "Kuzin served in Chechnya."

"Right again, two tours. The first with distinction, decorated twice. His second tour was…spotty, and that's the Russian write-up."

Bolan glanced through the file. It was thin and second copy in English even thinner. The Russian portion containing Sergeant Kirill Kuzin's fitness report and actions during his second tour of duty in Chechnya had been heavily redacted with black indelible marker. It wasn't a good sign. The Russians had been going the Attila the Hun route on the Chechens for more than a decade. Looting, raping, burning and torturing were standard operating procedure. For a soldier to have his private military file redacted indicated even the Russians felt he had gone too far. "So how did we get this?"

"Kuzin came back from Chechnya and got involved with the mob. The heroin trade. He got busted in Poland. Apparently he was getting high off his own supply and making mistakes. According to the Poles, the Russians gave them Kuzin's file in exchange for some information they wanted on an unrelated case. The Poles gave a copy of the file to Interpol. Kuzin was extradited and tried in the Russian courts."

Bolan shook his head as he read farther down. "He did his time at the Russian Military Hospital in Moscow?"

"In the psych ward. Four years."

Bolan shook his head. All too often the philosophy of Russian mental hospitals was to drug people into sanity. Failing that they would settle for quiet. "It says here he was released on a positive progress report and good behavior, given a bed in a state-run halfway house and a job in a lightbulb factory."

"That's right, but Kuzin jumped ship within two weeks and dropped off the planet."

Bolan closed the file. "What about the rest of the Russians?"

"Well, we're assuming most of the bodies from the Sierra de Juárez fight are indeed Russians. A lot of them have Russian tattoos, but like I said, the Russians aren't cooperating. We caught a break on Kuzin because Interpol had his prints."

"Did we get anything on our Spaniard?"

"We got nothing, just Memo insisting he's seen him somewhere before. The Mexican federal authorities have shared his prints and dental. He's not showing up on anyone's database."

"What about the nuclear fuel?"

Kurtzman sighed. "So far not much. Whoever stole the material transferred it into homemade containers. We believe it was during this process that the men in Mexico City were poisoned. The new containers themselves are of very high quality, but so far have proved untraceable."

Bolan knew they were grasping at straws. "The fuel itself?"

Kurtzman knew it, too. "Well, as of today's date there are four hundred and thirty-nine nuclear reactors in current operation on planet Earth located in thirty-one different countries. The good news is our fuel inventory looks secure. Bad news is that no one else is owning up to it, and some places, like our good friends the Russians and the Chinese, wouldn't no matter what happens. We're just going to have to hope the NSA can pick up some chatter or our friends make another mistake like they did poisoning those guys in Mexico City."

"That's not good enough."

"Well, Mack, you averted a nuclear terrorist attack. That's pretty damn good, but you and me? We're out of it. We're just going to have to let the big agencies collate data and try to work up leads. The CIA has field agents in Moscow discreetly digging up everything they can on Kuzin and his activities before he disappeared."

Bolan was pretty sure the time for discretion was over. "Read the file. No family, living out of a halfway house. They won't find out much. It would be better if I went to Moscow and did it my way."

Kurtzman suspected he knew how Bolan might make his inquiries. "Well, now, won't that irritate the Russians."

"I've irritated the Russians before."

Kurtzman snorted. It was hard to imagine a country on Earth where someone didn't want a man matching Bolan's description dead, and there happened to be a startlingly large concentration of them in Moscow. "You got me there, but right now the State Department is trying to get their cooperation on this one."

"Yeah, I hope they have good luck with that."

"Well, we do have Mankita. Sooner or later he'll—"

"He'll never talk," Bolan said. "Even if the Mexicans use blowtorches and jumper cables on him. He won't talk until we figure out what buttons to push."

"Well, Rubino Mankita has an extensive criminal record. I'm sure the psych boys are working up a profile on him."

Bolan suddenly saw it.

Kurtzman had seen this look on Bolan's face before. "What? What have you got?"

Bolan smiled. "What have we got?"

"Well…" The computer wizard pondered. "What we have is Kirill Kuzin and Rubino Mankita."

"And what do they have in common?" Bolan prodded.

"Well, Kirill Kuzin is a Russian soldier who came back from Chechnya with post-traumatic stress disorder and drifted into crime. Mankita is freelance hit man for the Mexican cartels and genuine sociopath."

"Yeah, but what do we know for a fact that both men have in common?"

Kurtzman saw the thread, but to his chagrin he couldn't see where it led. "The only concrete fact is that both men were in Mexico transporting the material to make dirty bombs, presumably to be smuggled into the United States."

"That's right. You said Mankita is an outwardly motivated maniac. Someone gave him a direction. Kuzin was a down and out. Ex-soldier, drug addict, and someone straightened him out, slapped him tall, made him a soldier again and motivated him enough to make that nuclear run through Mexico."

Kurtzman mentally flailed. He was the brains of this outfit, but if there was anything on the planet sharper than his intellect it was the instincts of Mack Bolan. He gave his friend a sour look. "You're going to make me do the math on this one, aren't you?"

"You can do it."

"Damn it…" Kurtzman savaged the facts of the situation like a terrier with a bedroom slipper but nothing was coming.

Bolan quirked an eyebrow. "Want a hint?"

"No!" Kurtzman muttered into his beard for several moments. "Yes!"

"Well, can you name another person in this situation who changed his attitude?"

Kurtzman was appalled. He should have seen it. "Memo."

"That's right."

"But you operated right alongside with him. You said he was a trooper. The FBI, the CIA and the DEA all debriefed him. The FBI is working up a new identity for him and they're cutting him loose. Word is he wants to go meet up with Najelli in Hawaii."

"That's right. We're going to delay that. I want Memo here, at the Farm, within twenty-four hours, and I want Calvin. He's good at this kind of stuff."

Kurtzman was having a hard time believing what he was hearing. "You're going to interrogate Memo?"

"I'm going to have a talk with him."

"But he doesn't know anything."

"I believe he does. He just doesn't know he knows anything."

"Okay…anything else?"

"Yeah, get me everything you can on some motivational, personal-empowerment guru named Gavi."

CHAPTER TEN

Stony Man Farm, Virginia

Bolan and Calvin James sat at the kitchen table drinking coffee. Kurtzman came wheeling in with a laptop and a thick stack of files across his knee. He spun to a stop at the place of honor at the head of the table and smacked down a file. "Gavriil Arkhangelov."

Bolan smiled over his coffee. "Gavi."

"That's what his adherents call him." Kurtzman passed out copies. "This guy has a real cult of personality thing going on in Russia and Europe, and he's started to make inroads into the Americas."

James peered at a photo of Arkhangelov sitting on a dais in a sarong, lecturing to an intimate audience of adoring teen groupies and middle-aged women. His shaved head and chiseled body gleamed like bronze. Beneath his hawk brows his dark eyes flashed with spiritual authority. The women were clearly clinging to his every word. "This dude is seriously pimping."

Kurtzman nodded with appreciation. "That's a screen capture from one of his DVDs. The man has lectured to packed stadiums in Russia, Asia and Europe. But on his television programs and DVD seminars he keeps it small and stocked with hot babes. Women watching his seminars only have eyes for him, and any guy watching wants to meet the babes. It's clever."

Bolan frowned at the photo. Arkhangelov was one of those guys who no matter how you held his picture seemed to be looking straight at you. Bolan had seen faces like that before. "So he's some sort of Russian Tony Robbins?"

"Try one-third Tony Robbins, one-third L. Ron Hubbard and one-third Rasputin. He's all about personal empowerment."

Something perked in Bolan's limited Russian. "Gavriil, that's…"

"That's Russian for Gabriel," Kurtzman said with a nod.

James dropped his copy in disgust. "The dude's name is Gabriel Archangel?"

"Oh, yeah." Kurtzman flipped a page and pulled a photo. "And this is his brother, Apollyon."

They all examined a photo of a shorter, stockier, even more muscular man with spiky, platinum-blond hair exhorting to a packed stadium with Nazi-like fervor. James sighed in disgust. "His brother's name is Apollo?"

"No, but good guess. Christian scholars often link Apollyon to the Greek god Apollo, but in the Greek and Russian Orthodox churches Apollyon is the name for the archangel Raguel. He's one of the archangels whose function is to take vengeance on the world of luminaries who have transgressed God's laws. In Revelation 10 he watches over other angels to make sure they are working together in harmony with mortals according to the Divine Order."

"And Apollyon is his brother Gavriil's chief enforcer."

"I'm still researching it, but Apollyon seems to have the chief administrator's job."

Bolan examined the photo of the shouting man. His spiky blond hair seemed to grow out of his head like nerve endings. "The sword behind the throne. I'm betting he was military."

"We just started researching these people and it's already pretty clear someone is protecting them. The cybernetic team is on it." Kurtzman flipped to a photograph of a beautiful redheaded woman leading a group of tanned, fit people in sarongs and head buffs in some kind of yoga practice on a tropical beach. "That's his sister, Michaela. The adherents all call her Mikki. From what I understand she's sort of the international den mother for the organization. The picture is from a retreat they had in Goa, India, last year."

"Damn," James said. "Where do I sign up?"

"Michaela," Bolan mused. "That's the Russian feminine of Michael, another archangel."

"That's right," Kurtzman agreed.

James sat up in his chair. "Dude, isn't Gabriel the Angel of Death?"

That had been preying on Kurtzman's mind all morning. "According to some interpretations of the Bible, yeah."

James poured himself more coffee. "This is wrong in so many ways."

Bolan flipped back to Gavi's photo. "What's this Gavi guy's action?"

"The name of the movement is Nebesa Sejchas, the rough English translation would be 'Heaven Now.' It's pretty much your textbook cult of personality-personal empowerment trip. I watched one of his DVDs and skimmed some of his literature this morning. He cherry-picks the parts of the Russian Orthodox canon that he likes, adds a huge infusion of New Age imagery, and then throws some pseudoscience, Eastern mystical practices and some good, old-fashioned Russian occultism into the mix. He has inspirational and guided meditation CDs, a 'spiritual fitness' program that looks a lot like yoga and pilates and tai chi all rolled up into one. The troubling part, given what we suspect, is that interspersed with his feel-good rhetoric there are some vaguely apocalyptic predictions."

James eyed the adoring women in the photos. "Except for middle-aged women and strippers in sarongs, and don't get me wrong, this Gavi dude had my profound respect for that, but man, who falls for this shit anymore?"

"Russians." Kurtzman shrugged. "By the thousands, and Europeans and Asians."

"Asians?"

"He's huge in Japan. He speaks the language. In fact it appears he speaks seven languages. A lot of very rich and influential people are into him. He's like a rock star in Russia and Eastern Europe. He's made inroads in South America, and while he isn't on PBS or NPR yet, he's starting to get U.S. marketing."

"What's his message?"

"Same old same old, it's a story as old as time. The rich get richer and the poor get poorer. Most poor people don't have much time to worry about their spirituality or the nature of their souls. They're too busy working for the man and putting food on the table. They work hard all week, go to church on Sunday and hope for their reward in heaven. The rich get richer, and in this day and age that includes the middle class, which is suddenly swelling up like yeast in the East. They don't worry about where their next meal is coming from, so they have the luxury to look around themselves, look at their toy boxes full of their possessions, realize they're going to die like everyone else and ask themselves that eternal question, 'Is this all there is?'

"And Gavi has the answers. Gavi knows why you're not happy and Gavi can fix it, and he isn't telling you to shave your head and renounce everything. He's telling you to enjoy the material life now while you give him your money to improve your spiritual life, and people are sending him their rubles hand over fist for CDs and DVDs and to attend his seminars. I have copies of his DVDs for both of you. You need to see this guy. One moment he's sitting in the lotus position lecturing like Buddha, the next he's standing up and dealing out the holy thunder and the next he's laughing and joking and taking questions from the audience. This Gavi guy could sell water by the river. He's a snake charmer."

"Can you connect him to Mankita or Kuzin?"

"Mankita? No, not yet. Kuzin? Not directly, but can you guess how Gavi made his reputation in Russia?"

Bolan smiled as he saw it. "Working with war veterans."

"You got it. First the Russians had their war in Afghanistan and then in Chechnya. The war in Chechnya is wildly unpopular and veterans got no respect. It's like jury duty—if you went you were too dumb to get out of it and when you come back the public at large assumes you're a drug-addicted psychopath. Gavi went among them like Christ among the unclean. Helping vets get off drugs, helping them find jobs, helping them band together to get benefits. A guy like Kuzin? On his last legs? He might just flock to a Gavi gathering just for the free food and then never leave. On top of that? The Russians have been on a nationalism kick in recent years.

"For all Gavi's good work they pinned the Hero of the Russian Federation medal on him. That's the highest award anyone can achieve in Russia, and there are some very high-level people in the Russian military and government who are adherents of his. In some ways Heaven Now is like Scientology. The more seminars you attend, the more money you give, the higher you rise. There's a whole hierarchy, and the rich and famous and powerful in the East are dying to get to the top. If you reach Gavi's inner circle, he makes you an archangel, and the list of publicly known archangels is pretty sobering."

"What do we know about Gavi personally?"

"Not much, and that's the scary part. We're having problems getting concrete information on him and his background. The CIA station chief in Moscow said Russian intelligence is watching Gavi very closely, and he also feels there are Gavi adherents in intelligence who are watching the watchers. I've asked Hal for the president's permission to hack some sensitive Russian databases. I also asked Akira to probe the Heaven Now database itself. He says it's as sophisticated as it gets." Kurtzman sighed. "Like you said, Mack. This may take footwork. To really get inside, we may have to do this your way."

Bolan had suspected that all along.

"Speak of the devil…" James glanced up at the ceiling as the kitchen window panes rattled with the sound of rotor noise. "The guest of honor?"

Out the window a black helicopter was circling into a landing in front of the main farm building. Bolan and James rose. Kurtzman turned to wheel himself back to the War Room. "I'll want a full report on his debriefing."

Bolan nodded. "You got it, Bear." Bolan and James took their coffee outside as Memo Dominico was led blindfolded from the helicopter by a pair of blacksuits. They walked him across the front lawn, and Dominico blinked in the sun as he pulled down his blindfold. He found himself face-to-face with Mack Bolan and Calvin James. Neither man was smiling. Dominico took an involuntary step back and bumped into large and unmoving Farm employees with automatic carbines. Dominico stared back and forth between the blacksuits, the green mountains of Virginia and Bolan and James in mounting panic.

"Hello, Memo," Bolan greeted.

Dominico's shoulders sagged. "Man…" His left arm was still in a sling. He tried once again to back up unsuccessfully. He turned at the sound of the black helicopter's mounting engine noise. He watched in consternation as the chopper rose into the sky, dipped its nose and headed east. He whirled and stabbed an accusing finger at Bolan. "You said we were square!"

Bolan nodded. "We are."

"So what am I doing here, man?" Dominico demanded. "I thought I was on a plane to Hawaii! Then two federal marshals sit down next to me and the plane flies east!" He flung his gaze around the alien landscape. "Where am I, man?"

"Can't tell you."

"You can't tell me?"

"No."

Dominico summoned fresh outrage. "Why am I here?"

"I need to talk to you."

"You could have asked!"

Bolan regarded Dominico dryly. "And what would you have said?"

"I would have said fuck you, *cabrón!*"

Bolan nodded.

"This is kidnapping! I have rights!"

"Actually, you are a wanted criminal in Mexico and your current status in the United States is, how shall I say, tenuous?"

Dominico went back to pointing fingers. "Man, you suck!"

"All I want to do is talk." Bolan shrugged casually. "Then we can go horseback riding and have dinner."

"What? Fuck you!" Dominico looked about ready to burst

a blood vessel. "Fuck horseback riding! Fuck dinner!" He whirled on James. "And fuck your…" Whatever Dominico saw in the black ex-navy SEAL's eyes made him think twice. He whirled back on Bolan. "Fuck you, man! What if I don't want to talk?"

Bolan raised his gaze to the helicopter disappearing across the mountains. "Well, I'll call the chopper back and put you on a plane to Molokai."

"So do it!"

"Except sooner or later the CIA will want to talk to you."

"I already talked to them!"

"Yeah, but they're going to question you one hell of a lot harder than I am. Like maybe they put you on a private flight from Molokai to Thailand where they put you in a very private CIA 'black site' prison where you're subjected to all sorts of Southeast Asian interrogation techniques. Bamboo shoots under the fingernails, hanging you upside down and going piñata on you with rattan canes… I've heard stories."

"Man…" Dominico drew himself up. "I can't believe you would do that to me. After all we've been through."

"I won't do it. You know me. I put my ass on the line for you with Colonel Llosa. He had a serious hard-on for you and you know it. I gave him my marker to save your ass. I don't know if I can save it a second time. I think I figured out something, and if I can, so can the CIA and so can your boys back home in S-2 Second Section, and some of these, on both sides of the border, play rough."

Dominico fumed.

"Speaking of markers, you owe me."

"I owe you?" Dominico waved his good arm in outrage. "I lost my house! I lost my stuff! I lost all my privileges in Mexico! I got nothing!"

"Rumor is you have millions in several offshore accounts in the Caribbean."

"I…"

"Actually, it's not a rumor. I have the account numbers. And I had some contacts in the DEA and CIA and some Mexican intelligence guys who owe me favors remove your stuff from your house in the hills before Llosa and the *federales* could get to it. It's all in storage containers on a freighter to Hawaii as we speak."

Dominico lost track of his rage. "Really?"

"When was the last time I lied to you?"

"Uhh…thanks?"

"Memo, come into the kitchen. Have a cup of coffee. We talk. Give me five minutes. You aren't happy? I call the chopper back."

"Okay, man. One cup of coffee. Because I owe you."

Bolan led them back into the kitchen and Dominico and James sat down as Bolan poured coffee. "Cognac?"

"No, man. Tequila."

"Coming up." Bolan dosed his mug of coffee with Patrón Silver from the liquor cabinet. Bolan sat down and the three men drank coffee for a few moments as hospitality was observed.

Dominico spoke first. "Ask your questions, man."

"Fair enough. These guys, Makita, Kuzin, they had your contacts and they had your routes."

Dominico bristled but there was no denying it. "Yeah, man, and I told you, I don't know how. I told you that. They had to have gotten to somebody."

"Who?" Bolan probed.

"I don't know!"

"I do."

Dominico blinked. "Oh, yeah?"

"Yeah."

"Who?"

"You."

Dominico stared in incomprehension. "Me?"

Bolan prepared himself for the verbal storm. "Memo? What did you tell Gavi?"

Dominico surged up out of his seat. "Fuck you, man!"

"What did you tell Gavi?" Bolan repeated.

"I only met him once! For a minute! He changed my life!"

Bolan accepted that. "What did you tell Apollyon?"

"What? I…fuck you, man!"

"Sit down," James suggested.

"And fuck you, too!"

James's voice dropped a dangerous octave. "Memo, sit down."

Dominico sat.

Good cop-bad cop had been established. Bolan gave Dominico a sympathetic sigh. "You've been Santo Solomon, King Solomon and a guy named Memo minding his own business trying to make a good life. Did you tell anyone from Heaven Now about your past lives?"

Dominico's facial muscles clenched so hard Bolan thought bones might break, and he knew he'd hit pay dirt. Bolan hurled what he suspected into Dominico's face. "Kuzin was Heaven Now. Mankita was Heaven Now. That's why they were in pickups with nuclear material in the Sierra de Juárez."

"Fuck that!"

"The Spaniard was Heaven Now. You saw him at a seminar."

"Fuck that! Fuck you! Fuck…" Dominico's face suddenly went blank. "Oh, fuck…me, man."

"Where? Where did you see him?"

"Oh, Jesus…" Horror crept across Dominico's face. "At the retreat. I saw him at the retreat in Argentina."

"Memo, at any point during your...adherence, did you tell anyone from Heaven Now anything about your past life as King Solomon?"

"I...told them everything," Dominico replied. "But they would never use that stuff! That's not what it's about! That's not what it's about at all!"

"Then tell me. What is it all about?"

Dominico shifted uncomfortably. "We're...not supposed to talk about it."

"You don't have to tell me everything that goes on or everything you told them, but can you just give me the gist of it?"

"Well, man, you want to change? First you got to own up to who you are and who you've been. You got to face it. You want forgiveness? You gotta apologize for the things you've done. You gotta have..." Dominico squirmed. "Convo."

"Convo?"

"Personal convocations," Dominico blurted.

That was a new one even for Bolan. "Personal...gatherings?"

"Yeah, you gather up all the people you've been, and you're assigned an Interlocutor..."

Bolan tried to keep the smile off his face. "Helps you bring it all together?"

"Personal convocation leads to personal harmonization," Dominico recited. "You are the Universe, man. When you gather yourself together the Universe gathers around you. When you gather your personal convocation, even the angels are watching."

Bolan didn't doubt that for a second. He suspected that an archangel was always watching during convo and taking down every word. "So what's a convo like?"

"Well...it's just you, your personal convocation and your Interlocutor. The Interlocutor gives you this special tea that relaxes you."

James rolled his eyes. "He drank the stuff."

Dominico scowled. "They have a machine. It looks like a lie detector but instead it helps you focus on your truth."

James threw up his hands. "Jesus, Memo! You drank the shit and you held the cans?"

"Gavi is a great man! He would never do any of the shit you're implying! Everyone always wants to shoot the messenger! Instead of getting the message!"

Bolan had met a lot of messengers who had required shooting. "Memo, I'm not trying to get down on Gavi's message. I'm not getting down on the man, yet. But unless you can tell me how else Mankita and Kuzin got all your information, I'm saying someone, somehow, got your convo info and used it. *Campesinos* in Mexico died, and someone was planning on killing who knows how many people in the U.S. I'm not saying Gavi did it, but it had to have been an inside job."

"No way! The people at Heaven Now are different, everyone there—"

"Every great man has his Judas, Memo!" Bolan let some fire kindle behind his eyes. "From Christ to Martin Luther King, they were all killed by their own. You're telling me that of all the people Gavi has helped, people like you, Kuzin and Mankita, not one of them could be a Judas?"

Dominico's spiritual crisis continued to deepen. "I hear what you're saying, man, but…"

Bolan went for broke. "Memo, I have to know. I think you do, too."

"Oh, man…"

"Just tell me who your Interlocutor was."

"That shit is private, man! I—"

Bolan roared. "You want to know or not! Give me a goddamn name!"

Dominico's knuckles went white. Sweat burst out upon his brow as he literally shook in his seat.

"That's it." Bolan stood. "Call the chopper. We do this without him."

James spoke quietly as he and Bolan's roles reversed. "Memo? You can't walk away from this. You've got to know. You were a player back in the day, and if you got played? If people died because of it? You got to do something, and you know that's a no-shit assessment. If you really turned your shit around, then this shit doesn't stand."

Dominico couldn't lift his head. "Ride."

Both Bolan and James blinked. "What do you mean, 'Ride'?" Bolan asked.

"Ride, it's short for Rider. Her name was Rider Anaya." Dominico stared into his hands as he betrayed everything he had believed in. "She wasn't my original Interlocutor, but when I went to Argentina for the retreat, everyone gushed about how lucky I was to get her. They say she'll be an archangel soon."

"And you told her everything?"

"My wrestling, my drug running, the people I'd hurt, the people I'd killed, wanting Najelli…everything."

"Let me ask you a question."

"What?"

"Do you believe someone got a hold of transcripts of your personal convocations and used them to perpetrate what happened in Mexico?"

Dominico closed his hands into fists. "Yeah."

"You know I'm going in."

"Yeah, man. I know."

"And you're my best shot at jumping to the head of the line."

"I know."

"So what do you say? You in, or you want me to call the chopper?"

"I…" Dominico looked deep into the middle distance. "I need to call Najelli."

Bolan took out his phone. "Be my guest."

"Thanks." Dominico took the phone and stepped outside.

Bolan turned to James. "What do you think?"

The Phoenix Force commando shrugged. "Man was a superstar in Mexico. He was a successful criminal, got his song, got his legend and turned his back on the life. You came calling, turned his shit all upside down and inside out and what does he do? He cowboyed up." James nodded thoughtfully. "Your boy Memo is an interesting cat."

Bolan poured them both a hefty shot of tequila in their empty coffee mugs. They both knew it would be their last social drink for a while. James took a long pull and savored the flavor. "So we're going in. With him or without him."

"Yeah."

They watched as Dominico had a very long and quiet call to a woman he loved in Hawaii. Bolan poured another round and shoved a mug forward as Dominico came back in. Dominico took the mug and tossed it back without blinking.

"And?" Bolan asked.

"I'm in, man."

Bolan had been betting on it. "So what did Najelli say?"

Dominico took a long breath and let it out. "She wants in, too."

CHAPTER ELEVEN

The War Room, Stony Man Farm, Virginia

"You sure this is a good idea?" Kurtzman asked.

Bolan thought it was a spectacularly bad idea, but he'd already made up his mind. "It's our best shot."

"Mack, this is like telling a Catholic terrorist the Pope is fallible and then taking him on a field trip to the Vatican."

"You know you have a way with words, Bear." Bolan shrugged. "Cal will have my back."

James nodded knowingly.

Kurtzman kept his eyes on Bolan. "You trust Memo?"

"I do. I believe he wants to do the right thing, and he's our ticket in. His exposure was minimal. Only Colonel Llosa, Dr. Corso and some Special Forces guys at Camp One know of his involvement. His place in Mexico City is vacated. He's got a bullet wound in him. He can show up at a Heaven Now center anywhere in the world and say he has no idea what's going on and he's on the run. He's got several million in offshore accounts, and I think that makes him an unknowing gold card member. I think they'll bring him in, and if they used his contacts and routes then they'll definitely want to talk to him."

"They'll most likely want to snuff him, you mean."

"I've considered that. So has he."

"And you and Calvin are his bodyguards?"

"That's how we'll play it. If our theory is right, somehow Heaven Now is involved in terrorism. If they were moving nuclear material across the Mexican border, then they must have had U.S. contacts waiting for them. If your theory is right and the men we fought in Sierra de Juárez were Russian vets, then I'm thinking they'll be wanting similar shock troops north of the border. Calvin and I will play the disillusioned U.S. spec-war operators and see if we can get ourselves recruited."

"I can do disillusioned," James stated.

"I know you can, both of you can, and let me tell you, that was a pretty good kitchen table deprogramming you had up there, but does the word *recidivist* mean anything to either of you two? What do you think is going to happen to our boy Memo when they pour the special tea down his throat again and Apollyon, Michaela or Gavi himself stares deep into Memo's big brown eyes and starts asking pointed questions?"

"I know it's not what you want to hear, Bear." Bolan sighed. "But I trust him."

"You trust him?" Kurtzman regarded Bolan frankly. "Why?"

"I fought beside him."

The computer expert had no immediate response for that.

"Besides, with Najelli with him he'll be motivated to stay on the straight and narrow."

Kurtzman didn't exactly consider Najelli Busto's involvement a red-hot idea, either. "You're okay bringing in the Busto woman on this?"

"Not so much, but her reasoning is solid. They're a lot less likely to think Memo is a plant if he brings his girlfriend with him. Plus, she's a better shot than he is."

Kurtzman still wasn't thrilled. "Well, the good news is that she'd barely had time to unpack her bags. We're arranging a private jet, we can have her here by tomorrow morning. Meantime the team is working up a decent back story about where she and Memo will supposedly have been during the Mexico mission."

"Speaking of women, what did you get on the Anaya woman?"

The cyberwizard clicked a key and a beautiful woman in a bikini top and a sarong appeared on the giant HD screen. She had golden-brown hair, golden-brown skin and golden-brown eyes. She was a study in vibrant health and happiness as she smiled into the camera.

"Damn!" James said enthusiastically. "This job is so right in so many ways! I want the Gavi sarong, the Gavi head buff, the Gavi shoes of the fisherman, the whole bit."

Kurtzman attempted to move on past James's enthusiasm. "Rider Maria Anaya. Born in Mendoza, 1980. Her father was an Argentine national, her mother is American. She was a model as a teenager in South America, she had a couple of pop songs that charted in the South American market, and had bit parts in a few Spanish-language films and a year as the bad girl in a popular South American soap opera. She was the girlfriend of a few Spanish-speaking actors and pop stars. Then she suddenly drops out of sight. There are rumors of drug addiction and some work in the Brazilian adult film industry, but nothing I can immediately substantiate. No criminal record. She reappears in Buenos Aires as a yoga instructor in the early 2000s, and next you know she's appearing on Gavi DVDs as adoring faithful, and then leading the faithful in their morning workouts on Gavi fitness and meditation DVDs."

Bolan had to give Rider her due. Arguably, the most beautiful women in the world came from South America, and arguably, most agreed the most beautiful of those came from Argentina, and no one in Argentina argued that the most beautiful women came from their Andean wine country, the province of Mendoza. Bolan had been there.

There was something in the water.

"Call it fate," Kurtzman continued, "but Heaven Now is having its South American retreat again in three weeks, in the Argentine Andes, at a ski resort in Bariloche."

"Man, tell me she's going to be there."

"Cal, we need to get you a bib, or a leash." Kurtzman pulled up the retreat's itinerary. "But yeah, she's leading several of the physical-spiritual fitness fusion seminars. She'll be there all week."

Bolan scanned the schedule. Gavi himself was going to be there to address the masses. "I think that's a party we're going to crash."

James reclined his chair. "So three weeks to the South American chalet seminar. What do we do with ourselves 'til then? I suppose I'll join up with Phoenix for a while."

"First I want a list of every possible name we can associate with the Heaven Now movement, no matter how big or small. Work them up for patterns and connections."

Kurtzman saw his evenings stretching out before him. "That's going to be thousands upon thousands."

"You have three weeks. Have Akira crack the Heaven Now database."

"I'm on it."

"Cal, David will just have to manage without you. Najelli should be here in the next twenty-four to forty-eight hours. I want you to work with her and Memo on getting their stories straight, forward and back. I think sooner or later all of us will have to pass a personal convocation. During breaks you can make an attempt at teaching Memo how to shoot."

"Cool, but what are you going to be doing?"

"I'm going to Moscow, and ask a few questions my way."

Kurtzman got a worried look on his face. "Mack, you better tread light and be real careful who you talk to. Like I said, this Gavriil guy is like a rock star in Russia at the moment, with rock star connections. Some very powerful people over there are true believers of his."

"I know, I'm going to need me a real Soviet-era believes-in-nothing nihilist."

Kurtzman's jaw dropped. "Not him."

"Yeah, Gavi works with the vets, and you yourself said I need to be careful of who I talk to. So I might as well start from the bottom up." Bolan rose from his chair. "I'm on a plane."

The Russian Federation

"YOU!" MAJOR PIETOR Ramzin, retired, strangled on his vodka as he suddenly found Mack Bolan before him.

Bolan had flown out of Dulles and arrived at Moscow's international airport at dawn. Bolan had found Ramzin in about as bad a bar he'd ever seen on the west side of the city around midafternoon. Ramzin had Georgian roots, and this was the kind of establishment he frequented. Ramzin looked like he had started drinking about the same time Bolan had debarked the plane.

"Ramzin." Bolan smiled. "You look like shit."

Pietor Ramzin had run an underground smuggling ring between the United States and Mexico with the help of cold war Soviet moles and ex-Special Forces soldiers. Bolan had destroyed his operation and put him in Leavenworth with four consecutive life sentences. Bolan had gotten Ramzin released to help hunt down a certain seven-foot-tall psychopathic acquaintance of his and then gotten him released back to Russia. They were not friends. Bolan had crushed Ramzin's criminal career, and had used bribery and coercion to get his cooperation afterward. He knew there was a deep, dark, dangerous part of Pietor Ramzin's heart that hated him.

Ramzin had looked better.

He was the same height as Bolan but was built on a thicker frame and well over a decade older. Ramzin had put on forty pounds since Bolan had seen him last, and it was in all the wrong places. Broken veins bloomed red beneath the skin of his nose and cheeks. Bolan had put Ramzin in prison and the Vandyke mustache and beard he'd assiduously cultivated there had grown out—along with his hair—into unkempt, ruglike masses. He was missing some teeth. His cheaply tailored corduroy suit was stained and shiny in the elbows and knees with long wear. He looked like some bad cross between a mad Russian poet, a drunken extra in a Viking movie and Santa Claus's ne'er-do-well brother. However, once the man had been a Spetsnaz officer, and in the burning cauldron of the Russian invasion of Afghanistan Ramzin had become a Hero of the Soviet Union and had the medal to prove it. He rose slowly from his chair. Even fat, dissolute and drunk he was like a great sagging bull. His scarred, hamlike hands creaked into fists. He was still formidable. The drunks at the nearby tables rose, clutching their drinks, and lurched away from ground zero.

Ramzin's bloodshot eyes went ugly. "I break you."

"I'll give you a job," Bolan countered.

Ramzin considered this for long moments before slumping back into his chair. "Fuck."

Bolan took a seat and took a pull from the bottle. The very cheapest vodka was distilled from molasses rather than potatoes or grain and the liquor burned on the way down like kerosene. "You have something better to do?"

"Yes." Ramzin nodded. "Drink."

Bolan refilled the Russian's glass. "I need you."

Ramzin eyed it steadily but showed some restraint. "And why do I take job from you?"

"You owe me," Bolan suggested.

"I owe you?"

"I got you out of Leavenworth."

Ramzin grunted derisively and drank. "You put me in Leavenworth."

"I'll pay you a thousand dollars a day."

That penetrated through the drunken haze. "A thousand?"

"Yeah."

"To do what?"

One look at Ramzin told Bolan the veteran soldier and criminal wasn't wearing the head buff or donning a sarong anytime soon. "You heard of Nebesa Sejchas?"

Ramzin hawked and spit on the floor. "Pussies."

"Well, that Gavriil Arkhangelov guy? It looks like I'm going to have to mess his shit up."

Ramzin spent a moment wrapping his pickled brain around this weird and wonderful turn of events. "And you pay me thousand dollars a day to help you?"

Bolan nodded. "Yeah."

"I want money in euros."

"Done."

"Cash."

"Of course." Bolan took out a thousand-dollar wad rubber-banded into a roll and dropped it on the table. "You mind the first day's pay in greenbacks until I can go to the bank?"

Ramzin stared at the cash on the table. "I want Stechkin machine pistol."

Bolan was well aware of Ramzin's weapons preferences and predilections. "You'll have it."

He gestured at the sea of squashed cigarette butts on the floor around him. "I need cigarettes."

Bolan tossed a pack of Marlboros onto the table.

"I need—"

"You need a bath." Bolan drained the last of the bottle into Razmin's glass. "Enjoy that. It's going to be your last for a while." Bolan looked to the surly, three-hundred-pound woman behind the bar wearing a Georgian apron and kerchief and spoke a little Russian. "Food, coffee, please."

Ramzin began chain-smoking Marlboros. "So, why Gavriil?"

"I think he tried to smuggle nuclear material into the United States." Bolan raised an eyebrow at Ramzin. "And you know how that is."

"I did not try." Ramzin raised a bleary brow back. "I succeeded."

The food arrived. The coffee was horrible, the borscht was fantastic and the pickled eggs were glorious or a monstrosity, depending on one's view of life. Ramzin ate about a third of the tureen and wolfed down giant chunks of brown bread slathered with some glistening mystery lubricant posturing as butter. Bolan watched. Ramzin had clearly crossed that line from heavy drinker to full-blown alcoholic. The fact that his appetite was good was a hopeful sign. "You think you can keep it together for the next two weeks?"

Ramzin combed food out of his beard with his fingers. "I keep together."

"Go home. Clean yourself up." Bolan finished his coffee, paid the tab and rose. "I'll pick you up tomorrow."

"I live—"

"I know where you live." Bolan stopped at the door. "Ramzin?"

"What?"

"If you're drunk tomorrow, you're fired."

Secure Communications Room, U.S. Embassy, Moscow

"SO HOW'S OUR OLD FRIEND Ramzin?" Kurtzman asked.

They had been enemies, but Bolan would admit to anyone Ramzin was one of the deadliest he'd ever had. If you didn't respect his abilities you were likely to end up dead, and no matter what his crimes, the man had earned Hero of the Soviet Union the hard way. It was disturbing to see him like this. "Honestly? He's in some gray area between the third and fourth stages of alcoholism."

Kurtzman stared incredulously into the video link. "And you're going to work with this guy?"

"Oh, yeah. In a way it almost makes him perfect for the job."

"Mack, this guy wants you dead, and that's on a good day."

"He wants a thousand euros a day a lot more." Bolan weighed the look he'd seen in the veteran soldier's eyes. "He's a criminal who's out of the life, and a soldier who's out of the action. I could be wrong, but I think he wants a shot at redemption more than anything."

"You're going to bet your life on an addict."

"Actually I'm going to bet on the Hero, but I'll keep my eyes open. What's the news on your end?"

"Najelli arrived. Calvin's been tweaking the back story and its pretty good. Memo's a wrestler who knows how to work with scripted behavior and Najelli is a natural. Cal's ninety-nine-percent sure that they'll be ready for the Argentine seminar."

Bolan took a wild stab. "How's Memo's shooting coming along?"

"According to Cal?" Kurtzman made a helpless gesture. "We still have a couple of weeks to work on it. How are things in Moscow?"

"The CIA is getting me a car and swears I'll have all the

gear I want by dawn. If Ramzin is in any kind of shape at all tomorrow, we're going in."

Kurtzman rubbed his temples as if he was starting to get a headache. "Mack, Hal needs something to tell the president besides 'Striker is going in with a drunken enemy of the United States and a trunk full of guns.' I mean, you can see that? You can see that, right?"

"Yeah." Bolan shrugged. "But that's what I'm doing."

The cyberwizard's symptoms seemed to worsen. "Tell me you have some kind of plan besides busting your way in during the middle of the day in the middle of Moscow with guns blazing. Tell me there's some sort of soft option here."

Bolan had been pondering his options the whole plane ride over. One look at Ramzin had given him what he considered a decent inside gambit on Heaven Now. "Tell Hal I'm going in soft on entry. If it goes hard after that, so be it. How's our list coming?"

Kurtzman was relieved for all of one second and his frown returned as he considered the enormity of the task on his end. "It's huge. Heaven Now isn't quite ready to knock Buddhism or the Catholic Church off their perches, but it's a global movement. I'm working up trees of adherents in Russia, Europe and South America and Asia and trying to make military or scientific connections. They have a cosmonaut adherent going up on the upcoming mission to the International Space Station. He's going to address the faithful from space and have a personal convo with Gavi on a live video link. You can see it at any Heaven Now center for free or buy it on pay-per-view."

"Swell. How did Akira's hack into the Heaven Now database go?"

"He hasn't done it yet."

Bolan could guess why. "It's pretty well protected?"

"State of the art. Akira says it would be easier to break into

Russian Military Intelligence's network, and he's done that before. He thinks someone outside of Russia developed Heaven Now database and is defending it. He's talking like top ten in the world."

"I gather we have a short list?"

"We're working one up."

"Can he get in?"

"Oh, he can get in, in fact he's raring to go. You know how he loves a challenge. But at the moment he can't guarantee he won't be detected, and we're going to be trying to get their most sensitive stuff. Chances are the second he's detected the entire Heaven Now network will go into lockdown. His question is, do you want him to go ahead and try now or wait while you try to get inside?"

Bolan considered. "Let's hold off, at least for twenty-four hours."

"He's going to be a very disappointed young hacker."

"Tell him to hold his mud and work the other angles. He'll be getting in the ring with the Heaven Now database soon enough. How's Memo's arm?"

"Our doctor admired Najelli's stitch-work. The nerve symptoms seemed to have gone away, but he needs to be careful of it. They gave him a physical-therapy regimen and he's hitting our gym. He says he'll be ready."

"Fair enough. I'm going to grab some chow here and get some rack time. Then it's off to Ramzin's bright and early. Striker out." Bolan thought about his afternoon meeting with Ramzin and what would be required tomorrow. He sighed. Kurtzman was right. He was going up against a globe-spanning cult during the middle of the day in the middle of Moscow with a drunken enemy of the United States and a trunk full of guns. Lady Luck had better be smiling.

CHAPTER TWELVE

Georgian Quarter, Moscow

Bolan arrived bright and early. Ramzin's neighborhood looked like the apocalypse had already come, lost interest and left for greener pastures. It was all Soviet-era block housing with raddled sidewalks and potholes like shell craters. Everything was uniformly rust-red or gray. Bullet holes and graffiti on the walls showed where the gangs had fought over territory. Georgians were one of the larger ethnic minorities in Moscow. Nevertheless life went on. Many of the windows had flowerpots on the sills and a gaggle of children were playing soccer in the middle of the street. They all stopped and formed a wary phalanx as Bolan pulled to the curb. He slid out and jerked his head at his car and held up a pair of five-hundred-ruble notes. At the moment that was approximately fifty bucks U.S. Two boys who appeared to be brothers came forward. One sat on Bolan's hood while the other took the money.

Bolan left his ride well guarded and climbed up sagging steps to Ramzin's apartment and banged on the door.

"Door is open."

Bolan entered to find Ramzin sitting at a tiny table in the room's one chair drinking tea and smoking. His combed and wet hair and beard were evidence of some bathing, and he was wearing a clean shirt. Bolan glanced around. There was almost nothing to see. He had a kitchenette with a hot plate, a bed in one corner and wardrobe in another. There was nothing on the walls except for an old, battered hunting rifle hanging over the hot plate and a giant Georgian kindjal double-edged dagger hanging over the bed. Winners of the Hero of the Soviet Union Medal were entitled to special privileges besides their pension. They were first priority on the housing list and entitled to an additional fifteen square meters of living space, which with the prisonlike crowding in most of Moscow's low income housing really meant something. They got a free yearly round-trip first-class ticket and a free yearly visit to a sanitarium or rest home.

Ramzin's current conditions told Bolan he was selling his hero's benefits to keep himself in booze into perpetuity.

At the moment Ramzin appeared to be sober and none too happy about it.

"Hard times?"

Ramzin rolled his eyes. "Perhaps Russia had good times. Perhaps before Mongol invasion. But even I am not old enough to remember."

Bolan was pleased to note Ramzin still had his sense of humor. It was as black as the ace of spades, but like an appetite for food it was a good sign. Bolan tossed a plastic sack of apples on the table.

Ramzin blinked at this anomalous event. "For what?"

"For you. According to Indian Ayurvedic medicine, apples help curb the appetite for alcohol and detoxify the body."

"Idol worshipping…" Ramzin muttered.

"Three a day. Fill your pockets and let's roll."

"You have guns?"

"I have guns."

Ramzin regarded the apples again. "You have money?"

Bolan tossed him an impressive wad of euros. "One thousand."

Ramzin dragged an uncharacteristically nervous hand through his hair. "I think perhaps I need haircut, and—"

"Gavriil made his rep working with destitute veterans. Between your Hero of the Soviet Union Medal and the way you look, you're ideal." Bolan turned and walked out. He went down the stairs and his security team seemed to be taking guarding his car seriously. He gave both boys another five-hundred-ruble note and a thumbs-up. The two boys stood about grinning, waiting to see what the American would do next.

They paled as Ramzin came down the stairs eating an apple. Ramzin smiled unpleasantly and accurately beaned the bigger one in the back of the head with the core as they ran off.

"Punks." Ramzin stared at the long black sedan. "This is your vehicle, a Volga?"

The Volga 3105 four-door was four years old and looked like it was going on twenty. That was one reason why Bolan had chosen it. Most Russians shared Ramzin's opinion of the state of the Russian auto industry. Anyone who could afford it bought an import. Russian carjackers often refused to jack native automobiles out of self-respect. That was in the car's favor, as well as the fact that it was one of the few Russian cars with a V8 engine and all-wheel drive. Bolan popped the trunk and unfolded a blanket to reveal the arsenal the CIA had acquired for him. Rifles, pistols, submachine guns, grenades and even folding rocket launchers filled the cavernous trunk. Bolan took out a Stechkin machine pistol in a shoulder rig with six spare magazines. "As ordered."

Ramzin strapped it on right in the middle of the street. It was the kind of neighborhood where people didn't call the cops, and the way the kids had reacted it was pretty clear that despite his current state Ramzin still walked with a lot of swagger. He took a little PSM pocket automatic and put it into his jacket for backup. He smiled nostalgically as he picked up an old NR-40 combat knife and tucked it into the back of his pants.

"You want a rifle?" Bolan asked.

Ramzin examined the shoulder arms Bolan had in the trunk and pointed at a stubby OC-14 assault rifle with an optic sight. "I take that one, and…" Ramzin stopped in midsentence. His pointing finger was shaking. He closed his eyes and closed his hand into a fist. It still shook. Ramzin had been one of the better riflemen of Soviet manufacture Bolan had encountered. Now the old soldier's hands shook with D.T.'s. He opened his eyes and shook his head in disgust. "Perhaps…I take shotgun."

"It's yours." Bolan handed him a TOZ pump shotgun and picked a Krinkov carbine with an optic sight for himself. "You want to drive?"

"Drive Volga?"

Bolan shrugged. "Sure."

"Very well."

He and Ramzin piled in and they headed toward central Moscow.

"So what do we do?"

"Tell me what you know about Heaven Now."

"Fucking cult—" Ramzin sneered "—for fucking pussies."

"Yeah, but what do you know about it?"

"I do not trust them. They offer too much."

"You have friends who have joined?"

"Yes, they offer you food, shelter, help you find job, and in return you give them…"

"Personal convocations?"

Ramzin considered the English words for long moments. "You give them everything. I told my friends you are giving them your soul. They are using you. They will use what you say against you. I was Spetsnaz. I was *mafiya*. I understand this technique. They did not listen. They did not want to. Now I am old and fat and drunk and alone." Ramzin stared bitterly out the window. "Now I work for you."

"Have an apple," Bolan suggested.

"I am already sick of apple."

"Have another."

Ramzin pulled an apple out of his pocket and bit into it. "So what is plan?"

"I want to go to a Heaven Now center. One that the vets go to." Bolan reached into a bag and pulled out a shag-style wig and clipped it in place. He hadn't shaved since he had decided to go to Russia and the lower half of his face had attained a nice underlying blue color. He clipped the wig in place and jammed an old Russian Army field cap down over it. He finished the ensemble with a positively filthy field jacket. "How do I look?"

Ramzin grunted in amusement. "Like Russian Rambo. But how will you explain accent?"

"You're going to tell them I'm a psycho from the neighborhood who was in Chechnya—and I don't talk."

Ramzin scoffed. "No one will believe."

Bolan let his arctic blue eyes go dead and gave Ramzin his best thousand-yard stare.

"Christos!" Ramzin threw back his head and laughed. "They will believe!"

"So how does it work around here?"

"How do I know? I never participate in this pussy shit besides showing up once for bowl of soup. Never go back."

Bolan smiled. "How bad were you when you went in?"

"Between pension monies." Ramzin shook his head ruefully. "Bad shape. I slapped Interlocutor to the ground. Was thrown out."

"Good. I want to go back to the same one. I'm betting these guys keep records on everyone who steps in or out. They know you're a Hero of the Soviet Union recipient. You're a potential success-story gold mine. I think if you show up in a clean shirt acting penitent and asking for help, they'll fall all over themselves to welcome you back into the fold, and if you even hint at your criminal activities outside of Russia, I think you're going to instantly make the A-list."

Ramzin nodded. "You want me to talk."

"And keep talking. I'm just going to sit around and drool, and when I get the chance I'm going for a walk."

"What is mission goal?"

"I have a couple, but most of all I want a laptop or a hard drive."

"You need more back story."

Bolan nodded. Ramzin's tactical brain was getting back in gear. "We keep it simple. My name is Roman. You don't know my last name. I'm a homeless vet. I sleep on your steps and am mostly harmless. You kind of adopted me and I'm along for the soup. That should do."

"And someone enters convo and say my friend Roman is missing?"

"Tell them I'll most likely be in a closet or the bathroom crying with the lights off. Help them look. That might keep the alarm level low for a few extra minutes."

"Very well."

"Listen, I think they're going to serve you some tea and I think there's going to be something in it. Can you make yourself throw up? Without using your finger?"

"I have vast experience with vomiting," Ramzin assured him.

"Drink the tea and then throw up. If they've been working with down-and-out vets they've seen lots of guys come in with D.T.'s. Act ashamed and keep talking. I want a sample of the tea if possible."

"I see." Ramzin's bloodshot eyes narrowed. "Rules of engagement?"

That was a potential mission-breaker. "Ramzin, this is a fact-finding mission. I have no proof. A lot of the guys in the center are going to be vets, guys like you, guys who need help. I'm going to have a hard time dropping a hammer on them."

"I, too."

"If it even starts to look like its going south, surprise will be our best option. Break a few bones and break contact. If we can't extract together we meet up back at the bar where I found you."

"I see."

"One more thing?"

"Yes?"

"You're going to be giving them your name and address, and no matter what happens you may be a marked man in Moscow."

Ramzin's own thousand-yard stare looked out hollowly into traffic. "I tell you. Week ago, I was drinking in room, with muzzle of hunting rifle under chin." Ramzin suddenly grinned malevolently. "We take these pussies."

"Good enough."

Ramzin took a few turns into increasingly ugly and narrow back alleys and stopped. "From here we walk."

They divested themselves of all their armament except the pocket pistols that they shoved into ankle holsters. Bolan pulled the filthy old cap down low, hunched into the field coat and checked their reflection in the car window. He would have shot what he saw on sight if it showed up at his door, but he was hoping Heaven Now was used to their kind of apparent riffraff. Ramzin led down a couple of twisting alleys. In the midst of the filth and refuse he pointed at a door in the back of a building. "That is door for losers. Where lowest come for food and clothing. We go in front door."

They stepped out of the alleys and out into the street.

The front of the facility wasn't terribly prepossessing. The old office building looked like a lot of old Moscow. Run-down and falling apart. The immediate difference was that all the windows were tinted dark and sparkling clean. The steps and sidewalk in front were swept and the two trees outside were a healthy green and well maintained. A small but gleaming bronze placard over the door had the words Heaven Now written in Cyrillic. Bolan let Ramzin lead and they stepped inside into air-conditioning and soft music.

The interior was fantastic.

By the same token it was nothing that would intimidate people like Bolan and Ramzin pretended to be. The foyer was clean, close and homey. The floors were wood with a narrow carpet that led one straight to the reception desk and a receptionist who was pretty, blond and appeared very earnest. Her eyes bugged at the sight of Major Ramzin and her hand reached for a hidden buzzer.

Ramzin seemed to get that reaction a lot.

He simply hung his head. The woman's hand hovered. Ramzin stuttered out some kind of speech in a very low voice. If he'd had a hat it would have been in his hands. Bolan couldn't hear any of the words, but Ramzin's voice shook with desperation and shame. The occasional D.T. shake only added to the effect. Bolan reminded himself not to play poker with Major Pietor Ramzin.

The receptionist began to cry and picked up her phone.

Bolan kept his eyes down and they took chairs and waited. They didn't have to wait long. Two men in suits came into reception. One had ex-Special Forces written all over him. They gave Ramzin a long, quiet dressing down for his past bad behavior. Ramzin nodded and would not meet their eyes. They finally nodded and clapped him on the shoulder. Ramzin pulled Bolan to his feet and he shuffled after them down the corridor. They entered a Spartan-looking cafeteria and Bolan recognized the door that opened into the alley. It was coming up on midmorning and the tables were roughly half-full with bums in varying states of decay who had come in early to beat the lunch rush. Their escort left and Bolan muttered low as they queued up for food. "What did you say?"

"I tell them truth. I tell them last week I had rifle to my chin. I tell them I need help." Ramzin gave Bolan a smile. "I tell them if I am not helping you I would soon be dead. They tell us to eat and someone will come talk to me soon." Bolan and Ramzin loaded their plates. The servers were more freshly scrubbed and fervent young Russians between the ages of eighteen and twenty-four who were improving their karma by serving food to the publicans. Bolan and Ramzin took a table by themselves and tucked in. As far as soup kitchens went, Heaven Now was first-rate. Someone was making a genuine effort to put real food into the afflicted. Bolan had never had better millet gruel with prunes and all the extra steps had been taken to process the creamed salt cod into something edible. Giant samovars kept army commissariat quantities of strong Russian tea flowing, and there were heaping platters of Russian pastries. Fresh fruit was always at a premium in Russia and the cafeteria had it here in abundance.

Ramzin shoved several pears into his pockets.

Bolan finished his gruel. "When they come for you, tell me to stay here. Then I'll go walk about."

Ramzin nodded and continued shoveling food into his maw. Despite the bloodshot eyes and gin blossoms of broken veins across his face, Ramzin was beginning to look human. He was in mission mode, and operators automatically took on food whenever they could. If anything was going to save Ramzin, it would be decades of Special Forces discipline.

Bolan saw the two suits coming toward their table and kept his cap over his eyes. "Here they come."

Ramzin rose respectfully and exchanged words with two well-dressed men. A third, powerful-looking man with a shaved head and navy blue polo shirt joined them. His muscles and demeanor screamed security. Ramzin patted Bolan on the shoulder. "Stay here, Roman. Eat. You are safe."

Bolan nodded dully without meeting anyone's gaze.

Ramzin left with the three Heaven Now men.

The big American drank tea and took his time cleaning his plate. No one paid any attention to him. Bolan noted the No Smoking signs and took his shot. He scooped up the cigarettes Ramzin had left for him as he dug for his lighter and shambled to the alley door. He stepped out into the alley. Two ragged-looking men who had already finished their meal were standing around passing a cigarette back and forth. Bolan tossed them his pack, pulled up his cap so they could see his eyes and used a choice Russian phrase.

"Fuck off."

The two men took the cigarettes and took the hint. Bolan glanced around the newly deserted alley and chose the drainpipe as his best mode of egress. The rusty screws creaked and the pipe shifted as it took his weight. Bolan scaled the back of the building and rolled onto the roof. He was interested to note the satellite dish and the helicopter pad. Bolan moved to the roof access. The door was thick security steel, but like most of the building it was old security steel with an old

Russian key lock. He took a pair of spring steel picks out of a wallet in his coat and worked the lock. It was a matter of heartbeats before he was in. Taking the little Makarov pistol from his ankle holster and putting it in his coat pocket, Bolan descended the stairs and spent a few moments listening at the first landing door before cracking it open.

The floor was a suite of offices. The tasteful paint job, niches for artwork and the wall-to-wall Persian carpeting belied the buildings ancient exterior. Bolan found the artwork rather pastel/pastoral/New Age and the bronze bust of Gavi again seemed to be looking at him judgmentally. One of the office doors was open and Bolan could hear the tapping of a computer keyboard.

Bolan decided on the head office at the end of the hall and headed straight for it. A thin blond man in a nicely tailored pin-striped suit inconveniently stepped out of the open office and blinked at Bolan in incomprehension. The Executioner's right hand came out of his pocket and cracked across the man's cheek. The Heaven Now man's eyes rolled as he sagged against the door frame and fell bonelessly to the carpet. Bolan rolled him back into his office and closed the door. The door at the end of the hall was beautifully polished blond wood and had several sentences in gleaming bronze Cyrillic that Bolan couldn't read.

Bolan put a dirty Russian combat boot to it.

The door flew open with a crack of splitting wood. A tanned, fit, fiftyish-looking man with a shaved head and man-scaped eyebrows was doing his best to look like his mentor. Unlike Gavi's piercing black eyes this man's brown ones flew wide as he looked up from his laptop and froze like a deer in the headlights. His mouth opened to say something. Bolan brought the butt of the Makarov down across the bridge of his nose. The man buckled as cartilage crunched, and he fell out of his chair clutching his newly deviated septum.

Bolan yanked the laptop out of the docking station. The crazy-war-veteran ruse was going to wear thin quickly, but Bolan wanted to bolster it as long as possible so he took the man's watch and wallet, as well. It was time to get the hell out of Dodge. He ran back the way he had come. Extraction was fairly simple. He would go back down the drainpipe, go inside, whine for Ramzin monosyllabically and they would hit the road. No other office doors were open. His luck was holding. Bolan hit the stairwell and snarled silently as the *thump-thump-thump* of rotors echoed down the concrete shaft from the roof.

The best laid plans…

Bolan went down instead of up. He had no idea what room or what floor Ramzin would be in, but he had to figure they would keep the newbie initiates on a lower level rather than upper. Bolan took the stairs three at a time and headed for the ground floor. He reached into his pocket and clicked a button on his cell phone. Somewhere in the facility Ramzin's phone had vibrated and signaled him that all bets were off. Bolan hit the ground floor and flung open the security door to the stairs and was relieved to hear the muffled screams of men and women.

Ramzin was extracting.

Bolan ran toward the sound of excitement. Down the hall Bolan could hear Ramzin roaring. The security guy with the polo shirt was coming down the hall the opposite way. Bolan waved his arms and howled tormentedly. "Pietor! Pietor!"

The security goon detoured and headed straight for Bolan, who cringed and pressed himself against a wall. The muscle ran up snarling. Bolan uncoiled and kicked him in the crotch. The security man bent in agony and Bolan kicked him in the face. As the man's head snapped up, Bolan gave him another snap-kick to the stones and the muscle went white and dropped liked he'd been shot.

Down the hall a door shattered and one of the original suits they had met in the foyer came flying out at shoulder height, borne upon the wings of Ramzin's rage. A woman in the room continued to scream hysterically.

Ramzin came trotting out holding a teacup and trying not to spill.

Bolan raised his eyebrows at the ceiling. The Heaven Now facility seemed to have an intercom system. A subdued sound between a bell and a chime began peeling quietly but insistently. "Ramzin, we gotta go! Alley exit!"

"Da!" Ramzin lumbered down the hall with one hand over the cup. "I come!"

The two soldiers sprinted for the soup kitchen. Two men came charging out the door. One was a kitchen staffer and another was security. Bolan flung himself into their legs in a chop block and toppled them like bowling pins. He rolled to his feet and burst into the soup kitchen.

A baker's dozen of bums and beggars rose from their seats like the living dead. Bolan was going to be forced to do something he didn't want to do. These men were veterans, soldiers who had lost everything. Most of them were simply here for a hot meal. Bolan had no desire to fight them, but he knew where their loyalties would lie. He drew his pistol. The leading homeless man spit and drew a rusted kitchen knife from beneath his coat in answer.

"Ramzin!" Bolan called back over his shoulder. "Little help!"

Ramzin ran into the cafeteria clutching his teacup and gave his summation of the situation. "Shit, son of bitch." The major took his cup, swallowed the contents down in a gulp and made a face as he tossed it away. "Piss test! Later!"

Bolan and Ramzin waded in.

The men had all been soldiers once but most of them were scarecrows or slack bags of alcohol and substance abuse.

Ramzin still had his mass, and by the reactions of people on the street he was still keeping his hand in breaking bones. Bolan was at the top of his game but trying to protect the purloined laptop hampered him. They took a few shots and Ramzin took a cut along the ribs but between the two of them Bolan and Ramzin smashed limbs and cracked heads. They left a small sea of moaning men behind them as they burst out onto the street.

Rifle fire cracked after them from the roof.

A bullet plucked at Bolan's epaulet and they turned a corner into the maze of alleys. Ramzin was red-faced, laughing, wheezing and bleeding as they ran for the car. The Russian operator was back in the action. Bolan pulled out his keys and pressed the button to unlock the Volga. They yanked open the doors and piled in. The V8 engine roared like some great beast from beyond the Ural Mountains as Bolan put the pedal down and they shot forward like a four-door shell out of a cannon.

Ramzin was turning purple and laughing so hard he was weeping. "So, comrade, what now?"

As far as Bolan was concerned, the situation was pretty simple. "We hit a CIA safe house I know, you take a piss and I drop off a laptop."

"And then?"

"Then we go back to your place, unload some ordnance, and see who comes knocking."

Ramzin's roar degenerated into a fit of strangled, vein-pulsing coughing.

Bolan had never seen the man so happy.

CHAPTER THIRTEEN

Georgian Quarter

"They come soon." Ramzin was fidgeting, though more out of need for a drink than nervousness.

"Sooner rather than later," Bolan agreed. They had hit the safe house, Ramzin had given the resident spooks a cup of number one and Bolan had turned the laptop over and both had been sent off for jet courier service to Virginia. While Bolan had arranged things Ramzin had gotten a haircut. His coif was early-Beatles now rather than Summer-of-Love-gone-homeless, and his beard had gone from mad Santa to satanic. He'd also bought a new suit off the rack. No one would ever mistake Ramzin for a solid citizen, but he looked better. In fact he looked downright dangerous. "Have an apple."

Ramzin took an apple from the bowl on the tiny table and shined it on his lapel before crunching into it. "I think I go to Georgia."

Bolan took an apple himself. "Oh?"

"Yes, when this is over. Moscow will not be safe. My

parents are Georgian. I speak language. Used to date Georgian girls from Georgian clubs exclusively. But I have never been. I am Moscow boy, born and raised. I used to receive letters from cousins. Perhaps I take money and go there."

Bolan had heard worse ideas. "I've been there. It's beautiful."

Ramzin chewed his apple meditatively. "So what is plan?"

"I'm going to hide in the cupboard."

"You hide in cupboard?" Ramzin rolled his bloodshot eyes. "Excellent. What is my part in this?"

"Actually I'm going to hide in the wardrobe. When they come, we need to determine if they're police officers doing their jobs or Heaven Now operators. Either way you're probably in a lot of trouble. Whoever it is, you tell them I'm a psycho, you're sorry, and haven't seen me since the incident. Tell them anything I stole has probably been sold for drugs. Gauge their reaction. I don't want to get in a gunfight with the Russian police. I won't be able to make out much of the conversation. If it's the cops, go along and I'll arrange a jailbreak. If it's Heaven Now, I want you to drum your fingers on the table. That's the signal. We hit them and hit them hard, but I want a prisoner. Got it?"

"I understand."

Bolan's highly modified touch-pad phone peeped at him. The picture wasn't high quality but a car had pulled up to the apartment building. Kurtzman's text said, "Company."

Bolan rose. "I'm in the closet." He turned off the sound on the phone and fastened it to his wrist before secreting himself in the wardrobe and filling his hands with a pair of Stechkin machine pistols. Ramzin's apartment was Spartan in the extreme, but every available niche was stuffed with weapons. Ramzin poured himself some tea and waited. His TOZ 12-gauge was duct-taped beneath the table with the stock folded, ready to cut anyone sitting across from him in two. Ramzin himself was concealing a remarkable number of weapons beneath his suit. There was a knock at the door and Ramzin called out that it was open.

Bolan watched through the cracked wardrobe door as four large men entered the apartment. Ramzin sat smoking and idly playing with a piece of twine. The twine was in a loose pile on the table before him. Ramzin's prodigious gut mostly hid the fact that the other end of the twine was beneath the table and happened to be attached to the trigger of his TOZ shotgun. Bolan frowned. The men didn't carry themselves like cops. Despite the heat and humidity, they were all wearing long coats. They didn't carry themselves like soldiers, either. Cops or soldiers would most likely have swept the apartment. These goons just walked in like they owned the place and beelined for Ramzin and surrounded him. They didn't look like they spent much time ladling soup at the Heaven Now homeless soldier kitchen. *Goon* was the operative word.

These guys stank like Russian mafia muscle.

The lead goon had a shaved head but there was nothing Gavi-like about him. He had bad teeth, a broken nose and violent little pig eyes. Two men with the word *leg-breaker* written all over them flanked Ramzin while a cadaverous-looking individual who was pushing the seven-foot mark stepped behind him. Scarecrow quietly pulled out a meat cleaver and waited for Pig Eyes' signal. Ramzin started to spin his story. Bolan heard his "Roman" alias mentioned twice. Pig Eyes wasn't buying it. Instead he was getting angrier by the second. He interrupted Ramzin with a slap that took out a tooth. Ramzin didn't bother to drum his fingers on the table. He scooped up the twine as he rocked back with the blow and yanked it savagely. The table jumped with the detonation and the blast of buckshot took off Pig Eyes left leg just above the knee. The other three threw back their coats and went for their guns. Bolan kicked open the wardrobe and came forward with a machine pistol buzz-sawing in either hand. The goons on either side of Ramzin staggered and tripped over themselves as Bolan's twin bursts walked up them like a ladder and hit the fatal top rung of their heads.

Scarecrow's cleaver stopped midrise and his head whipped around toward Bolan in shock and sudden terror. Ramzin took the opportunity to pick up the little table and snap it across Scarecrow's head and shoulders. The beanpole hit the floor moaning. Bolan reached down and pulled a revolver out of the man's belt and tossed it away. Ramzin ripped his shotgun free from the table debris. He snorted as he stripped away the remaining tape and pumped the action. "Punks."

"Yeah." Bolan reloaded his Stechkins. "That was too easy."

"Men such as these are easy for men such as us." Ramzin kicked the moaning beanpole. "Isn't this so?"

The Russian was right, but that wasn't the point. Bolan walked over to the man missing his lower leg and stripped him of his weapons. "Ramzin, what did Hoppy here say to you?"

"They wanted to know where the laptop was."

"No mention of Heaven Now, Gavi or anything about the fight at the center?"

"No. They just demand…" Ramzin saw it. "Bah! They are cutouts."

"These guys are goons. They were hired to retrieve a laptop and do a number on you without knowing who, what or why."

Ramzin spit disgustedly. "We have been probed."

"We've been set up. We got two dead and two wounded. Real Russian police are probably already on their way. If we're taken into custody, I don't think we're going to see a lawyer. I think we're going to be disappeared someplace in transit and then we start getting questioned for real."

"So, we shoot it out with cops and die like soldiers, or surrender and be tortured."

Bolan went to the wardrobe and grabbed his rifle and a web belt of magazines. "I don't kill cops."

Ramzin spoke like he was quoting scripture. "Spetsnaz does not surrender." He grabbed a bandolier of shotgun shells from the kitchen drawer. "Best we go now."

Bolan powered up his optics. "One problem."

Ramzin nodded. "Outside. Someone watches."

"What's in the warehouse across the street?"

"Abandoned." Ramzin shook his head. "How do we get to car?"

Bolan suspected a sniper. He glanced at Scarecrow. It was a mean thing to do, but the man had shown up to the meeting with a meat cleaver and a smile on his face. "Pull him to his feet. Tell him to run."

Ramzin yanked the man up and hurled him toward the door. Bolan went back to the wardrobe and pulled out the Russian airborne folding RPG-7. Scarecrow didn't need any urging. He flung open the door and ran down the hall. Bolan clicked the two halves of the launching tube into place and slid a rocket down the pipe. He went to the kitchen window and kept his eyes on the smashed-out upper windows of the warehouse. Scarecrow burst out of the apartment and took the steps down to the street four at a time. Bolan swung up his weapon. The tall man suddenly went limp like a fish and fell down the remaining steps sack-of-potatoes style.

"Sniper!" Ramzin called. "Third story, last window!"

Bolan had already seen. The sun was shining on the warehouse, and he caught the glint of optics. Bolan squeezed the RPG's trigger. Ramzin's kitchenette filled with fire and brimstone. RPG-7 back-blast was lethal up to twenty yards and the weapons were not supposed to be fired from an enclosed position. However anyone who had been to Iraq knew that safety precaution was often thrown to the wind. The heat wash of the rocket motor expanded to fill the kitchen and bounced back, enveloping Bolan in roasting heat. Gale-force wind blew in a cyclone of choking smoke as the rocket-propelled grenade hissed from the tube and streaked across the street. Bolan heard rather than saw the explosion in the warehouse.

"Hit!" Ramzin called.

Bolan staggered forward, blinking, choking and half-blind and deaf from the cloud of burned rocket propellant. Behind him Ramzin's cupboards and sink were seared black. The curtains were on fire. Bolan made a note to self not to fire rocket-propelled grenades out of kitchenettes.

Ramzin regarded Bolan with dark amusement. "Now I have lost cleaning deposit."

Bolan coughed and grabbed the spare rocket projectile out of the wardrobe. "Grab whatever you need and we're out of here."

Ramzin grabbed his kindjal dagger off the wall and stuffed his Hero of the Soviet Union medal into his pocket. "This is all."

Bolan tossed him the RPG and deployed his carbine. "Let's go." The Executioner moved down the hall with Ramzin on his six. Bolan kept his carbine shouldered and aimed at the warehouse as he moved down the stairs to the street. Smoke was pouring from the third-floor windows in clear indication that the building was starting to burn. Bolan couldn't imagine just one sniper assigned to this situation and the lack of incoming fire was worrisome. Up and down Ramzin's street people were screaming, dogs were barking and sirens were howling in the distance. Bolan and Ramzin charged for their Volga.

The enemy rocketeers emerged from behind a mail van down the street. Bolan swung the red dot of his optic onto the lead man's chest and squeezed his carbine's trigger. Ten rounds tore into the man's chest. He discharged his weapon as he fell back and the warhead shot skyward like a giant bottle rocket. Bolan swung his sights onto the second man and they exchanged fire. The rocket hissed from its tube and the second assassin fell as Bolan's burst slammed him back against the van. The antitank rocket streaked across the street, but the man had not been aiming at Bolan and Ramzin.

Bolan's shiny black Volga blew sky-high.

"Son of bitch!" Ramzin shouted.

"The van!" The delivery van had a few holes in it but seemed serviceable. Bolan knelt by the dead men and searched for keys. Ramzin's shotgun boomed twice. "Company comes!"

Bolan came up snake eyes. One man had keys to a BMW and one to a Lada. Neither man had the keys to a GAZ cargo van. Bolan drove the butt of his carbine through the driver's window and tossed the weapon to Ramzin. "Use this!" The Executioner yanked open the door and snaked an arm underneath the dash. The armor-piercing point of a fighting knife punched through the plastic of the steering column and a quick rip exposed the ignition wires.

The carbine began cracking in rapid semiauto in Ramzin's hands. "Quickly!"

Bolan spent a few seconds playing with Russian wiring and was rewarded by sparks and the engine turning over. "Come on! We're in."

The back window of the van exploded and a fist-sized hole erupted in the dashboard above Bolan's head. The van's engine promptly died. The Executioner sparked the wires but the engine had been assassinated.

"Anti-materiel rifle!" Ramzin roared.

"RPG!" Bolan snarled.

"Out of range!"

"Run!"

Ramzin ran. Anti-materiel weapons were giant sniper rifles firing anything from .50-caliber machine-gun bullets to 20 mm cannon shells. Their big disadvantage was that they were so big and heavy they were pretty useless against a moving human target. On the other hand, Bolan beneath the dashboard was a duck in a barrel. The GAZ shuddered as round after round hit it and the supersonic cracks of the huge bullets filled the interior like an echo chamber. The windshield shattered and rained glass. Bolan writhed across the foot wells and shoved open the passenger door. A huge bullet slammed the door and left it hanging by one hinge. Bolan heaved himself up and lunged out of the missing windshield and rolled down the hood to the street. Bits of grille peppered his head as a bullet ripped past, proving even the engine block was little defense.

Bolan rose and ran.

A chunk of asphalt shot skyward inches from his feet. Bolan broke left, betting the shooter wouldn't be able to traverse his weapon fast enough. He sprinted after Ramzin and quickly overtook him. "We need a car!"

"Yes…" Ramzin wheezed. "Not many…in neighborhood!"

Ramzin lived in a bad part of town, and Russia's poor depended on public transportation. They were just going to have to get to a busier street and carjack somebody. The problem was most incoming traffic was most likely to be more bad guys or cops. Bolan turned the corner into an alley. "Ramzin! C'mon!"

The Russian was still as strong as a bull, but the dash from the apartment left him sucking wind like a goldfish on the floor. Ramzin redoubled his efforts and trotted forward with the RPG over his shoulder and the carbine in his right hand like a giant pistol. Bolan peered around the corner. A BMW rolled out from a side street back the way they had come, and it was dripping gunmen from every window and the sunroof.

Bolan wanted the car bad but he didn't want what came with it. "RPG."

Ramzin gratefully unloaded the rocket launcher and sagged against the wall. One look told Bolan the major was in trouble. Ramzin was no longer pale or red-faced. He was as gray as a corpse and looked like he would fall into the first grave he found. Years of toxic living was flooding out of his pores in stinking rivulets of death-smelling sweat. Bolan had bigger concerns. The folding airborne version of the RPG had only remedial iron sights, but the BMW was coming head-on down the middle of the street. The shot was a no-brainer.

Bolan stepped out onto the street, put his front sight between the BMW's headlights and fired.

The vehicle's tires screamed as the driver stood on the brakes, and the gunmen in the windows whip-lashed like reeds in the wind. The rocket whooshed out of its tube and sizzled toward the BMW trailing smoke and fire. Men and machine disappeared in smoke and explosion. Bolan tossed the spent, smoking launch tube. He looked back to find Ramzin doubled over, vomiting on his shoes. Bolan waited suicidal seconds for the dry heaves to pass and yanked Ramzin upright. The sirens were getting closer. "We have to go!"

"I am…fine." Ramzin's legs wobbled and he dropped to one knee.

Bolan had no time to rehabilitate Ramzin. That would take weeks and months. Whether they lived or died would be decided in the next sixty seconds. Bolan needed the former Spetsnaz soldier, and he needed him moving. He hated to do it but Bolan reached into his jacket.

"No more fucking apple!" Ramzin gasped.

Bolan pulled out a 1.7-ounce airline bottle of Smirnoff vodka. "Buck up."

Ramzin grabbed for the liquor like a drowning man. He twisted off the cap and squeezed the contents of the little plastic bottle down his throat like mother's milk in a single long squirt. Ramzin coughed and wiped tears out of his eyes. Color returned to his cheeks as he returned to his feet. He grinned and squared his oxlike shoulders with the ephemeral confidence of an alcoholic who had braced himself. "May you have a hundred strong sons."

"Thanks." Bolan took back his carbine and slapped in a fresh magazine. "We need a ride."

Ramzin unslung the shotgun and began feeding it fresh shells. "We take alleyways. They open to main road. Road leads to third transport ring on-ramp."

Getting on the freeway and getting out of Moscow sounded like a real good idea. Bolan and Ramzin moved through piles of rubbish and potholes full of mystery moisture. Lines of limp laundry hung overhead between the fire escapes trying to dry in the humidity. The rattle of trucks and the noise of traffic echoing down the alleys let them know they were close. Bolan caught a momentary glimpse of an overpass before they turned and turned again through the maze of sagging pre-World War II architecture. "We are close!" Ramzin rasped.

The lines of laundry snapped and fluttered in the sudden fury of rotor wash. The helicopter circled above them like a telltale vulture circling the already dead. Bolan spun and raised his carbine, but the helicopter slewed out of sight over a rooftop. They'd been made. "There will be ambush!" Ramzin predicted.

There was nothing for it. There was nothing behind them except firefighters, cops and Russian Federal Police fast-reaction teams. If there was an ambush ahead, they would have to break through it. "Which way?"

"Around bend! Then straight ahead!"

The filthy corridor formed an elbow ahead of them that turned toward the open road. Bolan broke right and Ramzin left as they made for the freeway. The bad guys came around the bend first and these guys weren't *Mafiya* goons. There were five of them and they wore body armor beneath their jackets and carried stubby Russian submachine guns and folding stock shotguns. Bolan went for head shots and wherever the red dot of his optic landed heads broke like melons. Bolan took three men in as many heartbeats. A load of buckshot hit Bolan in the stomach and crushed him back into a row of trash cans. Ramzin's shotgun boomed, and Bolan's opponent fell with a red smear for a face. Bolan pushed himself up out of the refuse. His armor had held, but he still felt like he'd been kicked by a mule. Ramzin and the last assassin exchanged fire. The killer tottered back as Ramzin's pattern of buck printed him center mass, but Ramzin sprawled in the muck as a burst of bullets kicked his left leg out from under him.

Bolan's carbine sprayed brass and spewed lead as he held his trigger down and walked the rest of his magazine up the assassin from crotch to collar. He reloaded and ran to Ramzin. "Come on!"

Ramzin made a terrible face as Bolan pulled him to his feet and tottered on. His left pant leg was soaked with blood, but there was just no time to see to it. If they didn't break contact with the enemy, they were dead anyway. Bolan shoved one of his machine pistols into Ramzin's right hand and put his left arm over his shoulder. The helicopter had risen up high out of handgun range and slowly orbited as Bolan and Ramzin ran a bloody three-legged race for freedom.

They broke out onto a dirty street that lay in the shadows of the overpass and the on- and off-ramps. For a moment they were obscured from view overhead. The ambush vehicle was another GAZ van. The engine was running and the sliding door open. "There..." Ramzin gasped. "We go."

The driver sat upright in his seat and stomped on the gas. The GAZ's tires shrieked on the raddled pavement and the van shot forward like a drag racer off the line. The speeding vehicle had them dead to rights. Bolan raised his machine.

"Move!" Ramzin roared.

Bolan tumbled to the pavement as the Russian slammed one meaty hand into him and shoved him out of the way. Ramzin's pistol snarled off a burst, and then the front of the van met his body with a sickening thud. Ramzin flew over the hood and the driver stood on the brakes as the body hit the windshield. Bolan rose to his feet. Ramzin rolled down the sloping hood and flopped to the street. Behind the shattered, sagging windshield the driver ground his gears to grind Ramzin beneath his wheels.

Bolan put the front sight of the Stechkin machine pistol level where the driver's headrest should be and burned his entire magazine through the windshield on full-auto. The dead driver sagged and fell onto his horn. Bolan dropped to a knee beside Ramzin. He looked horrible. Blood was leaking out of every hole in his head. "Can you move?"

Ramzin's eyes focused. "*Da*...I will move." He made a horrible noise as Bolan helped him up and leaned him against the van. Bolan took his hand away from the back of Ramzin's head and it came away bloody. Ramzin peered at the crumpled front of the van and the bullet-pocked and raddled windshield. "This...will not do."

Providence arrived in the form of a Russian motorcycle cop screaming around the corner. His bike wobbled as he braked too hard at the sight of Bolan, Ramzin and the van. Bolan stepped forward and slammed his forearm across the cop's clavicles. The policeman did a full three-sixty in the air while his motorcycle continued another ten yards and fell over. Bolan peered down at the officer, who was blinking dazedly skyward and gasping. Bolan retrieved the bike and kicked the two-stroke Ural back into life. He pulled up to Ramzin and the Russian crawled on the back with great difficulty. "I thought…you do not…fight cop."

"I don't. I clotheslined a cop."

Ramzin made a gurgling noise that might have been amusement.

"Hang on." Bolan aimed the overloaded vehicle toward the on-ramp. He nearly lost the bike as Ramzin sagged to one side and toppled off to the pavement. Bolan spun the bike to a stop and jumped off. "Ramzin!" The Russian's mouth hung slack. Clear fluid leaked from the corners of his eyes and his pupils were blown.

Major Pietor Ramzin was gone.

Bolan gazed down at one of the most dangerous men he had ever faced. This day's events had been orchestrated by people with access to high-level power. What had actually happened would be covered up. Bolan knew Ramzin would be crucified posthumously. However there was one thing they couldn't take away from Ramzin, even in death. Bolan took Ramzin's Hero of the Soviet Union medal and it pinned it onto the dead veteran's chest. Sirens were screaming in every direction, and Bolan could see the flash of police lights on the overpass. Bolan jogged beneath the overpasses to the next street over. He ran to the corner and took the steps down into the subway. He lost his field jacket and cap in a men's room stall and then lost himself in the sprawl of the Moscow Metro.

CHAPTER FOURTEEN

U.S. Embassy, Moscow

The headline screamed War Hero Goes On Rampage! Bolan scrolled through the front-page article of the *Moscow Times* online. The piece was by necessity vague. The powers that be were indeed covering up most of the major details. The names of his victims were being withheld to "protect their families." Bolan shook his head. That would be *Mafiya* families being protected. Ramzin's suspected ties to organized crime were mentioned as well as his alcoholism and how he had been selling his hero's benefits and privileges. The Russian Federation was not on good terms with her former Republic of Georgia and thinly veiled racism helped to explain the soldier's fall from grace. Nevertheless, Major Pietor Ramzin was a Hero of the Soviet Union. He would be buried with full military honors at the Vvedenskoye Cemetery where many other Soviet heroes lay at rest.

Kurtzman spoke quietly across the link. "Ramzin was trained by the Soviet regime with NATO and the United States as his primary targets. God only knows the atrocities he committed in Afghanistan back in the day. He trafficked in guns, drugs, nuclear weapons and human life. He was a criminal and a terrorist, Mack. He wasn't a friend of ours."

Bolan was all too aware of Ramzin's résumé. "He was a Hero of the Soviet Union, Bear. He died going forward. That still means something to me."

Kurtzman had no answer. It was said that even more than his friends you could measure a man by his enemies. The two men were warriors. They shared history the computer expert knew he would never quite understand. He cleared his throat uncomfortably. "Well, you should probably read the op-eds."

Bolan clicked his mouse to the *Moscow Times* opinion page. His eyes went arctic as he read Gavriil Arkhangelov's full-page editorial with cold interest. It was a pretty standard "how could it have come to this" piece. In very humble fashion Gavi Arkhangelov cataloged all the good work he had done with Russian veterans and how if only Ramzin had come to one of his centers and gotten the help he needed all of this could have been avoided. Bolan smiled coldly. Gavi neglected to mention that Ramzin had been to Heaven Now centers twice and both times torn the place apart.

The rest of the editorials mostly decried the plight of Russian vets and called for stricter gun control.

"What did we get from our contacts in Russian security?"

"You were right about the first four who showed up. Low-level leg-breakers from the Praskovo Family, who themselves aren't very high up in the Moscow underworld."

"No one is going to miss them."

"No, like you suspected, they were perfect cutouts."

"Has Akira hacked the Heaven Now database?" Bolan asked.

"We're waiting on your call."

"How about the laptop?"

"The courier just dropped it off this morning. Akira says a

lot of the files are encrypted. Top-level job, just like the main database. I've already set him to breaking it."

"Good."

"And you're going in whether we break the Heaven Now data or not."

"Yeah."

"So you're sure in your mind this Gavi dude is dirty?"

"We probed one Heaven Now center in Moscow posing as crazy Russian vets. I stole wallets, watches and a laptop. The next thing the cops, the Russian Mob and some real private security hard cases were all over us. Heaven Now didn't call in the cops until after the firefight had started. This morning the whole thing has been swept under the rug. Oh, yeah, this Gavriil guy is a serious trouble, and I want a piece of him."

"What about you? You sure your cover will stick?"

"I wouldn't doubt that Heaven Now center security cameras have images of me, but I was just a field jacket and a hat that slumped a lot. I kept my head down and had long hair at the time. In Bariloche I'll be the suit-and-sunglasses kind of body-guard. It's Memo they want. I'll be a nonentity unless they try to hire me and Calvin, and by that time our back story will be well established. I'd call the recognition factor minimal."

Kurtzman accepted the assessment, but he wasn't alto-gether happy about it.

Bolan considered the next phase of the operation. "Has Memo made contact?"

Kurtzman nodded. "Yes, and so far that seems to be going well. He contacted the Mexico City Heaven Now center."

"What did he say?"

"Whatever else you say about Memo, he's a natural. He told them people were trying to kill him. That he was injured and on the lam with his girlfriend and didn't know what to do."

"What did they say?"

"They told him to hold tight and within the hour he got a call from his personal Interlocutor."

Bolan smiled. "The Anaya woman."

"Yes, apparently Rider Anaya was already in Argentina making arrangements for the upcoming retreat but she called Memo back stat."

"What did she say?"

"She asked if he was safe. He said he'd hired a couple of American private security men and he thought so, for the moment, but he was afraid the Mexican cartels were after him and there was no place safe from them for long. She asked him if he needed money, and he said no, his offshore accounts were still intact. She told him to come to Argentina. She said he would be safe there. She told him he had made great progress as an adherent, and that Gavi himself had taken an interest in him. She told him Gavi had said the best way to keep Memo safe would be to move him up in the organization and that he should come down as quickly as possible and help with the retreat."

Bolan suspected there was a good chance that Gavi had a personal interest in gassing up the dinghy and putting Dominico at the bottom of Lake Nahuel Huapí. "What did Memo say?"

"He gushed like a schoolgirl. I told you he was good."

"What about Najelli?"

"Rider said bring the girlfriend."

"And the bodyguards?"

"Ride told Memo he wouldn't need bodyguards once he was with Gavi, but she said to keep you two with him until he was safely in Bariloche, and that he could hold on to you until he felt he didn't need you anymore."

That was awfully damn reasonable. "Well, we have an open invitation."

"Seems that way. So what now?"

"I'm going to head back and take twenty-four hours R and R and work on our aliases with Cal. I was planning on hitting the retreat on opening day, but if Gavi wants Memo to come as quickly as he can then I say we don't disappoint the man."

Stony Man Farm, Virginia

EVERYONE LOOKED TANNED, fit and rested. Bolan was jet-lagged from the twelve-hour flight and covered with bruises that were blackening up nicely. Dominico and Busto were out horseback riding in the hills. Bolan had eaten, showered and slept most of the day. He stepped out onto the porch and gratefully accepted the beer Calvin James pulled out of the cooler. Bolan settled into a rocking chair and took a long pull. The two warriors sat drinking beer as the sun began to set over the old, rounded peaks of the Blue Ridge Mountains.

James spoke quietly. "Heard about Ramzin."

Bolan nodded. "Yeah."

"He was a bad son of a bitch."

"Lived it and died it," Bolan agreed.

James raised his bottle. "Well, here's to the man."

Bolan clinked bottles with James and drank to Major Pietor Ramzin. "To the man."

The Executioner watched the sun slowly sink, thinking of Ramzin dying on the streets of Moscow and Isidoro in the mountains of his birth. Some brave men were dying on this one. Gavriil Arkhangelov had some things to answer for. However, Bolan couldn't help but reflect on the fact that Isidoro and Ramzin were both bad guys whom he had called upon to step to the right side of the line. Karma occurred and both men had paid for their pasts. He doubted either man would thank him for it. Bolan couldn't help but note that Dominico was the last surviving member of this graduating class. Despite his scumbag past, Bolan genuinely liked Dominico, and the man was very likely living on borrowed time. Bolan turned his thoughts to practical matters.

"So how's Memo's shooting?"

"Well, I'll tell you." James gave his own interpretation of the thousand-yard stare as he peered off into the Blue Ridge Mountains. "We worked. We worked on that Uzi."

"And?"

"Cowboy gave him an H and K PDW."

The Heckler & Koch Personal Defense Weapon looked vaguely like an Uzi that had gone Star Wars. "And?"

"And with the folding stock and foregrip deployed, the selector firmly set to semiauto, and using a collimating sight…"

"Yeah?" Bolan inquired.

"Our boy Memo can hit the broad side of a barn."

"Well…that's good?" Bolan suggested hopefully.

James shook his head with infinite weariness. "Five times out of ten."

"Oh." If it came to a fight they would just have to hope there was a turnbuckle nearby for Memo to leap from. "How about Najelli?"

"Dude!" James immediately brightened. "If Memo doesn't marry her, I will. That girl is dog nuts with any piece of steel she puts her hand to. Cowboy and I talked it over. We're all going in with the German stuff. PDWs and P-2000s. H and Ks are the mercenary weapon du jour anyway. We have to expect getting disarmed initially, but we'll have full war loads from pistols to grenade launchers in safe houses from Bariloche to Buenos Aires."

"Cool." Bolan had high faith in Heckler & Koch kit. Weapons were something Germans always did well. "What's our cover?"

"Rubicon Solutions Group."

Bolan shrugged. "Never heard of them."

"That's because I invented them. Barb has arranged an office with a door and a telephone in San Diego."

"How does Memo know about us?"

"Najelli did private security in Mexico City. Our story is she met you when you were doing security work in the capital for some shady U.S. business contractors back in the day. You two slept together a couple of times and left it on good terms."

"Cool."

"So the story is when Memo went on the run he didn't know who to trust in Mexico, so Najelli called you. You and me are old war buddies who are starting our own merc-security business. Memo is Rubicon's first high-profile client."

It would do. Nice and vague but still solid enough to pass several once-overs of scrutiny. "Nice work, Cal."

James waved his beer dismissively. "It's what I do. Barb told me we're flying to Argentina first thing in the morning."

"Yeah, but we're going to stop in Mexico City first."

James looked askance at Bolan. "Isn't that town a little hot for our man Memo at the moment?"

"I'm trusting you to keep him out of sight. I won't be more than a couple of hours."

"Yeah? And what are you going to be doing?"

Bolan grabbed another beer out of the cooler. "I'm going to rattle Rubino Mankita's cage."

Mexico City, Federal Police Building

RUBINO MANKITA SMILED at Bolan when he walked in like he knew some private joke that Bolan didn't. He sat naked on a metal folding chair in an interrogation room with his hands cuffed before him. The steel table he sat before was bolted to the floor. Bolan would have preferred him shackled hand and foot, but they played by different rules in Mexico. The room had a one-way mirror and was miked for sound like it would be in the States, but the walls and floor were tiled and there was a drain in the middle of the room for whatever fluids occurred. An empty spigot in the corner attested to the need to hose down the room after particularly animated conversations.

Rubino Mankita looked like a poorly dressed side of beef with two eyes, a mouth and Mexican gang tattoos.

A pair of beefy *federales* stood on either side of Mankita with their sleeves rolled up. The surgical gloves they wore were stained with blood. Both men were sweating from exertion and didn't look happy. Despite their best efforts, Mankita was grinning through his mashed lips. By the varying colors and states of swelling, they had been working on him for days. This day's beating was a warm-up for Bolan's benefit. Colonel Llosa leaned against the wall smoking with an equally unhappy look on his face. One look at the colonel told Bolan the soldier had not ordered this. Mankita was now a Mexican federal matter rather than a military one, and both Bolan and Llosa were in the room only out of courtesy, and perhaps to see if Bolan could get something out of the sociopath that Mexican methods had failed to extract.

Llosa pushed himself away from the wall. "Striker, these are Agents DeBourbon and Diaz." The two agents nodded. They were not happy the subject had resisted their efforts and less so that an American intruder was here to see it. Llosa gestured toward the only good thing going on in the room. "And may I present Dr. Rina Talancon."

Dr. Talancon was tall and slim but filled out her white coat well. Her dark hair was pulled back in a severe bun, and small, square-framed glasses Bolan suspected her huge dark eyes didn't need were perched on her aristocratic nose. She had the lab assistant-seductress look down pat. Bolan had her pegged as the Mexican equivalent of an FBI Behavioral Analysis Unit agent. Talancon was a profiler. There were spots of blood on her lab coat and shoes, and she didn't seem to mind. Bolan took her offered hand. "Doctor."

Llosa had obviously seen enough today. "I will be right outside if you need me."

After the door closed Talancon glanced toward Mankita and raised a vaguely challenging eyebrow at Bolan. "You do not approve, either?"

Bolan let that one go. "I could have told you it would be ineffective."

Talancon sighed in acknowledgment. "I told my superiors the same thing. However Señor Mankita is involved in smuggling nuclear materials through Mexico. My superiors felt that direct methods were required to gain his immediate cooperation."

"I can understand that," Bolan said diplomatically. "The situation is urgent for both of our countries."

"Thank you. However, to be honest, I am not sure what you can add to this investigation. Nevertheless, both Agents De-Bourbon and Diaz and myself have been asked to offer you our every cooperation."

"Thank you, Doctor. I just want to talk to Mr. Mankita for a few moments."

"He hasn't spoken a word since his incarceration." Talancon gestured at the only other chair. "However, please, be my guest."

"Thanks."

DeBourbon and Diaz both took a menacing step up behind Mankita while Bolan took the seat opposite him. Bolan nodded at the maniac in a friendly fashion. "Hey, Rubino. Remember me?"

Mankita just smiled on like the psycho he was.

"Well, I just got back from Moscow."

Mankita blinked.

"Yeah." Bolan nodded. "I was at the Heaven Now center where they originally recruited your buddy Kirill Kuzin. Man, I tore that place apart."

Mankita's face went as blank as a cipher.

Bolan had seen this sociopath-who-just-had-his-movie-interrupted look before and knew he'd hit pay dirt. "You remember Memo? Well, he recognized your little Spanish pal from the retreat last year in Argentina."

Every muscle in Mankita's body tensed against his bones.

Bolan glanced at his watch. "I'm on a plane to Bariloche, and when I get there I'm going to rip Gavi a new rectum."

Mankita snapped his handcuffs and stood.

"Madre de Dios!" DeBourbon shouted.

"Shit!" Diaz swore.

The two agents lunged. Mankita threw a pair of elbows backward and both Diaz and DeBourbon sat down drooling teeth out of broken jaws. Mankita's smile returned, and it was all for Bolan. The Executioner rose from his chair to meet him.

Mankita showed Bolan his broken teeth. "You're too late, amigo."

Bolan hoped to keep the maniac monologing as long as possible. "Oh?"

Talancon punched a red button in the wall and began speaking in very calm but urgent Spanish into the intercom. Mankita picked up his chair and spun on the door. He turned the chair upside down and swung it back down on the doorknob like a guillotine, shearing it away. Fists pounded on the door, but it had been made to keep suspects like Mankita in. The glass was very likely bulletproof or close to it. Mankita turned back to business and his smile went from blank slate to beatific. *"Sí,* too late."

Bolan and Talancon were trapped in the room with a maniac.

The federal police had helpfully confiscated Bolan's pistols at the entrance and ran a wand detector over him to make sure he wasn't being a sneaky American. Fortunately, Bolan was about as sneaky as Americans got.

Bolan palmed six inches of black Grivory.

The fiberglass-reinforced plastic had been molded into the shape of a push dagger. The plastic blade wasn't sharp enough to shave with, but it was nearly unbreakable, weighed less than two ounces and could pass through any metal detector. Bolan was the kind of man who always liked to have something up his sleeve. He kept the black blade hidden flat against his wrist. "Too late? Yo, Rubino. We shut down your monkey-shines in Mexico. Argentina is just a question of taking out the garbage."

Mankita regarded Bolan bemusedly. "You want me to give something away."

"Well, amigo, you've already given away plenty. How about the whole enchilada?"

Mankita stepped around the table with the metal chair still in his hands. Talancon cringed against the wall as he passed.

Bolan waited. The problem with maniacs was normal pain and compliance techniques didn't work on them. In his experience shooting them between the eyes was generally the best option. Failing that you had to get up close and tangle with them. Mankita swung the steel chair up like a huge fly-swatter, and Bolan lunged. Mankita was moving with the unrestrained speed of the psychotic, and he got his swing going. Bolan caught the edge of the metal chair just as Mankita's swing passed his shoulders. The jolt of the metal slamming into his palm shuddered down Bolan's arm to the shoulder. He flipped the push dagger around his hand so that the blade protruded between his middle fingers like a dark, deadly version of flipping someone the bird.

Talancon leaped in from behind. Electricity arched between the probes of her snapping stun gun.

About 300,000 volts pumped into Mankita, passed through the metal chair and conducted straight into Bolan. Mankita screamed like a wolverine dying in the snow. Bolan's vision went white and he tasted tinfoil behind his teeth as his muscles rippled beneath his skin and tried to spasm themselves free from their moorings. His knees went to jelly against his will and Bolan dropped a knee on the tile. Talancon suddenly realized her mistake and compounded it by pulling the shock baton away.

"Hit him again!" Bolan snarled.

It was too late. Maniacs were not immune to being electrically short-circuited, but they were often oblivious to the pain and psychological shock once the current was gone. Mankita ripped the chair free from Bolan's shuddering grasp and swung. Talancon gasped and sagged against the wall as her arm snapped and the shock baton clattered away across the floor.

In Talancon's plus column she had bought Bolan several vital seconds.

Bolan rose as Mankita turned and threw a fistful of fiberglass in a wicked uppercut. No one was ever going to use a plastic knife to whittle themselves a duck decoy on a December night, but tests had shown a strong man could punch a Grivory blade through the side of a fuel drum. Mankita's soft and hard palate proved no barrier at all as Bolan hit him beneath jaw and lobotomized him from the limbic region up. Mankita's eyes went dead as his central processing unit cut out. Bolan ripped the blade free and the former contract killer and terrorist fell to the tile floor in a bundle of loose flesh and bones.

Talancon clutched her broken wrist to her chest. To her credit she was holding back the tears. "I am…sorry."

"No. It was good." Bolan put a hand on the table to steady himself. "But next time?"

"Yes?"

Bolan squared his shoulders and tried to shake off the post-electrocution heebie-jeebies. "Don't stop the juice until everyone is on the ground."

"I will…I mean, I won't."

Talancon started as the steel door banged like a drum as something heavier than a human shoulder hit. The tears spilled but her eyes were steady on Bolan. "You will tell me how this ends."

Bolan took a knee beside her and put a hand on her good shoulder. "You have my word on it."

The security door smashed backward as a *federale* with a battering ram gave it his best. Llosa and four men in full armor and riot helmets spilled in waving Berettas and screaming in Spanish. Bolan kept his hands open and in plain sight. "Dr. Talancon and Agents Diaz and DeBourbon need medical attention."

Llosa barked orders and two of the armored agents scrambled out the door shouting into their cell phones. Llosa lowered his pistol and put a hand on Bolan's shoulder. "Are you all right, amigo?"

Bolan nodded. "I will be."

Llosa took in the mayhem. "Did you get what you came for?"

"No." Bolan gazed down on Mankita's corpse. "But my suspicions have been confirmed."

CHAPTER FIFTEEN

Bariloche, Argentina

Bariloche looked like a cross between Santa's Village and Lake Tahoe. The area had been settled by German colonists at the turn of the nineteenth century, and the houses all looked like European alpine cabins and ski chalets. It overlooked Lake Nahuel Huapí, and every building that didn't resemble Santa's workshop was a hotel, disco or restaurant. It was Argentina's winter wonderland. It was half-truth/half-Argentine urban legend that the native, year-round population were all third-generation Nazi war criminals. There were certainly more blue-eyed blondes in snow-bunny attire than anywhere else in South America, and Calvin James looked about ready to burst into flames. The attention wasn't one-sided. Dangerous-looking black men were rare in the extreme in the Argentine Andes, and James was getting more cool stares of speculation than he knew what to do with.

James sighed. "I love this place."

Bolan shook his head. Calvin James was a man who was comfortable anywhere he went. On the fourteen-hour flight down he had watched all the movies, drunk all the international-flight free drinks, flirted with the flight attendants, chatted up Busto every time Memo had fallen asleep and been as happy as a clam. It had been another three-hour plane flight to Bariloche and shuttle bus hop to the downtown. In the last week Bolan had been on too many planes, taken too many beatings, been electrocuted, and despite the body armor he had worn he felt he had been shot just a few too many times. They were in Argentina and Calvin James was bright-eyed and bushy-tailed and on the hunt for babes and barbecue.

All Bolan wanted was to get the job done and leave.

Both warriors went frosty as Gavriil Arkhangelov walked straight out of a snow flurry and up to their party. Bolan had to admit the man was an imposing figure at six and a half feet in an ankle-length sable coat and matching fur hat. The Anaya woman and his sister stood arm-in-arm with him on either side, decked out in furs. The three of them looked like royalty. The royal guard accompanied them. In Russia the term for such men was "flat-heads." Large men, with improbably muscled physiques, straining their dark suits and the sheepskin jackets they wore over them. The big cities of Russia were full of such men. The question was, were they ex-military, Russian *Mafiya* or private security? It probably didn't matter. Whatever their backgrounds Bolan was betting their only allegiance would be to their personal messiah.

Rider Anaya and Michaela Arkhangelov melted away from Gavriil with synchronized precision as he opened his arms. "Memo! I am glad to finally meet you! Rider had told me so much." Gavriil had spoken in nearly perfect English and his face lit up like the sun as he smiled. Dominico was scooped up into Gavriil's fur-lined embrace and then kissed on both cheeks.

Dominico blushed beet-red.

Gavriil's sister gave Dominico the hug-and-kiss routine. "Rider has told me so much about you."

Rider walked up with tears in her eyes and hugged Dominico long and hard. "I am glad you are safe. I am glad you are here with us."

Dominico broke into a fit of stuttering and staring at his boots. Rider Anaya came forward and took both of Busto's hands. "Najelli, I am so glad you are here. I am so glad Memo finally found the love he was looking for."

It was Busto's turn to blush, and the girl from Culiacán didn't blush easy. Gavriil beamed down upon them all like a kinder, gentler, six-foot-six version of Pharaoh from *The Ten Commandments*. He turned his dark gaze to Dominico's own guard. "You must be Cal and Cooper. You have kept a member of our family safe. We are in your debt."

James grinned insolently. "No, man. Memo is in our debt. In fact he owes us money, and we aren't leaving until we get paid."

Gavriil threw back his head and laughed. It was a booming, startling laugh, as if both Santa and God were amused. It almost threatened to knock snow off the eaves, and people on the street stopped to stare and found themselves smiling at the sound of it. Bolan had met shamans, mystics and religious fanatics who had the juice.

Gavi was trouble with a capital *T*.

"Of course, Cal, you and your partner will be paid. Fulfill your contract with Guillermo, and please, stay as long as you like. You have our hospitality and consider yourselves welcome at any seminar or lecture during the retreat. I will be very busy, but call upon Rider for any needs you have. As for security?" Gavriil gestured and a member of his phalanx of guards fell out of formation. "This is Vanya Sychev, but we all call him Spartak. I suspect you will have much to talk about, and any question of coordinating security should be addressed to him. I believe he would like a threat assessment."

Spartak stepped forward out of the wall of muscle. The flatheads could all have had careers as NFL linemen. Spartak was built more like a tight end. Rather than projecting power he looked very relaxed. His every move said *soldier.* Bolan recognized the puckered scars on the left side of his face and neck. They were the results of shrapnel.

Spartak was Russian for the famed Roman gladiator Spartacus.

The Russian stuck out his hand. "I am pleased to meet you." His pale eyes gave both Bolan and James a measuring look. "I have not heard of Rubicon Solutions Group."

"Well, we're just getting off the ground," Bolan stated.

"How many men you field?"

"As of now?" James looked at Bolan, then grinned and held up a pair of fingers. "Two."

"Well." Spartak snorted. "You have cool name. It is good start."

"Thanks," James said. "Came up with that one myself."

Bolan found himself liking the man.

Gavriil gestured toward a three-car caravan of Toyota Land Cruisers. "Come, you must be very tired. Let us get you settled and we will speak more tomorrow."

Villa Huinid Resort y Spa

"PLUSH LIFE!" Calvin James was settling well with the accommodations. He mixed himself a screwdriver out of the minibar. Bolan accepted a beer and had to admit their digs weren't bad. Most of the hotels in Bariloche were old school German, but the Huinid had been built in 2005 and was a thoroughly modern vacation facility with all the amenities. The interest-

ing point was that the seminar was scheduled to take place in
the even larger and more modern Panamericano Hotel downtown. The Huinid was two and a half klicks out of town, very
private and had only fifty rooms. Dominico had made it into
the inner-circle A-list accommodations.

Or he was being culled from the herd.

They were in the suite right next to Dominico and Busto
with an adjoining door. Bolan checked over his weapons. The
CIA had arranged to have them delivered at the shuttle bus
from the airport. Bolan racked the action of the Heckler &
Koch PDW. It was stoked with ice-pick thin 4.6 mm armor
piercing ammunition. By comparison his H&K P2000 pistol
was loaded with fat, .40-caliber hollow-point rounds. Both
weapons were threaded for sound suppressors.

Bolan tucked his pistol away in a small-of-the-back holster
as Dominico gave the recognition knock at the door. "It's open."

Dominico was wearing a dark blue Savile Row suit. Busto
was wearing a little black cocktail number. Bolan restrained
a sigh. Dominico shrugged helplessly. "Najelli wants to go to
the casinos."

Busto beamed.

Bolan opened his garment bag. He wasn't going to get his
nap. Bolan switched into a black silk shirt and a dark green
herringbone sport jacket. He went with the black silk pocket
square and ignored the tie. James went all 1970s Shaft with
a black turtleneck and a toffee-colored leather blazer. Bolan
snugged his snub-nosed Centennial revolver into an ankle
holster and tucked away a well-used Mikov switchblade.
Bolan considered a knife a tool and chose whatever fit the
situation. Calvin James on the other hand was an aficionado
of fine steel. He was an accomplished knife fighter and his
skills had been learned the hard way, bought with stitches and
scar tissue on the streets of Chicago. His charmingly named

Randall "Letter Opener and Boot Knife" was a five-inch version of Randall's classic "Arkansas Toothpick"-style double-edged fighting stiletto, and the man could open an opponent with it like he was opening a letter. James made sure it slid in and out of the sheath with oil-on-glass ease and made the knife disappear. Bolan and James both checked their looks in the mirror and were satisfied. They looked the part of high-priced bodyguards.

They were ready to get their goon on.

The valet had their Land Rover LR3 waiting for them by the time they hit the lobby. James took out his tactical light and gave the undercarriage a once-over. "No bombs, but someone's attached a GPS unit with a magnet. You want me to deep-six it?"

"Not yet. We'll see what develops." Bolan took the wheel and drove the snowy, tree-lined two and a half klicks back to Bariloche proper and pulled into the parking lot of Casino Worest. It was more Euro-style than Vegas glitz, but to Bolan casinos were all the same—tied to organized crime, designed to relieve rubes of their money and ugly inside and out.

Busto squealed like a ten-year-old at Disneyland. "I need chips!"

Dominico reluctantly reached into his pocket and began peeling hundreds off his roll. Busto ordered champagne and ran to the blackjack tables with the gleam of a genuine degenerate gambler in her big brown eyes and Dominico in tow. Bolan and James both ordered club sodas and set about lurking and looking dangerous among the skiers and snowboarders. Busto wasn't a bad blackjack player, but she liked pushing her luck too much and over the course of an hour Dominico's wad withered considerably before they moved on to roulette. No one knew who Dominico was, but he was shelling out money like a high roller, had a beautiful girl on his arm and bodyguards and he was attracting attention.

Calvin James was attracting attention, as well.

Bolan had seen James's assassin come in about half an hour ago with four compatriots and line up at he bar and they had begun eyeing the Phoenix Force commando and laughing. The man was wearing a black suit and his long hair was pulled back in a ponytail. He wasn't particularly big and didn't have a soldier's vibe, but the casual ease with which he leaned back against the bar told Bolan the man was dangerous. The other men were drinking, but the man's whiskey sat by his elbow almost untouched. The men around him were a goon squad, but he was the hitter. The man said something a little louder. His friend's laughter rose in volume. Casino patrons in the vicinity began looking around nervously.

Bolan knew enough Spanish, particularly the swear words, to know that he was spewing some very ugly, racially motivated remarks.

"Looks like you have an admirer, Cal."

"Yeah, El Mariachi over there has been mad-dogging me for the last ten minutes." James sighed. "It's gonna be a fight."

Dominico had understood every word and he was furious. "*Madre de Dios!* Let me take this son of a bitch!"

Bolan put a restraining hand on his shoulder. "Not your job."

One of the man's companions pushed himself away from the bar and wandered over. "*Che!*" He spoke in thick English as he glanced back at the man in black. "My friend Waldero doesn't like you."

"You tell Waldero I think he is fan-fucking-tastic, and his next drink along with yours are on me."

Waldero's facilitator took a moment to process this. "You are a black *yanqui* monkey," he countered. "Go to Brazil. They have banana trees there, you can—" Patrons gasped and the man's eyes rolled midsentence as Calvin James dropped him with a short, sweet right hand to the jaw. Waldero eased himself off the bar smiling like the cat that got the canary. He sauntered over followed by a second, giddy and bald sycophant. Waldero's cheerleader stopped just short of jumping up and down and clapping his hands as they approached James. "You're going to get cut!"

Waldero pulled steel.

"You're going to get cut!" his fan chanted.

Argentine *facons* often had silver handles and silver sheaths. Waldero's knife ran to type, and rather than a ring or a hiss the foot-long blade made an ugly metal-on-metal rasp as Waldero drew it. It was shaped like a chef's knife and just as thin and even sharper. Argentine cowboys had been butchering entire cows and each other with *facons* for centuries.

Waldero's knife was thirty centimeters long.

The room went silent at the sight of it.

"You're going to get cut!"

Bolan was beginning to wonder if that was the extent of Skinhead's English. More importantly Bolan noted that casino security was doing nothing to contain the situation. Someone had paid good money to let the chips fall where they may on this one. The casino patrons were rapt. Bolan knew if he and James threw down with firearms the game was over, and they would be ejected from the country. Bolan had significant suspicions that was exactly what the bad guys wanted. This was Argentina. It was a macho culture. It was a riddle-of-steel thing. They were going to have to play it out, and as the challenged it was all James's play now. Bolan willingly resigned himself to fate. They were in a casino. It was going to be a knife fight.

He was completely prepared to double down on the skills of James in this situation.

James stepped up to the plate with a dramatic eye-roll. "Well, you know the old saying, Waldero."

Waldero's bald pal whispered a translation in his ear. Waldero turned his wrist sinuously and his huge butcher blade moved in lazy, hypnotic figure eights. *"Che?"*

Waldero's every move told Bolan he was a fencing master of the *facon*. They had probably pulled him from the pampas exclusively for this gladiatorial event.

James's smile dropped from his face like a rock as he spoke the Chicago, Lincoln Park, Puerto Rican gutter Spanish of his youth. *"¿Cuánto mas grande es el cuchillo? Mas pequeño es el hombre."*

The bigger the knife, the "smaller" the man.

The meaning wasn't lost on the Argentine. Waldero's face set in a silent snarl of offended rage as he came in with his big knife for the big kill.

The knife-fighter from Chicago was waiting. The glittering wedge of the little Randall boot knife appeared in his left hand like a magic trick, and he held it forward like a fencer. Waldero regarded the little dagger and Calvin James with open disdain. That in and of itself was fatal enough. However if Waldero had scouted his victim a little more thoroughly, he might have noticed as James sipped his club soda or tipped the cocktail waitress that the man from Chicago was not left-handed.

Waldero's eyes were still on the steel as James slapped leather.

The ASP expandable baton snapped open from its closed length of six and a half inches to sixteen and blurred around in an arc. Waldero blinked and moved with lightning reflexes that had probably made him the most dangerous knife fighter in Patagonia. He instinctively brought up his knife in defense. Just as James had known he would. The *facon*'s blade was wide and thin for slicing man and beast and the steel baton snapped it off an inch above the grip.

Waldero stared stupidly at the broken handle in his hand.

He blinked like an idiot as James dropped his knife and baton. He rubbernecked as the Phoenix Force commando hit him on the point of the chin with a left jab. James trip-hammered twice more. Waldero's glazed eyes followed the fist and James's bolo punch caught him flat-footed. The blow drove him six feet backward. Only a craps table held Waldero up as his eyelids fluttered like slot machines about to pay off into unconsciousness. An uppercut toppled Waldero over the craps table's rail and he fell into the chips.

Bolan kept his eyes on Waldero's companions, but they were hypnotized by the boxing lesson like most everyone else.

James leaned over the table. He took a handful of Waldero's shirtfront and cocked back his right hand. School was out. His right hand rose and fell. Chips bounced with each blow as James pounded Waldero like a nail. It was a pretty surgical beating. He left Waldero semiconscious, then stepped away and made a show of wiping his hands when he deemed Waldero had taken the required amount of punishment.

James walked up to the skinhead and nodded at the knife and the baton on the floor. "Pick those up."

The man shook his head in horror. "No, *señor,* no, I—"

"Pick them up!" James roared.

Skinhead shook like a leaf and picked up James's weapons. He rose slowly, holding them between his fingers and at arm's length like dead rats. "Yes?"

"Now give them to me."

Skinhead tremulously handed the man his weapons. James jerked his head at Waldero as he put his gear away. "Get out of here."

Skinhead and his pals ran to scoop up their fallen companions.

James raised his voice. "Next round's on me!"

He received a standing ovation. Bolan suspected he was

also going to receive some telephone numbers and room keys. Bolan shook his head. "That was grandstanding."

"I know." James grinned. "Wasn't it cool?"

Dominico was awestruck. "You are magnificent."

"God gave me a gift," James concluded modestly. "It would be disrespectful not to use it."

Bolan wasn't surprised as a wall of security finally arrived, followed by a very nervous-looking manager who told Dominico in Spanish they would have to leave the establishment. Busto was still smiling as they stepped out into the cold. "Well, I thought it was a lovely evening."

James scooped up some snow and packed it onto his knuckles as they waited for the valet. "What do you think?"

Bolan scanned the parking lot. The enemy had layered their attacks in Russia, and Bolan expected no less in Latin America. "They won't try it here on the strip."

The valet brought their vehicle, and James checked it for bombs again and shook his head. Bolan rode shotgun as they piled in. They drove down the snow-lined main drag. It was 3:00 a.m., and Bariloche was still alight and filled with people making the rounds between the clubs, casinos and bars. Darkness fell on them abruptly as they left Bariloche and turned onto the mountain road back to the hotel. The second attack came exactly where he expected it.

The headlights screamed up behind them on the mountain road back to the hotel.

James gently began braking. "Here we go."

Dominico looked back nervously. "Man, shouldn't we be going faster?"

Bolan reached down between the seats and drew his PDW. Cold air blasted and snow flurried into the car as James hit the switch and the sunroof slid open. Bolan rose into the freezing night and deployed the PDW's collapsible stock and foregrip. He squinted through his optic into the glare of the incoming vehicle. Bolan aligned the collimating sight's red dot onto the driver's side headlight and squeezed the trigger. Fire spit from the muzzle as he sent five rounds downrange and the light went out in a flash of sparks and breaking glass. The driver swerved violently, and James responded by slowing the Land Rover even more. It took Bolan two more tries but on the third attempt the other headlight went out. With the glare out of his face he could see the enemy was in a red Toyota Land Cruiser. The enemy driver stood on his breaks. James brought the Land Rover to a stop in response. Bolan called down to him. "Goggles."

James killed his headlights and the world went pitch-black. He handed Bolan up a pair of night-vision goggles as the bad guys shoved their SUV into Reverse. The world returned in grainy green and gray as Bolan peered through his optic once more. The PDW spewed spoon-tipped hollow-point rounds, and the tracer bullets drew laser lines in the air as they streamed into first one front tire and then the other. The Toyota's bumper dropped as the front tires burst. The driver desperately ground gears and stalled his vehicle. Bolan helped out by burning the rest of his magazine through the Land Cruiser's grille. "Cal, go around the next bend."

Men began jumping out the SUV brandishing weapons, but James pulled the Land Rover around the curve. The bad guys fired bursts into the dark as Bolan and the Phoenix Force pro dismounted. Bolan was interested to note that all of them had shaved heads. He gave out orders as he reloaded with a magazine of subsonic ammo. "Memo, get behind the wheel." He handed him a headset. "You let me know if we have any traffic inbound from the hotel. Najelli, your carbine is in the back. Get it and get up in the sunroof. We may be coming back in a hurry and we may need covering fire."

Bolan and James walked back around the bend threading sound suppressors onto the muzzles of their weapons.

The soldiers from Stony Man Farm stalked forward in the operator's world of ghostly night optics. The bad guys were operating in primeval night, and they were panicking accordingly. The driver had flooded his engine like an amateur and was stomping on pedals, banging on the steering wheel and only compounding his problems. He had also turned on his dome light. The men who'd deployed stumbled around in the darkness shouting at one another and shooting randomly into the trees at people they couldn't see.

James subvocalized into his headset. "Not exactly Spetsnaz, are they?"

"No they're not." Bolan had them pegged for local organized crime. He and James fanned out to either side of the road to put the killers into a cross fire. One of the gunmen pulled a road flare out of the Toyota and sparked it into life, illuminating himself, his compatriots and destroying what little night vision they had. He raised the flare like the Statue of Liberty and squinted into the darkness waving his assault rifle.

"Oh, please," James commented. His PDW hissed and clicked twice, and man and flare fell screaming and hissing into the snow by the side of the road. The three men still standing shouted obscenities in Spanish and fired wild bursts into the black in mounting panic. Bolan and James kept moving forward. These men weren't Russians, but Bolan could tell by the firing signatures of their weapons someone had supplied them with Kalashnikovs.

"Cal," Bolan said into the tactical radio, "take the rest of the tires. These guys are going nowhere."

"Roger that."

Bolan raised his weapon and started to fire. It took five shots of the lightweight low-velocity ammo to crack the windshield, but his sixth pierced the sagging glass and punched out the dome light. On the mountain road in the Andes there wasn't a single light in the world except for the spitting and guttering flare in the snow. James walked right past the three shouting men waving their rifles. He moved a prudent twenty yards behind the Toyota and shot out the rear tires. The gunners heard nothing until the tires blew and the Land Cruiser sagged onto its rims. More shots and shouts rang out.

James subvocalized into the tactical radio. "You figure these guys as Gavi groupies or straight-up third-generation Third Reich?"

"Let's find out." Bolan began to move forward. "Give me some diversion. I'm going to take one."

"Copy that." James raised his weapon. It was silenced but as he emptied the 40-round magazine into the truck the glass windows geysered and cracked. The driver screamed as the window glass erupted all around him. The shooters resumed screaming and ripped long bursts in all directions. Bolan dropped his PDW on its sling and snuck up behind one of the skinheads and snaked his right arm beneath his chin. The single choked gasp the assassin gave out was smothered by the AK blasts of his comrades. Bolan put his left hand against the back of the killer's shorn skull and shoved it deeper into the strangle. Skullface relaxed into oxygen starvation, and Bolan dragged him deeper into the Stygian darkness as his companions fired at nothing in particular. Bolan jerked him into a fireman's carry and walked back to the Land Rover while James covered the extraction. As Bolan walked around the bend, the remaining men became aware of the fact that one of their number was missing.

"Batata!" the remaining men howled into the darkness. "Batata!"

"You want me to take these guys?" James inquired hopefully. He really didn't have any use for skinheads of any stripe.

"No, let them panic. Let them freak out." Bolan opened up the back of the vehicle and tossed Batata in the back and cuffed and gagged him. "I want them pounding on the door of whoever hired them, and if they're local muscle I want the bosses freaking out and asking too many questions."

"Tension, apprehension and dissension have begun," James stated.

Truer words were never spoken. Bolan took shotgun and glanced over at Dominico as James climbed in. "Drive."

CHAPTER SIXTEEN

Batata Schweinsteiger was not a happy man. Bolan had strangled him unconscious again and carried him up to the room over his shoulder while Dominico told the front desk their friend was drunk. Bariloche was a party town, and the hotel staff hadn't batted an eye. Schweinsteiger sat naked and duct-taped to a chair. The swastikas and Nazi images tattooed over his torso showed that he was feeling his continental cultural inheritance. He shook and sweated as he stared back and forth between Bolan, Dominico and especially James. He looked down and blushed furiously every time he met Najelli's scathing stare.

Schweinsteiger wasn't being tortured, but the man just wasn't responding well to intimidation.

He jerked as Dominico lunged at him like a pit bull. "You staring at my girl?"

"No! I—" he mumbled under his duct-taped mouth.

Dominico slammed his hands on Schweinsteiger's back and began giving him a disturbingly friendly shoulder massage. "I think you're gonna be my girl."

The man twitched and whimpered under his restraints.

Bolan smiled at the short, hard rap at the door. He had been expecting the late-night knock. Not because they had carried an unconscious fascist upstairs to their room. It was the fact that they had returned at all that had sent Heaven Now spies scurrying. "I'll get it." Bolan picked up his PDW off the bed and went to the door. "Who is it?"

Spartak's voice came quiet but hard from the hallway. "Cooper, open door."

Bolan opened the door. "C'mon in."

Heaven Now filed into the room in force. Bolan had expected Spartak and his gladiators, but he was surprised to see Gavriil's brother Apollyon on point. Rider Anaya was with them looking confused and concerned. Apollyon Arkhangelov was even shorter in person. Where Gavriil was long and lean, Apollyon was built like a fireplug. His brother's dark eyes were strangely piercing and serene. Apollyon's pale blue eyes were always a little too wide open and darting about like he'd drunk just a little too much coffee.

Or he was tweaking.

Or he was nuts.

His manic eyes flicked to Schweinsteiger, then to the hardware in Bolan's hand, and locked back on Bolan. It was pretty clear Apollyon wasn't used to being regarded with casual, unblinking indifference. His normally red-faced look turned a deeper shade of rage. He spoke with a permanently angry English-as-a-second-language accent. "What has happened?"

"A guy tried to carve up Cal in the casino." Bolan waved his weapon at Schweinsteiger. "Then this asshole and some of his buddies tried to shoot us up on the road. Don't worry about it. We got it under control."

Apollyon went magenta. "It is untenable. You are guests. You do not take hostages and bring them among us."

"He's not a hostage." Bolan kept smiling, but he let his voice drop dangerously. "I have no intention of handing him back to the Hitlerites."

Apollyon purpled. Spartak gave Bolan a "nice knowing you" look, and his brute squad began to spread out. Rider Anaya put a restraining hand on Apollyon's arm and the effect was magical. It was almost like she had a secret pressure-release button. He turned his gaze upon her for just a moment and then looked back at Bolan.

Bolan went diplomatic. "What? You want him?"

Apollyon spoke through clenched teeth. "I want him."

"Take him, he's yours."

James slashed the duct tape but left on the zip cuffs and the tape across the man's mouth. Dominico shoved him from the chair and he stumbled into the waiting arms of Spartak's men. Busto came forward with Schweinsteiger's neatly piled clothes and belongings and gave them to Spartak. Anaya shook her head slightly at Dominico, who shrugged. "Old habits die hard."

"You need convo, Memo, and soon."

Dominico did a decent job of looking chagrined. Spartak glanced back as the Heaven Now entourage exited. "Cooper, Cal. I wish to speak to you tomorrow." Then he was gone.

JAMES PULLED A GPS unit out of his pocket and flicked it on. "I have joy on both signals. Tracking." They had taken the opportunity to put a pair of tracers on Schweinsteiger. There was a chance he would notice an extra card in his wallet, but it was winter in the Andes and he wouldn't be going much of anywhere without his boots. "You catch that dynamic between Apollyon and the girl?"

"Oh, yeah." Bolan had noticed. He had the feeling that maybe besides Apollyon's big brother that the only thing keeping him on his leash was Anaya. Despite the warmth and New Age love the young woman radiated, around the eyes she had a look Bolan had seen before. Rider Anaya looked like a woman in a cage. "It bears some investigation."

"Oh, man! I'll investigate it!" James warmed at the prospect of investigating Anaya. "And I mean, thoroughly."

"No, you're busy tomorrow."

"Busy doing what?"

"Taking a meeting with Spartak."

"Oh, yeah?" James gave Bolan a very suspicious look. "What are you going to be doing?"

"Investigating Rider, thoroughly."

James regarded Bolan with utmost seriousness. "You're no fun."

THE REAL DEVOTEES began arriving. They came from every corner of the globe and all walks of life. Bolan recognized foreign athletes, actors, pop stars and television personalities. There were also politicians, lawyers and businessmen. They all shared the fact that they had at least seven figures in the bank and were one-hundred-percent ga-ga for Gavi. International and Argentine paparazzi circled downtown like vultures as the hotels filled up. Gavi's security was nothing if not efficient. He had rented the entire Villa Huinid and Spartak had set up a checkpoint at the gates. No one without a golden Gavi ticket could get on the grounds. Gavi held a press conference for reporters, but they were shuttled in and out once a day, and the conferences were hosted by his sister while he stayed mysteriously aloof. So far Dominico had ducked his convo because Rider Anaya was besieged with people who wanted their personal convocations with her.

Anaya was a busy girl.

But a little surveillance showed that she did have a little

time to herself. When she wasn't leading spiritual fitness fusion classes or conducting personal convos, she managed to squeeze in her own daily practice at the crack of dawn. Bolan tracked her down at the hotel's sunroom where she was doing some yoga on her own. Anaya was currently standing on her head. Two very brief pieces of pink spandex covered her golden skin and the pink light of the sun bathing her body only added to the effect.

Bolan walked in and feigned surprise. "Sorry, I thought I had the place to myself."

Anaya smiled up at him. "No, I'm almost done."

Bolan stripped down to a pair of ancient khaki UDT-SEAL shorts, unrolled his yoga mat and began cranking off sun salutations. He moved smoothly from pose to pose, each movement done during an inhalation or an exhalation. It was a very basic twelve-pose sequence. Bolan would never be able to fold himself into knots like a Yogi on the streets of Mumbai or have his own instructional DVD and line of yoga wear, but he was pretty good at backbends and his standing poses were razor sharp. He could feel Anaya's eyes on him as he moved through the series of postures and started again. Bolan went through thirty-six cycles and stopped, facing the sun rising through the window with a healthy glow of his own.

Rider had come out of her inversion and was sitting in lotus pose. "I didn't know people like you practiced yoga."

Bolan grabbed a water bottle out of his gym bag. "People like me who don't practice yoga end up in wheelchairs."

Anaya ran her gaze over his body. "You have a lot of scars."

"You should see the ones inside."

Anaya perked an eyebrow.

It was true physically and metaphorically. "I'm always picking up new scar tissue. It always needs breaking up. I found out a long time ago that yoga beats a surgeon's knife or drugs, and it's a lot cheaper than a good physical therapist. Plus no matter how good a therapist is they'll never know your body better than you do if you take the time to explore it." Bolan gave Anaya his most rakish smile. "Plus you get to meet interesting people."

The woman blushed charmingly. They had both been exercising and they were in close proximity. The light in the solarium was transitioning from coral to golden as the sun began to clear the mountains. It was a magical, fleeting moment and they both felt it and felt the attraction. Anaya cleared her throat. "That's a very enlightened point of view."

"Oh, it was forced on me. It got to the point where I physically couldn't afford too many more surgeries or take drugs every day. Some changes had to be made."

Anaya looked sidelong at Bolan shrewdly and her not-so-hidden Heaven Now proselytizer came out. "Have you considered taking one of our classes?"

Bolan went for the jugular. "Have you considered getting out while you still can?" Anaya flinched as if she'd been struck. She dropped her gaze to the floor and began to cry. Bolan stood over her implacably. "I don't know about Gavriil, but Apollyon is a sociopath."

Anaya wept harder.

"In his twisted worldview he owns you. You're his, and because you help keep Apollyon on his leash, Gavriil and Michaela let him."

"He says…I must give him a child." Fresh sobs racked her. "I told him I didn't want to and…"

"He hurt you."

Anaya wouldn't meet his gaze.

"So you're using birth control without telling him." Bolan sighed. "When he finds out he'll kill you."

"You don't understand." Anaya rocked back and forth, clutching her knees. "You don't."

Bolan understood all too well. Rider Anaya was a beautiful woman who had gotten herself in trouble. Heaven Now had helped her clean up her act, but in doing so she had fallen into a far deeper and darker trap. She traveled the world but everything was paid for her. Bolan suspected she had nothing in the way of money to call her own. She was utterly dependent on the Arkhangelovs and their organization. She had seen the ugliness they were capable of, and she didn't see a way out.

"You can get out."

"No, I can't. Once you're in—"

"Memo got out."

Anaya blinked. "He—"

"He and Najelli signed up to help me take Gavriil down."

Anaya's eyes grew huge. "Take Gavi...down?"

"Gavi is involved in major international crime and terrorism. I think you've seen some of the people he surrounds himself with. I think you've had convos with some very bad people and learned a lot of very ugly secrets. Heaven Now is more than just a moneymaker. It's a genuine intelligence-gathering service. You got Memo's info and Gavi took it to do some smuggling of his own in Mexico. He ordered Dominico killed."

"No, that's—"

"We stopped it, but some good people died along the way, and I don't think Gavi intends to let Memo leave Argentina alive."

Anaya shook.

"I don't think I've told you anything you don't already know or suspect. If you want out, let me know." Bolan wrote a number on a napkin. "Your cell is probably bugged. Use a hotel phone. Memo is going to take his convo with you today. Don't spike the tea. The convos are bugged, but you know that so don't let on that we talked. I'll tell him." Bolan handed her the number. "You want out, you call me. Anytime, day or night, but do it soon or not at all."

Bolan threw his gym bag over his shoulder and left the solarium. He found one of the Russian security men out in the hall smoking. He wasn't one Bolan had seen before. Like all the Russians other than Apollyon he was a big man, built like a barrel with a brush cut. He looked genuinely surprised to see Bolan walk out of the solarium.

Anaya had a babysitter.

Bolan arranged a jilted look on his face and shook his head disgustedly. "Must be a lesbian."

The Russian minder snorted against his will and gave Bolan a sympathetic shrug.

Bolan walked to the elevator. He didn't hear the Russian move from his post, and he took that as a good sign. Bolan reviewed the morning recruitment drive. He was betting far too much on former cult fanatics. He had risked everything betting on Dominico, but Dominico was a big boy, and a genuine tough guy with a very Mexican sense of honor and payback. Rider Anaya was a very scared woman surrounded by very powerful people, and Bolan had rolled the dice again and let everything ride. Ratting them out to Gavi would be far easier than betraying the cult.

The question was how badly did Anaya want to avoid being Apollyon's personal slave and brood mare.

THE HEAVEN NOW retreat started for real the following day and Bolan had a very deep suspicion Gavriil had something up his sleeve. He pulled on a sweatshirt and headed down to the restaurant for some food. Culturally, Argentines weren't hardy breakfast eaters. Most drank coffee or tea and had a sweet roll. The restaurant was nearly deserted at this hour, but Bolan convinced a kitchen staffer to rustle him up some chorizos and eggs.

Bolan was shoveling it in when Spartak entered the dining room and walked up to his table. "May I?"

Bolan gestured at the chair across from him. "By all means."

"Thank you." Spartak took a seat. "It has come to my attention you have been paying attention to Miss Anaya."

"Jesus, that was fast."

The Russian's voice dropped low. "It will have come to Apollyon's attention, as well."

"Dude—" Bolan grinned guilelessly "—she's hot."

Spartak's scarred face arranged itself into a weary smile. "We are both professionals. So I will extend you professional courtesy. Stay away from Miss Anaya. Or you will end up at bottom of Lake Nahuel Huapí."

Bolan smiled back without an ounce of warmth. "That's mighty nice of you."

Spartak held up his hands placatingly. "Oh, it is not I who will be putting rocks in your pockets." The Russian's voice dropped low once more. "Apollyon has his own personal security. They are not professional like you and I. They will give no friendly warning, and believe me, they will be very… discourteous to you before they send you swimming."

"Well, I appreciate that."

Spartak lit a cigarette. "Perhaps you would like demonstration?"

Bolan was pretty sure there was some kind of communication breakdown here, but he went with it. "Sure, what the hell."

The Huinid was famous for its view of Lake Nahuel Huapí and most of it was lake-oriented to take advantage of it.

Spartak led Bolan to the back of the hotel and pointed out a window. There wasn't much of a back forty. The mountains ran nearly vertical behind the hotel. What there was of a back lawn was covered with snow. Exercise was going on but it wasn't "spiritual fitness fusion" with Anaya or Michaela. Apollyon stood stripped to his bikini briefs and was enticing four larger, similarly clad men to attack him. One was the man Bolan had met in the hall. Apollyon sent him flying. The Russians' pale skins were ruddy with cold, and steam rose off their bodies with furious exertion. The men came in with fluid attacks and grabs. Apollyon was like a Greek god beset by Titans. He sent one big man sprawling in the snow and instantly motioned for another. Bolan had encountered Russian sambo before. Usually it was practiced in a uniform like judo, but Apollyon and his posse had some kind of old school Siberian he-man style going on.

"The big man, Misha? Was army champion." Spartak gestured at the violent action. "His men, you understand, they do not let him win."

Bolan could tell. Apollyon might well have little-man's complex, but it was a dangerous case of little-man's complex. Bolan watched Apollyon and his playmates play rough. "You practice?"

"In my experience it is best to shoot a man. Better yet, blow him up. Better still, designate with laser and call in air strike. If I am reduced to homoerotic underwear wrestling in snow—" Spartak shrugged philosophically and chain-lit another cigarette "—somehow I have failed."

Again Bolan found himself liking the Russian enforcer. "Spartak?"

"*Da?*"

"You're okay."

Spartak nodded modestly.

Bolan felt certain that Spartak was hired help rather than a true believer, and the man had just as much as admitted he was ex-Special Forces. "Spetsnaz?"

Spartak blew a long stream of smoke and nodded. "In my day."

Bolan let the morning's winnings ride and threw the dice again. "You ever know a Major Pietor Ramzin?"

The Russian's pale eyes went flat for the barest of seconds and then he regained his usual, almost lackadaisical, persona. "Of course. The man was legend."

"You heard he's dead."

Spartak drew himself up and gave Bolan a very hard look. "*Da.* How do you know of him?"

Bolan had dealt with Russians many times. Any conversation like this was a chess game. Everything was move and countermove. Bolan had found it best in dealing with Russians to kick over the table and keep them off balance. "I was with him when he died."

Spartak's hand was in his pocket and Bolan knew it was resting on a gun. Bolan had his own pistol in his pocket and Spartak knew that, as well. The Russian spoke barely above a whisper. "So…the rumored second man. There are many in Moscow who wish to know who you are. Many who wish you dead."

It was nothing new in Bolan's world so he kept throwing Spartak curveballs. "How well did you know Sergeant Kirill Kuzin?"

Spartak gave Bolan an openly wary look. "I have not seen Kuzin in some time."

"He's dead. In a Mexican morgue."

"Mexico?" The Russian seemed genuinely surprised. It instantly turned to suspicion. "I suppose you were with him when he died."

Bolan swung for the bleachers. "No, but I saw Memo kill him."

He was rewarded with a genuine look of shock on Spartak's face. "You realize I should—"

"Fill my pockets full of rocks and put me at the bottom of Lake Nahuel?" Bolan suggested.

"No, I believe my employers would expect me to shoot you through kneecaps and hand-feed you to Apollyon and his boys."

"C'mon, you aren't buying any of this Heaven Now crap, are you?"

"I am devout Russian Orthodox."

"You're working for the wrong people, Spartak."

"I work for money," the Russian countered.

"Whatever they're paying you," Bolan countered back, "I'll triple it."

"You are asshole."

Bolan nodded. "I get that a lot."

"I am sure you do." Spartak lit another cigarette. "You ask me to betray Heaven Now and serve Uncle Sam?"

"I'm asking you to serve the Motherland and at triple the going rate."

Spartak put his poker face back on. "You must forgive if I do not take these revelations at face value."

"What if I could give you proof?"

"That would be interesting."

Dominico walked up wearing a Mexican national football team warm-up suit drinking a glass of orange juice. "Yo, Coop! On deck, man! Cal is taking Najelli shopping. It's your turn to guard me!"

Spartak gave Bolan another long look. "We will speak again."

Dominico watched the Russian walk off. "What was that all about?"

"I told him about Mexico and Moscow."

Dominico choked on his juice.

"I also told Rider earlier this morning. You're taking a convo with her in the next day or two. You need to establish your alibi with the Arkhangelovs."

"*Madre de Dios*... Man, why don't you just put up a sign?"

"I told you everything."

"Well...I'm me, man!" Dominico spluttered.

"That you are," Bolan agreed.

Dominico scowled out the window. "What's going on out there?"

"It's called sambo. Russian wrestling. Apollyon is taking his morning constitutional." Bolan raised a challenging eyebrow. "And?"

Dominico watched the snow savagery with the eye of a professional Mexican *luchador.* After a few moments of flying bodies he nodded, more to himself than Bolan. "I can take him."

Bolan nodded. Dominico might just have to.

CHAPTER SEVENTEEN

Bolan had been to a few cult proceedings in his time, but the Heaven Now opening convocation was something to see. They were in the convention hall at the Panamericano Hotel downtown. It was the middle of winter in Argentina, but the attendees were all in the adherent costume of purple sarongs and head buffs. Despite the sea of healthy and wealthy international glitterati, there were still a few matrons and a corpulent Russian general or two who Bolan could have spent his whole life without seeing in a sarong. The lights dimmed and an expectant hush fell over the crowd. The room was packed, and Bolan estimated there were perhaps eight hundred souls in attendance. Even though they were standing in the back Bolan was surprised that he and James had been allowed to attend the standing-room-only, inner-circle adherent event.

Bolan gazed bemusedly as James kept adjusting his sarong distractedly. A crotch holster was about the most uncomfortable way to carry a handgun and both soldiers were packing snub-nosed Smith & Wessons next to their packages. "What? You don't dig the threads?"

"I look like the towel boy at a Tunisian bath house," James muttered. He noted Bolan's amusement and wasn't pleased. "Man, I won't even tell you what you look like."

Bolan ignored James's discomfort and scanned the crowd. They all seemed very happy and very expectant in a very strange, touchy-feely sort of way. He wondered if it had anything to with the military-size samovars of tea the faithful were drinking. "Your lab guys send us anything on the tea sample?"

"Yeah, it came in while you were messing with Rider's head. The main ingredients are *Camellia sinensis,* that's green tea to you, and *Jasminum sambac.*"

"Jasmine flowers?"

"Check out the big brain on Bolan."

The faithful weren't all bright-eyed and bushy-tailed over antioxidants and flower petals. "And?"

James's smile flashed. "And what I am currently calling Herbal X."

"What's the chemical makeup on your Magic X?"

"Well, it's definitely botanical as opposed to a synthetic, and looks like it's a member of the amphetamine class."

"They're putting meth in the tea?" Bolan scanned the crowd again. "Cal, these people look more like they've been eating magic mushrooms than tweaking."

"No, we're talking a subclass of amphetamine, probably some sort of phenethylamine. Whatever this stuff is it's an empathogenic-enactogen."

"In English?" Bolan suggested.

"Think of it as a very mild form of Ecstasy. From the chemical breakdown you can reliably predict effects like mild euphoria, a sense of increased intimacy with others and diminished feelings of fear and anxiety."

Short of strong liquor Bolan would be hard-pressed to

think of a better nonconfrontational interrogation drug. "Not bad."

"I'm telling you, sodium pentothal has nothing on this shit."

"So what is it?"

James leered. "Man, if I knew I'd be growing it and rolling my own. I'm figuring it must be some local specialty, east-of-the-Ural-Mountains herb we just haven't encountered yet."

"You get the flash drive to Spartak?" Bolan had gotten Aaron Kurtzman to put together a file of the pertinent events in Mexico and Moscow with photos and run it through Russian translation software.

"Yeah, I palmed it to him in the restaurant this morning. He took it. Didn't bat an eye. He's a cool one."

The assembled throng suddenly gave a collective little gasp as the lights dimmed.

"Showtime," James announced. Vaguely eastern music slowly became audible. A spotlight fell on the stage and lit Michaela Arkhangelov. She smiled lovingly at the crowd with open arms and was greeted with a passionate ovation. People in the packed room pressed toward the stage. She let the applause go on for a few moments and then slowly lowered her arms. The applause fell in cue with her limbs. Given the international clientele Bolan wasn't surprised to hear her speak in English. "Thank you, thank you all for coming."

A young woman screamed. "We love you, Mikki!"

"Mikki!" A chorus of calls joined her. "Mikki!" "We love you!"

"If she starts singing 'Stairway to Heaven,' I'm outta here," James muttered.

Bolan watched as Michaela absorbed the hysteria with calm benevolence. James was right. The room was starting to take on a rock-concert-like fever. The beautiful redhead on the stage lifted one graceful hand and the room went silent except for a pervading sense of expectation that could be cut with a knife.

"Let us give invocation." Michaela spoke with quiet power and she led the assembly in a fairly typical call and response. "Gavi brings us blessings," she called. "Our blessings onto Gavi."

"Gavi brings us blessings, our blessings onto Gavi," the assembly chanted.

"Gavi tosses my salad, bless you Gavi," James murmured.

Bolan rolled his eyes.

"Gavi shows us our truth," Michaela intoned. "So we show our truth to Gavi."

"Gavi shows us our truth, so we show our truth to Gavi," the throng responded.

"Gavi will suck my fat black one, so I will show my fat—"

Bolan jabbed an elbow into James's ribs.

The opening invocation went on for a few more rounds, but it was short and sweet. Bolan was interested to note that even as they all slavishly poured their blessings and truths onto Gavi, the recurring theme was not that Gavi was a god, but that he was a key or a path and that the adherents only had to unlock the blessings and truths they already had. It was all about empowerment, it was slick and it made Gavi's mostly privileged converts feel good about themselves, and it let Chechen veterans and other disadvantaged adherents feel justified in wanting some. After the invocation Michaela thanked everyone for coming again and then singled out a half-dozen individuals for all the good work they had done. She suddenly shot the audience a sly look. "I believe my brother is here."

Cheers, screams and applause met the announcement.

"Shall we invite him out?"

The calls, applause and ovations shook the wall of the conference facility.

Michaela smiled impishly. "Where is my brother?"

The sound of the crowd turned into a thunder of expectation demanding release.

Apollyon walked onto the stage. The hall rocked with laughter as he stared out into the crowd in mock confusion. "What? What?" He heaved a theatrical sigh. "Ah, I see. You want my brother, Gavriil."

Once again the throng surged toward the stage.

"Well, you know what?" Apollyon gazed stage right and smiled charmingly. "I believe my brother is here."

The house erupted into chant once more. *"Gavriil! Gavriil! Gavriil!"*

A spotlight hit the stage outlining a small Persian rug with a mediation cushion on it. Michaela and Apollyon stepped back into the shadows as the music rose once more. A carpet and cushion were just visible stage right and left and the brother and sister folded themselves into lotus positions on them. They would be watching the crowd while Gavriil held forth. The chant was lost in a communal roar of ecstasy as Gavril stepped out onto the stage wearing nothing but a purple breechclout.

"Oh, my God! Gavi! Gavi!" was girlishly squealed in a dozen languages.

"Damn," James observed.

Gavi folded himself into the lotus position on the cushion center stage and adjusted the floor mike before him. "Thank you all for coming."

Other than Bolan and James the entire assembly screamed *"Gavi!"* in unison.

Gavriil smiled in bemused embarrassment at the waves of love being sent his way. Bolan had to give the guy credit. In his time Bolan had seen everything from fire-and-brimstone self-proclaimed messiahs, to slick holy rollers to rabid fanatics demanding human sacrifice. Gavriil was a class unto himself. He gazed out benevolently on the audience until the chants started again. The chants died like a knife cut as he reached for the mike once more. "Let us talk about the Path of Love."

Well over a dozen adherents in the front fainted dead away.

THE OPENING reception was turning distinctly bacchanalian. The Panamericano Hotel was closed to everyone except Heaven Now devotees who paraded around in uninhibited glory in the sarongs and head buffs. The casino was closed, but the bar, indoor pool and spa were open. The Herbal X magic tea and Gavi's performance had loosened up everyone, and over a thousand of the faithful were exploring all avenues of immediate Heaven Now gratification. There were debates, prayer groups, sing-alongs and orgies depending on what room you visited. Bolan nursed a beer and kept an eye on Dominico and Busto as they spoke animatedly with Anaya and a gaggle of fellow adherents on a circle of couches in the bar. Anaya was sending Bolan far too many searching looks over the heads of the adherents, but there was nothing to be done about it at the moment without compounding the problem.

James sat book-ended by a pair of buxom blondes in sarongs on a couch across the room. One was passionately discoursing on something while the other nodded emphatically. James was doing his utmost to maintain eye contact and look utterly fascinated by what she was saying. He had managed to get a hand on the hip of each of them, and they leaned in closer, wide-eyed, as James said something undoubtedly profound.

"I fear your friend will never make a true adherent."

Bolan found Gavi himself looming at his elbow. Bolan was

not used to being snuck up on, and he filed the experience away. Normally Gavriil was the sort of man who commanded a room the moment he walked into it. He had slipped in unobserved and stood with Bolan in the corner. Bolan glanced at his happy friend and shrugged. "Yeah, well…"

"Fear not. One may earn merit through service, and through service true devotion can come."

Bolan nodded. "Enlightenment through selfless action."

"Yes." Gavriil's black eyes beamed at Bolan. "Your friend's actions are far from selfless at the moment, but through continued service he might learn to take action selflessly, with no thought toward the fruit of his actions, and it is then he shall partake of the fruit of wisdom."

"Merit through service." Bolan shot Gavriil a sly look. "You recruiting?"

"Always." Gavriil nodded. "Our movement is growing. The world will change. We will need reliable people in the United States to perform a variety of roles. As you know I have helped many veterans of the war in Chechnya. I believe many veterans of the American war in Iraq are similarly troubled."

"Well, like you said, Cal would be something of a wayward adherent. To be honest so would I."

"Many in our employ are not adherents. However, most come around once they experience Heaven Now and feel its worth and power." Gavi raised a speculative eye at Bolan. "You speak as if you have received some spiritual teaching."

"I read a few books." Bolan knew he was treading on thin ice. Gavriil had the same X-ray eyes as the nuns Bolan had encountered in Catholic school in Pittsfield, except this wasn't grade school and Gavriil Arkhangelov wasn't going to crack his knuckles with a ruler. This was life and death. Bolan knew the best lies were seamlessly woven with truth. "I met a monk during a stint in Southeast Asia. He used to say all kinds of crazy shit."

Gavi smiled tolerantly. "Crazy shit?"

"I was raised in a religious household. Then shit happened to my family, and you know? God wasn't there. That soured me on religion. Then I got involved in some real ugly conflicts, and I saw real ugly things. Things I could hardly believe. Things no one would believe if I told them. Things that would sour a man on God and humanity altogether."

"And then?" Gavriil probed.

Bolan stared into the distance. "And then some bald man in an orange bedsheet starts telling you stuff that makes so much sense it scares the hell out of you."

Gavriil cocked his head with interest. "What scares you?"

Bolan locked eyes with Gavriil. "When that monk looks at you and you know you're a pussy. That he's right, and everything you ever did was wrong, and you know that you're too much of a coward to change or do the right thing. That you'll keep doing the same thing you always did, keep screwing up your karma because it's all you know how to do. Because you're too old to start over, and this is all that puts bread in your jar, but you know that you're an empty vessel, you're the tyranny of evil men, and you're damned." Bolan cast his eyes down. "Just like the nuns always told you you'd be when you were a kid."

Gavriil sighed knowingly. "Mr. Cooper, I was raised Russian Orthodox. I know all about nuns."

Bolan snorted. Gavriil Arkhangelov was a charming son of a bitch. One minute he was a spiritual guru and the next he was like your best beer buddy.

Gavriil sighed again, but this time it was filled with compassion. "Your hands may well be stained with blood, my friend, but you are far from damned. Have you ever thought about what is it you truly want?"

"Don't know." Bolan shrugged helplessly. "I mean, I like what you got going on here. It feels right. It's not some monk in a temple talking about karma, this is immediate, it's…" Bolan searched for the words.

"Nebesa Sejchas?" Gavriil suggested dryly.

"Yeah," Bolan agreed. "It's not shaving your head and renouncing everything. It's embracing everything. Heaven now."

"It is that," Gavriil agreed. "But I do not ask slavish devotion or ask you to take my word for it. Move among us. Speak with our adherents. It seems to me you wish to talk. Perhaps you might wish to receive personal convocation. Unlike the confession of your youth, you would speak only of that which you wish to. Our only requirement is that if you choose to speak you do so with honesty."

"It's not the worst offer I've had."

"I will proselytize no further." Gavriil put a huge hand on Bolan's shoulder. "All I ask is that you think about it."

Another smaller, much more feminine hand fell upon Bolan's arm. Michaela Arkhangelov wrinkled her delightful nose in mock reproach. "All I ask is that you two men break up this tea party."

Bolan put on an embarrassed face. "I'm sorry, Miss Arkhangelov. You're right. There are over a thousand adherents here who have traveled across the world for just a moment with your brother, and I'm monopolizing his time."

Michaela's smile showed the gleaming white teeth of a predator. "On the contrary, Mr. Cooper. I feel it is my brother who has been monopolizing your time. This is a retreat, not a recruiting drive. Life is to be enjoyed."

Gavriil's all-encompassing laugh boomed as he threw back his head. "I stand chastised on all sides." Heads whipped around at the sound of his laugh, and the faithful in the bar surged toward their messiah. The Russian strode forth with open arms to meet them.

"Your brother is quite a guy."

Michaela nodded seriously. "He is the most important man on Earth."

Bolan shrugged internally. Gavriil Arkhangelov was making a serious bid for Public Enemy Number One, but most important man on Earth seemed like a bit of a tall order.

Michaela smirked. "I can see you doubt me, but wait and see. Soon, he will change the world forever."

Bolan gave her a good-natured leer in return. "I did like what he said about the Path of Love."

The woman's fathomless blue eyes drank in Bolan's frame. "Did you know we conduct seminars on the proper ways to make love for maximum fulfillment?"

"I saw something about that on the flyer." Bolan took in Michaela's physique measure for measure. "Where do I sign up?"

"Seeing as I am the instructor…" She pressed her room key into Bolan's hand. "You may sign up anytime after midnight."

Bolan watched the beautiful Russian woman's hips sway as she walked over to the crowd gathered around her brother. Calvin James ambled over, grinning from ear to ear. He held up two Panamericano room key cards like he'd hit twenty-one at the blackjack table. "Marika and Lotta, from Sweden."

Bolan looked across the room and reviewed James's conquests. Marika was built like a supermodel and as for Lotta…there was a whole lot of Lotta. "Not bad."

James snorted. "Not bad. What did you get out of Michaela?"

Bolan held up the key to the bridal suite at the Huinid.

James gazed at the ceiling for strength. He had just scored

a pair of perfect tens, but Bolan had trumped him with the queen of hearts. "Whatever, man."

"Yeah, and you're going to have to delay the Swedish bikini team tonight."

"What!"

"I'm going to see what I can get out of Michaela later tonight. You've got to stay on deck and keep a watch over Memo, Najelli and Rider."

"You see? This is just one more example of the man trying to keep the brother down."

"We can switch off tomorrow."

"Man! They'll be with some Brussel sprouts tycoon from Belgium by tomorrow!"

"It's the happy hunting grounds around here," Bolan told him. "You'll have other opportunities. Believe me."

"Happy hunting grounds my black…"

Bolan left James grumbling and walked over to the bar. It was ten o'clock. He ordered a roast beef sandwich and draft beer.

He had a feeling tonight he was going to need his strength.

CHAPTER EIGHTEEN

Michaela Arkhangelov's tawny frame was spooned into Bolan's side. They were both awake and both aware of it though neither said anything as they basked in the afterglow. The night they had spent together had had very little to do with spiritual enlightenment. It had been far more about heat, friction and animal physicality. Nonetheless Bolan had to admit that the fulfillment had been pretty much maximal.

He was glad he had taken up yoga.

Michaela murmured into his chest. "What are you smiling about?"

"I'm just hoping I don't have to fight anyone today or ride a horse."

She laughed and spooned in closer. Her laughter was musical and something to hear. To have a woman as beautiful as her lying in his arms and laughing like that was a powerful thing. Bolan had been the target of some top-drawer seductions, and he knew Michaela Arkhangelov was the Heaven Now pinch hitter for cleaning up men of means.

The redheaded Russian had the power to make men love her.

Bolan stretched. "I can't wait for the seminar on Friday."

"I believe there is little I can teach you."

Bolan trailed his fingernails lazily down her side and felt the flesh goose-bump beneath his fingers. "I'd still like to review the course materials."

"Sunday will be the grand day."

"That's when the retreat gets addressed from space?"

"Indeed, on the last night of the retreat, Colonel Renat Khokhlov will address us from the vault of heaven itself. The day when the world will change."

Heaven Now adherents kept saying that. Even Gavriil and Michaela were saying it, and it was starting to send up red flags on Bolan's internal early-warning system. He smiled. "What? You're koo-koo for cosmonauts or something?"

"Of course, what Russian isn't? Americans are not?"

"Oh, I came from that generation of American kids who drank Tang and got up early to watch every space launch on TV. I'm all about astronauts."

"Mmm. I enjoy imagining you as a little boy watching rocket launches." Michaela dragged her nails down the skin of Bolan's stomach in return. "But that is the past."

"You're more interested in the here and—" Bolan groaned as Michaela started preparations for a rocket launch of her own "—now."

"I am interested in heaven." The woman rolled on top of him and her blue eyes bored into his with undisguised lust. "Now."

The War Room, Stony Man Farm, Virginia

"WE HAVE TO GET SOMEONE UP on the International Space Station, Bear, ASAP."

Kurtzman stared blankly at Bolan's image on the video link. He appeared to be serious. Aaron Kurtzman had fielded some pretty strange requests from the big guy in the past, but this was the mother of all tall orders.

"Mack? Listen very closely. *Endeavor* is going up in three days. Three days. I can't secure you a berth on her. Neither can Hal. Frankly I doubt the president of the United States could do it without blowing the cover off whatever you're trying to accomplish."

"We have to get someone up there," Bolan repeated.

Kurtzman couldn't believe he was even having this conversation. "Mack, we've gotten you and some of the lads orbital and suborbital in the past, but we always had some wiggle room. *Endeavor* is going up in three days, and it would take weeks to prep *Discovery* or *Atlantis*."

"Something is going on up there. On *Endeavor*." Bolan shrugged. "Has to be done."

"Do you mind telling me what you're basing this on?"

"I've had some suspicions for a while about this address to the retreat from space. My gut tells me I have confirmation."

"Your gut?"

"Yeah, and something that Michaela Arkhangelov said to me."

"You really think she would let anything important slip?"

Bolan gave Kurtzman a weary but satisfied half smile. "It was pillow talk."

Kurtzman heaved a mighty sigh, and one that was tinged with a little jealousy. Mack Bolan had been with more beautiful women than Kurtzman had had hot dinners. Nevertheless any intelligence agent would tell you that pillow talk was one of the top five methods of intelligence gathering. "Okay, let's just assume the president is going to call that sufficient. The nominal crew size, including this mission, is seven, and all the seats on that flight are full, Mack. Just exactly who do you propose we replace?"

"Dr. David Nunn, computer science engineer."

The big guy had done some research. Kurtzman pulled Dr. Nunn up on his computer out of habit, but he knew all about him. He was one of the United States' best minds when it came to cybernetics and information systems. On several occasions Kurtzman had been tempted to try to recruit him for Farm activities, but his politics were somewhat liberal. Various countries had built modules for the ISS and not all of the computer systems were meshing at one hundred percent. Nunn was being sent up to help synchronize things. "And if our man Dr. Nunn doesn't want to give up his seat for king and country?"

"I know some people who would be willing to sit on him."

So did Kurtzman, and he suspected they were the same people. "I see, so we're going to send you up the gantry posing as the good doctor?"

"No, he's going to take sick and be replaced at the last moment."

Kurtzman found Bolan's calm surety about the whole situation deeply disturbing. "Mack, let me explain something to you. Going up on the space shuttle, much less to the International Space Station, is the Holy Grail of science. It doesn't matter what your field is. Physicists, rock stars, billionaires—everyone and their brother wants to go up into space. You know even Akira would like to go up into space. So—"

"So that's why we're going to send him." Bolan nodded.

Kurtzman had no prepared response.

"Come on, Bear. He's as good as Nunn if not better."

Kurtzman exploded. "We agreed! No more sending Akira into the field. Nearly every time we do he gets shot at and the crap kicked out of him. He's been captured twice, Mack! The last time he was subjected to chemical torture and interrogation! You remember that? We agreed! No more sending Akira into the field!"

"We're not sending him into the field. We're sending him into space."

"You think that's funny?"

"Yeah, kinda. But why don't we ask him?"

"Oh, sure! Ask him if he wants to go up in the shuttle on a mission to the International Space Station!" Kurtzman was livid. "What do you think he's going to say?"

Bolan clicked keys and a video window appeared. Akira Tokaido looked up from his workstation into the video three-way. "Hey, Bear. What's up, Mack?"

Kurtzman waved his arms in a near conniption fit. "Don't listen to him!"

Bolan smiled. "Akira, do you want to go up in the shuttle on a mission to the International Space Station?"

Tokaido's face went blank. "You kidding?"

Bolan shook his head. "No."

Tokaido shot from his seat and pumped both fists skyward. "Shit, howdy, yes!"

Kurtzman's face sagged into his hands. It was happening again. Tokaido was almost bouncing up and down in his seat. "So, what do I do?"

"Well, ostensibly you're going to do some programming and systems integration for the Space Station. You up to that?"

Tokaido scoffed. "Dude, their computer architecture is archaic. I could fix that stuff in my sleep. I could probably do it from my cell phone."

Bolan smiled at Kurtzman. "See?"

The computer wizard seethed.

Tokaido couldn't believe his luck. "That's it?"

"No, you do that in your spare time. The main mission is to find out what Heaven Now is up to."

"Okay, yeah, right and then I contact you?"

"Most likely you need to stop it."

"Ohhh…kay."

"You see!" Kurtzman pointed a condemning finger at Bolan. "You see?"

"Colonel Renat Khokhlov will be your main target. Aaron will give you files. He'll have had combat training so be careful."

"Right…" Tokaido's enthusiasm dimmed slightly. "How many Russians are going up on *Endeavor?*"

Kurtzman scanned the mission profile. "Just Khokhlov."

"What's his mission profile?"

Kurtzman grunted unhappily and pulled up files. "It's more of a PR stunt than anything else. Khokhlov is Russia's current most famous cosmonaut. He won the Hero of the Soviet Union piloting MiG attack fighters during the war in Afghanistan. He's also won the Order of Merit for outstanding contributions to the development of Russian Statehood. Word is the Russian government is going to push for a moon shot and they want to prime their people for the announcement. Our sources say his address to the Heaven Now retreat will be taped and edited by the government and then shown on the Russian news channels." Kurtzman read Bolan's face. There was something the big guy wasn't buying. "What?"

"How many Russians are up on the station already?"

Kurtzman clicked keys. "One—Mission Specialist Dr. Denis Treschev."

"What's the doctor's specialty?"

"Virology."

Tokaido's eyes flicked between video screens. "Virology?"

Bolan ignored him. "Bear, assuming everything we believe about Heaven Now is true, and that Colonel Khokhlov's address on Sunday isn't the main attraction, why would Heaven Now be excited about a virologist who's four hundred miles up in space?"

Kurtzman frowned mightily as his brain pounced on the problem and collated data already in storage there. "I can think of one reason."

"I was hoping you could."

"One of the main areas of scientific research on the ISS is the effect of weightlessness and space on terrestrial organisms. Humans, animals, plants, as well as microorganisms."

"And?"

"Weightlessness has some very strange effects on living creatures, and not just the loss of bone density and muscle strength you read about astronauts suffering. All life on Earth is ruled by gravity. You remove it and it affects all of the biological processes. We're just starting to investigate what effect it may have on human DNA. On top of that, no matter how good the shielding is up on the ISS, anyone who spends any time up there is being exposed to far more cosmic rays than a human being protected by the Earth's atmosphere."

"And what happens to microorganisms, like bacteria or viruses?"

"There have been several studies conducted so far."

"And?"

"They mutate, wildly and unpredictably."

Tokaido's eyes flicked back and forth. "Mutating viruses?"

Bolan ignored him. "Do we have anything on Colonel Khokhlov's itinerary once he comes down?"

Kurtzman saw things with terrible clarity as he pulled it up. "He's scheduled to address the UN Assembly about the peaceful and cooperative exploration of space between nations. Reception to follow."

"And then?"

"He's embarking on a four-continent speaking tour of nations with active space programs."

"Call it a gut instinct, but I don't think the colonel has a clue. He may be a starry-eyed Heaven Now adherent, but he's a Hero of the Soviet Union and belongs to the Russian Federation Order of Merit. I'm willing to bet he wouldn't willingly commit genocide."

"I agree. His record doesn't fit suicide plague bomber. Colonel Khokhlov is an unwitting biological vector. Dr. Treschev is the Heaven Now agent."

"What could he be cooking up there?"

Bolan scanned what little they had on Treschev. "He's worked on top secret Russian military projects. A lot of his file is redacted. We're going to have to assume he could have samples of any active biological culture Russia has ever considered weaponizing. For that matter, it doesn't have to be smallpox or Ebola. Given a few genetic twists the common flu could be turned into a doomsday disease."

"Uhhh…" Tokaido raised his hand like he was in school. "Doomsday?"

Bolan turned his attention to the young man. "You need to get up there."

"Right," Tokaido said uncertainly.

"We don't have much time."

"Right."

"Bear, you need to make a call."

Kurtzman picked up his phone and dialed Hal Brognola's preset number. "Right."

The Huinid

BOLAN CLOSED THE LAPTOP at the knock on the door. "Open."

Dominico, Busto and Anaya came in, followed by James.

They had come back from Dominico's morning convo and the Mexican was puffed up with pride. "I aced it, man! Best performance of my career!" Bolan gave Anaya a measuring look. The young woman was looking more fearful and trapped by the day. Bolan had to hope she could hold it together, and hope Heaven Now chalked up her behavior to Apollyon's winning way with women. James was openly scowling.

"So," Bolan asked, "did the blond twins give you a rain check?"

"No, the blond twins did not give me a rain check!" James slammed the door behind them. "They went upstairs with some dreadlocked Brazilian soccer-playing dude. I saw him in the restaurant this morning. They're going to have to surgically remove the smile from his face, if I don't do it for him. Jive-ass, manioc-eating…"

Bolan interrupted James's grumbling and gave them the short version of his conversation with Kurtzman.

"Madre de dios!" Dominico exclaimed.

"Well…just…crud." James stared up at the ceiling. "Still, Akira in space. That's something. So how do we play it?"

"We play it cool. Memo goes to seminars and appears to work on his karma and recruiting Najelli."

Dominico was still wearing his game face. He was ready to win. "Cool, but what does Najelli do? Should she convert or something?"

"Not yet. For now she should just go shopping and play blackjack."

"Yes!" Busto pumped a gleeful fist in victory.

Anaya looked back and forth between them. "And what about me?"

Bolan had been waiting for that question. "Who do you report to about your convos?"

"I work only with the A-list adherents, and I take my own convos with Mikki."

"Tell Mikki that Memo is scared after the attack on the road. Tell him he's fully committed and you think you can get him to make another million-dollar contribution and that you need to spend time with Najelli to get her to join up and make it happen. That should allow them to monopolize a lot of your time and give you excuses to ditch Apollyon. Cal and I will never be far away."

Anaya dropped her gaze to the floor. Apollyon's presence haunted her every moment. "And what about at night?"

"If there's a problem, you text me. If you're worried, if you think you're in danger, you just text 'I need you.' If you're doing it under duress, if it's a trap, you text 'I need you now,' and we come for you. Guns blazing."

Anaya wouldn't lift her eyes. "All right."

Bolan looked to James. "What's the status on Schwein-steiger?"

James pulled out his cell and pressed an icon on the keypad. An NSA satellite fed him a map of Bariloche. A red dot sat unwinking on the Huinid. "We're out of the satellite window, but as of forty-five minutes ago he was still here in the hotel. I'm thinking he's most likely dead or they're keeping him under wraps. We better plan on him and some of his head-bangers being around if things go south."

"Right." Bolan nodded toward the terrace. "Cal, I need you for a second."

Dominico was outraged. "Hey! We're all in this, man!"

"This is a what-you-don't-know-won't-hurt-you kind of thing, Memo."

Dominico wasn't happy about it, but he didn't protest.

Bolan and James walked into the Andean winter morning. "Have you seen Spartak?"

"Yeah, he was in the restaurant this morning, too."

"Did he say anything?"

"No, he just gave me one of those inscrutable Russian stares. You know, the kind that keep burning into your back even after you've left the room." James chewed his lip as he weighed the Russian in his mind. "I don't know, man, I don't know if we can bet our lives on this guy. He's a merc, and chief of security for Heaven Now is probably the best gig he ever had or ever will."

"We did drop a bomb in his lap."

"Yeah? And what happens if he goes all hot potato with that bomb and tosses us into Gavriil's hands? I heard rumors of goin' all Greco-Roman with Apollyon and his pals in the snow and then swimming Lake Nahuel with pockets full of rocks."

"Spartak may be a jaded merc, but he's deep Special Forces. If he believes Ramzin was murdered and Heaven Now is risking world war with terrorist acts, I'm betting he chooses the path of righteousness."

James wasn't completely convinced. "You're betting our lives on that Russian?"

"Yeah," Bolan agreed. "And one million euros."

James brightened. "Oh?"

"Yeah, on the flash drive there's a Web link to a Caribbean offshore account. Five hundred thousand euros in Spartak's name. I gave him the account number for a second account with another five hundred thousand, but not the password. He gets that when he mucks in. If loyalty to the Motherland, avenging a Spetsnaz legend and a million euros isn't enough, then he's fooled us all and he really is a Heaven Now true believer."

"Okay, I feel you, but the man could send up some smoke signals. He's playing it awfully close."

"Russians always play it close, Cal."

"Well, that is a fact." James suddenly grinned. "So… tonight I'm going out to 'investigate' and you're going to pull guard duty, right?"

"No. Unless you have a higher-level contact, I'm going to work Mikki for some more pillow talk. You're still pulling sentry, soldier."

James pointed an accusing finger. "You suck!"

"Well…" Bolan shrugged helplessly. "Tell you what. You go seduce Apollyon or Gavriil, I'll get out of your way. Hell, I'll want to get out of your way."

James stalked back into the suite. "Jive-ass, blue-eyed, white-devil…"

CHAPTER NINETEEN

Bolan's eyes flicked open. His internal clock told him it was around 4:00 a.m. His cell phone was vibrating. Michaela Arkhangelov shifted against him as he slid the phone from beneath his pillow. It was 4:07 a.m. and he had a text message.

i need you now

They had Rider, and she was messaging under duress. It was a trap. Bolan's thumbs skimmed over the touch screen.

im coming

Michaela murmured into his chest. "What is it?"

Bolan put weariness into his voice as he text-messaged "game on" to James.

"It's Dominico again. He's been freaked out since the attack on the road. He jumps every time the wind blows outside his window and then someone has to hold his hand."

"Mmm." Michaela nestled in. "You should go."

Bolan's eyes flared wide. "All right."

Michaela rolled over as Bolan sat up. He slid his right arm beneath her chin and she made a happy noise. She jerked and started flailing as Bolan vised his forearm and bicep against her carotids and used his other hand to push her head deeper into the strangle. Bolan waited until just before she went slack and released the hold. Michaela sucked air like a landed fish as he tore the pillowcases into strips and hog-tied her. He shoved a wadded strip of bedding into her mouth as she gasped and bound it in place with another. Her glazed eyes focused and gazed up at him in blue-eyed bloody murder as he put on his clothes. She shrieked in muffled rage as Bolan picked her up and unceremoniously dropped her in the closet. "Gotta go." Bolan drew his snub-nosed Smith as he walked out into the hall.

A startled lookout by the elevator nearly dropped his phone as Bolan emerged without a signal from Michaela. The man dropped the phone and began pleading for his life in Russian as Bolan stalked forward. The Executioner cut off the begging by ramming the barrel of the revolver into the man's belly and then slapping him unconscious with the cylinder. Bolan picked up the man's fallen phone and dropped a dime on Spartak.

The Russian answered on the first ring. "What?"

Bolan dropped the bomb on Spartak. "Rider is in trouble. She contacted me with the code that she's doing it under duress and it's a trap. I just choked out Mikki and hog-tied her. One of your men in the hall is down. Cal is on his way."

Spartak was silent on his end.

"I'm going in. I'm burning down Heaven Now," Bolan advised. "Pick a side."

"No. Wait."

"Why?"

"You say it is trap?"

"That's the way it looks."

"Does Rider know we are in contact?"

"No, I've been keeping you as my ace in the hole."

"Then let me go to door. As head of security, I will demand to know what is going on. It will cause confusion. You and friend Cal climb down from roof onto balcony. We put them in cross fire."

It was the best offer Bolan was going to get at 4:00 a.m. in the Andes. Assuming Spartak could be trusted. "My ass is going to be hanging out in the breeze, Spartak."

"It is all our asses now."

"How many of your men can you rely on once the shooting starts?"

"None."

It was a sobering assessment. "How soon can you be at the door?"

"I am just down the hall. I will give you and Cal two minutes from time you signal me you are on roof."

"Done." Bolan tapped off and called Dominico.

Dominico mumbled sleepily. "What?"

"Rider's in trouble. Cal and I are going after her."

Dominico snapped awake. "On my way!"

"No, sit tight. You and Najelli gear up. We may be leaving in a hurry."

Dominico didn't like it but he didn't argue. "All right. We'll be ready."

James's voice came out of the stairwell. "Striker!"

"Clear!"

James appeared dripping in armament and dropped a bag to the floor with a clank. Bolan dipped in and pulled body armor over his black T-shirt and strapped into web gear and tactical radio. He slung one PDW over his shoulder and took up a second one. James checked the loads in his assault rifle and grenade launcher. "What's the plan?"

"We go to the roof. Rider's room is on the second floor, seven doors down from here. We climb down. Spartak is going to knock on the door for us."

"Nice."

The two soldiers grabbed their gear and sped up the stairs. The access to the roof was locked. James kicked it off its hinges. Cold air blasted against Bolan as he stepped out onto the steep, snow-covered shake-shingle roof. James was wearing his full raid suit. He grinned at Bolan in his T-shirt. "Nice night for a walk on the roof!"

Bolan ignored the cold. He pulled on a pair of gloves and fastened his phone to the back of his left wrist while James fixed a rope to a roof vent. Bolan peered over. The orange glow three stories below told him the lights were on in Rider's room. He touched the screen of his phone. "Spartak, we're in place."

"*Da*, two minutes."

James took the rope and began to slide down the side of Villa Huinid. Except for the darkness and freezing wind, it was an easy descent. Ten seconds later James gave the rope a double tug to let Bolan know he'd landed on the terrace. Bolan climbed down two floors and he kicked out to land lightly next to the Phoenix Force commando. The drapes were closed, but Bolan was able to peer through a gap. The room was full of goons. Eight were immediately visible, including Batata Schweinsteiger and Apollyon's largest playmate, Misha. Anaya sat sobbing on the edge of the bed. Her clothes were torn and her face was bloody and swollen from a severe slapping. Everyone else was smiling, smoking, fondling their pistols and waiting to do some damage to an American.

Apollyon himself was nowhere in sight, and it gave Bolan a cold feeling that had nothing to do with the wind and snow.

Bolan's phone vibrated. He touched the screen and read Spartak's text.

at door

Bolan typed back.

in place

Everyone in the room jumped as a fist hammered on the door. Even out on the terrace in the howling winter night Bolan could hear Spartak roaring his indignation at parade-ground decibels. The men all looked at Anaya, the door and then one another in alarm. Misha stabbed out his cigarette and nodded at Schweinsteiger and the door. Schweinsteiger lowered his pistol and opened the door. Bolan had to suppress a smile as Spartak immediately slapped the skinhead to the floor. Spartak stepped over the skinhead, marched up to Misha and began reading the big man the riot act.

"You know, I like him." James picked up a deck chair and hefted it. "Now?"

Misha wasn't taking the dressing down lightly. He leaned his face down into Spartak's and began bellowing right back. Bolan put a Personal Defense Weapon in each hand. "Yeah."

James flung the chair through the sliding-glass door. Everyone except Spartak just about leaped out of their shoes. Glass crunched beneath Bolan's boots as he stepped in. He leveled his weapons like a high-tech gunfighter. James had his six with the rifle-and-grenade combo shouldered. Bolan tipped his muzzles at the floor. "Drop the guns."

Spartak produced a Pernach machine pistol and aimed

the gleaming slab-sided weapon up at Misha's head. "Do as he says."

One of Schweinsteiger's skinheads dropped his pistol and raised his hands. Misha snarled a disgusted obscenity in Russian and exhorted his men to shoot. Spartak cracked Misha in the teeth with the slide of his weapon for his trouble. "Guns! Now!" Spartak boomed.

The men looked around at one another and began lowering their weapons.

War broke out on the floor below. Bolan recognized the rapid-fire snapping of Dominico's PDW and the louder *crack-crack-crack* of Busto's carbine. Both were drowned out by the roar of shotguns. The spell of intimidation in Anaya's room broke at the sound, and the suite turned into the OK Corral. One of the skinheads spun and raised his revolver. Bolan's PDWs chattered in his hands as his twin bursts tore through the skinhead's chest and hammered him into oblivion. A Russian raised a sawed-off shotgun, and James burned him down before he could thumb back the hammers. Misha rose from the floor into a tackle that carried Spartak across the room. Bolan lowered his aim and blew Misha's left knee out from under him. Anaya screamed as the two embattled Russians fell onto the bed on top of her. Schweinsteiger ran screaming out the door. Bolan felt the hard jab of a bullet against the left shoulder of his body armor. He rammed his right-hand PDW out at arm's length and put a burst through the man's brainpan.

Another shotgun boomed and Bolan felt a burn across his cheek. He and James drilled the shotgunner at the same time and the three simultaneous bursts shoved him backward. James held down his trigger and burned the rest of his magazine through the man and into the remaining skinhead behind him. The shotgunner collapsed back across the Misha-Spartak-

Rider puppy-pile on the bed. The victim of James's blow-through burst fell with a crash through the folding closet doors.

The remaining Russian had fallen to his knees with his hands shaking in the air. *"Nyet! Nyet! Nyet!"*

James strode toward the pyramid of dead and struggling humanity on the bed. "Cal! Downstairs! Go!"

James slammed a fresh magazine into his rifle and drove the butt of it into the surrendering Russian's face to keep him out of play. He stepped out on the terrace, grabbed the rope and stepped out into space. Bolan slung one PDW and yanked the dead man off the top of the pile. Spartak was busy punching Misha in the side of the head, while Misha had bitten half of Spartak's ear off. Anaya was moaning and yelping as the two big men fought on top of her. Misha's face lurched into view as he tried to avoid a punch, and Bolan drove the butt of his weapon into his face. Spartak rose up to give himself some room and began raining down blows on Misha in earnest. The Russian's eyes glazed over into unconsciousness but Spartak kept hitting him.

Bolan hooked Spartak into a half nelson and hip-tossed him off the bed. Spartak spluttered angrily, but Bolan ignored him and kicked away any firearms within reach before man-handling Misha onto the carpet. Anaya crawled to the head of the bed and curled up like an injured animal. The Russian who had surrendered had risen to his hands and knees. Spartak cupped a hand to his mutilated ear and began stomping the man out of a general sense of rage.

James spoke in Bolan's earpiece. "Striker! Najelli is down! Memo is gone!"

Bolan ran to the terrace. A three-car caravan of white Land Cruisers was pulling out of the parking lot and onto the mountain road. Bolan raised his weapon and slapped the folding stock and foregrip into position. He shouldered the weapon and peered through the optic just in time to see the rear vehicle pull away into the darkness. There was nothing to shoot at but floating red taillights disappearing into the distance, and Bolan didn't know which car Dominico was in.

James spoke urgently over the tactical radio. "Najelli is bad! We need to get her medical! We need to extract now!"

Throughout the Huinid people were screaming in their rooms. Someone pulled the fire alarm and old-fashioned fire bells began ringing on every floor. There was a hiss and rattle of pipes, and then the ceiling sprinklers began spritzing the room. Bolan sighed heavily as he felt the water begin to freeze on his flesh from the mountain wind howling in from the balcony. His assessment of the situation was colder. They'd ruined the retreat, but Gavriil had won the round. He'd sacrificed a few pawns. Bolan had lost players, and ones he cared about. All that was left was to salvage whatever he could from the situation, regroup and extract before the local authorities entered the mix. "Spartak, you staying or going?"

Spartak stopped stomping his hapless victim. "I go with you."

"Then get us a vehicle. Something big enough for five." Bolan groaned wearily as he heaved Misha into a fireman's carry. "We're out of here."

Stony Man Farm Armory

ARMORER EXTRAORDINAIRE John "Cowboy" Kissinger stared across his workbench at Akira Tokaido with a mixed sense of vague jealously and genuine pride. "Going to have to call you Space Cowboy now."

Tokaido smiled smugly back. "Darn tootin'."

"Well, Akira, bad news is we can't smuggle any guns up there with you, and we wouldn't even if we could."

"You wouldn't?"

"No, you can't hit dick, and everyone knows it. Can't have you punching holes in the International Space Station."

Tokaido's face fell. "Well, what about, like—"

"Like frangible ammo?" Kissinger suggested.

"Yeah, frangible ammo. Like federal marshals use, on airplanes."

"Well, now I considered that but it still came down to the fact that you can't hit dick. Even if you don't breach the hull we can't have you blasting apart things like guidance control or life support. Some of that stuff is kind of vital."

"So what do I do if I have to make a citizen-of-space arrest? Challenge the guy to a game of chess?"

"No, these guys are Russians. You'd lose."

"Great. So, harsh language?"

Kissinger shoved out a plastic equipment case and flipped the latches. "You'll use this."

Tokaido looked at the contents. It was an MP3 player, and top of the line. "It's an MP3 player."

Kissinger picked up the device, aimed it at a striking dummy along the wall and pressed the click-wheel. The MP3 player made a "chuff!" noise. A dart shot out of the jack, un-spooling wire. The dart hit the dummy and the device *tack-tack-tacked* as Kissinger held down the click-wheel and gave it juice. "It's a stun gun."

"Dude..." Tokaido was giddy once more.

"Just remember the problem is you can't hit dick, and you only get one shot."

Tokaido's shoulders sagged.

"Also, keep in mind that you'll be in zero gravity and every action has an equal and opposite reaction. If you wuss-hand your stun gun like you do with pistols on the range, it's going to squirt right out of your grip and hit you in the face. Also, keep in mind, you'll be in zero G, so if you fire and you're not braced, the compressed air jet will move you backward. Just like the air thrusters the astronauts use."

"So do I have a backup stun gun?"

Kissinger sighed at Tokaido's lack of tactical sense. "No, each astronaut is allowed only one personal stereo and every piece of equipment and every ounce of weight is accounted for on a mission. But since you can't hit dick, we're giving options. Pull the handles off the case."

Tokaido stared at the equipment case. The black plastic spade handles did seem a bit oversized. "What?"

"I said pull them out, and pull hard. It's a friction fit."

Tokaido took the handles in his hand and yanked. One handle came out in his right hand. The left one took an extra tug. The straight handles filled his palms. An arc of hard plastic covered his fingers. A pair of flat electric leads gleamed at each apex. His jaw dropped. "Oh, no way!"

Kissinger nodded proudly. "Way."

"Electric stun knuckles!" Tokaido squeezed the handles and sparks flew between the leads. "Dude! Batman so used these in *Justice League: Secret Origins!*"

"Does talk like that get you laid?" Kissinger inquired.

"Dude, these would so get me laid at Comic-Con!"

"I have no idea what that means, and I don't want to, and stop wasting the charge."

Tokaido reluctantly took off the stun knuckles.

"Now, we all know you can't hit dick with your fists, either."

Tokaido had begged several members of the Stony Man teams to take him to the dojo and teach him some self-defense. His forays into the manly arts had ended up pretty ignominiously.

"So I want you to keep a few things in mind. You don't have to duke it out. All you have to do is touch your opponent. No one up there is wearing anything except T-shirts and sweats so you get contact anywhere you can light them up with 950,000 volts. Let them come to you.

"Remember this—you can't swim in zero gravity. So always keep a wall or a bulkhead within arm's or leg's reach so you can pull along or push off. If you get stuck in the middle of a compartment with no momentum? You're a sitting duck."

"The guy Treschev's a science geek," Tokaido scoffed. "What's he going to do?"

"You're a science geek."

"Yeah, well."

"And he's been up there for months already, and knows every inch of the station like the back of his hand. You'll be in his yard. Also, keep this in mind. There's a survival kit in the escape module and the Russians keep a pistol in it. You'll have a diagram to where it is. There's a survival kit in the shuttle, as well, and it's packing a NASA space knife about the size of a machete." Kissinger waved a dismissing hand. "I doubt it'll come to any of that. What you have to worry about is that there are plenty of screwdrivers, spanners and other heavy tools to make mayhem with if our friend Dr. Treschev decides to take a sudden, violent dislike to you."

"Great."

"Listen, kid. I've read your mission profile." Kissinger grew serious. "Remember your mission. You'll have all access 24/7 up there. You hack into his computer system. If for some reason you can't, just go into the lab when he's sleeping and access it. With any luck there won't be a fight at all."

Tokaido began to feel some apprehension. "Yeah, well, we all know how things go when I go out in the field."

"Kid, you aren't going into the field." Kissinger sighed wistfully. "You're going into orbit."

CHAPTER TWENTY

CIA Safe House, Bariloche

Bolan, James and Spartak gazed down in judgment upon Misha Tetriakov. The man's face looked like hamburger, and his knee was swathed in bloody field dressings. He sat bound to a chair and sweated with the knowledge that three very dangerous men had found him wanting. But it wasn't enough. Bolan watched Tetriakov steel himself for what he thought was to come and knew they were dealing with a true believer. Tetriakov was full-on Heaven Now. They had learned from Spartak that Michaela had briefly been his lover to cement his membership, and when she had broken it off there had been Heaven Now groupies aplenty to soften the blow and keep him in. He'd been seduced by Aphrodite, been anointed the right hand of Apollyon and obviously regarded Gavriil as Zeus enthroned on Olympus. The only problem was that rather than ancient Greek mythology this was the twenty-first century and Heaven Now was a death-cult focused on the apocalypse. Bolan turned away and walked into the kitchen with James. "Can you snap him?"

"Snapping" was the name for making a fanatic realize he'd been lied to and used by the cult that had recruited him. James was a master at it, and the man wasn't happy. "We need something to rattle his cage like you did Mankita, but I don't know what that is. The cat's out of the bag and he knows it. He's beyond kamikaze. He's in Samurai mode. He isn't just ready to die. He's ready to endure. It could take days, weeks, to snap him through normal methods." James looked Bolan dead in the eye. "What do you want me to do?"

James was one of the best interrogators Bolan had ever met, but his technique was ninety-five-percent psychological and five-percent pharmaceutical. The man wasn't a torturer and both warriors despised men who were. They had been at this impasse before. Sometimes, you had to give the bad guys a pass if you wanted to stay a good guy. Even if it cost you. Despite the most heinous threats, it had never come down to going medieval on someone. Bolan had never asked it, and he really didn't know what James would do if he did. Even if James did it, Bolan knew it would end their friendship, and end James's relationship with Stony Man Farm. Bolan also knew in his heart that if the situation required it, he would do it himself and take the karma rather than dump it on one of the most honorable soldiers it had been his privilege to work with.

Spartak walked into the kitchen. James had sewn his ear back on, but the Russian was still in a bad mood. "I know of what you speak."

"Yeah?" James challenged. "And?"

Spartak glanced emotionlessly at the butcher block full of kitchen knives. "Give him to me."

James eyed the Russian coldly. "Fuck you."

"Go for walk," Spartak scoffed. "This is no longer only American matter."

James and Spartak glared at each other.

Bolan smiled with sudden inspiration. "You know what?"

The two men spoke in unison without taking their eyes off each other. "What?"

"Well, it's just that there's no reason we can't be civilized about this."

"What are you talking about?" James asked.

"*Da.*" Spartak was equally confused. "What?"

"You know." Bolan looked past the knives to a large plastic bag. "Why don't we just brew a pot of tea and have a nice chat."

James and Spartak glanced at the dime bag of personal-convo Herbal Magic X tea that Rider Anaya had pilfered for them for further analysis.

"Live by the tea?" James grinned from ear to ear. "Spill your guts by the tea."

Spartak nodded grudgingly. "I enjoy irony of it."

"Good, you two have yourselves a tea party. Cal, you're the good cop. Spartak, you're the bad cop. Tea Misha up and then get him babbling. I'm going to check on the girls and phone head office."

Spartak began filling a kettle while James hefted the bag and began considering dosage.

Bolan went into the cabin's back bedroom. Like Bolan, Busto had gotten herself on the bad end of a pattern of buckshot, only she had taken a whole lot more of it. Bolan had four stitches in his left cheek. Busto had ten. She had a hole through her left shoulder and had taken two buck balls along the side of her skull, inducing a significant concussion. The worst was the ball of lead that had nicked her left carotid. James had managed to stop the bleeding and stabilize her, but she had lost a lot of blood and between shock, concussion and blood loss the woman wasn't in good shape. They needed to get her to Buenos Aires and a real hospital stat.

"How you doing?"

Busto was awake, but she was on military-strength morphine. "Where's Memo?" she asked.

It was the tenth time she'd asked, and each time it was like the first. Bolan sat down on the edge of the bed and gave her hand a squeeze. He gave her the same answer. "You'll see him soon."

Bolan pulled the comforter up around her as Busto drifted back into her opiate fugue. He swore to himself for the tenth time she would see him again. Alive or at his funeral. It was a promise Bolan made to himself and her. Guillermo Dominico had chosen the good fight and fallen. Dominico would be rescued or revenged. Bolan rose and went to Anaya's room. She was curled up beneath the covers. She had been slapped around, and two Russians determined to kill each other had used her as a wrestling mat. Her beautiful body was one massive bruise. Her blackened eyes were closed, but by her body language he could tell she was awake. She tensed as he put a hand on her shoulder and relaxed as he gave her a gentle squeeze. "Hey."

Fresh tears squeezed out of the corners of her eyes. "Hey."

"How you holding up?"

Anaya cringed deeper into the covers in answer.

"It's okay. We're getting out of here soon."

She ground her face down into her pillow miserably. "Where am I going to go?"

"Well—" Bolan leaned in and whispered in her ear "—how about Molokai?"

Rider's misery fell from her face and was replaced by shock. "Hawaii?"

"You'd prefer busing tables in Minnesota?"

Anaya giggled. "No!"

"Hawaii's where Najelli, her daughter and her mother are going. Memo, too, if I can save him. Memo and Najelli both like you. They'll be strangers in paradise. They could use a friend. So could you."

"I love Hawaii."

"Have you been?" Bolan asked.

"No, but when I was a little girl—" Anaya blushed through her bruises "—my friends and I all watched *Magnum, P.I.* every week on television."

"I can't promise you Tom Selleck, but I can promise you good surf and plenty of yoga students."

Anaya suddenly shuddered. "They'll come for me. He will come for me."

"No. Heaven Now is going down, and Apollyon is right at the top of my hit list." Bolan took Anaya's chin in his hand. "Believe me. They're all going down."

Hope moved in the woman's big brown eyes. "I do."

"Get some sleep. We're going to have to move soon."

She clutched Bolan's hand. "Will you stay for a little while?"

"I will."

It didn't take long. Fear and pain had ridden Rider Anaya for days. For a few moments now she felt safe, and exhaustion took her seconds after she closed her eyes. Bolan waited until her breathing became regular with sleep before slowly extricating his hand. He tucked a pillow between her arms as a surrogate and went into the back room. He connected his laptop to the satellite link and sent for secure live-video feed to the Farm. Bolan found himself facing mission controller Barbara Price. "Where's Bear?"

The willowy blonde gave Bolan a bemused look. "Fretting like a hen, and since Akira is off to Cape Canaveral, he's taken on his share of the cybernetic work here at the Farm. Right now he's trying to break the encryption on that hard drive you picked up in Moscow. May I be of some assistance?"

"We need ASAP extraction out of Bariloche."

"Bariloche has been in lockdown since your gunfight last night and its biggest paying customer of the season fled the scene. The airport is out of the question. The news services worldwide are blowing up saying that an attempt was made on Gavriil Arkhangelov's life."

"What's Gavi saying?"

"Very little. He extracted by private jet to Brazil, where's he's quite popular by the way. His press person made a statement that it appears that someone tried to kill him, but they are not sure, and they don't wish to return to Argentina while his life may be in danger. The Argentine police don't like it much, but he's already out of the country. The blogosphere is going crazy, as well. The most popular conspiracy theory is that the CIA did it."

"Can you get us out, or are we hiking to Chile?"

"The good news is that Bariloche doesn't have much of a police force, and there are several private airstrips we can extract out of. Chile is likely to be your best bet. Bad news is that the provincial police are on their way and federal teams are flying out of Buenos Aires. We either get you out now or you have to plan on being bottled up for a few days until something more elaborate can be arranged."

"Then we go now, but we need medical for Najelli. She's stable, but she got shot up pretty bad."

"Well, that complicates things, but I'll make it work."

"We have a prisoner who requires medical attention, as well."

"Okay…"

"I'm going to leave Rider with Najelli. When Najelli is well enough, I'm sending Rider with her to Molokai."

"You're handing out a lot of tickets to paradise."

"She earned it. Arrange it. You know I'm good for it."

Price knew from long experience that Mack Bolan didn't forget debts. "I know."

"You say that Gavriil extracted to Brazil?"

"Yes, and if you're thinking—"

"He has Memo," Bolan said.

Price also knew Bolan didn't leave people behind. "I see."

"Cal, Spartak and I will ditch our weapons here. Have the CIA collect them when they can. I need you to arrange armament to be waiting in Brazil on-site and a mission profile to get in wherever Gavriil is at."

"You're moving awfully fast."

"They're going to hammer Memo for everything he knows, and they're not going to be nice about it. Particularly not if Apollyon is involved. According to Spartak, he likes the rough stuff. If we're very lucky they may keep him alive to use him as a hostage. Either way he doesn't have much time. I want to be in Brazil and kicking down a door in twenty-four hours."

"Jesus, Mack, we—"

"Make it happen."

Price went into mission control mode. "All right, to expedite things you need to split up and your strike team has to go now. I'll send a CIA asset along with a doctor they trust to take care of Najelli and Rider. When things cool off we'll smuggle them into Chile."

"Do it," Bolan agreed.

"Like I said, police presence is light in Bariloche, but there aren't many major roads and they're all closed. I'm sending you a map to the nearest airstrip. I suggest you, Cal and Spartak lace up your boots and get hiking. It's fifteen klicks through the snow. Just take your passports and all the money you have on you. I'll have the CIA Buenos Aires station work up a list of private pilots who don't ask too many questions and frequently fly to Chile." Price's fingers flew across her keyboard. "Your quickest flight will be to Puerto Montt. From there we'll get you a shuttle to Santiago. Santiago will be our best bet to get a private jet for Brazil. You're going to burn some hours on puddle jumpers, but there's no helping it. We just don't have the assets that far south to get you a straight shot. Getting you to Buenos Aires would be quicker, but if your descriptions haven't been circulated yet they will be."

Bolan would've liked the straight shot to Buenos Aires, but Calvin James stuck out like a sore thumb in South America's Christmas-tree country, and Spartak was known by his real name. Bolan and Spartak both were bandaged and bleeding. "Your call, Barb. Make it happen."

Price raised a critical eyebrow. "What about your prisoner?"

That was a good question. He wasn't going to leave a three-hundred-pound fanatic with the girls even if he was tied up. "We'll have to take him with us."

"You're going to tote a three-hundred-pound Russian fanatic cross-country through fifteen kilometers of snow?"

"If we can't get him all the way we'll drop him off someplace."

Price looked at Bolan askance across the link.

Bolan sighed at the lack of faith. "Someplace warm."

"Contact me when you have visual on the airstrip. I will advise from there."

"Copy that. Striker out." Bolan closed up the satellite link and returned to the front room. Spartak and Tetriakov were snarling at each other in rapid-fire Russian. Bolan noted that Tetriakov's eyes were slightly glazed and he was slurring some of his words. James stood to one side with his arms folded and seemed very pleased with himself.

Bolan leaned close. "How'd you get the tea down him?"

"I just told him the truth. I told him Spartak wanted to carve him up, but that we're Americans and we wouldn't allow it. I told him I'm a medic and I knew he must be in a great deal of pain but I didn't have any painkillers to give him. I asked him if he'd prefer tea or whiskey. He couldn't hide his reaction when I mentioned the tea. I think a lot of the Heaven Now adherents are at least psychologically addicted to it."

"You brewed it strong."

"Oh, yes." James smirked. "Yes, I did."

Bolan watched as Spartak picked a fight with Tetriakov. They had done a bang-up job of breaking the big man's stoic silence. "How's it going?"

James leaned back against the wall. "Don't know. It's all in Russian, but our man Misha is three teas to the wind and Spartak has him all riled up. Spartak knows the drill. We just have to hope he can get him to blurt out something useful."

Tetriakov was blurting out a lot and angrily. Bolan hoped it was more than just theories about Spartak's mother's sex life. Tetriakov's words became more slurred and he began to reel in his chair. Spartak gave him several helpful slaps, but Tetriakov's head just rubbernecked. Spartak looked over to Bolan and James and shook his head. Tetriakov was going down for the count. Spartak picked up the notepad next to the phone and began quickly jotting down notes in Cyrillic.

"You get anything?" Bolan asked.

"I am not sure." Spartak continued to write. "Perhaps. Wheat must be separated from chaff."

James shot Bolan a look, but as far as Bolan was concerned Spartak had risked death and dismemberment and joined the winning team. He was in it for the duration. Bolan walked out onto the porch and gazed out into the snowy morning. The wind had blissfully stopped. The world was gleaming white. James followed. "What are you thinking?"

"About how to get the big man out of here."

"What have you got?"

"Don't know. You're the medic. What have you got?"

James considered the logistics of the situation and the intricacies of his patient. "We can splint his leg and do some kind of modified three-legged race, but he'll fight us every step of the way. If we dope him up enough so that he doesn't, he's deadweight. A whole ass-load of Russian deadweight. Either way it's gonna be a long fifteen klicks across this mountain."

Bolan's eye fell on the old-fashioned corral fencing surrounding the property. "How about that?"

"How about what?" Cal asked suspiciously.

"Fence post."

James was appalled. "You want to try and ride him out of town on a rail?"

"No, more like pack him out of here like porters on a safari."

James wasn't pleased.

Spartak walked out onto the porch. "Misha has lapsed into unconsciousness. What is plan?"

James jerked his thumb at Bolan. "The man here wants to string the prisoner across a pole like an elk and Sherpa his ass across the tundra."

Spartak nodded. "I have done this before."

James's eyes narrowed. "I'm sure you have."

Cape Canaveral

"L-MINUS TWO MINUTES and thirty seconds," came through the headset. "Visors down, turn on oxygen."

Akira Tokaido fumbled with his visor and cool air began to circulate in his helmet. He sat 190 feet up in the air. Nice men in the equivalent of white NASA surgeon's scrubs had firmly strapped him into a horizontal chair. He found he was having problems dealing with the fact that he was sitting on top of approximately 2,200,000 pounds of rocket fuel. That was just the boosters. He didn't even want to think about the giant orange marital device-shaped balloon of liquid oxygen and hydrogen that fueled *Endeavor*'s own trio of engines. Tokaido admitted to himself his fears were somewhat skewed.

He wasn't sitting on top of all that energy potential like an Apollo astronaut. He, the shuttle, the solid fuel boosters and the immense external tank were more bundled together like a giant package of bottle rockets.

There had been no time to give the young man any real training. All they could do was give him a forty-eight-hour crash course on what to expect and two rides on the simulator. Strangely enough his biggest fear had been about the acceptance of his peers. He'd been to none of the months of training exercises and practices this team had been through and none of the team building. NASA astronaut training was rigid and ritualized. He had worried that everyone else on the flight would think he was some interloping hack who had licked boots or done something unspeakable to get a tourist visa to space. It was true the *Endeavor* team had looked at him askance on arrival. The jean jacket, ponytail and cowboy boots might have had something to do with it.

Tokaido did not look like astronaut material.

He was aided by the fact that everyone else considered Dr. David Nunn a walking rectum; most were pleased that someone with a sense of humor had replaced him. Within an hour of the initial meet-and-greet everyone had taken to calling him "Kid." What he had done with the computer simulations, and his suggestions about the station's computer architecture and integration issues, had led to multiple job offers from various agencies once he came down.

They had risen early on launch morning and had the traditional prelaunch breakfast. He had been advised to eat hardy. Space cuisine had come a long way from reconstituted powdered orange juice and food tubes, but it was still nothing to write home about. Tokaido had been giddy as the *Endeavor* team had suited up like space gladiators into the orange launch-and-entry suits. When they had done the *Right Stuff* astronaut walkout from the Kennedy Space Center for the press, his heart had threatened to burst out of his chest.

It was all real.

Last minute or not Mrs. Tokaido's boy was a genuine American astronaut.

He was going into space.

"L-minus one minute and counting." The astronaut in mission control who interfaced with the shuttle crew began ticking off the countdown in five-second intervals. "Fifty-five…"

Tokaido's eyes flicked around his surroundings rapidly. The flight deck seemed to be growing smaller. He squeezed his eyes shut and that made it worse. His breakfast was threatening to launch before the shuttle did.

Mission Specialist Gretchen "Sparky" Sparks leaned over as much as she could given the parallel to the ground seating arrangements. Without a space suit on she looked like the long-lost Kennedy cousin who had posed for *Playboy*. She knew more about low Earth orbit engineering than any other human being on the planet. This would be her third trip into space. She was widely rumored to be a member of the very exclusive club of human beings to have had sex in a zero gravity environment. Even in the shapeless orange suit with a goldfish bowl on her head she was total space-hottie material. Astro geeks the world over peered into the starry sky and dreamed of being on a shuttle flight with her. Tokaido had been one of them. Now he was actually doing it. It was a dream come true. To his undying shame he didn't want Gretchen Sparks anymore.

He wanted his mother.

Mission Specialist Sparks gazed at Tokaido sympathetically. "You okay?"

He cleared his throat. "Why do you ask?"

"You're sweating, and they've turned on the coolant tubes in our launch-and-entry suits."

"Oh."

"And you're hyperventilating in an oxygen-rich environment."

"Ah."

Sparks cocked her head solicitously. "Would you like to hold hands?"

"Yes." Tokaido shoved the frog in his throat down. "Yes, I would."

Sparks's hand reached out and closed around his. Tokaido closed his eyes, and this time it brought relief rather than a spinning sensation.

Final countdown began.

Far below the water deluge system rumbled like the world's biggest toilet. Tokaido instantly felt the need to relieve himself, but he had sworn to himself he wouldn't use the mission "diaper" all the astronauts wore.

The main engines throttled up and everything started to vibrate and rumble.

"You have to let go of my hand now."

Tokaido opened his eyes. "What?"

"We're about to pull three g's. You really want to use the armrest."

That seemed to make sense. "Oh."

The rumbling and shaking began in earnest.

"5...4...3..."

"Mr. Tokaido?"

"Yes?"

"You need to let go of my hand."

"Right." Tokaido let go of the woman's hand and slapped his own on the padded armrest.

"Lift off!"

Tokaido had been afraid he might scream. He needn't have worried. They instantly pulled two g's and it was impossible to scream with an elephant stepping on his chest. He managed a gargling noise through his locked jaws.

Mission control was triumphant. *"We have liftoff!"*

Endeavor shook, rattled and roared. God seized Akira Tokaido and flung him like a rock toward the stars. The elephant stepped harder as they pulled their third g, and seven million pounds of thrust accelerated *Endeavor* to the full 17,500 miles per hour they needed to escape Earth's grasp. Tokaido could feel every ounce of that force right behind his seat ramming him heavenward. The shaking and rattling continued unabated, and he was sure they were going to fly apart at any moment. It went on forever, and he was absolutely sure now that something was definitely wrong.

The elephant hopped off his chest.

The shake, rattle and roar died away and everything was suddenly very quiet except for the four men up front in the cockpit congratulating one another. Tokaido jumped as *Endeavor* rang like a bell. He had been in the simulator twice. That was the separation of the fuel tank. The giant orange external tank was empty, and it was beginning its long fall back to Earth. Tokaido twitched as reaction control jets began firing like cannons and *Endeavor* began making initial alignments needed to meet the International Space Station. He heaved a sigh.

Captain Steven "Special Delivery" Davis spoke through the mikes. "You can raise your visors and turn off oxygen."

Tokaido managed that without too much trouble. He was on the back passenger deck. There was very little for him to see and absolutely nothing for him to do.

"Hey, kid."

Tokaido looked over at Gretchen Sparks. "Yeah?"

"You want to see something neat?"

"Um…yeah."

"Grab your pen."

"What?"

Sparks sighed tolerantly. "On your kneeboard. Grab your pen."

All of their suits had a small kneeboard with a pen and pencil. Tokaido drew forth his gleaming NASA space pen. It had its own pressurized ink cartridge and could write in zero gravity and on nearly any surface. "Okay."

Sparks grinned. "Let go of it."

"What?"

"Let go of it."

He let go of his pen. The pen floated a foot in front of his face. Tokaido's heart surged in his chest for the second time that day. "Yay!"

Sparks nodded knowingly. "Welcome to space, Mr. Tokaido."

The computer hacker was as giddy as a schoolboy. "Yay!"

Davis spoke across the intercom. He didn't need to look behind him to know what was going on. "Mission specialists will please secure all objects until orbit is established."

"Oh, sorry." Tokaido retrieved his pen and slid it back in place on his knee.

"Newbies," the captain muttered, but he didn't sound displeased. For people like Captain Davis and Specialist Sparks, space was their playground and the shuttle one of their favorite toys. They liked showing it all off.

"When we get to the station I'll show you some cool tricks," Sparks said.

Tokaido's mind blurred. "Thanks."

"Keep your mind out of the gutter, Mr. Tokaido," Sparks suggested.

Tokaido blushed to the roots of his hair. "Um…I will."

CHAPTER TWENTY-ONE

Salvador, Brazil

Bolan emerged from the Phenom 300 Executive jet. As private jets went the little twin-engined Brazilian was a sweet ride. More importantly it had the juice to make Santiago, Chile, to Salvador, Brazil, in one hop. Probably the most important factor was that the seats were plush and reclined all the way. Bolan and his team had spent most of the flight sleeping except for the fifteen minutes it had taken to demolish every prepackaged corporate snack in the refreshment center. Bolan stopped on the steps and let the ocean breeze hit him. It was winter in Bahia, which meant that by Brazilian standards it was currently a frigid eighty-six degrees. Bolan took a moment to savor the tropical sun. After the death march across Bariloche he had been fairly sure he would never be warm again.

Bolan stepped down to make room as James and Spartak manhandled the comatose Misha Tetriakov out of the cabin and propped him up on the bottom step. Jack Grimaldi stepped out of the cabin and stretched expansively. He had been waiting for them on the tarmac in Santiago. The pilot patted the side of the Phenom happily. Grimaldi liked Brazilian jets. He liked Brazilian beer. He liked Brazilian girls. He liked the province of Bahia in particular. Any mission to Brazil was a trip on a gravy train with biscuit wheels as far as he was concerned.

They all turned as an ancient black Ford Falcon pulled up to the private plane hangar. A black man as tall and dark as James but five times as wide emerged. His head was moon-faced with fat but his broad brow, cheekbones and nose along with his short, combed-back spiky dreadlocks gave him a lionlike demeanor. Despite his obesity the man radiated power. He rumbled forward like a sumo wrestler in khakis, a 4XL Hawaiian shirt and flip-flops and held out a hand like a catcher's mitt. "Luisao Love."

Bolan's hand was engulfed. He had read the man's résumé. His mother was American from Harlem and his father Brazilian. He'd spent about half of his life in each country. Right around the invasion of Kuwait he had been a United States Marine. After being tapped by the CIA the last ten years of his life were either vague or deliberately redacted. "Cooper." Bolan nodded back at his team. "Jack, Cal, Spartak."

"Nice to meet you." The CIA's man in Salvador grinned at Tetriakov as he swayed on the jet's lowest step. "And this one?"

"You read the briefing we sent you?"

"Yeah, and you know? My girlfriend listens to Heaven Now inspirational tapes." Love shook his head sadly. "I have to say I find this all deeply disturbing."

"We've gotten about all we can out of this guy, but they have an asset of ours. It may come down to a trade."

"Trade? I got the impression this was going to be a gunfight."

"Oh, it's going to be a door-kicking situation, but we didn't know what else to do with him. A trade is plan Z, and I don't think the bad guys will go for it."

"Well, I'm glad to hear that. Trades always turn into ambushes and gunfights, and the tradees always get perforated. Call me old school, but I prefer a good old-fashioned rescue where we start the gunfight and we finish the gunfight."

"You're a man after mine own heart, Mr. Love."

"Call me Lou." Love rolled around to the back of his car and popped the trunk. "It was short notice. What do you think?"

The weapons were right out of a Sean Connery-era Bond film. They were a 1960s copy of a 1940s Danish Madsen submachine gun. The weapons were strangely long, flat and angular. Most of their finish was missing. Their most distinguishing feature were the equally antique silencers wrapped in canvas mounted on the barrels. Bolan hefted one and noted the gaping muzzle. "A forty-five?"

"Colt forty-fives come fat and subsonic, right out of the box, baby!" Luisao shrugged modestly. "Just like me."

Bolan liked the big man already. Love began handing out Brazilian .45-caliber pistols like party favors and the team tucked them away. "Take it all out." The team took out the weapons, ammo and bags of gear as Love heaved the huge Russian over his shoulder like a sack of potatoes and tossed him in the trunk. He slammed the lid happily. "You know, you just aren't any kind of spook in South America until you've tossed someone bound and gagged into the back of a Ford Falcon." The big man sighed with satisfaction. "I finally got my street cred."

They piled into the car and drove at reckless speed through the private plane hangars. They pulled onto the freeway and shot like an arrow straight for the coast. They turned north up the coast road for about half an hour before Love pulled up to a construction site. Several beachside condos were going up. He waved at the white sand and blue water. "Welcome to my office."

Bolan stepped out and gazed out over the ocean. "Nice."

"My uncle owns a construction business. We're all alone here. C'mon." They unloaded Misha and walked in past bare walls and open electrical outlets to a patio. Love fired up a gas-fueled portable barbecue and began pulling foot-long hot dogs and wine-bottle-sized Xingu black beers out of a cooler. He seared the dogs up like a pro and then piled them precipitously high with a relish made of corn, tomatoes, peas, black and green olives and chopped eggs. It was nothing short of spectacular. But that described Brazilian food in general and the food of Bahia in particular. Bolan wolfed his food and nodded for more. "You got a bead on Gavriil's whereabouts?"

"Oh, yeah." Love turned a dog and pointed his tongs across the little bay. "He's right over there."

Bolan looked across the water. The beach was pristine, but through the greenery the Executioner could see the windows and balconies of mansion-sized houses peering out tastefully through the tropical hardwoods. A small dock held a few small boats. "Gated community?"

"Oh, yeah."

Bolan calculated. Kidnapping wasn't quite the national pastime in Brazil as in some parts of Latin America, but crime was bad. The guards would at the very least be ex-cops and soldiers, and being a pocket of wealth police response time would be fast. "What kind of security is he keeping close?"

"The man has protection. I used some connections among the cleaning ladies and hired help. Gavi's got Russians as big as me and nowhere near as friendly."

"How many?"

"From the outside looking in, at least six, and those are just the ones visible from the front and the back. We better count on more inside. Word is Apollyon's no slouch and God only knows what his brother Gavi is capable of. They say the man walks on coals and lays on nails and shit."

Bolan had dealt with mystics run amok before. They died like everyone else, but it often took a lot more effort. "What's security like on the beach?"

"None to speak of, but it's considered private water. Shore patrol drives by a couple of times a night. They roust out boats and beachgoers that aren't supposed to be there. For the past twenty-four hours it's been double and tripled up. I doubt we can sneak a boat past."

"All right." Bolan's plan solidified. "Jack is going to park a float plane a few klicks offshore. We swim in from here and make our assault." He turned to Love. "Can you get us something amphibious?"

"There's a lot of them around." Love handed Bolan the tongs. "Jack, you're with me. We'll drop Misha off with nice folks I know and then go shop for a plane. I leave you with it and then go accessory shopping for tonight's swim."

Grimaldi hopped up. "Let's go kick some tires."

Bolan applied two more dogs to buns and went heavy on the relish and served up seconds to James and himself. Spartak glanced around. "So what do we do while we wait?"

Bolan had taken note of several hammocks strung between some of the open support beams where the construction workers most likely took their siestas. "I suggest we take a nap."

BOLAN AND HIS TEAM went down to the beach at 4:00 a.m. Love had gone to the scuba shop. They each had swim fins and a kickboard to support their plastic-bagged weapons and gear. The thin, formfitting warm-water skin-suits in black and contrasting neons made Bolan and James look like superheroes. Spartak looked like a supervillain. Luisao Love looked like a cross between an elephant seal and a blood pudding.

With racing stripes.

"Hey." Grimaldi spoke across the tactical link. He was already somewhere out on the waters in an old Grumman Widgeon amphibious plane. "You guys want to see something cool?"

"Um…" Bolan considered just what that might entail at this particular juncture of the mission. "Sure."

"Look straight up. Two o'clock. Near the Southern Cross."

Bolan looked up into the starry night over Brazil. It took a second and then he noticed. One of the stars was moving.

"You see that?" Grimaldi asked.

Bolan found himself smiling up into the night.

James echoed his sentiments. "You're kidding."

Grimaldi was obviously delighted with himself. "Nope. I checked the ISS tracking Web site while I was waiting. That's Akira at one hundred and eighty miles up at seventeen thousand miles per hour."

"It is something," Spartak admitted.

Love looked back and forth between the warriors on the beach. "What are you guys talking about?"

Bolan pointed upward and drew a line tracking the ISS's path. "You see that?"

Love craned his goggled, leonine head toward the stars. "Is that a satellite?"

"No, it's the International Space Station."

"Oh?"

"Yeah, we have a friend up there."

"Really."

"Yeah."

Love spent a few moments contemplating this. "That's pretty cool."

"Yeah," Bolan admitted. They watched the point of light move swiftly across the sky until it disappeared over the Atlantic horizon. Three very dangerous men returned to the matter at hand, and that was Dominico's rescue or his revenge. They strapped on their fins, tied their war loads down on their boards and entered the Atlantic. It was a fine night for a swim. It was about a three-thousand-yard swim, and Bolan had been a bit worried about Love but for all his bulk he was a strong swimmer.

"Boat," James called out softly.

The beam of a searchlight broke out between themselves and the shore, and the putter of a patrol boat became audible. The boat bisected their path, but it was hundreds of yards away, and its searchlight was sweeping the beach rather than the sea. They broke the surface of the dark water as it passed and began kicking once more toward shore. It wasn't long before Bolan and his team emerged from the surf. Bolan took his board and bag and shed his fins above the waterline. His bag held a life vest in case they found Dominico in no condition to swim. The men unwrapped their weapons and strapped web gear over their skin-suits. Bolan clicked his tactical as he kicked off his fins. "Jack, comeback."

"I read you, Sarge."

"We're on the beach. We're moving in on target."

"Copy that. Holding position."

Bolan and his team padded silently up the sand. The community was gated, but it was open to the private beach. They mounted the series of low stone steps that wound up into low hills the community was built upon. The gates that separated the paths to individual houses were more ornamental than functional. The walls and gates of the individual houses themselves were quite substantial, and Gavi had a pair of very large men with rifles standing outside his.

"Spartak, you know those two?"

"Yes," the Russian replied. "Boris and Vytel. Apollyon's men."

Boris and Vytel were talking casually, but their weapons

were in hand and their eyes were constantly scanning. They seemed to be on a fairly high state of alert. It wasn't unreasonable, but there was something here Bolan didn't like. Boris suddenly laughed at something Vytel said. "Spartak, you catch that?"

"*Da*," Spartak said. "Vytel say the Mexican is fucked."

That didn't sound good, but there was some room in the statement for Dominico to still be among the living. "You were head of security."

"This is so." Spartak agreed.

"You have either one of those guys phone numbers?"

Amusement crept into Spartak's voice. "*Da,* what would you like me to say?"

"Call laughing boy. Offer him a million to let us know where Memo is. Wait until we're close."

"I see."

Bolan, James and Love crept uphill through the underbrush into striking range of the two Russians. Boris reached into his pocket as his phone rang. Bolan waited for the magic moment when Boris's face went blank, and Vytel turned to ask him what was going on. The team burst out of the undergrowth. Spartak's assessment that Apollyon's personal guards were goons rather than soldiers proved true. Boris and Vytel went wide-eyed and froze for a fatal moment. Love put both hands into Boris's chest and bounced him off the compound wall with brutal force. James kicked high and Bolan low. Vytel failed to block either blow, and he dropped as his brain and his scrotum temporarily went haywire. Bolan turned his attention to Boris because he wasn't vomiting.

Bolan dropped to one knee beside Boris. "Offer still stands," he said in Russian. "A million bucks. Where's Memo?"

"Wishing he were dead," the Russian gritted.

Bolan narrowed his eyes. True believers. "Lou?"

Love rolled the Russian over and gagged and zip-tied him. James had finished up Vytel and taken his remote for the gate. "Front or back?"

Bolan looked at Love, who was eyeing the wall. It had been a while since the big man had run the obstacle course at Paris Island. "Uhh…"

"Cal and I will insert over the wall in back. We'll let you two know when we're in."

Love was visibly relieved as James handed him the remote. "Right."

Bolan and James moved beneath the trees and circled toward the back of the house. The building was nestled against the hill so the backyard was really the side. They vaulted atop the wall and paused to observe the grounds. They were lit with low garden lights and the lights were on in the swimming pool. The lights were on in the kitchen and at least two armed men were inside. The living room was lit but other than that the windows were all dark. "Don't like it," James said.

"Me, neither."

"Too easy."

"Way too easy. Let's do it." Bolan dropped from the wall to crouch in the shadows between two flowering bushes. James dropped down one slot over. Bolan spoke across the tactical. "We're in. Hold positions."

The rest of the team came back in the affirmative.

Bolan took one step out of the shrubs and the side yard went lunar glare. Passive motion sensors were becoming the bane of Bolan's life. All hell broke loose.

"Nebesa Sejchas!" a dozen men roared as they spilled out of the mansion, spraying the night with automatic rifles.

"Jesus, these guys have a war cry," James muttered. The two warriors raised their weapons and took out the floodlights in short bursts. It wouldn't be enough. Between the lawn and garden lights, the pool and the moon and stars above, there was enough light to fight by. The good news was the Brazilians were confirmed barbecue hounds, and the mansion had a Stonehenge-size pit made of brick. Bolan and James broke for it, firing as they went. He took one Heaven Now gunner on the fly and Bolan took another. They baseball-slid behind cover and brick chips flew as the enemy spied them and poured in fire.

"Lou! Spartak! I need a flank attack on the east side!"

"Inbound!"

"I think they're going to charge us," Bolan opined as the Russians roared their battle cry again.

"No shit," James said. "You take right, I take left?"

"Roger." Bolan dropped prone and rolled to the right corner of the barbecue pit while Cal rolled left. "Now!"

The two men stuck their heads and shoulders around the corner as the eight Russians charged them. Bolan's weapon clicked and coughed in rapid-fire. Russians fell. Over their shouts and their automatic weapons they were unaware of Spartak and Love reaping them from the side. The charge was sliced apart before it got fifteen feet from the back porch. Bolan slammed in a fresh magazine and rose up into a run. "Spartak, with us! Lou, fade back! Hold the front of the house!"

"Copy that!" Love pulled a fade for the front. Men fired rifles from the back doors and windows, but Bolan was wearing night vision and their muzzle flashes lit them like strobes. Bolan and his team were swiftly moving shadows whose weapons made almost no noise and less light. Two of the three men who had stayed back on the porch to provide covering fire fell face-first. The third threw down his weapon and screamed in Spanish. *"¡Me entrego! Me entrego!"*

Bolan pointed the muzzle of his suppressor in the man's face. "You surrendering, Schweinsteiger?"

The man flinched from the smoking muzzle. "*Sí!* Yes."

"Where's Memo?"

Schweinsteiger shook. "I don't know!"

Bolan pushed the suppressor against his face and let him smell the brimstone. "What does that mean?"

"He's not here! I swear, amigo! He's not here!"

"Gavriil?"

"Not here!"

"How about Apollyon?"

"Where's Apollyon?"

Schweinsteiger shivered and sniveled and couldn't look up.

Bolan toppled the man onto his back and curled his finger around the trigger. "If you want to live, tell me."

"He's inside."

"How many men with him?"

"Two…he has two."

James spit. "Don't like it."

"Me, neither."

"Too easy."

"Way too easy. Spartak, what's he planning?"

"Apollyon?" Spartak grunted. "Apollyon is no planner. If there is plan, it is Gavriil's, and he is a deep one."

"He saw our attack." Bolan eyed the angles of the house. He doubted he'd seen Love. "Lou, stay frosty and out of sight. Memo's not in the house. They're up to something. Apollyon may be coming your way."

"Copy that."

Bolan shot out the chandelier in the vast living room, and it fell in a rain of glass and sparks. Two men hurtled forward shouting and firing from the hallway. *"Nebesa—"*

Bolan, James and Spartak cut them down. Bolan heard running footfalls on the hardwood floor and heading toward the front. "Cal, Spartak, sweep the house." Bolan moved in pursuit. "Lou, one coming right at you. I'm right behind. Take him alive if you can."

Love whispered. "Oh, I see him. I got him." Bolan heard the front door fling open and then furniture and glass broke. Love's voice boomed through the house. "Got you! I got you, motherfucker! I—" A tremendous crash shook the walls. Bolan heard the muted clicks and bullet smacks as Love fired.

"Lou!" Bolan shouted as he skidded to a halt in the hall. Love was flat on his back in the foyer sucking wind with his weapon across his chest. His night-vision goggles were askew, and blood was pouring down around them from his split forehead. "You all right?"

"Goddamn, overcompensating, muscle-bound little midget…tossed me on my head." Love heaved his massive frame to his feet and swayed uncertainly. "Sorry, man, he got past me."

"Which way?"

"He's heading down…" Love sagged to one knee. "To the water."

"Cal! Lou's hurt! He isn't swimming anywhere. You and Spartak need to get him and get him down to the beach ASAP."

"Copy that!"

"Jack! We're out of here! No time to swim out. I need you to bring the plane right up to the sand!"

"Roger that!" Grimaldi replied. "ETA five minutes!"

Bolan suddenly stopped and picked up a black box. It had a retractable antenna and a pair of switches. "This isn't yours?"

"What? No. He must've dropped it when he threw me. I managed to get off a burst from the floor. Must've took off without it."

Bolan loped out of the compound. He wanted a talk with

that overcompensating, muscle-bound little midget. The soldier stretched out his legs and flew down the stone path scanning from side to side. He stopped when he reached the sand. Bolan scanned the footprints his team had left. An extra pair dug into the sand going the wrong way and with the length and depth of a man who was running. At a hundred paces the footprints broke right and circled back for the tree line.

Bolan spun as Apollyon exploded out of the underbrush.

The Executioner could have given him a point-blank burst, but he needed him alive. He swung his submachine gun at the Russian's head and lost it as Apollyon hit him in a flying tackle. Getting a foot beneath him, he levered himself up. Bolan swung a knife-hand blow at his adversary, but the Russian's arms were already up in a guard. Bolan pumped a jab at his face that Apollyon easily avoided, and the two men locked up collar and elbow.

Apollyon got beneath Bolan's guard and things went south directly. The Russian maneuvered himself up and behind the soldier with breathtaking ease, and suddenly Bolan felt the man's massively pumped-up arms sliding around his neck into a chokehold. He dropped to one knee and went for the shoulder throw but tugged to no effect as the Russian set himself. Apollyon's arms writhed around Bolan's head like pythons. The soldier let his head be pushed forward because it gave him a little room. Then he jerked his thumb straight back over his shoulder. Apollyon screamed as his adversary's thumb rammed into his eye.

Bolan reached back a little farther and found Apollyon's ear. A second scream ripped out of the Russian as the Executioner vised it between his thumb and forefinger and ripped it off with a twist. He violently shrugged out of Apollyon's suddenly enfeebled embrace, rose and rammed his elbow once, twice, three times into his opponent's face. Cheek and orbital bones cracked. The Russian staggered back moaning and holding his face in one hand and holding the other palsied hand before him.

Bolan grabbed the offered hand and bent back Apollyon's thumb until it broke. Apollyon keened and snatched back his maimed hand against his chest. This rather conveniently exposed his left collarbone and Bolan took the opportunity to swing his fist down upon it like a hammer. The long, thin bone snapped like a stick.

Apollyon fell to his knees and collapsed with a whimper.

Grimaldi and his twin-engine amphibious plane came roaring up to the beach spewing spray. Bolan looked back to see James and Spartak making a heavy going of it through the sand with Love sagging between them. Spartak gaped in amazement at the wrecked Arkhangelov moaning in the sand and then at Bolan. "You took Apollyon? With your hands?"

Bolan picked up his submachine gun and dusted the sand off of it. "I wanted him alive."

The seaplane crunched to a halt in the sand, and a moment later the Stony Man pilot flung open the door to the passenger compartment. Wedging a semiconscious Love into the cabin took James and Spartak far longer than Bolan had hoped. The Executioner gathered up their gear from the beach and watched the flashes of police lights speeding up the coastal highway. Getting Apollyon aboard was far easier, and neither Spartak nor James were particularly gentle about it.

Bolan waded out into the water and slung their equipment into the cabin and then joined Spartak and James in pushing the plane back out into the surf and turning it around. As mission leader, Bolan was the last man in as Grimaldi thrust his throttles forward. The twin two-hundred-horsepower engines roared as the ace pilot took them out to sea and they howled as the plane tried to take off. The Widgeon bounced and skidded across the surface. "Jack! Get us up!"

Grimaldi shouted over the straining engines. "The specs on this bird are one pilot and five passengers!"

"Yeah?" Bolan scanned the cabin. They were in spec. "And?"

"Yeah, and we got some very big passengers and this is a very old airplane!"

Spartak nudged Apollyon roughly. "I know a way we can dump one hundred and ten kilos right now!"

It was tempting. "Lose the guns! Lose the gear! Lose everything!"

The cabin howled and wind and water sprayed inside as James opened the door and people began passing him their submachine guns, loaded magazines and knives. It all went out the hatch and into the drink. The cooler, fins, kickboards and then watches and tactical links followed them. It was about to come down to stripping naked and haircuts when the struggling seaplane finally shook off the Atlantic's grasp and lumbered into the air. James slammed the door shut.

Grimaldi shook his head at his instruments. "We're still overloaded. We aren't going anywhere far or fast this loaded down! We need an alternate landing zone and soon!"

"Just head north for a bit. Cal, how's Lou?"

James lifted Love's eyelids and peered into them. "The bigger they come the harder they fall, and Apollyon inverted our man headfirst and hard. He definitely has a concussion."

"Can you wake him up?"

"I am awake, goddamn it!" Love growled and batted James's hands aside. "Jack, do what Coop said. Go north up the coast for now." He sagged back into his seat from the effort and surrendered to James's ministrations. "I'll tell you when to turn left."

Grimaldi aimed the nose of the struggling plane north while James applied field dressings to Love and Apollyon.

Bolan glanced back at their prisoner. They had yet to interrogate him, but Bolan already knew some of the answers. The mansion had been a trap. The Heaven Now faithful had laid down their lives to draw them in, and then Apollyon was going to bolt and blow them sky-high. If Dominico was still alive, he was in a world of hurt and most likely on his way to Russia.

CHAPTER TWENTY-TWO

Harmony Module, International Space Station

Tokaido hacked into the ISS mainframe. Actually hacking was a misnomer. He was simply patching in. There was no need to hide his movements. It had taken him all of ten minutes of subtle reconnaissance to learn that his three fellow space farers knew very little about computers. The outgoing American commander turned out to be a closet gamer, and Tokaido's first task as an International Space Station mission specialist was to resolve issues his laptop was having with the latest World of Warcraft patch.

After that he had the run of the ship.

Harmony module was the utility hub of the station and acted as the main power conduit to the rest of the station. It was a central connecting point for several other station components, and the Canadian robotic arm could be operated out of it. Most importantly, it contained racks for busing electronic data. From here he could clandestinely plug into any computer system he wanted. Not that much clandestine behavior was required. He literally was a NASA mission specialist and this was his job. Nothing on the ISS was considered top secret. There was nothing that needed breaking into. He could patch into anything he wanted. If he felt the need he could cover his tracks with childlike ease.

Tokaido's main problem with the mission was the human side of the equation. He did most of his hacking from the security of his cybernetic suite at the Farm. Now he was officially undercover. He was finding out very quickly that he wasn't good at sneaking around or lying to people. He felt like everyone could see through him and knew he was up to something. He had spent most of the night sweating, and his stomach turned as he worked on the ISS computer suite's integration issues, all the while trying to work up the nerve to wait until no one else was in Harmony module and access the biolab's computer.

There wasn't much to access. Tokaido's Russian translation software digested the lab files and spit them back out in English. There were no biohazard flags or tags on any of the files in the computer and no warning stickers in the lab itself. A second, more sophisticated application in the hacker's laptop began crunching the data in the biolab files in both English and Russian and looking for hidden codes. Tokaido had designed the decryption software himself and he frowned as it came up empty. Dr. Treschev appeared to be experimenting on molds and yeasts, specifically for the development of renewable sources of food for extended space flights and Mars and lunar bases. Tokaido snorted to himself. Dr. Treschev was making space Vegemite. In fact earlier in the day Treschev had offered him a sandwich made with a brown goolike spread right out of one of his petri dishes.

Tokaido had politely declined.

He found nothing of any relevance to his mission in the lab data. That of itself didn't mean anything. If Striker was right and Treschev was up to no good, then he was most likely keeping two sets of books, and just like Tokaido knew more about computers than the rest of the crew put together, no one besides Treschev could tell one tube of brown goo from another and the doctor had a minifridge full of them. Tokaido began covering his tracks so that Treschev wouldn't see that he had examined his files. He was just going to have to access Treschev's laptop and—

"What are you doing?"

The young hacker jumped right out of his skin.

He'd been caught red-handed. Tokaido panicked and grabbed for the MP3 player stun gun around his neck and promptly lost contact with his laptop and the mainframe panel he'd been working with. He shot out his spare hand for the wall of the module and came up six inches short. Like most ISS modules, Harmony was shaped like a beer can on the outside with a uniform cubelike interior. Tokaido oozed backward a few more inches at snail-like speed to find himself in the exact epicenter of the module. There was absolutely nothing to push off from.

Gretchen Sparks shook her head from the hatchway. "A little jumpy this morning, Mr. Tokaido?"

The Stony Man cyberexpert windmilled his arms and kicked his legs and absolutely nothing happened. "I'm—" he tried the breaststroke, then furiously tried the backstroke "—resolving integration issues!"

"You do seem to have some issues at the moment."

Tokaido finally stopped struggling and hung weightless in the middle of the module. In his few outings into the field he had been tied up and subjected to chemical interrogation, however this was without doubt the most profoundly helpless moment of his life. "Don't sneak up on a guy like that!"

Sparks gazed with highly suspect sympathy at his predicament. "You can't swim in space, kid."

Tokaido glanced about helplessly. He was pretty much

exactly equidistant from all four sides of the module. The hatch at either end might as well have been miles away. "So, what do I do?"

"Well, I could give you a push...."

Tokaido saw no mercy in the woman's big brown eyes. "You're going to make me work for this, aren't you?"

"In space there are certain survival skills you just have to master."

She was going to make him work for it. "So, what do I do?"

"Well, you could just hang there. The environmental and life support system vents oxygen into the modules. That creates air currents. Sooner or later you'll drift into contact with something."

Tokaido didn't like the sound of that. "Sooner or later?"

"Yup."

"Or...?" he asked hopefully.

"Or there's Newton's third law of motion," Sparks suggested.

Tokaido mentally ground gears. It had been a few years since high school physics. Suddenly the Cowboy's lecture on firing the stun gun in zero gravity leaped to mind. "For every action there is an equal and opposite reaction!"

"That's my little mission specialist!" Sparks announced proudly. She raised an eyebrow. "Now, how will you apply it?"

"Uhh..." Tokaido reached for his stun gun and stopped. Firing it would require a whole lot of explanation, and he didn't want to throw it against the wall and break it. "I've got it!" His newest, proudest possession was his NASA mission cap. He pulled it off his head and with a snap of his wrist tossed it at Sparks, who caught it. The young man wafted diagonally a few inches to his left and came back in contact with the control panel he had been hacking into.

"Mr. Tokaido." Sparks spun his hat back at him. "You get an A."

He flushed with pride as he caught it.

"So what are you working on?"

Tokaido flushed even redder and began stuttering. "Uhh, I'm integrating." He hoped Sparks would just chalk it up to embarrassment and a puppy-love-type space-crush.

She would only be half-wrong.

Aracaju, Brazil

"I'm setting up the trade for Moscow," Bolan said.

"Moscow?" Kurtzman shook his head. "You don't want to go back to Moscow right about now."

Bolan and his team sat in a beachside cottage and took a video conference with Kurtzman. Bolan had no desire whatsoever to go back to Moscow. He and his team were exhausted. Heaven Now had circulated the descriptions they had of Bolan, James and Spartak, and they were individuals of interest in the investigation of the shootout in Salvador. They had limped north to Aracaju in their overloaded amphibian to where Love had friends. More importantly they had a private lagoon with a boat shed that could hide the plane. Love was at the local hospital. Bolan sighed. It seemed to be a rule this mission that if you befriended Bolan you got a concussion, or shot or both. Spartak had contacted the Moscow Heaven Now center and they had allowed Apollyon to leave a quick message that he and Misha were alive and unharmed.

Bolan considered his bargaining chips. Misha was going to need a new knee and his samba days were over. The biggest problem was that he was still back in Bahia and in a very bad mood. Smuggling him from Brazil to Moscow would be a logistical nightmare. Apollyon's eye was unsalvageable, and no one had bothered to retrieve his ear from the beach. His shattered shoulder was bound to his chest with a bandanna. Like a lot of violent bullies given power over those around them, once Bolan had broken him down physically, Apollyon's mental and moral deterioration soon followed. The youngest Arkhangelov swung in bipolar fashion between making wild threats and sniveling for mercy and more painkillers.

Bolan didn't want to speculate on what kind of shape Dominico might be in at the moment.

"You're right. I'm not going to Moscow. What are the dispositions of Able and Phoenix?"

"Phoenix is deployed. Able is standing down at the moment. Carl and Pol are here right now."

"I need them to collect Misha and Apollyon and take them to Moscow. They need to set up the trade. Take a picture of them with a recognizable landmark in the background so Gavriil knows we're for real."

"But you're not bargaining for real."

"Big Lou said it himself two days ago. Trades almost always go bad, and the tradees usually end up dead. We're going to assault."

"That's nice. Assault what? And where?"

"Sos'va, or actually the farm that the Arkhangelovs keep outside of it. According to Apollyon, that's where they grew up, and that's where Gavriil would have gone if he wanted to lie low."

"A farm? In…" Kurtzman pulled up a map on his computer and gazed upon the Russian province of Tyumen. "Mack, that's on the other side of the Urals!"

"Well, according to Apollyon, they've made improvements on the old place. Swimming pool, airstrip, reprogramming cabins in the woods, interrogation rooms in the cellar complex, the whole bit. Gavi didn't stint on anything."

"Mack, there's nothing there. Whatever is there *is* mountains. Whatever isn't mountains is forests, and whatever isn't forest is swampland. We're talking severe isolation and slim-to-nonexistent assets for you to call upon."

"I know."

"But you want to know what Tyumen does have? Oil. The province is the nexus of the Russian oil and natural gas industries. The capital city of Tyumen is the second richest city in Russia behind Moscow. That means *Mafiya*, Mack. If Gavriil is feeling lost and lonely out there, he can probably call on a sizeable army if he wants to, and no one is going to know the difference or do anything about it."

"I'm sure he can," Bolan said. "That's why I need to divert his attention toward Moscow."

"Okay. How are we going to do this again?"

"I'd prefer to infiltrate down out the Urals, but I don't think we have time. Gavriil has an airstrip. We'll need a plane. Gavriil will most likely have lookouts at the nearest airports and railheads. I suggest we fly out of Vorkuta or Yarega on the western side of the Urals. Both cities have international airports and both are about four hundred miles equidistant from the target."

"Mack, just getting you there and getting you a plane is going to be a monumental task. What are you going to do for equipment?"

"Like you said. There's a lot of money up there and it's very rough country. The roads are awful. Most people and freight are moved by private planes and there are lots of airstrips. Even Gavriil has one. A plane shouldn't be too hard to come by. Don't bother trying to get us a war load from the States or Europe. Spartak will buy for us locally on the black market. I also need satellite images of the Arkhangelov farm and recon on activity and force estimates up until the time we take off."

"Satellite imaging will probably be the easiest part of the

bargain," Kurtzman said. "I'll get on that and get Barb on your itinerary."

"How are the girls doing?" Bolan asked.

"The CIA medic cleared Najelli to move forty-eight hours ago. They smuggled her to Buenos Aires and sent her stateside. She's at the naval hospital in San Diego and they say she's recovering nicely. Rider is staying with her. They both have tickets to Hawaii as soon as Najelli is ambulatory. They've been asking about any word of Memo, and you."

"What about me?" James asked.

"You?" Kurtzman shrugged. "Not so much."

James sighed heavily.

Spartak shrugged philosophically. "They did not ask of me, either."

"Actually Rider sends along her thanks. She wants to thank you in person. She said she never would have had the strength to get out if she didn't know you were with her."

Spartak leaned back in the couch and gave one of his rare smiles. "In person?"

James opened another beer. "Left out in the cold once again."

CHAPTER TWENTY-THREE

Tol'ka Revolyutsii Aerodrome

"You're kidding." Calvin James wasn't happy. There was very little revolutionary about Tol'ka Aerodrome. It had taken them forty-eight hours to reach it by private plane, helicopter, aircraft carrier, military transport and finally Russia's Aeroflot airline. The tower was made of Lincoln Logs. Part of the airstrip had been chopped right out of the forest. The hangar looked suspiciously like a circus tent. Grimaldi took it all in with his characteristic good humor and was off examining planes. He'd flown in and out of far worse airfields, and he gave Bolan the thumbs-up. James didn't care much about the airfield. That was Grimaldi's concern. The Phoenix Force commando was staring at the equipment Spartak had acquired sight unseen from some shady source in the closest town of Sosnogorsk. "How much did we pay for this?"

"You do not wish to know," Spartak said.

Bolan took an SKS carbine from the crate in the back of the truck. It was old school, blue steel and wood rather than the black metal and plastic of modern weapons. It fed from stripper clips shoved down from the top rather than magazines from the bottom and held only ten rounds. The folding bayonet was permanently attached. The SKS had first been adopted by the Soviet Union in 1949. They had finally phased them out of their second line and noncombatant units in the 1980s, but the Russians never threw anything away. They had made millions of the weapons and untold thousands were still in storage in bases and depots throughout the Russias. Bolan racked back the bolt and held the action up so that sunlight poured down the barrel. "The bore looks all right."

"Dude." James was still disgusted. "This stuff is 'Saving Private Ivan' issue. You want to storm Heaven Now farm with this crap?"

Bolan didn't, but he was going to. "We've worked with less."

James gave Bolan a "How do I get transferred out of this chicken-shit outfit?" look and set about choosing a weapon.

Spartak checked his own weapon with a satisfied grunt. "SKS is solid kit. We have one hundred rounds for each weapon." He snapped out the folding bayonet and frowned at the edge. "In Moscow, or Tyumen, I could get you anything you want. Here in countryside you must settle for what is pilfered from local military bases."

"Oh, for God's sake." James reached into a crate and held up an equally ancient-looking Tokarev pistol that still had Cosmoline on it from storage. "Tell me we have RPGs."

"No. No RPG, but I acquired these." Spartak pulled off the towels covering a pair of canvas pails. They were loaded to the brim with an assortment of obsolete Russian offensive, defensive, antiarmor and incendiary hand grenades.

James reserved comment, but he did pull out a set of well-worn Russian web gear and began stuffing the pouches with ordnance. Bolan pawed through some Afghanistan-war-era titanium and fiberglass body armor. "We don't have any night vision?"

"Hard to find east of Urals," Spartak said.

"Daylight raid." James heaved a mighty sigh. "This gets better and better."

"When did you turn into such a doubting Calvin?" Bolan asked.

"Oh, I'm no doubting Calvin," James replied. "It's just that so much of this shit is turning into a joke I figured you needed a straight man." He turned his straight-man gaze on the three executive jets parked beneath the tent. "And how are we going to get a jet in there undetected?" he asked. "And you know how hard it is to jump out of an executive jet? The opportunity to get splattered through an intake is spectacular."

"Right!" Grimaldi appeared out of nowhere and lit a Cuban cigar. "And right again!" He pointed his cigar at a hoop of corrugated iron that passed for a hangar. "And that is why *that* is our ride."

Everyone looked over at their ride. It was big, had one giant four-bladed propeller on its nose and two sets of wings. James blinked at the ancient-looking aircraft. "It's biplane."

"It's an Antonov An-2," Grimaldi agreed.

"You know ever since that Grumman Widget—"

"Widgeon," Grimaldi corrected.

"Ever since that Grumman *whatever,* we've had sucky rides."

The ace pilot looked hurt. "The An-2 is the biggest and bestest single-engine biplane ever built, and you, my friend, will refer to her, and only with the deepest respect, as *Annushka*."

Spartak nodded at the *Annushka*. It was the name that Russian soldiers and airmen had given the An-2 for half a century and with fondness. "It is good plane."

Bolan agreed. He'd jumped out of an An-2 before. "Spartak, you've been to this place?"

"Only once. Farm is big, and is working farm. Wheat, cows, horses. Though people who work farm come from village down the road."

"What kind of resistance are we looking at?"

"With luck your ruse has worked, and Gavriil's eyes are upon Moscow, and he feels safe behind his mountains. Normally I would have been sent to Moscow to retrieve Apollyon and Misha and kill you. Now he will send Baitrov."

"Is that good?"

"Baitrov is like me. Mercenary. Dangerous man. Perhaps it is good to have him away. If I am right, he will have keep Samvel and cadre of veterans by his side."

"And what about Samvel?" Bolan asked.

"Samvel is experienced soldier. Fought in Chechnya. Trained sniper. He was recruited out of veteran center when he was drug addict by Gavriil himself." Spartak spit. "The not so good? Samvel is fanatic. He and men with him will fight to the death."

"How many?"

"Six, or twelve. I believe given situation he will have twelve. All handpicked. There will also be regular security men. They usually number six, but they will be ex-cops and the like. Mostly scum. Perhaps some local Mafia, as well. Gavriil generally does not like to have them associated with him, but given situation—" Spartak lit a cigarette "—we should expect it."

"So let's just call the odds ten to one to be on the safe side," James said.

Spartak nodded and smoked.

Bolan glanced at the satellite photos Kurtzman had sent. "Tell me about the airstrip."

"It is big, but not suitable for jets. Has own gas truck and a shack, but no hangar. Gavriil currently flies in P180 Avanti."

Grimaldi whistled. "Now that is one sweet ride. World's fastest turboprop business aircraft. Stand up cabin. Pure luxury, I'm telling you." He unfolded a satellite map onto the truck bed. "Here's the way I see it. It's all river, valley, river, valley where we're headed. Heaven Now manor has a little valley of its own. So we cross the Urals and go nap of the earth, low and slow. Then we pop up right over them before they know what happens and you guys drop LALO, and I'm talking base-jump height. We're on them before they know what hit them. I'll pull spotter duty until you ask me to land."

Every waited for James's reaction to a Low Altitude Low Opening jump east of the Ural Mountains. He shoved a stripper clip through the top of his carbine and sent the bolt home on a live round. "Flyboy is the only man making a lick of sense around here."

Bolan nodded. The die was cast. "Let's do it."

Grimaldi stared upward toward the vault of the sky. "I wonder what Akira's doing?"

Columbus Module, International Space Station

"WHAT ARE YOU DOING?" Dr. Treschev asked.

Tokaido managed to remain calm. He was breaking into Treschev's laptop. He had waited until both Treschev and Commander Khokhlov were asleep in their zero-gravity sleeping bags and quietly gone off with his laptop and tools to the Columbus module. Columbus was the science laboratory designed by the European Space Agency. The biolab was part of it, a single rack science station that was the size of a refrigerator and covered with dials, buttons and drawers and had an articulated arm to hold a laptop in place. Tokaido's laptop was currently mounted on the arm, and Treschev's floated a little off to one side tethered by USB cables. It had taken Tokaido's personally designed machine very little time to get past Treschev's passwords, break his encryption and then translate the Russian data into English. Treschev's laptop told a very different story than the data on file in the ISS mainframe.

Dr. Denis Treschev was not working to improve sandwich spread for space travel. The doctor was mutating tuberculosis bacteria. Tokaido had barely skimmed the data but just from the little he'd read, the TB strains Treschev had personally nurtured in space were proving remarkably resistant to the most current antibiotic regimens and his space bacterium bred like bunnies.

"Mr. Tokaido?" Treschev peered at the young man quizzically from the hatchway.

"I'm…" Tokaido turned beet-red and began sweating and stuttering. He had the poker face of a twelve-year-old boy caught mooning beneath a girl's window at midnight. "Resolving…integration—"

Treschev slid smoothly through the hatch and closed it behind him.

"Hey! I—"

"I believe that is my personal laptop."

"I…well…" Tokaido swallowed with difficulty. "Yes. Yes, it is."

"I see." Treschev was a wiry man in his fifties, bald on top, and zero gravity made the curly hair he had on the sides stick out like a clown. Tokaido had no doubts whatsoever the cosmonaut could kick the living crap out of him. The young hacker's right hand went to the stun gun Velcro-tabbed to the front of his ISS sweatshirt. His left moved toward the intercom button.

Treschev reached behind his back and pulled out a Soyuz survival machete.

Tokaido made a noise that stopped just short of being a squeak.

The Russian floated forward. The ten-inch-long black blade was shaped like a knife with an ax on the end and a saw down the back. It occurred to Tokaido that it was probably a perfect tool for lopping off someone's head. "You won't get away with this."

"You were fooling around in the lab. You had an accident. You start a fire. It required venting to put out, and you, improperly trained, tragically asphyxiated. Once we are back on Earth, it will no longer matter what the investigation reveals." Treschev got a very ugly gleam in his eye. "Khokhlov will return to Russia. Sparks will return to the United States, and the Dance of the Archangels will already have begun."

Moral outrage stiffened Tokaido's spine. He shoved out the stun gun at arm's length, sighted using his thumb knuckle like the Cowboy had shown him and pressed the click-wheel. Treschev blinked for one heartbeat as Tokaido boldly presented what appeared to be a portable media player at him like a crucifix at a vampire. But whatever he saw in the younger man's eyes made him instinctively snap his weapon up before him. The stun gun made a spitting noise and the barbed probe arrowed across the module and smacked into the machete. The probe jammed directly into the hole used for pulling nails.

Tokaido clamped the click-wheel down and delivered the juice.

Blue sparks jumped across the black blade as 950,000 volts pumped into the steel and arced across the saw teeth.

The young hacker's stomach sank as Treschev stared at his machete and then at Tokaido and his stun gun. "Fascinating."

The *tack-tack-tacking* of the stun gun slowed and died as the battery drained. Treschev pulled out the probe. The barb and the wire drifted away sadly like a spent strand of silvery seaweed. The Russian gave the younger man a professorial look. "The handles of all cosmonaut tools are insulated, Mr. Tokaido."

Treschev kicked off the module wall and shot toward the hacker like a torpedo.

"Shit!" Tokaido kicked backward and dug into the pockets of his sweats. His fingers curled around the grips of the stun knuckles. He ripped forth the one from his right pocket. The left one caught. He tugged on it furiously, but his pocket wound around it. Treschev swung the machete down at the crown of the younger man's head in a butcher's blow. Tokaido shoved up his right hand awkwardly to block and his arm ached to the shoulder with the force of the blow. The machete blade chopped into the high-impact plastic and stopped half-way through. Tokaido reflexively hit the trigger and more juice went uselessly into the blade. He tried to shove the blade toward Treschev's face while freeing his left-hand weapon, but the cosmonaut was stronger than he was and better at mul-titasking. Tokaido's head snapped back as his opponent punched him in the face.

Treschev punched him a second and a third time. Tokaido saw stars as the Russian ripped an elbow across his jaw. He drifted backward, blood ribboning from his mouth and forming little ruby-red spheres. Treschev ripped the split stun knuckles off his blade and tossed them behind him. "You are like a very poor James Bond, Mr. Tokaido. You know, I recognize the case these came from. In fact—"

He stopped monologing as Tokaido finally managed to free the set of stun knuckles and slid them over his right hand.

"Ah, yes, I should have known there would be two." Treschev sighed. "I guess I am no James Bond, either." He punched a few buttons on the biolab rack and a drawer containing test tubes and petri dishes slid out.

"Hey! What are you—"

Treschev slashed the blade across the top of the tray beheading beakers, tubes and sample jars. Broken glass flew and the air around him filled with globs of blue culture medium that instantly formed into spheres. Treschev floated in space, smiling. Winking bits of glass, blue marbles of biohazard and contrasting BBs and marbles of Tokaido's blood surrounded him.

"Oh, shit."

The Russian scientist looked like something out of a very bad science-fiction movie and Tokaido was his very unhappy costar.

"Oh, well, there will be no accident, no fire, and you will not asphyxiate due to incompetence. I fear I shall not see the fruits of my labors." Treschev floated out of his cloud of blood, plague and glass toward the young hacker. He shrugged, but his eyes stayed on the stun knuckles. "I guess the story will be I went space-crazy and murdered you."

"You went space-crazy and want to murder the whole planet!" Tokaido held up his fist and gave the stun knuckles a squeeze. The electrodes arced. "But that isn't going to happen!"

Where this bravado was coming from the young hacker didn't know. He realized it wasn't bravado. He wasn't a soldier, and he made a very poor James Bond. But the plague was floating right in front of him and Akira Tokaido was going to be good and goddamned if he let Gretchen Sparks, much less the rest of the citizens of Planet Earth, be exposed to it.

Treschev cocked back his blade and soared forward to commit murder.

The hatch behind them opened. Sparks stuck her head in. The mission specialist surveyed Tokaido, bloody and battered, with his fists held up before him. She saw Treschev with a machete in his hand and in the center of the module was a dancing mobile of glass and blood and goo. "What in the blue hell is going on in here!"

Treschev checked himself. "Gretchen, Mr. Tokaido—"

"The Russkie's doing biowarfare experiments!" Tokaido blurted. "It's out of containment!"

Treschev started to say something but looked at the machete in his hand and the carnage in the module. He turned and put a foot against the wall to kick off and go for Sparks. The mission specialist slammed the hatch shut. Treschev sighed. "No matter."

Tokaido gestured Treschev in. "Come get some."

The Russian slowly slid toward him, always keeping a hand or a foot near a module wall. Tokaido cocked back his right hand and realized he was very likely about to have it cut off. His mouth kept filling with blood. He kept swallowing it and felt like he was about to throw up. He searched his mind for anything he could do. The men of Stony Man Farm weren't much for boasting, but they were all fond of him, and he constantly pestered them for stories of their battles. His mind spun as he sought for a dirty trick he heard. He could kick Treschev in the nuts. The Russian would just as likely cut off his foot in the attempt. Maybe he should throw a jab, just let Treschev cut off his left hand and then hit him quick with the right.

No, after the left hand got lopped off Tokaido knew he was going to lose most of his gumption. Kick in the nuts… Treschev came gliding forward. Throw something… Treschev kicked against the wall and shot forward. Poke in the eye…

The eyes!

Treschev came into range.

Tokaido hawked up from the back of his throat and spit.

Unfettered by gravity the wad shot like a viscous comet of blood and spit straight into Treschev's face with a splat.

Tokaido leaned away from Treschev's blind swing with the machete. He squeezed the grip on the stun knuckles and the probes arced electricity as he threw a wild haymaker into the Russian's face. The young hacker's armored fist crunched into Treschev's left eye and cheek.

Treschev screamed as 950,000 volts shot straight down his optic nerve and into his brain.

The Russian went into violent convulsions and his limbs herky-jerked in every direction at once. The back hatch flew open again, and Sparks reappeared and promptly screamed.

Tokaido cocked his fist for another punch. "Gretchen, get out of here!"

"Go high!" Sparks shouted and threw a fire extinguisher in a perfect spiral over the winking, multicolored swarm of death in the middle of the module and past Treschev's flailing form. The fire extinguisher clanged off the ceiling wall and bounced toward Tokaido. He caught it awkwardly and the momentum swung him around into a wall.

"Sweep it all toward me!" Sparks slammed her hatch shut again.

Tokaido fired the extinguisher and shot like a rocket to the back of the module and bounced against it with impressive force. It was turning into a very hard day in zero gravity. He braced himself against it and cut loose once more. The chemical storm blasted the shattered disease culture back quite efficiently. The culture it was suspended in was sticky, and once it hit the far wall it stuck. Treschev had stopped his flailing. Tokaido grimaced but held down the trigger and hosed his fetal form tumbling back toward the far hatch.

Sparks's voice came across the intercom. "You all right?"

Tokaido spit some more blood. "Yeah. I think so."

"Have you been exposed?"

"Umm. Good question." Tokaido looked himself up and

down. He had beads of blood stuck to him, but careful examination showed no blue goo. "I don't think so. I know I didn't breathe any, and I don't see any on me."

Sparks's voice dropped low. "Do you think the commander is involved?"

"Umm, dunno. I don't think so. If they were in it together, you'd think they would have come down together."

"Probably." There was a pause on the other side of the intercom. "Okay. Listen. There's an emergency panel to your right. Open it."

Tokaido turned and twisted the two bolts holding the panel closed. Inside were two air bottles and respirators. He took out a mask. "Got it."

"Put it on. Turn on the oxygen dial to the green marker on the gauge."

Tokaido winced as he fit the respirator over his swollen mouth.

Sparks didn't wait for him to try to reply through the mask. "Listen, I'm going to override the module's life support and tell the computer the module is on fire. We're going to do an emergency vent on Columbus. One, that should vacuum most of that crap out, and two, if that crap likes living in humans, it likes it warm. The temperature in there is going to drop real quick."

"What about Treschev?" Tokaido glanced at the dry-chemical-coated man hanging suspended near the hatch. "I don't know if he's still alive or—"

"Fuck him," Sparks said.

"Right."

"Listen, you're blood's not going to boil and you're not going to explode, but you're going to be in a weightless vacuum. It's going to be very uncomfortable and very cold. Watch the environmental control panel. When it hits absolute zero get out of there."

"But if I open the hatch—"

"Air will come blasting in. The overpressure will keep any residual material from coming out with you."

"Grab on to something. Brace yourself when you open the hatch."

"Right." Tokaido wrapped his hand around the spar of an open load rack. "I'm ready."

He wasn't but—

"Beginning emergency vent."

Slats shot open and Tokaido suddenly felt like he was inside a vacuum cleaner with the motor reversed. Everything that wasn't nailed down went flying. His feet flew out from underneath him, and he almost lost hold of the spar. Glass, extinguisher powder, blood droplets and most importantly bits of blue jelly shot toward the vent in ribboning streams. Treschev spun about grotesquely, but nothing animated him except the buffeting suction.

Tokaido watched the temperature gauge drop like a rock. The blood he had swallowed was already making him sick, but as the outside air pressure dropped to zero every hollow in his body expanded with his own internal pressure, including his stomach and his bladder. The shuttle was currently on the dark side of planet Earth, so rather than the internal environmental controls and shielding keeping the modules cool they were busy keeping the inhabited sections warm. Columbus had shut down the heating and the vastness of space was sucking the air and heat out of the module like a cosmic sponge.

Tokaido breathed with difficulty. His blood was making funny noises. Despite all of his other discomforts, he could have sworn his hair hurt. He wore a sweatshirt, sweatpants and wool sock-booties, but he shook uncontrollably as the temperature plummeted past freezing. His vision blurred and teared over as someone tried to inflate his eyeballs like balloons. The spar he was holding on to began burning into his hand with cold. The buffeting stopped as the air-pressure needle pegged back at dead zero. The temperature hit absolute zero and crept lower. The drops of blood on his clothes had crystallized. The light on the intercom was blinking. Without air there was nothing to carry sound waves from the intercom, but Sparks was signaling him the only way she could.

It was time to go.

Tokaido pushed off and sailed to the far hatch. His hands burned as he grabbed the latch and the wall support next to it. The hatch opened with blissful ease, and he was suddenly blasted by the worlds biggest hair dryer as the warm air in the module beyond blasted in. He pulled himself past the torrent with his hands and into the next module. He waited for the pressure to mostly equalize and then pulled the hatch shut.

"Tokaido!" Both Sparks and Khokhlov were shouting over the intercom. "Tokaido!"

He would have collapsed, but there was nowhere to collapse to in zero gravity. Denied that terrestrial comfort, he just curled up in a fetal ball in midair and shook. He wondered if he would ever be warm again. He wondered what Bolan and his team were up to.

He was positive it had to be easier than this.

CHAPTER TWENTY-FOUR

East of the Urals

They dived in at dawn. The good news was that they had contacted the Farm before takeoff and they knew of Akira's success in space and it buoyed men who knew they were flying into a very bad situation. Carl Lyons had contacted them and told them today was the day for the exchange in Moscow. This was going to be their best shot at beheading the Heaven Now serpent.

"Going in!" Grimaldi said. They had topped the Urals' peaks and then threaded the plane down through the river valleys scant feet over the treetops. The ace pilot had swung southeast around the Arkhangelov's valley, then taken the An-2 into a steep climb straight into the rising sun before turning to make his deployment run at the valley. The team had scrubbed and oiled their ancient weapons. Each man had fired a hundred rounds through them, declared them fit and then cleaned and oiled them again. The folding bayonets of the carbines were not particularly good steel, but the dull gray blades now bore edges that were mercury bright and razor sharp. Each man wore his web gear beneath locally manufactured sheepskin jackets. They were carrying so many grenades in their pockets and web gear they looked like they were trying to smuggle grapefruit into Siberia.

"Jumpers!" Grimaldi shouted back. "Thirty seconds!"

The An-2 swooped straight out of the sun like a hawk.

Bolan, James and Spartak checked one another's rigs and strapped down weapons one more time and then filled their hands with their drogue chutes. Bolan opened the cabin door and the wind whipped into the unpressurized cabin.

Grimaldi whooped like an invading Mongol. "Go! Go! Go!"

James shoved himself out the cabin door and Spartak went out a heartbeat behind him. As team leader Bolan went last. He stepped into the doorway and saw both soldiers arch into textbook freefall position as he stepped into the void. The world fluttered and roared around Bolan in the orange light of dawn. The Urals rose in smoky purple to the west. The Arkhangelovs had a working farm, and the gleaming white, futuristic-looking Avanti aircraft on the airstrip was clearly visible.

Bolan and his team dropped like stones toward the immaculate farmland.

The Executioner watched as James let go of his drogue at eight hundred feet and Spartak instantly followed above him. It was just enough altitude to give them a few seconds of maneuvering as they glided toward their objective. Bolan released his drogue and felt the vibration in his back as the lines unspooled out of his pack. The main chute suddenly deployed, and Bolan's straps cinched against him like a rubber band suddenly drawn full taut. He grabbed his handles and went from falling to controlled descent. They slewed out of the sky straight for the stables.

Damn, Bolan thought.

A woman came out of the cattle barn. She had a yoke across her back with two huge pails of milk balanced to either side. She looked up at the sound of the plane and froze as she saw the jumpers. Bolan saw the tiny splashes of white in the red dirt as she dropped her load and ran for the main farmhouse. Bolan had hoped to be on the ground before they were spotted, but there was no use crying over spilled milk. He had also hoped to alight right in the driveway, but they would most likely be shot out of the sky if they tried. Bolan chinned his tactical. "Hot LZ and we have civilians! Land at the barn!"

"Copy that," James answered.

"Da!" the Russian said.

James slid down out the sky and flared his chute behind the cover of the main barn. Men began spilling out of the main house. Spartak hit the ground and rolled as the milkmaid pointed and screamed. Bolan flared his chute. Bullets ripped through the fabric as the ground slammed bone-jarringly into his boots. He shucked out of his straps and unslung his carbine. Bolan pushed off the safety as random bullets chopped into the barn. The range from the house to the barn was about 150 yards. He pushed the slide on the rear sight of his rifle to the 150 mark. "Cal! Spartak! Each of you take a corner! Put the house in a cross fire! I'm going in!"

The two soldiers moved into position as Bolan entered the barn through the back door and dropped prone. Shafts of sunlight speared through the dark interior as bullets riddled the walls. Bolan kneed and elbowed his way through hay and manure. He moved his way to the front of the bar and found a fist-sized knothole low to the ground and to his liking. He peered through it at the house.

The enemy was armed with pistols, submachine guns and shotguns and they blazed away like amateurs. Like most non-soldiers they were hypnotized by the doors and windows of the barn and poured fire into them with random shots going through the walls and hammering the loft. Bolan counted seven men clustered on the porch firing between flowerpots and deck chairs.

It was no cover at all from one of the foremost riflemen on the planet.

It was way too easy. They were cannon fodder. Bolan clicked the Russian walkie-talkie clipped to his web gear. "Yo, Spartak."

The Russian replied through the static-ridden equipment. *"Da?"*

"These guys are amateurs."

"Da." Spartak agreed.

"You told me Gavriil doesn't go anywhere without a squad of picked veterans."

"This is true. I trained them."

James spoke from the southern corner. "They're waiting for us to declare our numbers and firepower before they open up."

"House is fortress. They suspect we are few and wish to count our guns," Spartak grunted stoically. "It is what I would do."

"Give them a few shots. I'm going to see if anyone declares themselves."

"Copy that."

The deeper bark of rifle caliber weapons cracked from either corner of the barn. Hails of submachine-gun fire responded. Bolan sighted through the knothole. It was a narrow lane of fire, but at 150 yards it gave him command of the front of the house. Two men on the porch fell to James's and Spartak's marksmanship. The others continued to spray back indiscriminately. Bolan kept his eyes on the windows and was rewarded with movement on the second floor. It was little more than shadow but the rising sun was shining on the front of the farmhouse, and then Bolan caught reflection off an optic or steel.

Bolan squeezed his trigger three times rapidly. Sparks flew within the room and the shadow fell. James and Spartak each dropped another shooter on the porch. Bolan took a quick target of opportunity and a flowerpot flew apart as did the head of the shooter behind it. Bolan kept one eye scanning the windows and doors. The glass shattered out of the window at the peak of the farm's loft and the cone-shape of an RPG-7 warhead thrust outward. Firing a rocket-propelled grenade from indoors was gutsy, as Bolan well knew. The Executioner fired six shots in rapid succession. His SKS racked open on an empty chamber but bullets kept hitting the loft window as James and Spartak saw the threat. The weapon fell out of the window and clattered to the roof of the porch below and slid off to hit the ground.

Bolan shoved a stripper clip into the top of his weapon and the bolt slammed home. One of the men on the porch leaped out and dived for the fallen rocket launcher. His dive turned into a boneless flop as Bolan put two rounds into him. The other two men lost their nerve, turned and lunged back in the house. One made it. One didn't as James and Spartak both fired.

The board beside Bolan's head exploded.

"Sniper on the roof!" James shouted.

Bolan didn't need to be told. Dagger-sized flinders of barn flew like shrapnel all around him. The barn offered a degree of protection from the pistols, shotguns and submachine guns arrayed against them on the porch. It might as well be tissue paper to the semiautomatic sniper rifle on the roof. The barn was no cover but it did conceal him, and Bolan rolled as the sniper sought him out by educated guess. The sniper's guesswork was good. A bullet plucked at the sleeve of Bolan's sheepskin. He rolled behind a hay bale but it was little more than psychological comfort. Straw flew. The assault on him suddenly ended and he saw wood flying at either corner of the barn. James and Spartak would be hugging mud. "Cal! Spartak!"

They both came back.

"Either of you have a shot?"

"Only if we stick our heads out!" James replied.

That was exactly what the sniper was waiting for.

Grimaldi's voice crackled across the radio. "I see him. I got him."

The roar of the An-2 circling grew very loud as the aircraft dived. Bolan rose as the fusillade against the barn ended. He kicked open the barn door and raised his rifle. Grimaldi was diving straight at the farmhouse. The sniper had risen and was discharging his weapon into the approaching aircraft as fast as he could pull the trigger. He should have dropped and rolled, but he was Heaven Now faithful and he sought to bring down the enemy. It would take a lucky shot for the rifle bullets to smash anything vital enough in the An-2's massive radial engine to stop the attack. The man fired his rifle empty and turned to jump a second too late. Grimaldi dipped his starboard wing and suddenly pulled the nose of the aircraft up. He missed the peak of the roof by four feet. His starboard landing wheel hit the sniper between the shoulder blades at 150 miles per hour. The sniper's arms whipped behind him and he flew from the roof like a superhero. Gravity finally pulled him relentlessly earthward, and the sniper bounced on the drive with a crunch of bones Bolan could hear from the barn.

Grimaldi waggled his wings in victory as his biplane roared over and banked into a tight turn. Bolan shouted. "Go! Go! Go!" James and Spartak burst around either side of the barn, and the team ran in a wedge for the farmhouse. "Covering fire!"

James and Spartak both dropped to one knee and sought targets. Bolan charged on. He pulled a grenade from a pouch and whipped it through a porch window.

"Man on the roof!" Grimaldi radioed. "He's got an RPG!" Bolan watched as Grimaldi sent his plane soaring upward out of range. An RPG thumped and rushed from the roof and a rocket sizzled upward after him. It exploded a hundred yards from Grimaldi's tail.

Bolan shouted behind him as he kept the front covered. "Spartak!"

Spartak charged forward and scooped up the fallen RPG on the drive. James hung back and kept the entire front of the house in his sights. Spartak took half a second to inspect it and then aimed it at the roof. The rocket launcher thumped and the chimney, the rocketeer and a section of roof disappeared in fire and smoke. The doors to the stables blasted open beneath the steel bumper of an ex-military GAZ jeep. The passengers all began firing guns at once. The driver concentrated on running James down. The Phoenix Force pro was caught in the open. He snapped his carbine around and began firing at the oncoming jeep. Spartak tossed away the spent launch tube and whipped his carbine around on its sling.

James pitched forward as a shotgun blast from the house hit him squarely between the shoulder blades. A second shotgun blast kicked up earth a foot from his head. Bolan shot-putted a second grenade through the porch window, and a man shouted in alarm and then screamed as shrapnel filled the front room of the farmhouse. Spartak's carbine cracked at the oncoming jeep. The man riding shotgun in the jeep sagged over the dash. One of the men standing in the back was trying to aim an RPG. He toppled backward and fell off the speeding vehicle with a bullet from Spartak in his brain. The other man in back collapsed an instant later.

Bolan punched hole after hole in the jeep's windshield. He knew he was hitting the driver. Blood sprayed across the cratered glass, but either the man had the soul of a kamikaze or the jeep had a life of its own. Bolan's rifle ran dry. "Cal!"

James rose just in time to go flying over the jeep's hood. He slammed into the windshield and it buckled with the blow. The jeep slowed and came to a halt with nothing but the departed for passengers.

"Cal!"

James rolled off the hood and fell to the earth with a groan. Bolan ran forward. The Phoenix Force commando shook his head and pushed himself up. "I'm fine, my armor took most of it, I'm…" James sat back down again. "Shit."

"Spartak! I need—"

Spartak sat down in the dirt with red stains spreading on the front of both pants legs.

"Shit," Bolan said. They'd attacked a fortified position at over ten to one odds. By Bolan's count they'd taken down sixteen men, but the odds had finally caught up. "Cal, how you doing?"

"Dunno, maybe some cracked ribs. I feel like throwing up. Maybe I'm bleeding inside."

"Stay put." Bolan trotted over to Spartak. The Russian was already binding his legs with field dressings. He looked up at Bolan and shook his head. He snarled as Bolan picked him up and put him in the back of the jeep. The Executioner cleared the driver's seat and dropped down the collapsed windshield. James grimaced as Bolan put him behind the wheel. The soldier retrieved the fallen sniper rifle and gave it to Spartak with a couple of spare magazines. "I think there's a tunnel between the house and the stable. If they're going to make a break for it, they either go for the horses and ride into the hills or they'll go for the plane. Cal, take the jeep out about five hundred yards. Maybe to that hill over there. Keep the farm covered."

"You're going in," James said.

"Yeah, what the hell. It was ten to one. The way I figure it's only seven or eight now." Bolan sighed. "Things are going our way. Let me borrow your pistol."

He took James's Tokarev and clicked his radio. "Jack, keep flying spotter. I'm going in. If you don't hear from me within ten minutes, land and pick up Cal and Spartak. Keep an eye on the road. Someone inside had to have made some phone calls by now. We're out in the boonies, but reinforcements or the law will be on their way."

"Copy that."

James painfully shoved the battered GAZ into gear and headed for the grassy knoll. Bolan picked up the fallen RPG-7. "Jack?"

"Yeah," the pilot said.

"Close your eyes. This is going to hurt your feelings." The range was about five hundred yards. Fairly long for an RPG-7, but Bolan's target was a forty-seven-foot-long airplane. He put his crosshairs on the wing root and fired. The rocket-propelled grenade hissed across the intervening distance. High explosive and aviation fuel were a heady mix. The gleaming Avanti luxury plane blew up in spectacular fashion.

"The was cold-blooded murder," Grimaldi pronounced.

Bolan dropped the smoking tube and took up his carbine as he began walking toward the house. The roof was on fire from Spartak's rocket. Bolan stepped inside. Grenades and gunfire had ripped the vast living room apart. Smoke was beginning to fill the air. Bolan heard sudden screaming and the back door slamming. "Cal, what have we got?"

"I make it mostly civilians. Four women, three men. The two men are old and the other is just a kid. They're heading for the road. Wait." James's voice hardened. "Two more.

One's a guy in a suit with a gun. He's with the milkmaid. He's heading for the hills."

"She going willingly?" Bolan asked.

"He's dragging her by the hair."

Sentence was passed. "Spartak, drop him. Let the girl run."

Out in the fields a high-powered rifle cracked once.

"He's down," James confirmed.

The smoke was starting to get thick. Bolan looked for the door going down. It was in the kitchen as he had suspected. He kicked in the cellar door and dropped a frag down the wooden stairs, which were narrow and rickety. Bolan slung his carbine and drew his pistol and another grenade and began his descent. He pulled the grenade's pin and stepped inside. He had to duck his head in the low cellar. The space smelled of vinegar. His frag had done a lot of damage among the pickling jars. Bolan stepped through beets and broken glass to the door at the other end.

It wasn't locked.

Bolan threw it open and lunged to one side but no bullets sought him. He descended another flight of steps, only these were concrete. The door at the bottom was heavy oak and it was open. Bright light poured up the stairwell. Bolan descended and surveyed the torture tomb. It was as bright, white and clean as a medical facility. Michaela Arkhangelov smiled at Bolan sweetly. "Hello, lover."

Two men stood stone-faced and shoulder-to-shoulder in front of Michaela and Gavriil like human shields. They wore armor and held their folding-stock shotguns at the ready. They were clearly a couple of the Arkhangelov royal guard and looked completely ready to die for their deity. Michaela and Gavriil stood behind them with pistols in their hands. Next to her, two goons Bolan made as Mafia held Dominico up between them. Dominico had been pounded. He raised his head and his face had been beaten almost beyond recognition. He choked words from between mashed lips.

"Just…fucking…kill them."

"He is very brave. Very strong. It was a pleasure breaking him." Michaela Arkhangelov's smile was sickening. "Not that he had anything worth saying."

Bolan glanced at Gavriil. "So, what was it going to be? The Four Horsemen of Apocalypse? Conquest, War, Famine and Death and then you and Heaven Now as the savior?"

Gavriil gazed at Bolan very seriously. "For the Hindus Shiva must do the dance that destroys and remakes the universe. The Old Testament had Noah and the Flood. The Vikings had Ragnarok. All faiths know that a new age requires a culling."

Bolan had dealt with megalomaniacs with worse plans.

Michaela's beautiful blue eyes were as cold as death. "Now drop your weapons, or we start shooting Memo to pieces. One joint at a time."

Bolan knew she wasn't bluffing. He couldn't shoot through the goon squad in time to save Dominico. There were too many of them to try to charge and go hand to hand. He had no choice. He had to drop his weapons. The Tokarev pistol dropped to the concrete floor with a clatter.

"You…stupid…shit," Dominico groaned.

Michaela's face was triumphant. It was disturbing to see such an ugly smile on such a beautiful face. "Now, step forward, slowly. Samvel, take his rifle and—"

The cotter lever pinged away as Bolan let the grenade roll out of his left hand. The egg-shaped explosive bounced once and rolled toward the middle of the room.

Michaela screamed. The Mafia goons shouted and dropped Dominico. Michaela screamed again as Gavriil grabbed his sister and shoved her in front of him as a shield. Samvel shouted "Grenade!" and leaped to smother it with his body. The other guardsman shot Bolan in the chest. The pattern of buckshot smashed Bolan and knocked him back through the doorway. He sat down on the stairs and took the opportunity to kick the door shut before the man could shoot him again. The door shuddered as a blast of buckshot impacted. The muffled *crump* of the grenade rattled the heavy door on its hinges. Bolan drew the pistol James had loaned him and flung the door open again.

Samvel lay mostly headless on the floor. The grenade had detonated before he finished his leap and his face had failed to contain the blast. The other guard lay on his back staring sightlessly at the ceiling. One of the Mafia men sat blinking, stunned stupid. The other was reeling toward the open back door. Dominico and Michaela lay on the floor entwined like lovers. The Russian RGN-86 hand grenade had only a thin aluminum casing and did little in the way of shrapnel damage. It did its work with the 110 grams of TNT it packed and in the enclosed room that work was ugly.

Bolan shot the goon going for the door and dropped to one knee by Dominico. He rolled Michaela off him. Blood leaked from the corners of the woman's eyes as well as her ears. Her mouth hung slack and her pupils were blown. Offensive grenades were also called concussion weapons. Michaela Arkhangelov's concussion had been lethal. Blood leaked from every orifice in Dominico's head, but that had pretty much been the case when Bolan had entered the scene. "Memo, can you hear me?"

"I hear…angels."

"That's just me."

Dominico smiled. "That *cabrón,* Apollyon. I thought I could take him." He coughed and blood spattered his lips. "Sorry, man…I couldn't."

"It's all right. I took him out for you."

"Good. He killed Najelli."

"No, she's alive."

"Really?"

"Yeah, really," Bolan assured him.

"Well, I'm glad he's dead anyway."

"No, he's still alive."

Dominico's eyes focused and unfocused. "You didn't kill him?"

"No, but I broke his thumb, broke his collarbone, poked out his eye and ripped off his ear." Bolan gave Dominico a grin. "No one messes with my friends."

Dominico's eyes would have widened if they hadn't been swollen to slits. He gave Bolan a split-lipped grin in return. "You called me friend."

"Yeah, what the hell." Bolan nodded reluctantly. "You'll do."

"Gavi... I think he went out the back."

"Yeah, I know. You just sit tight here a minute while I finish up." Bolan clicked his radio. He compared the mouth of the dark tunnel to his mental map of the farm. "Cal, Gavriil's probably in the stables by now."

"Copy that, I—" Bolan heard Spartak's rifle fire twice over the radio. "Copy that! He's in there. Spartak just shot his horse out from under him. He got back inside."

"Keep him in there." Bolan took his carbine and snapped the bayonet into place as stepped into the darkness. The tunnel was a rough concrete tube that Bolan had to crouch-walk. There was a blood trail, and halfway to the stables he encountered a pistol with blood on the grips. There was light ahead coming down from a hatch. Bolan examined his assortment of grenades. He had a frag, an antitank, another high explosive and a smoke. Bolan pulled the nine-inch, waxed cardboard tube, scraped the friction igniter against the wall and popped smoke. He tossed the tube up the hatch and waited a few moments. The horses were already upset by all the action, and the smoke set them to rearing and neighing in dismay.

Bolan mounted the steps and stuck his head up for a quick peek. No one was visible, but the stable was swiftly filling with blinding white smoke. Bolan emerged in a crouch and tried not to breathe. He shoved up his carbine as Gavriil dropped from the rafters with an ax in his hands. Gavriil chopped into the SKS weapon with maniacal strength and the force of it knocked Bolan to the ground. Gavriil's shaved head and face were a skull-like mask of blood as he raised his ax like the Reaper's scythe. "Now! Now, you—"

Bolan snapped his carbine around and shot Arkhangelov in the chest. The SKS fired the round in the chamber and then jammed up solid. The fixed magazine and the springs and cartridges within had been chopped in two.

Gavriil staggered back a step and raised the ax for another blow.

Bolan leaped to his feet and lunged. The point of his bayonet punched through Gavriil's solar plexus. Bolan felt the blade grate against Gavriil's spine and punch out the back. He gasped and dropped his ax. His huge hands shot around Bolan's throat and began to squeeze with horrible strength. Bolan twisted his weapon and Gavriil's hands went feeble.

Bolan ripped his blade free and Gavriil Arkhangelov fell dead to the straw.

The Executioner tossed away the broken carbine and clicked his radio. "Cal, one coming out. Jack, land her and let's get out of here."

"Copy that."

"Roger."

Bolan felt heat at his back and saw that the straw where the grenade had landed had caught fire. He slid open the barn

doors and then let the horses out of their stalls. Gavriil's farmhouse was burning to the ground. Black smoke billowed and
rose from the burning hulk of the Avanti executive transport.
Bolan walked toward the airstrip and James picked him up on
the way. Grimaldi brought the An-2 in for a landing. He took
as wide a detour as he could around the burning aircraft and
pulled up next to the fuel pump. James parked at the shack,
and Bolan and Grimaldi eased James and Spartak into the
plane. Bolan gratefully took the canteen the ace pilot handed
him and drank it dry while the pilot refueled. Grimaldi
checked his watch, and Bolan knew he was mentally review-
ing the extraction routes they had discussed. "So, you got a
favorite destination?"

Bolan stared up into the morning sun. "How about Hawaii?"

EPILOGUE

Molokai

Bolan's cell phone rang. He didn't particularly want to answer it, but the theme from *Shaft* told him it was Calvin James. Bolan groaned and shifted in his hammock. The palm trees supporting it swayed in the breeze above him. He reached for his phone. "Calvin James."

"My brother."

"Wish you were here, man. You back on your feet?"

"Taking walks in the hills, doing some shooting with the Cowboy on the range, mostly taking it easy," James replied.

"Any word from Akira?"

James laughed. "Too much information. He's a genuine secret agent who saved the world and Mission Specialist Sparks is suitably grateful. He keeps texting me about how he's a black belt now and how great zero gravity sex is."

"The boy was due."

"How you doing?"

Bolan glanced over at his hut. "Just waiting for my girl to bring me my next Blue Hawaiian."

"Your girl—" Bolan could hear James bolt upright in Virginia. "Oh, man, tell me you're not hitting Najelli! Our man Memo is all jacked up in the hospital and that boy is in love."

Bolan glanced down the beach. Busto's daughter was running up to the surf, shrieking and running away when it rushed up against her feet. She chased it back happily as it receded. Busto and her mother were laughing and following suit. "I wouldn't do that."

James grew bitterly suspicious. "Not Rider. You know I had my eye on that."

Rider Anaya had just finished applying sunscreen. Bolan watched as she ran to join Busto's clan frolicking in the surf. "Wouldn't do that to you. As a matter of fact, she's been asking about you."

"Really!" James lost all pretense of cool. "What'd she say?"

Bolan smiled as his drink approached. "Get your ass Hawaiian-side and ask her yourself."

"Oh, you know I'm all over that. I'm…" James paused quizzically. "So who's bringing you your next drink?"

"Gotta go."

"But—"

Bolan tapped his phone off. Dr. Rina Talancon walked toward him with one arm in a sling and two Blue Hawaiians crooked between her fingers. The black hair that had been severely restrained moved in a long wave with each step she took in the sand. Her bikini revealed the lush proportions her lab coat had barely restrained in Mexico City. "You promised me a story."

"You promised me a Blue Hawaiian."

She glanced down at the drinks. "I have two of them."

"Well, then, let's see. Where to begin…?"

Don Pendleton
SKY SENTINELS

**A new spark in the Middle East could ignite
the ultimate global conflagration....**

Iran is flexing its military muscle, kidnapping
U.S. journalists and openly daring America to retaliate.
When Iranian intelligence officers kidnap three prominent
Americans from D.C., Stony Man gets involved.
Dispatched to free the hostages and get a handle on
the main event, Stony Man discovers the planning
stages of a radical multinational plot that could
ignite the next—and last—world war.

STONY MAN®

*Available October
wherever books are sold.*